To Peter

PART ONE

In a Good Light

Clare Chambers

arrow books

Reissued by Arrow in 2021

13

Arrow Books
20 Vauxhall Bridge Road
London SW1V 2SA

Arrow is part of the Penguin Random House group of companies
whose addresses can be found at global.penguinrandomhouse.com.

Penguin
Random House
UK

First published in Great Britain by Century in 2004
First published in paperback by Arrow in 2005
This edition published in paperback by Arrow in 2021

www.penguin.co.uk

A CIP catalogue record for this book is available from the British Library.

ISBN 9780099469186

The authorised representative in the EEA is Penguin Random House Ireland,
Morrison Chambers, 32 Nassau Street, Dublin D02 YH68.

Printed and bound in Great Britain by Clays Ltd, Elcograf S.p.A.

1

YOU NEVER GET OVER A HAPPY CHILDHOOD, ACCORDING TO Donovan. What we all need is a little disappointment. I think I know what he meant. But this isn't about Donovan. It's about my brother, Christian. And Penny, of course.

It's funny, because I hadn't given Penny a thought for years, but on the very day Christian made his announcement I had an odd experience which made me remember.

It was a Friday in late February. There was a soapy smell of hot-house hyacinths outside the front door when I went to fetch in the milk, and in the kitchen there was the musky smell of Elaine, Christian's carer, preparing his breakfast. She doesn't actually need to do that. He's quite capable of making his own. Everything in the house was designed so that he can manage in his wheelchair. He's what they call a T2 paraplegic, which is nowhere near as bad as it could be.

Elaine's the latest (and the least agreeable) in a series of people whose job it is to come in daily to help out. Christian's not an especially demanding employer, but it's heavy work and doesn't pay well, so naturally staff turnover is high. I preferred the last chap, Mike. The three of us used to sit around and play Scrabble in the afternoon; he had a good vocabulary for a home help. You wouldn't catch Elaine playing Scrabble, not that I've asked her.

She didn't come through the usual channels. She was passing the house one day when Christian was out front salting the driveway in case of frost, and she took the trouble to stop and talk. In the course of their conversation it emerged that she was looking for work as a carer and had some experience, so Christian took her number. A fortnight later Mike handed in his notice and Christian got straight on the phone. No references: her last patient couldn't oblige as he was dead.

When I saw her standing at the hob stirring a pan of scrambled egg that morning it occurred to me that Christian must have given her a front door key. That made me feel rather uneasy. I didn't like the thought of her coming and going as she pleased – in fact, I'd been considering asking Christian if we couldn't advertise for somebody new, even though it would mean some short-term upheaval. I've nothing against Elaine, but when she's around I feel as though I'm an intruder in my own house. I can't relax. There's so much of her. I don't object to her size – a waif would be no good in a job like this – but she always has so many bags and hats and scarves and appurtenances; it's as if she's trying to fill up as much space as possible.

Conversation is another sticky area. It's a choice between long, haunting silences and a bombardment of unwanted advice on everything from pedicures to pensions. It's something I've often observed about members of the caring professions: they tend to interpret jovial self-deprecation as a cry for help. I think Elaine sees me as someone who needs taking in hand. The other day she even suggested it was time I got a foot on the property ladder. I said I was afraid of heights. She said, 'Are you really?' So I had to explain that it was a joke. She said, 'Oh. Your sense of humour,' and gave me one of her caring smiles. Naturally Christian hasn't picked up any of these signals. Men are notorious for not seeing what's under their noses and he is no exception.

I suppose what annoyed me about Elaine's remark was the implication that I must be just dossing here temporarily until I've sorted myself out, when in fact this is my home. I've lived here since it was built in the mid-Eighties. My studio is at the back of the house, facing south-east, so I get the sun in the morning, and the box room is quite adequate as a bedroom. I've always been able to sleep anywhere. Sometimes, when I've been watching a late film in the sitting room, I can't be bothered to go to bed at all. I just flop over fully dressed on the couch – another big advantage of not sharing a bed.

I suppose our domestic arrangements might strike an outsider as odd. Living with your brother wouldn't be everyone's idea of fun, but we know each other better than anyone else alive, and if he needs me I'm always there to help. In fact we're happier than most married couples I come across. I suppose that's why none of my boyfriends have outlasted the initial surge of euphoria; it would take a truly exceptional man to compete with Christian.

On this particular Friday I was dressed more formally than usual because I was going to give a talk to a group of primary school children in Surrey about my work as an illustrator. I'd never been asked to do anything like that before, but my latest book had just won a prize so in the miniature world of children's publishing I'm suddenly somebody. I should say 'our' latest book, since it's a collaborative effort. Words by Lucinda Todd. Pictures by Esther Fairchild. Lucinda Todd bashes out the text in about a week and it takes me the best part of nine months to do the illustrations. This inequality of effort is supposed to be addressed by a forty/sixty split of the royalties. I'm no mathematician, and I'm not saying I've been stitched up, but someone has and it's not her.

'You look smart. Are you going somewhere?' said Elaine, glancing up as I hovered in the doorway, wondering whether to retreat to my room until she was out of the way. I was wearing a linen trouser suit, fresh out of the dry cleaner's. I could still feel the stapled ticket grazing the back of my neck.

'Oh, just to a primary school,' I said, advancing into the kitchen and slopping milk into a glass. 'I don't know why I've dressed up for a load of eight-year-olds.'

The newspaper was on the table, still folded. I sat down with my milk and started to read the headlines.

'For a minute I thought you had a job interview,' she said. This wasn't the first time she had implied that in her opinion painting by day and waitressing by night did not constitute a proper career path. 'That colour suits you,' she went on. 'You should wear it more often.' With Elaine even a compliment comes welded to a piece of advice.

I decided to play along. 'Do you think so? I'm not sure.'

She tipped the scrambled egg onto a slice of toast and ground pepper over it with a vigorous wringing action that put me in mind of someone killing chickens. 'Definitely. It goes with your eyes.'

The suit was green. My eyes are blue. It occurred to me she was either colour-blind or having a laugh, but her expression was sincere. Before I could think of a suitable reply she was off again, with another suggestion. 'I've got a friend who could do your colours for you. She holds up these fabric samples to your face and works out what season you are.' She poured orange juice into a tumbler and put it on a tray with the plate of scrambled egg. 'She did me before Christmas and it turned out I'd been wearing the wrong colours for years. Everything was fighting with my skin tone. Where do you keep your napkins?' she said, opening and closing drawers on cutlery, teatowels, pegs and balls of garden twine.

'I don't think we've got any,' I said, which was not quite the truth. I *knew* we didn't have any. 'We're not big on napery,' I added, in case she was after a tray-cloth next.

'Oh well. He'll have to do without,' she replied, in a voice as crisp as new linen.

'Why are you taking him breakfast in bed, anyway?' I asked, watching her balance the tray in one hand while she swept up the newspaper that I'd been reading and tucked it under her arm. 'You don't need to indulge his every whim, you know.'

'It's just a one-off treat,' she explained. 'I won't be making a habit of it.' And she shook her long, copper hair back, rather like a horse flicking off flies, clip-clopped down our wooden hallway in her Dr Scholls and disappeared into Christian's room, closing the door behind her.

IT TOOK ME ABOUT AN HOUR TO GET TO WEYBRIDGE BY CAR. I don't like driving on the motorway, but I had my portfolio of paintings and a box of books which was too heavy to carry.

It was breaktime when I arrived and the kids were all out in the yard. I could hear the high, echoing shouts as soon as I opened the car door. I'd have been happy to stand and watch them all day: the boys charging around, colliding with each other like a herd of maddened sheep, the girls decorously skipping, or sitting on the benches in little huddles. And the loners, standing with their backs to the wall or, worse, plum in the middle of a football game, petrified or oblivious.

'All in together, girls,
Never mind the weather, girls,
When it's your birthday
Please jump IN,'

went the chant as I staggered past the skippers with my boxes. A teacher with a whistle round her neck stood on the steps leading to the entrance, hugging a coffee mug, while a group of girls stood around her, very close, clamouring for her attention. I wouldn't have admitted it to Elaine, but I was extremely nervous at the thought of addressing a classful of eight-year-olds. People always assume that children's authors must have a natural affinity with children, and understand just how their minds work. It's not an unreasonable assumption I suppose, but it doesn't apply in my case. I don't even know any children. When I get to work on a book it's myself as a child I'm thinking of, not modern children, real or imagined. In truth I find them a little scary, as if they might somehow unmask me.

In spite of this attack of self-doubt, I must have looked like a legitimate authority figure because before I'd advanced very far a small boy accosted me and asked if I could peel his satsuma. I found this rather touching, so I put down my

baggage, and was presently besieged by half a dozen other peti-
tioners wanting me to open packets of crisps, or prise plastic
straws from the back of drink cartons. I couldn't remember
this sort of free-range snacking being encouraged when I was
at school. On the contrary, milk was just coming off the menu.
The only source of refreshment was a crippled drinking fountain on the outside wall of the toilets, which yielded a slow
drip of metallic tasting water which swelled to a trickle when
someone inside pulled the chain. In any case, our mother
would never have stooped to crisps: she would have sent
Christian and me to school with something nutritious and
embarrassing like a hard-boiled egg or a stick of celery.

Somewhere a bell rang and the crowd around me melted
away, leaving me with a handful of orange peel. I put it in
my suit pocket and picked up my boxes again. The teacher
blew her whistle and two hundred children stood rooted to
the spot. For a second I froze too, and then I remembered
that I was an adult, and therefore not bound by the same
rules, and I picked my way self-consciously between the
little statues to the door, my progress followed by two
hundred pairs of eyes.

I had over-prepared for the event of course. Having fixed
on the notion that I would need to fill the time with chat
and avoid awkward silences at all cost, I had rehearsed an
hour-long lecture, written up on twenty cue-cards as if I was
addressing the Royal Society. I had the confused idea that
eight-year-olds might be withdrawn and uncooperative creatures like the teenagers they would one day become, but I
couldn't have been more wrong. They were still buzzing
from their workout in the fresh air; at least half a dozen
hands shot up before I'd even unpacked my case. Everyone
wanted to ask a question, or just tell me what they'd had

for breakfast. Half the time they were repeating the point made by the previous speaker, but I found their enthusiasm and lack of inhibition totally disarming. Pretty soon I abandoned my notes and the lesson descended into an amiably anarchic free-for-all, only loosely tied to the subject of illustrated books.

The teacher, Miss Connor, who looked as though she was straight out of college, had withdrawn to the back of the room to listen. Occasionally she threw out a warning cough if any of the children became too boisterous but, after a while, even she began to relax, when it was clear I wasn't going to dry up altogether and need rescuing.

Quite often, having almost dislocated a shoulder in the process of stretching up to secure my attention, some poor kid would then forget what it was he wanted to say and collapse back into his seat, mumbling in confusion. It was at this stage, when I had stopped feeling nervous and was beginning to enjoy myself, that instead of addressing my remarks to Miss Connor, or the back wall, I started to pick out individual faces.

'Has anyone any idea what this book might be about?' I asked, holding up a painting done in acrylics, which had formed the cover of my last book. It showed, from above, but with a skewed perspective, a summer garden full of trees and flowers in full bloom. In the middle of the lawn was a greenhouse, from which a cloud of butterflies, balloons and parrots was emerging.

Whoosh. Up went thirty hands.

'Yes?' I singled out a boy with white-blond hair and colourless eyelashes. He reminded me of a hamster I'd once known.

'Um . . .' He subsided, covering his face. I could see the

veins on his arms, thin blue tributaries through the skin. 'A garden,' he finally spluttered, inspired.

'Good idea,' I said. 'Any other offers?'

'A garden,' said the next contributor, a scruffy kid with a number two haircut.

'Ye-e-es,' I replied smoothly, moving on to his neighbour, a girl.

'Oh. I was going to say garden too.'

'Was anyone not going to say "garden"?' Miss Connor put in, and several hands fell.

'Football?' came a suggestion from the back.

'Football,' I said, looking over at my painting as if I couldn't remember what was in it. 'Interesting. Why do you say that?'

'Because I always play football in the garden.'

There's no arguing with the logic of personal experience.

Only one hand remained up, but its owner, a girl with dark, shoulder-length hair, had her head down, writing, which was why I hadn't noticed her earlier.

'Yes?' I addressed the top of her head as her neighbour gave her a terrific nudge.

'Oh!' She looked up at me with wide, grey eyes, and the moment I saw her face an electric jolt went right through me, and I thought *I know you*. But of course I didn't know her at all. I'd never seen her before in my life. What startled me wasn't just a striking resemblance to someone I'd once known: it was more complicated than that. It was Penny I had recognised, not as she was now, or as I'd ever known her, but *as she must once have been*. It was the strangest feeling, remembering something I'd never actually experienced, and I was still recovering when she spoke again.

'I think it's about a magic greenhouse,' she said, meeting my eyes, and I felt the ripple of another strange current between us. *The Magic Greenhouse* had been my title for the book, ditched at the last minute in favour of *Gordon's Garden*.

For the rest of the session I tried not to stare at her, but felt my gaze pulled in her direction time and again. Her answers, it seemed to me, were always the most perceptive, the most intelligent. The dinner bell took me by surprise. I had meant to wind up in plenty of time, possibly set them a little task – a drawing competition or something. But Miss Connor stood up and told the children to leave their things exactly as they were on their desks, and then she thanked me for coming and they all gave me a short round of applause before stampeding for the door.

While Miss Connor tidied up, I packed my things away, and then on the pretext of admiring the displays – a whole wall of papier-mâché humpty-dumptys and stuffed sock puppets – I had a quick look at the exercise book on the dark-haired girl's desk. A chewed pencil lay in the fold of the open pages, which were covered with laboriously joined-up writing. I flipped the book shut with one finger and read the name on the front. Cassie Wharton-Smith. That surname alone, long since expelled from memory, settled it, but I remembered, too, right back before everything went wrong, when Penny and Christian were still together and happy, Penny used to say, 'If I ever have a daughter I'll call her Cassandra.' And Christian, who used to cringe at the thought of children, even hypothetical ones with sensible names, would cringe even harder and say, 'People like you should be sterilised.'

'She's a bright little thing,' I said to the teacher, pointing to the desk Cassie had recently occupied.

'Oh yes, she's a lovely girl,' she replied, shouldering her handbag and opening the door for me. 'She's got a wonderful imagination.'

She locked the classroom, one of those Portakabins reached by a flimsy wooden staircase. The tiny, grey lobby in which I stood waiting was cold and cluttered. Padded jackets ballooned from a double row of pegs on either wall, almost meeting in the middle. Through a chink in the floor I could see the grass below. When I stamped my foot experimentally, the whole structure seemed to quake.

'You don't know the parents, do you?' I said, as Miss Connor caught me up. 'I only ask because I used to know her mother. Ages ago.'

Miss Connor shook her head. On the top of her open handbag lay a packet of cigarettes. She was obviously dying to escape for a smoke. 'I don't think the father's around any more,' she said, and then stopped, blushing at this indiscretion.

'You couldn't let me have her address, could you?'

She gave an apologetic grimace. 'Sorry. Not allowed to do that. You understand.'

'Of course. It doesn't matter,' I said, embarrassed to have asked. For all she knew I could be some mad stalker with a grudge. 'It was so long ago. I don't know what I'd say to her, anyway.'

I WAS TAKEN BACK TO THE STAFFROOM AT LUNCHTIME AND introduced to those few teachers who were in there eating their sandwiches. Someone fetched me a plate of cheese flan and potato croquettes from the canteen and everyone laughed at my gratitude, which was genuine. I must be the only person alive who likes institution food: I find spam fritters comforting in a way that rocket leaves can never be.

The staffroom was even more of a hovel than the wobbly Portakabin I'd left behind. The chief comforts were twelve low, padded vinyl chairs without arms, arranged around three square tables, the tops of which were exactly level with the seats, so it was impossible to draw up to the table – to reach your coffee for example – without kneecapping yourself. The rest of the staff, already wise to this, were sitting back, eating off their laps and using the table as a footstool. The workbenches around the edge of the room were buried beneath sloping piles of paper and books and ring-binders. The draining board of the aluminium sink was crowded with unwashed cups. On the floor, the carpet tiles were starting to curl up at the edges, like stale slices of bread.

I'd brought two boxes of books along with me to sign and sell at the book fair in the afternoon. This was meant to be a golden opportunity for me to make a profit. I'd envisaged a hall full of affluent, book-loving parents, eager to demonstrate their support for the school's literacy programme, but I had sadly misjudged the market. Most of the children seemed to be picked up by au pairs, who naturally carried no spare cash and were deaf to the demands of their little charges. I was in any case having to compete with the tie-ins for some new cult Japanese cartoon movie, which took care of most of the boys. One of my first customers, though, was Cassie. She was unaccompanied, and produced a crumpled-up ball, which turned out to be a five pound note, from her cardigan pocket. She spelled out her name without waiting to be asked, and I dutifully inscribed it on the title page.

'Do you like reading, Cassie?' I asked, looking up at her serious face.

She nodded. 'I like Roald Dahl.'

'Well, this will probably be too easy for you then.'

'That's all right. I like easy books too.'

'Do your mum and dad read to you at bedtime or do you read to yourself?'

'Mummy does. Daddy doesn't live with us any more.'

'Oh.' Just as Miss Connor had surmised. I was on the point of asking what her mummy's name was, but I lost my nerve. It seemed creepy somehow, to be prompting a strange child to divulge personal details. For all I knew it could be a criminal offence. Besides, once she'd spent her money Cassie didn't linger to chat, but said goodbye with one of those frank, appraising stares that children often deploy to make adults squirm.

When the rest of the browsers had melted away I did a quick tally of my takings. The results were as follows: Sold – fourteen. Misappropriated/nicked – five. I reckoned the day's receipts would amount to a loss of £2.50. Rather than lug the boxes of unsold books back to the car I told the teacher on duty I was donating them to the school – proceeds to the staffroom refurbishment fund. She laughed gaily as if I was joking. I don't know why I suddenly came over all charitable. It must have been something of my mother rising to the surface at last.

I DROVE STRAIGHT FROM SCHOOL TO THE RESTAURANT SINCE there wasn't time to go home first. I've worked five nights a week as a waitress at Rowena's in Crystal Palace ever since

it used to be the Grill Rooms. Back in those days there was
sawdust on the floor and the music was so loud I used to
wear cotton wool in my ears and lip-read the orders. I got
quite proficient at it until the manager told me I could stay
away until the infection had cleared up because I was putting
people off their food.

There was live comedy on Friday nights, and live music
on Saturday. It would be pleasing to think that I had seen
some of today's great comic turns in their infancy, but
unfortunately none of the Friday night acts from the Grill
Rooms has ever to my knowledge made it onto the TV.
One old chap who used to do daft things with a sliced loaf
was a hit at the Edinburgh Fringe about five years on from
his Grill Room debut – I think he won a 'Best Newcomer'
award, but I haven't heard of him since. The murky waters
of obscurity must have closed over his head soon
afterwards.

Nowadays Rowena's serves pizzas and pasta and plays light
opera. The comedians have gone, along with the rock bands
and the cocktails. There's more light, and less smoke and
no sawdust. It's a different clientele. Or maybe it's the same
clientele, now ten years older, married with children. We
don't get stag nights any more and I can't say I'm sorry.
Even lavish tips didn't feel like adequate compensation for
the harassment and groping.

Waitressing may not seem like a great job, but evening
work suits me fine. I can be at home during the day if
Christian needs me, and I can paint in the mornings when
the light is good and I'm at my best. It's physically tiring
being on my feet from six until midnight, but my mind is
free to wander and there's no stress. Even when there's been
a scene and a customer has got drunk or belligerent it

doesn't carry forward to the next day. I sleep well and every morning's a new beginning. The money's terrible but I can usually double it in tips, and I'm an optimist by nature: I try to look at it as a wage-packet half full rather than a wage-packet half empty. Since I don't have to pay for my accommodation my living expenses are small, and I'm not extravagant. Sometimes when I'm turning the pages of Vogue in the hairdressers I might find myself hankering after a pair of fuchsia pink beaded slingbacks for £600, but the moment soon passes. It's the long reach of my mother again, jangling the charity tin under my nose and turning my thoughts to the Less Fortunate.

Elaine finds my lack of ambition hard to understand. It's another area of my life she'd be keen to tackle if I let her. A fortnight ago she brought in one of those career profiling questionnaires designed for school-leavers. She had come out as an ideal headmistress or prison officer, so I couldn't fault its acuity. I filled it in later when she'd gone and it turned out I was a born librarian, which depressed me. I must have overplayed the stuff about working on my own and liking peace and quiet. Another complaint Elaine levels against my choice of job is that it gives me no time for a social life. This is unfair: Rowena's is my social life. Without it I wouldn't have one at all. There's Rowena herself, the chefs – who are generally young and male and never last more than six months – and the other waitresses, mainly students of nineteen or twenty, for whom the six to twelve shift is just a warm-up to a night of drinking and clubbing and shagging, if their conversation is to be believed. I'm occasionally invited on these raids, but never go. They are desperate to show me a good time. Poor Esther, stuck at home with her crippled brother, they think, when

I cry off, yet again. All this pity and sympathy are entirely undeserved. There's no need for me to hurry back to Christian, who is well looked after. And if I want a date the restaurant is as good a place as any to meet men: people who are out for a meal are usually relaxed, in a good mood and ready to have fun, and the atmosphere at Rowena's seems to be conducive to flirtation. It's very different from the Grill Rooms, where the pounding rock music, and the whoops from the Tequila Slammer girl, not to mention my earplugs, made conversation all but impossible. I've met a few blokes that way, in the line of duty, though I never took any back home. Then for the last four years there's been Geoff.

Again, it's not a conventional arrangement, but it suits us remarkably well. Round about my thirtieth birthday I went through a low period. I couldn't seem to work up much enthusiasm for anything; I was trying a new style of painting and it wasn't going well; I found myself crying a lot for no particular reason. There was a bleakness about everything. Eventually I went to my GP but she was off on maternity leave so I saw the male doctor instead. Geoff. He was sympathetic and reassuring and let me ramble on for ages, well beyond my allotted time, so that every other appointment that day would be late. He looked about fifty, slightly overweight and absolutely not what you'd call good looking, but with a nice, interesting face. I noticed the pictures on his desk: a wedding photo, and a boy and a girl in their early teens, their smiles glittering with heavy-duty orthodontics. Anyway, at the end of our chat he prescribed me some mild anti-depressants and told me to come back two weeks later, or sooner if I felt bad.

It's annoyingly hackneyed, but I started to entertain

fantasies about him from that point. Not desperately ambitious ones: more romantic than erotic. He seemed so kind,
so capable. I often find myself attracted to people who come
to my aid in however humble a capacity: plumbers, AA
men, the bloke from Dyno-rod. Perhaps gratitude is an
aphrodisiac.

I went back to see him as arranged and we talked some
more. He was interested to hear about my illustrating work,
and my set-up with Christian, and wondered if my role as
carer might be putting me under strain, so I was able to set
him straight on that score. He offered to put me in touch
with the community psychiatric nurse for a spot of counselling, but I didn't feel my case warranted it. I said just
talking to him had made me feel better, and I would perse-
vere with the tablets.

A few weeks after my last appointment, he came into
the restaurant with another bloke. When I went to take
his order he gave me a discreet nod of recognition, but I
made the mistake of greeting him openly with a cheerful
hello, just to let him know that I was in good spirits,
which I was, now that I'd seen him. His friend immediately pounced on this. He was a coarse, boozy type, as
unlike Geoff as could be imagined. 'She one of your
patients?' he said as I walked away. 'Wouldn't mind getting
her on the couch, heh heh.' I was suddenly conscious that
in my black mini skirt and tight T-shirt I probably looked
cheap and trashy, and cursed myself for having acknowledged him.

When I brought their food Geoff looked absolutely mortified and kept his eyes on his plate. His friend said, 'Thanks,
darling,' and made an infuriating clicking noise with his
tongue, as though urging on a horse. I felt like clubbing

him over the head with the pepper grinder, but I just gave him a chilly glare instead.

He got progressively drunker and more lecherous as the evening progressed, and every time I approached the table he would come out with some innuendo while Geoff shifted about on his seat in agonies of embarrassment. It was hard to ignore now, as there were only a few remaining diners, and my relief when they finally paid (leaving a tip of exactly ten per cent) and left was immense.

Another twenty minutes had passed by the time I had finished clearing up and wiping down the tables, so when Rowena let me out of the now-locked front door I was completely taken aback and a little alarmed to see Geoff loitering in the shadows like an assassin. He was carrying a rolled golf umbrella, which he made no move to put up, even though a light drizzle was falling.

'Esther!' he said, hurrying over, and I was flattered that he'd remembered, until it occurred to me that I'd been wearing my name-tag all evening. 'I'm sorry about earlier.'

I glanced around in case his friend might still be lurking. 'I've put him in a taxi,' he added, guessing my concern.

'It's all right,' I said, congratulating myself on this unexpected reversal. I now had the power to reassure him.

'It must have sounded as though we were discussing you. I promise that wasn't the case.'

'I know.'

'Everything that takes place in the consulting room is completely confidential. I'd be struck off if I . . .'

'Don't worry. I shouldn't have said hello. It put you in an awkward position.'

'It's not your fault at all. My friend is a male chauvinist

pig, especially when he's had a few.' The rain started to come down more heavily now, and he remembered the umbrella, which sprang open at the touch of a button. He held it over me so I was forced to take a step towards him to spare him an unnecessary drenching, and we stood, in awkward and unfamiliar proximity, blocking the narrow pavement so that passers-by were forced to step around us into the gutter. I glanced at my watch, a gesture that seemed to bring him up short.

'I'm sorry,' he said. 'It's late and I've made you even later. Can I give you a lift anywhere? I'm parked round the corner.'

I couldn't help laughing at such a recklessly unprovisional offer. 'No. I live miles away. In Caterham. Near the surgery.' What I didn't say was that my own car was parked, like his, around the corner. Normally I would have considered this sort of feminine scheming to be beneath me, but I was intrigued to see just how far out of his way he would be prepared to go. It would give me an index of his concern.

'Of course,' he nodded. 'Obvious really.' And he started to walk in the direction of his car, so that I was obliged to do the same, drawn along by the overarching embrace of the umbrella. 'It's not far from me,' he said. 'Warlingham.' Even without a map I could work out that Caterham would represent a detour and I felt a quite immoderate surge of happiness, so that I had to bite my cheeks to suppress a smile.

His car, parked an immaculate three inches from the kerb, was a newish Rover saloon, smart but not flashy; the car of a professional man who isn't interested in cars and has nothing to prove. He opened my door first, a gesture which made me think of my father, who always had perfect manners. The interior was clean, but not fanatically so, and equipped with sensible things like a fire extinguisher, blanket, ice scraper and another small umbrella with a Liberty print.

On the journey we talked about impersonal things: the health service, the election, but without committing ourselves to a particular political allegiance. At one point he said, 'How would you have got home if I hadn't offered? Public transport's hopeless down this way,' and I wondered if he'd twigged.

I didn't want to compound my deceit with an outright lie, so I said, 'Oh, I'd have managed.'

There was a tape protruding from the jaws of the cassette player, and I was dying to see what it was. I would have put money on it being Neil Diamond, or someone similar. It was all I could do to stop myself having a look, but presently Geoff said, 'Do you want some music on?' and snapped the tape into place, filling the car with the unmistakable snare-and-treble sound of Oasis. Before I could register my surprise and approval he had shuddered and hit the eject button. 'My son's,' he said by way of apology and went on to tune the radio until he hit on a wailing soprano, which was obviously more to his taste. 'Do you know *Der Rosenkavalier*?' he asked, and I was forced to confess my brutish ignorance of opera and all other branches of classical music.

'I never go myself any more,' he admitted. 'I just sit slumped in front of the TV like everyone else.'

When we got close to home I asked him to drop me at the corner. Ours is a private road and it wasn't worth unlocking the gate for the sake of an extra fifty yards. As the rain was still scything down he insisted I take his umbrella. I noticed he didn't offer me the ladies' one.

'Well, thank you...Doctor,' I said, as I didn't know his first name at this stage, and he gave me an oblique smile and raised his eyebrows.

'My pleasure,' he said. And although there hadn't been the shadow of any flirtation between us, I *knew*.

The next day at the restaurant there was a bouquet of yellow roses waiting for me. There was no card, so I was able to answer Rowena's inquisitive stare with unfeigned ignorance. The flowers lasted a week, but much longer as fuel for my daydreams. I still had the umbrella too. I'd kept hold of it deliberately to maintain that slender thread of connection between us: every time it rained he would think of me – though possibly with diminishing affection.

Then about a month after the flowers an envelope arrived for me at the restaurant. It contained one ticket to the Coliseum for a performance of *Der Rosenkavalier*, and no accompanying note, but its provenance was perfectly obvious.

He'd even gone to the trouble of discreetly obscuring the ticket price, an act of exorbitant courtesy, which again reminded me of Dad. Now and then I would take it out of my purse and be assailed by anxiety. Would he be waiting for me in the adjoining seat, or was it just a quirky gift from an opera-lover bent on converting the heathen? Was he, in fact, demented?

Right up until the very last moment I entertained the possibility that I might not go: after all I would have to change shifts with one of the other waitresses, and find something respectable to wear (but what?). Curiosity won of course, as I had always known it would, and the appointed evening found me perfumed and painted, in a smart dress and uncomfortable shoes, standing in the bar, toying with a glass of orange juice that I was too sick with nerves to drink.

There was no sign of him there or in the foyer, so I went to my seat, which was in the dress circle, one in from the aisle, and made an attempt at reading the programme notes, losing the plot in about the second paragraph. I couldn't shake off the feeling that I was about to be exposed as an impostor and thrown out, that people could tell just from looking at me that I'd thought there was no Strauss but Johann.

I'd bought a big bag of wine gums at the station, in case he didn't turn up and the performance was boring, but I felt too inhibited to take them out of my handbag. All around me the auditorium was filling up, but the aisle seat remained unoccupied – oppressively so, it began to seem to me. Then the house lights dimmed and the orchestra began tuning up, and just as the first notes of the overture rose like balloons from the pit, he came down the steps, with silent, hasty tread, and slipped into the seat beside me, flinging his coat across his knees, and there was no chance to do more than exchange a quick nod until the end of the first act.

'Aren't you taking a bit of a risk?' I said, as we fought our way back to the bar at the interval.

'I suppose I am,' he replied. 'It's completely out of character.' He had gone to the trouble of pre-ordering drinks to avoid the crush – it was what had made him fractionally late – and it took him a while to track them down: one red wine, one white.

'You choose: I didn't know which you'd prefer.'

'I can't drink alcohol at the moment,' I replied, and I

could see the light dawning even before I added, 'not while I'm taking the tablets you prescribed.'

He looked appalled at his error. 'I'm so sorry,' he said. 'I wasn't thinking of you as a patient.'

'Good,' I said. 'Perhaps if I knew your name I could stop thinking of you as a doctor.'

That was how it began, with a curious mixture of impulsiveness and calculation. For an extra-marital affair it was incongruously restrained. It was weeks, for example, before we got around to making love, and even after that it was something that could only be infrequently achieved. Opportunity and location did not often present themselves. His house was out of the question. I wasn't completely comfortable with the idea of bringing him home for sex-in-the-afternoons with Christian in the next room. Although I had done the ethical thing and registered at a new practice, Geoff was still Christian's GP and I couldn't help feeling there was something questionable in the arrangement. Since Geoff's free time was mostly incompatible with mine the relationship had to be conducted to a large extent by telephone. Every fortnight he would make some work-related excuse for not being at home on a Wednesday night – my weeknight off – and we would meet up for a drink.

We never discussed his family. He made no complaints about his wife's failure to understand him, as adulterers are widely believed to do. In fact he made it clear that he was not prepared to take any risks that might cause her suspicion or pain. 'You know I'll never leave my wife,' he said, right at the outset, to which I replied, 'I'll never leave my brother,' and we laughed out loud, to find ourselves in such perfect accord.

* * *

SINCE ROWENA TOLD THE OTHER GIRLS THAT I AM AN 'ARTIST' they have stopped calling me Sad to my face. I can't see the logic of this: some of my favourite artists were famously sad: Van Gogh, Dora Carrington, Mark Rothko . . . Rowena herself keeps badgering me to do some freelance (and, I suspect, free) artwork for the restaurant, principally a giant mural of the Italian Riviera on the back wall. I've tried explaining that I'm a miniaturist: I don't do big pictures. It's detail that's my thing.

She was on about it again that night, while I was in the staff loo, struggling into my waitress costume, which was slightly crushed from having spent the day in a plastic bag in my car boot. She's one of those people who doesn't find a toilet door any barrier to conversation.

'You could do it the week we're away,' she was saying while I buttoned my shirt and peered at my face in the mirror, which was lit by a single, flickering neon strip. 'The paint smell would have gone by the time we re-open.'

'Have you got a coat hanger?' I interrupted. My green linen suit was hitched over a hook on the door like a giant tea-towel, and I didn't want anyone drying their hands on it. I heard her footsteps retreat and then advance and a wire hanger was thrust under the door.

'I've got a teacher friend who could lend you an overhead projector,' she went on, undeflected. 'If that's how you do it.'

'Mmm,' I grunted, dabbing face powder over the remains of that morning's foundation. The gold compact was my mother's, and my grandmother's before that. It had a particular smell, sweet and cloying, like the inside of an old lady's handbag. All at once I could see mum's dressing table back at the Old Schoolhouse, with its set of tortoiseshell brushes and her few cosmetics, so infrequently and inexpertly applied.

'We've got to do something about that light,' I said as I emerged, zipping up my skirt. 'It adds on about ten years.'

'I think I'll just take down the mirror,' said Rowena. 'Until this frizz grows out.' She was recovering from one of those deep-fried perms, which had reacted badly with her previous regime of bleach and colour, to leave her hair as brittle as spun sugar. It looked as though it might melt in the rain.

'Listen. Have you ever got back in contact with someone after a long silence?' I asked her.

She put her head on one side to consider, happy to abandon the matter of the mural. She is used to my strategy of refusing to engage with topics that don't appeal.

'No, I can't say I have,' she said finally. 'I think I'm probably still in contact with everyone I've ever known, apart from my ex-husbands, I mean. I sort of collect people.'

'Well, I seem to mislay them,' I said, as we made our way upstairs to the restaurant. I explained about coming across Cassie. 'So what's the best way of tracing an address?'

'You could get her number from Directory Enquiries, if her surname isn't too common.'

'I'm not sure I want to phone in the first instance. I'd rather write.'

Rowena chewed her lip. 'Do you know anyone corruptible who works for the police or the DVLA?'

I raised my eyebrows. 'I didn't realise you were such an expert at subterfuge.'

'Well, it's all my divorces. They've made me devious.'

'Evidently. But for someone like me who doesn't have your underworld connections . . .'

'The internet. You can get anything off the internet,' she said confidently.

'How?'

'I don't know. We'll have to ask one of the geeks in the kitchen. Who is this woman anyway?'

'She was my brother's girlfriend. His first real girlfriend. When I was fifteen they . . . split up.' I hesitated over the phrase: it made their predicament sound so ordinary. 'It was a horrible, disastrous split that should never have happened. I think he got over it quicker than I did. Anyway, he had bigger things to worry about – like being paralysed.'

IT WAS TWENTY TO ONE BY THE TIME I PULLED UP OUTSIDE the house and, unusually, Christian's light was still on. This slight deviation from our routine gave me a moment's anxiety, and I wondered if he might be feeling ill, but as I approached the house I could hear Ella Fitzgerald singing Cole Porter, loudly, so I guessed he must be okay. Playing music at an unneighbourly volume in the early hours is one advantage of living in a detached house on a large plot that we don't exploit often enough.

Christian rolled into the hallway to greet me while I was still on the threshold trying to free my key from the lock. He was wearing his blue towelling bathrobe and his hair was sticking up in wet spikes as if he had recently been in the bath, and he had a curious expression on his face – an unnerving combination of smugness and guilt.

'Hi Pest,' he said, cheerfully, reverting to a childhood nickname that fell out of use at least twenty years ago. This only fuelled my suspicions.

'Are you all right? What's going on?' I asked, slinging my bag over the corner of the settle.

'Nothing. Well. Come in and sit down. Do you want some wine?'

I glanced at my watch. We quite regularly exchanged news and conversation over a drink, but not at this time of night. Sunday evening is Happy Hour. Christian opens the drinks cupboard at about six o'clock and starts mixing cocktails. About a decade after they went out of fashion we're suddenly hooked. He's working through a recipe book I bought from the remainder shop next door to Rowena's, and sometimes he'll throw in one of his own invention, just to catch me out. The Tequila Mockingbird is probably his best creation.

I was wide awake now, and if he was in confiding mood, I decided it might be a good time to bring up the matter of replacing Elaine, so I followed him into the sitting room and sat on the couch. The music cut out while he fiddled with the controls, and then resumed at a friendlier volume. On the coffee table, beside an open bottle of claret, were a couple of wine glasses, but as I went to help myself I realised they had both been used. One of them bore the imprint of a lipstick crescent at the rim. *Company.*

'How has your day been?' Christian went on, bringing a fresh glass from the recess in the wall. 'How did you get on at the school?'

'Fine,' I said, warily. 'The kids were sweet.' I made no mention of my encounter with Cassie. Penny is a subject that is never raised any more. I upended the wine bottle and a scant thimbleful of black dregs slid into the bottom of my glass.

'Oh,' said Christian. 'We must have finished it. Shall I open another?'

'No. I wasn't desperate,' I said. 'So what is it, then?'

'Nothing bad. I just want your advice about something. Because it affects you. It's Elaine.'

'Oh, I'm so glad you've brought this up,' I said, and was about to launch into my plea for her dismissal, when something in Christian's eager expression stopped me.

'I'm going to ask her to marry me,' he said, and a faint blush spread over his face.

I must have been gaping like a netted fish because he gave my knee a squeeze and said, 'Are you all right? You look a bit shocked.'

'Wha . . . Well,' I stammered, as the art of speech returned by degrees. 'I am a bit. Surprised. To tell you the truth.' All the while I kept giving these irritating gasps of laughter. 'I had no idea. I didn't realise you were even keen. I obviously haven't been paying attention.'

'There wasn't anything to notice. We haven't exactly been all over each other. We've been out together a few times while you're at work. Most of the time we just sit in watching videos.'

Or taking baths, I thought. 'Why didn't you tell me before? How long has it been going on?' In spite of my best intentions I'd managed to sound disapproving instead of simply intrigued.

'There was nothing to tell until now. It wasn't love at first sight or anything. In fact, when she first came I thought she was a bit abrasive.'

At last, some common ground!

Christian drew his dressing gown, which was starting to gape, more tightly around him. 'But then after a while

I found I was really looking forward to seeing her, and I realised I'd never felt that way about any of my other carers.'

'They were blokes,' I pointed out.

'Yeah, but even so. And then that week she was off with flu – do you remember that?' (I did: I'd done some of my best work in ages.) 'I really missed her. I think that's when it started to dawn on me that she might be The One.'

'But, I mean, *marriage*. You've only known her three months.'

'Well, three months is quite a long time in my circumstances. When someone helps you to get your pants on from day one, intimacy builds up pretty quickly.'

'Do you think she'll say yes?' Suddenly I found myself looking at Christian through fresh, unsisterly eyes, as a potential partner. When I was a child I had assumed he was the most handsome man on the planet, but hadn't given the subject much thought in recent years. Of course, the wheelchair might put some people off, but in spite of it he still looked fit and strong. He worked out with weights twice a week and his upper body was broad and muscular. A stranger might have put his age at thirty-two, though he was nearly forty. His hair was still thick and showed only the first incursions of grey. He was funny and talented; he made plenty of money designing and testing computer games, without ever having to leave the house, which was spacious and tasteful and paid for. Now I could see that to someone like Elaine, he wouldn't be an unattractive proposition.

And then it hit me, like a snowball full in the face, what it would mean for me if Christian and Elaine did get married, and how insanely oblivious I must have been to all their hints and signals. Elaine had been here bright and early cooking breakfast this morning because she'd just spent the night. And all the suggestions about the property ladder and the friendly careers advice were nothing but veiled warnings of my imminent eviction.

'. . . thinking of asking her on her birthday, but I'm not sure if I can wait that long,' Christian was saying, as I tuned back in, still spitting out snow. 'What do you think?'

'What does it matter what I think? It's your life,' I said, in much the same tone that Mum used to say, 'It's your money,' whenever as a teenager I proposed buying some piece of trash from Miss Selfridge.

'Well, it's your life too, and your home. I didn't want to spring it on you as a done deal.'

'No, but...'

'And I don't want you thinking you've got to find somewhere else to live. You can stay here as long as you like.'

'Don't be daft, Christian. Of course I'd have to move out. You can't start married life as a threesome.'

'But Elaine wouldn't mind. I know she wouldn't. She understands our set-up and she's not territorial. Anyway, she really likes you.'

I shook my head at his naivety. How little he knew of his intended bride, and womankind in general. 'You know what they say about two women sharing a kitchen,' I said, as light-heartedly as I could.

'But where would you go?'

'I could move in with Dad for a while,' I said, with more enthusiasm than I felt. 'Hone my backgammon skills. Immerse myself in Classic FM.' It occurred to me that from what I earned from the books and Rowena's I wouldn't be able to afford to do anything else. Without the considerable subsidy

that my rent-free existence represented I wouldn't even be
able to live in the same part of the country any more.

'You do like her, don't you?' I could see the first shadows of doubt pass across his face.

'Of course I do,' I lied valiantly. 'We get along fine. I'm
just so amazed that you want to marry her. I mean, no one
gets married nowadays.' That wasn't what I meant at all. I
really wanted to say: marry, by all means. But not her.

'I know. I've surprised myself. But she's so *inspiring*. She
really believes she can get me walking again one day. She's
downloaded tons of stuff off the net about new treatments
in America. I've already seen most of it, and it's no good
to me, but the fact that she's so wholehearted, when everyone else has lost interest—'

'I haven't lost interest!'

'Okay, not lost interest, but got used to things. Elaine's
still got that crusading enthusiasm.' This would have worked
very much in her favour. I know there are some people who
manage to reach an accommodation with their disability: a
few rare souls even claim it has enriched their lives, made
them more appreciative of life's pleasures, but Christian is
not one of those. He has never grown comfortably resigned
to not walking. Regaining the use of his legs remains a goal,
however distant, that he won't relinquish. 'I've tried both,'
he says simply. 'And walking's better.'

'But you don't need to marry her to get the benefits of
that.'

'I'm not putting it very well. I feel like any time I spend
apart from her is time wasted. Plus, there's the sex. I mean
regular sex.'

'Yeah, well, don't go into details.'

'Anyway, we've got no reason to be pessimistic about

marriage. Our parents are still together and happy.'

'They're living six thousand miles apart!' I protested.

'That's just circumstances. And it's only temporary. In fact it's a testament to the strength of their relationship.'

'When did you say Elaine's birthday is?'

'Three weeks' time.'

'How old will she be anyway?'

'Forty-seven,' Christian said, with a trace of defiance.

This surprised me. I had assumed she was older than me, but not by that much. 'Well, she'll definitely say yes then,' I assured him. 'When women get past thirty-five they panic and marry anyone who asks.'

'Really?' Christian looked sceptical, and not especially flattered. 'How do you know?'

'There's a whole publishing industry dedicated to the subject. Where have you been?'

He shook his head, at a loss, then he grinned at me. 'You've only got a year left then,' he pointed out. 'Better start panicking.'

I DIDN'T SLEEP WELL THAT NIGHT. I LAY AWAKE UNTIL THREE, fretting, and then I made myself a cup of hot milk and took it into the studio and sat with it in the dark. I could hear the distant swish of traffic on the bypass, and the occasional screech of tyres and slamming of car doors that signalled the homecoming of Caterham's youth.

I allowed some tears to pool up in my eyes. I wasn't sad for myself, exactly. I just felt confused and disorientated and slightly foolish. But I was sad that Christian, who could have done so much better, should have lowered his sights this far. And I thought of Elaine, that impostor, who would soon be sharing my name and living in my house and planning how to refurnish my rooms and telling me what was good for Christian, and me, and the world in general. Then I thought of Penny, who had been marked down as my sister-in-law from the day we met, and who had wielded such influence over me, and whose path had crossed mine this very day, as if by design. Occasionally, over the years, I had entertained the fantasy that she and Christian might meet up again and there would be some gesture of reconciliation. Now, as I reviewed these two apparently unconnected events – Christian's intention to marry Elaine, and my rediscovery of Penny – it was impossible not to see the workings of Providence. It was my job, evidently, to bring about this long overdue reunion. For Christian's sake I would take a deep breath, dive back down through the cloudy waters of the past and bring up the pearl.

PART TWO

2

CHRISTIAN WAS FIVE WHEN I WAS BORN, BEFORE I HAD EVEN learned to smile he could read, write his name, catch a tennis ball one-handed and run like a hare, and a quarter of the best part of his life was already in the past. The age gap was such that there was never any competition between us. Christian surpassed me in every accomplishment, so rivalry was pointless. I worshipped him; he endured my worship. According to family lore it was Christian who taught me to read when I was three and he was eight. (Mother was a great delegator.)

We lived on the border of Kent, where the London suburbs trickle into the green belt, in what we liked to call a village, bordered as it was by an approximation of countryside: common land on two sides and a scrubby, pick-your-own farm on the other. Ours was the largest house and garden in the area by some stretch – a grade two listed Victorian schoolhouse, set in an acre of weeds. It had been left to Dad by a maiden aunt, a piece of good fortune he endured with his usual stoicism.

Though picturesque from the outside, the house had fallen into a state of disrepair during Aunt Edie's lifetime, a trend which our tenancy, unfortunately, did nothing to reverse. One of the seven bedrooms was out of commission all the time I lived there because of advancing damp. Black clouds of mould grew on the bulging ceiling and sweaty walls; cardboard boxes stored there would turn soft as felt overnight. In the end the door was locked on the problem: it didn't matter; there were plenty of other rooms.

There was something wrong with the plumbing, which meant that hot water was sometimes available and sometimes not, according to the mood of the boiler, a black monstrosity called The Beast, which bent us all to its cast-iron will. It was always threatening to expire, like a querulous elderly relative, and had to be fed regularly with shovelfuls of coal and given artificial respiration with a pair of bellows. Dad was often to be found first thing in the morning on his knees before it, as though at prayer.

Electricity, too, was subject to an air of randomness rare in other houses. The wiring was clearly ancient and temperamental, and had probably suffered interference from rodents over the years. Switches and sockets wobbled like loose teeth, and it wasn't unusual for us to be plunged into darkness if more than one appliance was running. There were always candles in jam jars standing around in readiness. When the blackouts came in 1974 we hardly noticed.

Dad worked as a chaplain at a young offenders' institution near Gravesend. He once told us that one of his altar boys was a murderer – a fact we used to parade with some

embellishments before our friends, to their great admiration. Mum had trained as an optometrist and once worked
in a mission hospital in Cameroon. To hear her talk you'd
think she had removed cataracts with her bare hands.
Perhaps she had: she wasn't squeamish. Now she worked
as a volunteer in a local charity shop, and did odd bits of
typing and other menial jobs (unpaid) for different overseas aid organisations. There wasn't much money around.
The generous maiden aunt had also left Christian – then
a baby – £100, which Mum duly confiscated and donated
to famine relief, an act whose legality Christian still
disputes. Mum took little interest in housewifery: her mind
was fixed on nobler things. Every ledge and rail in the
house was richly lagged with fluff and dust, huge spiders
squatted in cobwebbed corners, and windows were cloudy
with smears. Once a year, in late spring, Mum might launch
a brief but futile assault on the dirt. Rugs would be dragged
into the garden, hung over the washing line and beaten
with a broom. A feather duster would be twitched along
the picture rails and twirled into corners, momentarily
unsettling the dust and sending the spiders skating for
cover.

Cooking was another household chore performed dutifully, but without enthusiasm or skill. Ever since working
at the mission hospital and witnessing poverty and starvation daily, Mum had had an uneasy relationship with food
and took no pleasure in handling it. The fact that human
beings required so much of it, so often, seemed to her a
design flaw that she would have liked to take up with the
Maker at the earliest opportunity. She would never use
cookery books, which were in her view decadent and waste-
ful of ingredients, but instead followed her instincts,

invariably driven by thrift or haste, and often wrong. I remember the recriminations that followed Christian's discovery of a whole snail shell in one of her blackberry crumbles. In one respect she was ahead of her time, undercooking vegetables decades before it became fashionable. Unfortunately meat and poultry frequently came in for the same treatment. The phrase 'avoid the pink bits' became something of a family motto. Dinner was often bread and cheese.

Perhaps it was hunger that accounted for my early habit of promiscuous grazing. By the time I was two I had, according to family legend, eaten:

1 earthworm
1 Christmas tree bauble
1 fir cone
2 pieces of coal
the cardboard cover of *Ant and Bee*.

When I was little, this was held up as an example of my irrepressible character and prodigious appetite. Years later it occurred to me that it also signified a certain level of neglect: how long would a toddler have to be left unattended to dispose of an entire book cover?

THIS IS MY EARLIEST AUTHENTIC MEMORY: BROKEN GLASS.

It was the summer of '73: the year eleven-year-old Janine Fellowes murdered little Claudia Lyle and was sent to prison for ever. Christian told me she put a pillow over her face, and then hid the body in the wardrobe and *went to the cinema*. That was the bit that made me shiver. I was glad to think she was locked away, and not prowling the lanes with her pillow, looking for other little children, but Dad said it was a terrible thing to imprison a child, shocking beyond words, and he couldn't sit back and say nothing.

On this particular night I came down to the sitting room after lights out because I was having a nightmare. Janine Fellowes again. A strange woman with damp, waist-length hair was sitting on a stool on an island of newspaper in the middle of the floor. My father was on his knees behind her, endeavouring to trim two inches from the ends of her hair by following the horizontal stripe of her shirt. Christian was lying on the couch under the front window, reading *Shoot*.

'Where's Mummy?' I asked.

'Here,' the woman replied, smiling, and now I could see and hear that she was. 'What do you want?'

'You don't look like you.'

'That's because you're used to seeing me with a bun,' she said.

'Keep still,' Dad instructed, pausing to readjust the position of her head. 'Or it'll go skewiff.'

'Why don't you leave it like that all the time?' I wanted to know. She looked so lovely, like my Tressie doll, who had a thick blonde plume that you could pull out of a hole in the top of her head by pressing her belly button.

Mum smiled. 'Because I'm too old. When women get to a certain age long hair doesn't look nice any more.'

'Mrs Blewitt's got long hair,' I said. Mrs Blewitt ran the Mothers' Union and wore an Alice band.

'Yes, well,' said my mother.

'All done,' said Dad, whisking the towel from her neck and shaking it out with a flourish, sending up a shower of bristles.

'How old is too old?' I wanted to know.

'Thirty,' said mother decisively, brushing herself down.

'Is thirty too old for everything?' I wondered aloud. I could hear Dad chuckling away. He always found these question and answer sessions highly amusing. I could make him laugh without even trying.

'Certainly not,' said mother. 'Only some things, like long hair.' She swept the pile of drying fluff into a dustpan and tipped it into the bin, losing some in the process. 'And short skirts.' Her own skirts came from the Nearly New shop in West Wickham and fell in a stiff cone of earth-coloured tweed or corduroy to three inches below the knee. She stroked my plaits and then gave me a gentle pat on the back in the direction of the door. 'So make the most of your lovely long hair while you're young,' she ordered, and then turned to include Christian in the dismissal. 'Bed, young man.'

He made grumbling noises, and rolled reluctantly off the couch onto all fours, before slouching after me. Moments later the central window pane exploded, and in the very spot where he had just been lying sat half a brick, surrounded by shards of smashed glass.

'Was that my fault?' Christian said, when the pieces had been swept up and wrapped in newspaper. He had broken windows before, usually with a football, but never by just lying down.

'No,' said Dad, peering into the darkness through the empty frame. 'It was mine.'

A MONTH LATER MY LOVELY LONG HAIR WENT IN THE BIN. Our school had been raided by the nit nurse not long after I started as a pupil in the reception class and Christian and I were identified as carriers. We were taken aside quietly and given some leaflets, which we were told to take home to our parent-or-guardian.

'What's a guardian?' I asked.

'Someone who looks after you who isn't your mummy or daddy,' the nurse explained kindly.

'I haven't got one of those,' I said, and started to cry.

Fortunately Christian was on hand to explain our domestic arrangements and try to comfort me. 'Stop crying, stupid,' he said, and made a move to ruffle my hair, then thought better of it.

We ran to meet Mother at the school gate, waving our sheets of local authority literature on *pediculus humanus capitis*, invalidating all our teacher's efforts at discretion.

'Oh, that's a nuisance,' said Mother serenely. She was never one to fuss over matters of hygiene: her dealings with malaria and leprosy had left her unimpressed by lesser ailments. We stopped at the chemist on the way home to pick up a nit comb and some lotion.

'They only go to clean heads,' said the woman behind the till, in what she imagined to be a comforting tone, as she counted out Mother's change.

'What nonsense,' said Mother, who had no time for such platitudes. 'The soldiers on the Somme were crawling with head lice and you don't think they had clean hair.' And snapping her purse shut, she led us out of the shop with our dirty, infested heads held high.

At home the scissors were produced and Mother cut my long, looping curls to a ragged two-inch crop. Christian laughed when he saw me shorn and smeared with lotion, then shut up when Mother turned the scissors on him.

'You look like a boy,' he said afterwards, as we gazed at ourselves in the big gilt mirror above the fireplace. I was standing on a chair, so our heads were level, and I noticed for the first time that we had the same large, crumpled ears.

Since much of my time was devoted to the business of emulating Christian I didn't take his remarks as an insult. On the contrary I was delighted. Boys had all the best games: they could climb onto the shed roof, throw tennis balls right over the apple trees, ride a bike no-handed, and swarm up to the top of the rope swing and sit in the oak tree, miles above my head, pretending not to hear anyone calling.

'Let's play death-sticks,' I suggested. This was a game of Christian's own invention, involving rolled-up magazines which functioned as treasure and weapons. The object was to impound each other's hoard by any means possible – principally force. There were no rules. Daring raids on one another's territory usually ended with the two of us brawling in the long grass and thumping each other with tattered copies of *Shoot*.

Christian pulled a face. 'It's too easy. I always win.'

This wasn't boastfulness, but simple fact. His five-year head start meant that there was no game at which I could beat him, no skill I could ever teach him. Nothing I did could ever impress Christian, but the effort of trying seemed to rule my whole childhood.

3

OUR PARENTS WERE DIFFERENT FROM OTHER PEOPLE'S, AND they had different rules. They didn't mind if we were noisy or boisterous, or if we traipsed mud through the house, or slid down the compost heap, or caught nits. They didn't rant and fume when we came home from school with indelible ink on our uniforms, or pockets torn loose, or our shoes scuffed grey. When we left our pens all over the kitchen floor, Mum and Dad stepped over them, and when we trampolined on the beds and crippled the springs, and left footprints on the wall from sliding down the banisters, they just shrugged.

Dad's position on discipline owed much to his job at the prison. He spent all day among young people for whom rage was the normal mode of expression; he had no wish to witness or participate in angry scenes at home. His sternest reproof was likely to be 'Now, now . . .' and a telling off was referred to as 'a kind word'. Mum's attitude to child-rearing – in fact

to everything – had been shaped by those years with the
mission. She had seen so much poverty and suffering, and
so much resilience of spirit, it had left her with a contemp-
tuous disregard for life's petty problems. What was faulty
wiring, or a dirty carpet to a woman who was in mourning
for a whole continent? Her view – not one widely held in
the suburbs at that time – was that children in good health,
who had food and shelter, were already thrice blessed and
needed no further cosseting. Money that could be given to
charity was not to be wasted on frivolities like television,
sweets and trashy plastic toys.

Instead, we had the run of the garden and its amenities:
the trees, the rope swing with the tyre on the end, the shed
and its collection of ancient tennis rackets, bats and balls,
the nettle patch. We seldom had other children back to
play. Mum had tried it once but it hadn't worked: a girl
from my nursery school had come to tea and got an electric shock from one of our loose light switches. She had
cried so much that Mum had to take her home early. The
invitation was never returned and the experiment wasn't
repeated.

In return for considerable latitude in the matter of dirt,
disorder and noise, we were expected to observe three
general rules: we were not to moan; we were not to be bored;
we must share everything and hoard nothing. Although we
were rarely told off and never smacked, there existed a
powerful deterrent to misbehaviour in the form of Mother's
patiently delivered lectures. She would sit the offender down
and explain, at great length and in fine detail, the historical, moral and sociological reasons why certain actions were
undesirable, citing many examples, and alluding frequently
to the Less Fortunate.

The Less Fortunate were often a spectre at our feasts, and were sometimes there in person. Since the house was large, and our parents had philanthropic tendencies, the spare rooms would occasionally be offered as temporary accommodation to the homeless of the parish, visiting clergy, or young offenders at the end of their stretch.

The most recent lodger was a plump teenager called Cindy, who was having 'problems at home', the details of which were known only to Mum and Dad. She was introduced to visitors, for tact's sake, as our au pair, although she never lifted a finger in the house, and seldom climbed out of bed. She passed most of the days in her room listening to Capital Radio, making the odd foray into the kitchen to raid the fridge. Sometimes she let me perch on the window sill and watch her applying her make-up, from a staggering array of bottles and tubes, ranged in height order on the dressing table. She had tan foundation to cover her red cheeks, and red blusher to paint them back on again, lipsticks in every colour including black; a whole paint palette of eyeshadows, and a tiny brush and comb for eyebrows. For someone who never went out, she spent an awful lot of time on grooming. Her knowledge of the subject was encyclopaedic, and she enjoyed nothing more than passing on her wisdom to a novice. The relative merits of block or wand mascara, and the difference between cream and powder blusher were secrets I would never hear from my mother's unpainted lips. Mother was evidently less impressed with Cindy than I was: one afternoon I caught the tail-end of one of her famous lectures. They were in the kitchen; Mother was tending a pan of blackberry jam; Cindy was staring at her with her painted peacock's eyes, bottom lip drooping, in an attitude of helplessness.

'The point is, Cindy,' Mother was saying, dripping hot jelly onto a plate and prodding it with her finger, 'by sitting around here all day listening to pop music you aren't really fulfilling your potential, are you?'

Cindy's bottom lip, glossed to a high shine with Midnight Cherry, drooped still further.

'You mustn't let the terrible experience you've had ruin the rest of your life. It's never too late to make amends. You have talents . . .' Mother snapped off the gas under the preserving pan. 'You mustn't let them go to waste.'

'I don't think I've got any talents,' Cindy said.

'Nonsense. Of course you have.' Mother set to writing labels for the jam jars. *Bramble – September '73.*

'Like what?'

'Well . . .' A frown gathered on Mother's brow, then she spotted me eavesdropping from the doorway. 'What are you doing skulking there, young lady?' she demanded.

'I smelled something nice.' I pointed at the stove where the jam sat resting. 'Is that for us?'

'No.'

Of course it wasn't. On the rare occasions our kitchen was filled with appetising smells, the end product of all this baking, bottling and preserving never ended up in our stomachs. Cakes, chutney and jam were packed up and handed over to the church fête or the Scouts' bazaar, and sold in aid of the Less Fortunate.

A WEEK AFTER THIS CONVERSATION I WALKED INTO CINDY'S room uninvited early one Sunday morning and found a strange man lying in her bed. I made the mistake of mentioning him to my parents over porridge, and that was the end of Cindy's sojourn in the Old Schoolhouse and the end of my introduction to the cosmetic arts. Having taken to heart Mother's advice about using her talents, and decided that casual sex was their natural outlet, she was now sent packing for her trouble.

'Where's Cindy?' I asked, when I came in from school to find her room bare and abandoned, and Mother stripping the bed. The chair was no longer draped with clothes, and all the colourful lotions and potions had vanished. Only a few traces of her presence remained: a talc footprint on the carpet, the stencilled outline of her bottles picked out on the dressing table in loose powder, and the fairy-dust glitter of crumbled eyeshadow.

'She's gone to stay with relatives,' said Mother, peeling the undersheet away from the mattress and tossing it downstairs.

'Is she coming back?'

'No, I'm afraid not.' Mother folded the blanket into a neat square, hesitated a moment, and then chucked that over the banisters too.

'Why not?'

'Well, it didn't really work out,' she replied evasively.

'Was it because of that man?' I asked, drawing an E in the fluff on the bedpost.

'Partly. We couldn't have her bringing people back to the house.' Mother held the eiderdown out of the window and gave it a good, hard shake.

'You have friends back,' I pointed out.

'Yes, but that's different. This man could have been anybody.'

'Do you mean a burglar?' I said, suddenly full of fear and excitement.

'No, not a burglar,' said Mother, who was beginning to

tire of this line of questioning. 'Go and bring me a clean pillowcase from the trunk.'

'Will we be getting someone else?' I wanted to know.

'Oh, I expect so,' Mother sighed. 'Sooner or later.'

4

OUR FATHER WAS THE ONLY PERSON WE KNEW WHO WENT TO work on a Sunday, apart from the man in the newsagent's on the green.

He took two services at the prison every Sunday – Holy Communion and Evensong. Attendance was voluntary, and sometimes the homicidal altar boy would be the only person to turn up. 'God was there,' Father used to say.

If we were very lucky he would bring home stories from work. One thing he told us, which made my scalp tingle, was that you could never let a prisoner so much as *glimpse* a key. Some of the young men in there were so desperate and so cunning that they could memorise the exact shape and dimensions of any key in the blink of an eye, and reproduce a perfect replica when it was their turn in the workshop.

But our favourite was the one about the prisoner who took a warder hostage in his cell. Father was the only person who had been able to talk him into releasing the warder and giving up. He had succeeded where the trained negotiator had failed, because months earlier he had given the prisoner, who was going out of his mind in solitary confinement, a pack of cards. The moral of this story, Father said, was that even the most hardened criminal could be moved by a small act of kindness. 'No,' said Christian. 'The moral of this story is: never let a prisoner get between you and the door.'

We liked to imagine our father as a hero. Chaplaincy didn't generally offer much scope for heroics, so those few incidents that qualified tended to be somewhat exaggerated. By the time Christian and I had retold the story a few times we had managed to convince ourselves as well as our audience that it had been Father himself who had been taken hostage and very nearly murdered.

I don't think Mother would have made a good chaplain. She wouldn't give a man a pack of cards even if he was on Death Row: she'd have him knitting blankets for earthquake victims. She refused to go to our local church, saying that it was just a club for middle class people who liked singing hymns. Instead she had a very intense and personal relationship with God that didn't require her attendance at acts of public worship. She was happy rattling collecting tins or knocking on doors for a good cause, but you wouldn't get her within half a mile of the Young Wives or the Mothers' Union. Not that they were exactly clamouring to have her.

I remember one incident in particular. It was the year after the headlice and the departure of Cindy, so I would have been six. Christian had been dragooned into the church pantomime owing to a desperate shortage of males, and we went along to watch his performance as 1st Footman in Cinderella. We were sitting near the back of the hall, and even perched on top of my folded coat I could only see the actors if they advanced to the very edge of the stage. Just before the interval I had begun to weary of my obscured view, and the elderly lady in front had twice turned round and asked me not to kick her in the back, so my parents allowed me to slip around to the back to see Christian. It was coming up to the big chorus number at the end of Act One, so most of the cast were on stage or in the wings. There was no one in the dressing room except the women who were helping with wardrobe and make-up. They were whisking between the rails of costumes, picking up discarded clothes and putting them back on hangers. Before I had a chance to make my presence known one of them held up a limp, grey rag.

'Look at Christian's shirt!' she said, holding it up, to display its many rends and missing buttons and dark tide-mark around the collar and cuffs. 'Did you ever see anything like it?' Her companions laughed and shook their heads.

'He must have had it on all week. Do you think she ever does the laundry?' one of them said.

'Too busy worrying about the ragged urchins of Timbuktu to notice the ragged urchin under her own roof,' the first woman replied.

'Such a nice boy,' said the third woman, who had not so far contributed. 'But, oh those shoes! It wouldn't surprise me if they'd never been polished since the day he got them.'

I didn't hear any more on the subject, because at that moment there was a loud burst of applause from the auditorium and the three women looked up and flinched violently when they saw me.

'Esther!' said the first to recover. 'Why aren't you watching the show?'

'I can't see over people. I'm looking for Christian.'

'He'll be out in a minute. It's the interval now.' One of them fetched me a drink of squash from the cast's tray of refreshments, and they all said wasn't I getting tall, and how nice my hair was looking now that it had grown back, until Christian came out and told me I wasn't supposed to be backstage.

'Did you see my bit?' he asked.

'No, but I heard it.' I glanced down and noticed for the first time that his shoes were rather bald and tatty, and that mine were just the same. For the rest of the interval I kept my eyes fixed on people's feet, counting the shiny shoes as they passed, until at last I saw a pair of scuffed and gaping pumps more disreputable even than ours, and I looked up with a belated jolt of recognition into Mother's smiling face.

5

ON SUNDAY EVENINGS MUM AND DAD WENT DOWN THE LANE
to Mrs Tapley's to watch the Classic Serial, leaving
Christian and me alone in the house. We took this opportunity to stay up late and play Monopoly and pontoon,
and other games regarded by Mother as liable to encourage the sin of avarice. We didn't have any money of our
own so we gambled with the bag of silver milk bottle tops
that mum was collecting for the blind. I loved the feel
of them, and the noise they made, shimmering together
in the bag.

'What do blind people need milk bottle tops for?' I
wondered aloud.

'They hang bunches of them in their doorways,' Christian
said confidently, 'so they can hear them rattling when
anyone comes in.'

He had broached the subject of pocket money once, without success. Instead of agreeing to hand over ten pence

every Friday, mother proposed delegating a quarter of the family budget to Christian. He would, of course, be responsible for his share of the food bills, rates, gas and electricity, not to mention clothing and household repairs. They sat down together with pen and paper to calculate how much change he might look forward to at the end of each week: the result was a deficit of £3.75 and the idea was shelved.

These Sunday evenings were especially precious because so much of Christian's time was taken up with matters more important than Monopoly or me. It was his final year at Junior School, and he seemed to spend every waking moment being drilled by Mother in Maths and English in preparation for some great test. After school, instead of tearing around the garden with me or practising new ways of getting from the attic to the cellar without touching the floor, he would sit in the dining room, chewing his pencil over *Fletcher Book Three*, and *More Verbal Reasoning*. At first I was allowed to be present at these lessons, in the hope that I might pick up some crumbs of knowledge as they fell. I would sit next to Christian while he wrestled with sets and sequences, and dash off crayon drawings one after another. In half an hour I might have produced twenty pictures, and Mother would be muttering about paper not growing on trees. Eventually I was expelled from the sessions for disruptive behaviour. My habit of clamping my tongue between my teeth and humming while I drew was too much of a distraction to the would-be scholar.

On Saturdays Mum would put on the newest of her nearly-new dresses and drag Christian off to various open days run by local schools. On her return she and Dad would withdraw to the dining room to confer, while Christian tore off his shirt and tie and joined me in the garden. The few free hours remaining to Christian during this period were spent outdoors, practising one or other of the sports at which he excelled. He was the sort of boy who could spend hours quite happily chucking a tennis ball against a wall, or bouncing a football on his head. He even took his cricket bat to bed with him and hugged it while he slept. He couldn't stand still for a minute without his arms wheeling around in a burst of imaginary spin-bowling, or walk down the street without dribbling a pebble along at his feet. On one occasion we rigged up a badminton net in the garden using two bamboo canes from the runner beans and a gooseberry net. Dad chewed a rectangular court out of the long grass with the rotary mower and for weeks we did nothing but chase shuttlecocks as the wind sent them swooping into the rough. Then the birds started eating the gooseberries, and that was that. Instead we put a wellington boot on the end of the bamboo poles and used them for jousting on our rickety bicycles. We faced each other at opposite ends of the garden, lances balanced on handlebars, and rode like the wind, until – Whump! – I'd feel the impact of a boot in my chest and I'd be on my back in the grass, gazing at the sky through a spinning pattern of oakleaves.

THE LETTER OFFERING CHRISTIAN A SCHOLARSHIP TO THE best boys' school in the area arrived on a Saturday morning in spring. Having exerted themselves for some months with just this end in mind, Mum and Dad were oddly subdued. Success, of the sort that comes in envelopes, was always to be treated with caution, it seemed. They sat Christian down to break the good news.

'Well done, son. You've got a scholarship to Turton's,' Dad began, offering him a hand to shake.

'Was that the one with the pool and the squash courts?' Christian asked, punching the air when Dad confirmed that it was. 'Magic.' He mimed a forehand smash.

Mum, already totting up the cost of another variety of racket, not to mention the uniform, smiled bravely. 'It's a great opportunity for you, Christian,' she said. 'You're very fortunate.'

Having dispensed with the congratulations, Dad launched into the first of their reservations. 'The thing is,' he said, folding and unfolding the letter mechanically, 'if you do go to Turton's, you'll be mixing with boys from much wealthier families.'

'So?' To Christian, other boys' families were a matter of complete indifference, wealthy or not. 'I don't care.'

'What we're trying to say is that the friends you make there will be able to afford things that we can't,' Mum explained.

'What sort of things?'

'Well, pocket money, television, new bicycles, expensive toys, parties, foreign holidays.' Mum got quite carried away counting off potential areas of deprivation on her fingers until Dad interrupted.

'These are unimportant material things, of course, we all know that,' he put in hastily. 'The point is, if you go to Turton's you'll have to accept that there will be times when you feel left out. And we won't be able to buy you back in.'

'Doesn't bother me. If people like me, they'll like me, won't they?'

'Exactly. That's just the right attitude. Good lad,' said Dad, hoping to wrap up the discussion and post off the acceptance slip before Mum had a crisis of conscience and changed her mind.

'The other problem with schools like Turton's,' she said, stalling, 'is that they tend to give the boys who go there the idea that they're a cut above.'

'Is that bad?' asked Christian. He had, after all, spent the last six months hunched over those test papers trying to ensure he was a cut above the other three hundred or so applicants.

'In the eyes of God everyone is special,' Dad said.

'But not boys at Turton's?'

'No, no,' said Dad, conscious of having muddied the waters. 'You'd be special whichever school you went to. And children who don't go to Turton's are no less special than anyone else.'

'Can I go to Turton's one day?' I asked.

'No, darling,' said Dad, patting my hand. 'It's a boys' school.'

'Are boys specialler than girls?'

'Absolutely not,' said Mum.

'So can I go there or not?' Christian wanted to know.

'I don't see why not,' Dad said, uncapping his pen.

'Now that we've ironed out those few little worries,' Mum added. We all watched as Dad drew a squiggle on the dotted line. It was Christian who broke the silence of this solemn moment.

'Can I have a squash racket?' he said.

THE EVENING BEFORE THE FIRST DAY OF TERM, CHRISTIAN WAS made to parade in front of us in his school uniform. Grandpa Percy – Mum's dad – had sent a cheque for the whole kit: even the socks were new. Christian stood scowling in the middle of the sitting room, a cardboard doll, hung with his press-out clothes. The blazer sat stiffly on his shoulders; his trousers held twin creases like the blade of a sword. He held his head awkwardly as though wearing an orthopaedic neck brace. On closer inspection it was discovered that he had failed to remove the cardboard packaging from the shirt collar.

A flash cube splintered and popped as Dad took a photo to send to Grandpa Percy, as proof that his funds had been properly deployed and not diverted to the Less Fortunate, as had sometimes been known to happen.

'Right, that's enough preening,' said Mother, giving Christian a gentle push. 'Off to bed.'

I was the only one who remembered his shoes. Mum found me ten minutes later in the cupboard under the stairs, picking through a box of rags. 'What on earth are you doing in here?' she asked.

'Looking for shoe polish,' I replied, still rummaging. 'Have we got some?'

'I don't know.' She looked helpless. 'It would be here if anywhere, I suppose. What do you want it for?'

'To clean Christian's shoes for school,' I explained, hoping she might take over.

'That's a nice thought, dear,' she said, and left me to it.

Eventually, after further ransacking, I turned up a dented tin of black Tuxan containing a couple of fossilised pellets of polish. I carried it into the kitchen along with one of the fresher rags, and set to work.

So it was that Christian began his career at Turton's with shiny shoes, and I went into the top infants with black finger-nails and was called a dirty little tinker by the dinner-lady.

6

OUR SUMMER HOLIDAYS WERE SPENT AT THE SAME PLACE every year – a caravan on the Pembrokeshire coast, just upstream from Milford Haven. The owner was a friend of Dad's from his college days who had disgraced himself by abandoning his wife and young son for another woman. My parents, who strongly disapproved of his behaviour, had allowed the friendship to lapse, but his ex-wife, Barbara, still maintained irregular contact by letter, and insisted we continue to use the caravan. They evidently shared my parents' horror of anywhere 'commercialised' – a term whose broad sweep took in everything from the Blackpool illuminations to a solitary gift shop – as the caravan was parked, by arrangement with the farmer, at the edge of a field on a river estuary, several miles from the nearest settlement. It was reached by a rutted clay track full of deep potholes, filled in wet weather with tea-coloured water. The car would often get bogged down, its trapped wheels spinning helplessly, and we would have to fetch stones and slates to build up the collapsed path beneath the tyres. In dry weather the car crunched over sharp chippings and sagged onto punctured rubber. Dad would say, 'Hey-ho,' and reach for the jack, while we unloaded the luggage onto the side of the path to dig out the spare wheel. None of this ruffled Mum and Dad, who accepted all such minor inconveniences with perfect serenity. Holidays were not an opportunity to wallow in luxury, but a chance to renew our appreciation for the comforts of home.

We bought milk and eggs daily from the farm and filled our giant canisters with drinking water from the outside tap. Every morning we would hike across country, over stiles and streams to the village shop and return carrying bread and fresh meat and vegetables. The round trip took most of the morning; the rest of the time Christian and I spent mudcombing along the shoreline at low tide, or fooling around in our rubber dinghy when the water was high, trying to stop the outboard motor snagging the reeds. Dad, safely upstream of our splashing, dozed over his fishing rod, while Mum sat on a canvas deckchair peeling through a pile of library books, or knitting six inch squares for an aid project known as The Universal Quilt.

In the evening Mum would cook dinner on a two-ring primus stove, using whatever we had managed to buy that morning, along with our supplies of dried food from home. Some of these combinations were more successful than others: chicken with mushrooms and rice we liked; pork chops with spaghetti and marrow we didn't. Plates had to be cleared either way, as there was no larder or fridge for raiding later. Dad would boil a kettle to wash the dishes in a bucket, and then we would sit around the table by the light of a whining gas-lamp and play non-competitive games until bedtime.

One night, on our first visit there, I woke up to a darkness so complete I thought I'd gone blind. My screams must have been audible in Milford Haven, and caused pandemonium in the confined space of the caravan, as the other three blundered around, stubbing their toes and colliding as they hunted for the torch. After that episode I was never comfortable in a blackout again, and Mum had to leave a candle burning all night to placate me.

Caravan life favoured those with a strong bladder. It was a half-mile hike to the chemiloo in the farmer's spidery shed, which had no light and the bottom half of a stable door which didn't shut. If you applied any pressure it was likely to come adrift from its one hinge altogether. For emergencies there was a bucket behind the caravan. I don't remember washing: I think we went without.

We seldom left our immediate surroundings, except on foot. That stony track was a powerful deterrent to unnecessary travel, particularly if we'd used the spare tyre on the way in. One glorious day, though, when the temperature was in the nineties, Mum and Dad contained their revulsion and took us to a seaside resort, where we dug fortifications against the incoming tide and threw our grubby little bodies off the collapsing ramparts into the surf. Mum changed into an ancient flowered swimsuit with an attached skirt and moulded cups like half coconuts, and showed off plucked-chicken skin to the sun. Dad, who was red-haired and likely to burn, stayed covered up and did the crossword. When Christian and I started to wrinkle from too much time in the water we scratched ourselves dry on thin, prickly towels and played tennis on a court drawn in the sand with the edge of a spade.

In the afternoon we walked along the front and bought 99s from a fat man in a kiosk. The ice-cream swirled onto the cones, whiter than anything in nature, and tastier too.

'Forty new pence!' mum muttered, shaking her head as she handed over the cash. 'That's eight shillings.' It nearly broke her heart to give that sort of money to someone who looked so well-fed.

'Still, it's only once a year, eh?' Dad said, seeing the rapture on our faces as we licked the pointed white peaks into smooth hills.

'You're right, you're right, I should just shut up and enjoy it,' Mum sighed. 'But what a price.'

Lured by the flashing lights and the chink of coins, Christian and I hung back at the entrance to the amusement arcade, gazing at the slot machines, with their tempting overhang of copper pennies. Anyone could see that it would only take one more penny to bring the whole lot crashing down, but we knew better than to ask for something that didn't grow on trees, especially after that ice-cream.

There was a whoop from an old woman beside the door. The one-armed bandit had started to pump out silver: *ker-chunk, ker-chunk*, went the beating of its metal heart, as the woman scrabbled to collect her winnings. Christian's eyes gleamed as she moved away. He could see one she'd missed – a ten pence piece winking in the corner of the tray. He waited until she had gone and then ducked inside to claim it.

'Where did you get that?' Mother demanded, pouncing.

She had been looking at postcards a few doors down and only just noticed we weren't with her.

'From in there. It was just lying there,' he said defensively, his fingers closing round the coin. Up ahead I could see a man holding a box of flags and a collecting tin in the shape of a lifeboat. Christian saw him too. 'Please can I keep it?' he begged, knowing how Mum's mind worked.

'Well,' she looked to Dad for a ruling, but he just shrugged. 'All right,' she relented. 'But you'd better pray you're never shipwrecked!'

It was an exceptional day in every way. The early start meant we hadn't had time to buy food for the evening meal, so on the way back to the caravan we stopped for fish and chips, which we ate out of paper with little wooden forks. Frizzled nuggets of golden batter, and soft, fat chips, stinging with salt and vinegar: nothing would ever taste as good again.

'When I'm earning money,' Christian whispered later, as we followed Dad's swinging torch beam across the field to the chemiloo before bedtime, 'I'm going to have fish and chips and white ice-cream every night. You wait and see.'

I kept that little fork wrapped in a piece of tissue in my pocket until we were back home again, when I transferred it to the empty Germolene tin that held all my treasures.

WHEN IT WAS TIME TO LEAVE AND RETURN TO THE OLD Schoolhouse and what remained of the summer holidays, Mum told us we would be stopping in Bath for lunch with the owner of the caravan, whom we were to address as Aunty Barbara, though she was no relation. Although I'd never met her, I knew the name from birthday cards, which she sent several weeks late, if at all. These cards were some-times accompanied by an inappropriate gift – indoor fire-works, for example, or a glassblowing kit. Her latest present to me had been a model of a silver Aston Martin, as driven by James Bond. On the bottom of the box was a label read-ing: To Donovan, love from Daddy.

'Will I have to kiss her?' asked Christian, who at twelve was starting not to enjoy being slobbered over by grown-ups.

'No. Not if you don't want to,' Dad promised him.

'If she gives us mash will I have to eat it?'

'Of course. She'll have gone to a lot of trouble to give us lunch.'

'Will we have to sit and talk to her?' Christian wanted to know. We were just turning up the hill to her house, one of a sand-coloured terrace, with black railings and steps leading up to the front door.

'Do stop worrying,' said Mum. 'It'll be perfectly fine. 'She's got a boy about your age. You can talk to him.'

'Whose age?' I said, brightening at the prospect of young company and strange new toys to play with.

'Oh, in the middle, I think,' Mum said vaguely, as we pulled up outside number twelve Clifton Villas. A terra-cotta plant pot containing some bruised petunias stood awkwardly on the third step, partly blocking the way. Dad bent to move it and then stood up sharply as a fat drop of water hit him on the back of the neck. We looked up to see a steady drip, drip, falling from the overflow pipe to land squarely in the flower pot. 'Ah,' said Dad, stepping round it to ring the doorbell.

From within the house a voice called, 'Get that, Donovan,' and a few seconds later the door opened an inch or two and snagged against a chain. A boy bigger than me stood in the gap, frowning.

'What do you want?' he said.

Dad rocked nervously on his heels, holding out the box of Genuine Welsh Fudge he'd just bought at Aust Services. 'Hello. We've come to see Mummy.'

'Hang on,' the boy said, slamming the door on us. We could hear his retreating footsteps and then a muffled exchange of 'Who is it?' 'Some people to see you.' 'Find out what they want. Oh never mind, I'll do it myself.'

Mum and Dad rolled their eyes at each other, and then there was a clatter as someone fumbled the chain off and the door flew open. Although it was nearly lunchtime the woman standing before us was still in her dressing gown, which was pink satin and decorated with coffee-coloured stains. Her hair was half in and half out of a bird's nest arrangement on top of her head, and her eyes were two squashed spiders of smudged mascara.

'What the F—', she began, and then as the moment of recognition dawned her face seemed to collapse with embarrassment. 'Oh Christ. It's never today already,' she said, and shrank back behind the door, emitting a strange whimpering noise.

'Look, why don't you lot wait in the car,' Dad said, taking control. He handed Mum the keys and the fudge and we trooped back down the steps, while he slipped inside and closed the door.

'What was wrong with her?' Christian asked, when we were all safely inside the car.

'I don't know.' I could see Mum's face in the mirror, her eyes pinched shut. 'She may have only just got out of bed. Clearly she's not expecting us for lunch.'

'I'm hungry!' I wailed.

'Here.' Mum passed back the box of fudge, an uncharacteristic gesture which showed the full measure of her preoccupation. 'You might as well have some of this. There'll be nothing else for a while.'

Christian and I fell on the box, clawing at the cellophane, before she could change her mind. On the front was a woman in fancy dress – a black and white checked skirt and a sawn-off witch's hat with a frill, superimposed on a background of mountains and blue, blue sky. It wasn't a scene we recognised from the mudflats of Milford Haven, but the fudge was everything we could have wished for: smooth and buttery and sweeter than sugar itself. We ate piece after piece, our heads lolling in ecstasy. Mum hunted in the bag at her feet and produced her knitting needles from which hung the beginnings of another square for the Universal Quilt. Her fingers began to work, quickly, rhythmically, the ball of wool jumping beside her.

Half an hour passed. The woollen square was finished and cast off and another one begun. A pound of fudge sat heavily in our stomachs, the box lying empty on the seat between us, proclaiming our guilt, our greed, our lack of restraint. Any second now Mum would notice and we'd be in disgrace for the rest of the day.

'What do you think he's doing in there?' Christian ventured to ask.

Tick, tick, went the knitting needles. 'I don't know,' Mum replied. 'Just lending a hand.'

'How much longer will he be?'

'I've no more idea than you, darling. We shall just have to wait patiently.'

As she said this, the front door opened and Dad emerged,

holding a small suitcase. Behind him stood the boy whose frowning face we had glimpsed briefly. Dad gestured to me to move across onto the uncomfortable ridge between the two back seats. 'This is Donovan,' he said, ushering him in. 'He's coming to stay.'

We exchanged quick, embarrassed smiles, sizing each other up, then Donovan turned back to stare at the blank windows of his house. His mother had not come out to wave him off. Mum raised an enquiring eyebrow.

'She's suffering from the . . . er . . . wrath of grapes,' Dad replied in a whisper. 'I've rung her best friend, Joan. She's on her way over. It's not the first time, apparently.' And then at full volume: 'Everyone comfortable in the back? Ha ha. Just say if it gets too breezy.'

The small matter of lunch seemed to have been forgotten, but I could hardly raise it without reminding Mum about the fudge. In any case I was feeling slightly sick. I concentrated on stealing glances at Donovan's profile. He had light brown hair, thick and close cut, like the pelt of a small mammal, so that it was all I could do to stop myself stroking the furry nape of his neck. His nose was straight and sprayed with freckles, and when he finally turned his head and caught me staring I could see that his eyes were pale green like the pebbles of glass that wash up on the beach after years and years at sea.

'Are you a boy or a girl?' he asked, squinting. His confusion was understandable in the face of my unisex shorts and T-shirt, and androgynous haircut – a result of Mum's ongoing war against nits and one-style-fits-all technique.

'A boy,' I replied, and he nodded, relieved.

Christian gave a little snort from his corner, but didn't give me away.

'How old are you?' I asked. I could see he was some years older than me: his mouth was full of large, new teeth, while I still had gaps top and bottom.

'Ten,' he replied.

'Ten,' Dad sighed. 'That's a wonderful age.'

Donovan looked unconvinced.

'How long is he staying?' I asked Mum, who was usually in charge of visitors. I didn't want him vanishing without warning, like Cindy.

'Oh, well, Donovan's welcome to stay as long as he likes. Until his mummy's better.'

'Is she poorly?'

'Yes. She just needs a little rest,' Mum said lightly, though how she knew this I couldn't imagine. She hadn't even spoken to Aunty Barbara but had been in the car with us all the time. Sometimes it took your breath away what adults knew. Until that day I don't think it had even occurred to me that grown-ups could be ill. I thought it was something to do with childhood, like having nightmares, or crying over nothing, that you grew out of. Mum and Dad certainly never complained of feeling unwell or took 'little rests'.

'I was sick in a bucket once,' I confided to Donovan, who continued to stare out of the window.

'My mum's often sick in buckets,' he said, without turning round.

'Wh . . .'

'Do you play cricket, Donovan?' Dad cut in heartily.

Donovan said he did, but that he couldn't be in the school team because he didn't have any whites. 'I'm the third best batsman in my class,' he said, with punctilious honesty.

'Splendid. There you are, Christian. Now you've got someone to bowl at,' Dad said.

'He's already got someone!' I protested, a whole summer of wicket-keeping stretching before me.

About a quarter of an hour into the journey, Donovan gave a gasp and said, 'Chewy!'

'What did you say, dear?' Mum asked.

'We've forgotten Chewy, my hamster. Mum won't remember to feed him.'

The car slowed down fractionally. 'I'm sure she will.'

'She won't,' Donovan said vehemently, his green eyes growing wide with alarm. He looked as if he might cry.

'We'll turn round. It's no problem,' Dad said, and at the next exit we swung off and headed back towards Bath. 'I can check that this Joan has turned up,' he said in a whispered aside to Mum.

Twenty minutes later we restarted our journey with an extra passenger: a fist-sized furball who stayed wedged in a plastic tunnel at the bottom of his cage all the way home and refused to wake up and entertain us or show any gratitude for his rescue from certain starvation.

ON OUR ARRIVAL AT THE OLD SCHOOLHOUSE WE FOUND THAT in our absence a jay had fallen down the chimney into the dining room. Sooty streaks and smudges on the walls and ceiling were evidence of its suicidal panic to be free. A row of beheaded stalks was all that remained of a dried flower arrangement on the mantelpiece, and a pair of china figurines lay shattered on the tiled hearth.

'Good-ee. Shan't have to dust those again,' Mum said – as if she ever did!

The jay itself was discovered in a dishevelled state,

patrolling the top of the Welsh dresser. Dad threw open the French windows and it took off like a rocket into the garden, almost scalping him.

'Well!' said Mum, as the five of us stood there surveying the debris. 'Who'd have thought a thing that size could do so much damage?'

7

'YOU'RE A GIRL!' DONOVAN SAID, WATCHING ME CHANGE into my nightdress. Mum had put him in Cindy's old room, but as soon as she'd gone we dragged the mattress up to my room in the attic.

'So?' I laughed, pleased to have got the better of him.

We had spent what was left of the daylight showing him over every inch of the house and garden, enjoying his evident admiration. 'Is it all yours?' he asked, taking in our overgrown acre with a sweep of his arm. 'Lucky you,' he muttered when we assured him it was. He was up the top of the rope swing in an instant, and swarming to the outermost branches of the oak. When he finally slid down the rope, scorching the palms of his hands, Christian treated him to an 'up and round' – a terrifying ride in which the tyre traced a dizzying elliptical path, passing inches from the tree trunk. His shrieks of laughter, or possibly fear, brought Mum to the window. 'Don't break

Donovan's neck the minute he arrives,' she reproved mildly.

After supper – shepherd's pie containing generous amounts of carrot and swede but only traces of mince – we unpacked Donovan's suitcase and inspected its contents. One toothbrush, one flannel, soap, *Whale Adventure* by Willard Price, clothes, a deck of cards, a compass, a wallet, a book of matches from a French hotel, bearing the enticing message *Bienvenu à Biarritz*, and a brown felt sausage dog which leaked chopped tights from a hole in its belly. He stuffed the dog under his pillow, embarrassed, but we weren't going to laugh anyway. Christian still had an old teddy somewhere in his room and took items of sports equipment to bed with him, so was in no position to mock.

'What's the compass for?' he wanted to know.

'In case I get lost,' Donovan explained. 'I'll know where I am.'

'No you won't,' said Christian, who at twelve was turning into something of a pedant. 'You'll just know which way you're facing.'

The most exciting discovery in Donovan's case, from our point of view, was the wallet containing two five pound notes. The last time I had seen a fiver it had slipped out of a birthday card from Grandpa Percy. Mum had swiped it and put it in a special one-way bank account, which I couldn't touch until I was eighteen and had learned, somehow, without any practice, the Value of Money.

'Wow,' said Christian, holding them up to the light to marvel at the watermarks. 'Ten quid. Where did you get it from?'

'My dad sends me pocket money sometimes. If he hasn't seen me for a while I get more. Or if I do something good at school, like when I passed my piano exam, and I write and tell him, he sends me money then.'

'That's not fair,' said Christian, full of envy and indignation. 'I do loads of things at school and I never get money for it. All the other boys in my class got bikes and stuff, just for getting into Turton's, and I got a *scholarship* and Mum and Dad didn't give me a penny.'

'I'd rather have my dad at home and not have the money,' Donovan pointed out.

'Yeah, well,' Christian said. We didn't know what else to say.

WE INSTALLED CHEWY'S CAGE ON TOP OF MY CHEST OF drawers. He gave off a sweet, musty smell and made scrabbling noises during the night, which woke me up. In the morning, the cage was surrounded by wood shavings and pellets of food that he had kicked through the bars. Donovan made a miniature obstacle course for him on my bedroom floor, using empty toilet rolls and Lego bricks. Chewy proved quite proficient at show-jumping over pencils, but his career as an entertainer was cut short when he escaped from the arena and did a wee on my eiderdown. Dad built him a run in the back garden using four planks from a dismantled cold-frame and the gooseberry netting that had once served us briefly on the badminton court. Unfortunately Chewy lived up to his name and nibbled through the mesh one afternoon while unsupervised. After a frantic search, during which Donovan and I combed the garden on hands and knees, while Christian patrolled the gap-toothed perimeter fence, the runaway was finally discovered asleep in a pile of dried grass cuttings at the base of the compost heap. Further experiments in free-range hamster care were subsequently abandoned and Chewy was confined to his cage.

I was the one who had found him, and as a token of his gratitude Donovan gave me one of his five-pound notes *and* the book of matches from Biarritz. They seemed to me a symbol of everything exciting and forbidden: fire, foreignness, hotels.

'You're my best friend for ever,' he promised. He really loved that hamster.

'I can't really keep it, can I?' I said, feeling uneasy about the money.

'Yeah. You need it more than I do,' Donovan replied. Although impressed by the size of the house and garden, he had noticed a certain deficiency in its contents. There wasn't much among our collection of home-made toys to tempt him. It had already emerged in the course of conversation that he had a colour television in his bedroom at home, as well as one downstairs. He laughed scornfully at my set of wooden farm animals – the only inhabitants of an unfurnished Victorian dolls' house – and the warped bagatelle board with its rusty nails, but pounced on the James Bond car. 'Oh cool, I've got one of these.' He frowned. 'I did have.'

He couldn't believe that we didn't have and had never heard of Mousetrap, Twister, Battling Tops, Ker-plunk, Haunted House or Ricochet Racers, and then admitted that he hardly ever played them because there was no one to play with except his mum, who was seldom in the mood.

'She gets these sad feelings,' he explained. 'And she can't play Mousetrap or stuff like that when she's got sad feelings. She has to lie down.'

'Our mum has sad feelings too,' I said.

'No she never,' Christian retorted. 'You're just saying that.'

'She cries when there's been an earthquake or something on the radio,' I protested. 'And when Grandma Percy died.'

She did her crying standing up, though. That was the difference. She would never lie down during the day.

DONOVAN MAY HAVE BEEN THE ALL-ENGLAND KER-PLUNK champion, but he was something of a disappointment when it came to more traditional games like chess and draughts. Christian, who occasionally found his invincibility a burden, was hoping he might at last have found a worthy opponent, but Donovan appeared not to know even the general principles. Dad gave him a cribbage board and he looked at it, mystified, turning it over and over to see where the batteries went. 'Thank you,' he said at last. 'What does it do?'

Christian took it upon himself to put right this deficiency in Donovan's education and taught him a few essential games like pontoon and five-card brag, with the aim of fleecing him of that last fiver. However Donovan proved too much of a card-sharp to fall victim to this scheme, and moreover refused to accept Christian's marker, sensing instinctively that he was a man of straw. His real talent, though, was for bizarre party tricks: he could play the recorder through his nose and juggle with three lightbulbs, skills only achievable through the sort of dedicated practice born of chronic boredom.

If the weather was fine we were encouraged to spend as little time as possible indoors. You only had to walk from one room to another without a sufficiently purposeful stride to be accused of 'mooching' by Mum and turfed out again. Most days were spent riding round the spinney, the wooded end of the common that abutted our back garden.

'I wish I'd brought my Raleigh Chopper,' Donovan said, looking at our rusty bikes, which Mum had acquired third or fourth hand from the charity shop. He said the same thing every time my gears slipped or the chain fell off, making him skin his ankle. I thought his complaints showed an annoying lack of gratitude, given that I was having to make do with balancing on Christian's crossbar or running alongside the wheels like a dog.

It was down at the spinney that Donovan instructed us in the art of smoking, using a single Embassy that he'd pinched from his mum's handbag, and kept hidden inside the casing of a defunct biro. We were allowed one drag each before it was extinguished and put away for another day. Then he showed us how to make our own by collecting shreds of tobacco from discarded butts and rolling them up in the rectangular pieces of tissue paper that came from a tiny packet in his wallet. In truth the foulness of that first burning breath had been enough to put us off cigarettes for good, but we were nevertheless pleased to have learned a new skill. Trying to make something out of nothing was in our blood.

Sometimes, when we didn't feel inclined to wander, we concentrated on various home-based projects. Christian had heard on the radio that a man called Percy Grainger had been able to throw a cricket ball right over his roof from the front garden, and run through the house in time to catch it in the back. He and Donovan spent many hours practising this, imperilling the upstairs windows and dislodging several roof tiles in the process, and finally came to the conclusion that the Graingers must have had a smaller house, or at least a less cluttered hallway. It was dodging round all the bags and boxes that mother had offered to store for the Girl Guides' jumble sale, which was costing them valuable seconds. The game ended when a ball thrown by Donovan failed to clear the roof, bounced down the tiles and lodged in the guttering, one storey above the flat roof of the kitchen, making it inaccessible by ladder. Attempts to free it by poking it with a rake from the attic window above also failed. It still lay a yard or so out of reach. Christian was desolate: how were the days to be filled without his precious cricket ball?

'That was your lousy throw, you spastic,' he accused Donovan.

'Well, it was your stupid idea in the first place,' Donovan retorted, and pretty soon the two of them were rolling around my bedroom floor, fists flying, while I jumped up and down yelling at them to stop. Christian, who had the advantage in bulk, soon had Donovan pinned to the floor. 'Repeat after me: "I, Donovan Fry, am a useless spaz,"' Christian instructed, from his superior position astride Donovan's chest.

'Get off me,' the victim replied, through clenched teeth.

'Only when you've said it.'

Donovan stopped thrashing and slumped back, defeated. Christian smiled a victor's smile and slackened his grip a fraction, at which point Donovan raised his head and spat in Christian's face: a perfect shot which caught him open-eyed and open-mouthed and left him gasping with shock. Christian's loss of grip was only momentary, but it was enough for Donovan to push him off and scramble to his feet, running down the stairs, three, four at a time and away into the garden out of sight.

'I'll kill you,' Christian shouted over the banisters after him, then shut up smartly as Dad peered up the stairs and raised an enquiring eyebrow. 'He gobbed at me,' Christian explained. Dad pulled a face to indicate his disapproval of spitting in general, and the word 'gobbed' in particular.

'You were sitting on him,' I protested, my loyalties uncomfortably tested by this incident.

'No doubt you were both behaving in a thoroughly discreditable manner,' Dad said, in the mock-solemn voice he used when he wanted to tell us off without seeming to. 'If it happens again you'll be on a three-man lock up.' Threats were often couched in the language of the prison: a three-man lock up was reserved for the most dangerous and violent inmates, who required a minimum of three warders to supervise the opening of the cell. 'Come on,' he finished. 'Let's go into town and get you a new cricket ball.'

Donovan was nowhere to be found and didn't respond to our calls, so had to be left behind. By tea time he still hadn't returned. Mum saved him a slice of pork pie and some salad on a plate and said not to worry: he'd be out somewhere cooling off and would come back in his own good time. Dad was more anxious: there were some funny people out there, he said.

At nine o'clock, as dusk was falling, Dad and Christian – who was now feeling guilty and uncomfortable – volunteered to search the spinney and surrounding lanes. 'He may be lost,' said Dad. 'If there's no sign of him we'll have to call the police.'

'You don't think he'll have tried to go home?' Mum suggested. 'Perhaps I'll just give Barbara a ring.'

'He wouldn't leave Chewy,' I said.

'No, I don't suppose he would,' Mum agreed. 'But I think I'd better tell Barbara. Just something else for her to fret about,' she said to Dad as she went out to the phone in the hallway, closing the door behind her.

'What if the funny people have got him?' I asked.

'No, no, don't say that,' said Dad, tugging at one eyebrow – something he often did when abstracted.

'He's probably up a tree somewhere, sulking,' said Christian. 'Or hiding out, watching us all and laughing.'

Mum returned a moment later and we turned to face her expectantly. 'Barbara says not to call the police. He does this disappearing act quite regularly apparently. He has been known to stay out all night. I didn't enquire into the circum-stances. She said he won't have gone far: he just does it for effect. I told her I couldn't promise not to call the police once it gets dark.'

Dad nodded. 'Come on, Christian. Get your shoes on.' He rummaged in the kitchen drawer for the torch, which gave out the feeblest yellow glow with its dying batteries.

I stood in the garden to watch their departure. The ground had given up the last of its heat and the grass felt cold beneath my bare feet. Somewhere an owl hooted, and I had a powerful sense of being watched. It made my skin tighten and the hairs on my arms stand out like cats' fur, but when I looked around there was no one.

'I know you're there,' I said loudly.

A spray of gravel hit me on the back and I spun round. Donovan was sitting on the flat roof of the kitchen, swing-ing his legs. He laughed at my surprise, and then lowered himself over the edge and dropped to the ground beside me.

'You're for it, Donovan,' I said, indignant on behalf of Dad and Christian, who had gone out in the dark to rescue him from the funny people for nothing. 'Mum's really cross with you.'

Donovan's smug expression melted away: he had never seen my parents tell anyone off. 'Why?' he said. 'I haven't done anything bad.'

The sound of our voices brought Mum to the kitchen window. 'Ah, good, you're back, Donovan. Can I have a little word?'

I went to follow them but Mum held out a hand to let me know I wasn't included in the invitation.

Twenty minutes later the rescue party returned to find me curled up on the settle outside the dining room. Mum and Donovan were still in conference. My attempts at eaves-dropping had been thwarted: their voices were low and the door was solid.

'Donovan's back. He was hiding on the kitchen roof,' I explained, enjoying my role as newsbreaker. 'They've been in there ages.' Christian and I exchanged significant looks: we knew from experience that one of Mum's 'little words' could run on to many paragraphs.

'I almost feel sorry for him,' Christian said, kicking off his shoes.

THE ODDEST THING WAS THAT WHEN THE PAIR OF THEM DID finally reappear it was Mum and not Donovan whose eyes were wet.

'Didn't she have a go at you at all?' I demanded later when we were in our beds. 'What did she say?'

'Nothing much,' Donovan admitted. 'She told me not to stay out after dark while I'm here and she's in charge of me. Then she was just asking me questions about Mum, and home and stuff. She wasn't cross.'

'Why did she come out crying?'

'I don't know. I didn't say anything to make her sad. I

actually kept saying I liked it here *better* than home. You'd think she'd be pleased.'

8

ONE FRIDAY AT TEATIME WE CAME BACK FROM THE SPINNEY
to find Dad in the sitting room adjusting the dial of a small
television set. A new acquisition perhaps? Christian and I
traded hopeful glances.

'Gather round,' Dad said, tweaking the piece of bent wire
that sprouted from the back of the set. In spite or perhaps
because of his fiddling, the picture kept scrolling up to the
top of the screen and then reappearing again at the bottom,
the two moving images divided by a broad black strip. 'We're
going to see something interesting in a minute.'

'Is that ours?' Christian asked, pointing at the set. 'Did
you buy it?'

Dad shook his head. 'No. I borrowed it from Mrs Tapley.
Just for tonight.'

Christian's face fell, his hopes of becoming a regular television viewer extinguished. Mrs Tapley lived in the village.
She was immemorially widowed and had wiry black and

white hairs on her chin and a houseful of cats. Christian always said it was well known that she dabbled in the black arts.

After making more adjustments to the dial and dealing a slap to the top of the box, Dad managed to bring the picture to a halt. We crowded closer and the screen began to flicker and disintegrate. 'Step back,' he commanded. 'It must be the floorboards.'

Eventually, when we had managed to dispose ourselves around the room in positions that didn't threaten the television's fragile equilibrium, the grey and white fuzz resolved itself into a picture of women in bell-shaped dresses, whirling around a vast ballroom.

'In a moment,' said Dad, sitting between me and Donovan on the couch and putting his arms around us, 'we're going to see Donovan's mummy.'

'On telly?' I said.

'Is she an actress?' Christian asked, turning to Donovan. 'You never said.'

'You never asked,' he replied. 'Anyway, she's not famous or anything.'

'She must be if she's on telly,' I said.

The door opened and Mum came in, bringing a plate of malt loaf, lightly greased with margarine.

'Aunty Barbara's going to be on telly,' Christian told her.

'She's an actress,' I explained.

'I know.' Mum smiled at Donovan. 'And a very good one too. We used to go and see her on the stage in London when we were first married.'

'You must be filthy rich,' Christian accused Donovan. 'Actors and actresses earn billions.'

'No we're not,' Donovan replied in some indignation.

'Mum says if it wasn't for the alimony we wouldn't have a pot to piss in.'

This remark, and our parents' astonished expressions, sent Christian into convulsions.

'What's alley money?' I asked, feeling sure that this must contain the germ of the joke.

'Quiet now everyone, or we'll miss her,' Dad said, leaning forward to turn up the volume. Five pairs of eyes swivelled back to the screen. The minutes passed. Scenes changed and characters came and went with no sign of Aunty Barbara. When the appearance of any female between the ages of eight and eighty had prompted the question 'Is that her?' once too often, Dad plucked the newspaper from the jaws of the magazine rack. 'Are we watching the right programme, do you suppose?'

'Well, I don't think it was a major part,' Mum reminded him, reaching down beside her for the knitting bag. 'She was only twenty at the time. Donovan,' she went on. 'Mummy rang last night. She's feeling much better and she's coming to pick you up tomorrow.'

Donovan's face darkened. 'Do I have to go?'

'I'm afraid so, dear. Though we've loved having you. School starts on Monday. And besides, your mummy's been missing you and wants you back.'

'Did she say that?' he asked, brightening.

There was a second's hesitation before Mum said, 'Yes', then Dad said, 'Oh there she is!' and we all leaned towards the screen with one movement. A young woman in a maid's costume of black dress and white pinafore had entered a large drawing room where some sort of concert party was in progress. She minced across the room with that double-quick way of walking that women did before comfortable shoes were invented and said to one of the men standing at the wall, 'There's a gentleman to see you, sir, name of Jessup,' and then tip-tapped out again.

'She looks so young,' said Dad.

'That was before I was even born,' Donovan said.

'She's got a look of Audrey Hepburn about her,' said Mum. 'I've never noticed it before.'

'This is exciting isn't it?' said Dad, trying to stir up a show of enthusiasm for Donovan's benefit. 'It's not every day we see one of our friends on the television.'

'It's not every day we see a television,' Christian pointed out.

We watched on, waiting in vain for Aunty Barbara's reappearance, until finally Christian, who wasn't finding the film much to his liking, said, 'Is that all?' and Mum and Dad conceded that it probably was.

'Good,' said Donovan, checking his watch. 'Can we have BBC One now? It's *Crackerjack*.'

9

THE AUNTY BARBARA WHO ARRIVED THE NEXT DAY TO CLAIM
Donovan looked quite different from the one with the bird's
nest hair and stained dressing gown, who had forgotten to
make us lunch and didn't have a pot to piss in. Different
again from the lady's maid with a look of Audrey Hepburn,
who had flitted briefly across the TV screen the day before.
This time she was washed and brushed, with her dark hair
twisted into a rope over one ear, and she was wearing a long
fur coat even though it was just September and the rest of
us were still in T-shirts. It wasn't one of those plush black
coats that go with diamonds and Rolls Royces, but a brown
patchy thing that looked as if it might have been made from
hundreds of Chewy's relations stitched together. Mum hung
it up in the downstairs cloakroom with our anoraks and the
weight of it brought the rail off the wall so that the whole
lot collapsed in a heap on top of our muddy wellingtons.

Once Aunty Barbara had been divested of this pelt and

a number of interesting packages she treated each of us in turn to a bony one-armed hug. In her free hand was a smouldering cigarette in a tortoiseshell holder, like the back end of a fountain pen, which she continued to suck long after the butt was ground out in a saucer.

'Donovan, have you been a massive nuisance?' she said to her son by way of greeting.

'Of course not,' said Mum, seconding Donovan's grunt of denial. 'He's been a treasure. Hasn't he, Gordon?'

Dad nodded vigorously. 'He's welcome here any time. Any *time*,' he said, laying his hand on Donovan's head.

'Well, it was very good of you. I can't tell you,' said Aunty Barbara. 'You'll have to let me have your two in return some time.' And she gave Christian and me a menacing wink with her twiggy eyelashes, while Mum and Dad exchanged glances.

There were presents next, which was the main thing: a Mary Quant doll in a black and white suit for me, a dartboard for Christian, and a bottle of vodka for my teetotal parents, which would go straight in the box for the tombola the minute Aunty Barbara had gone.

'Have you got anything for me?' Donovan asked, when the bags were emptied and we'd said our thank yous.

'Don't be so grasping,' said his mother. 'As a matter of fact I have, but it's at home.'

'Why didn't you bring it?'

'Because it's a fish tank, that's why. Satisfied?'

'A fish tank! With fish in it?'

'No – with parrots in it. Of course fish, you dunce.'

'Oh, cool.'

As soon as introductions were over and Christian and I had endured Aunty Barbara's compliments on the rapidity of our growth and striking looks, we were allowed to escape upstairs with our gifts.

'She's gorgeous,' Aunty Barbara said to Mum before we were quite out of earshot. 'I wish I'd had a girl.'

In his bedroom Christian removed his framed scraper-board etching of a hedgehog from the wall and hung the new dartboard in its place. Pretty soon the surrounding wallpaper – and even the ceiling – was pitted with tiny holes, evidence of our enthusiasm and inaccuracy. Occasionally one of the darts would strike the metal frame on the board and come flying back to spear the floorboards at our feet.

'Does anyone know the rules of darts?' Christian said after a while, when he had become slightly more proficient at hitting the target. We looked blank.

'Hey, Esther, you could stand against the board and we've got to throw the darts around your head without hitting you,' Donovan suggested.

'No way,' I protested. 'You can't even throw straight.'

'We'd blindfold you so you wouldn't see them coming,' he added kindly.

'It might be a bit dangerous to use a real person,' Christian conceded. His glance fell on my new Mary Quant doll, still in her cellophane box. I could well imagine the fate that would be in store for her. Donovan had already told me that he had set fire to his Action Men because he liked to watch them melt.

'I'm going downstairs to talk to the grown-ups,' I said, snatching Mary up and taking her with me.

'Spoilsport,' said Donovan.

'*Girl*,' said Christian.

* * *

MUM, DAD AND AUNTY BARBARA WERE SITTING OUT IN THE garden drinking iced coffee. Aunty Barbara had the comfortable sun-lounger, which always had to be given up for visitors or the elderly. Mum and Dad were sitting – very carefully – on the lethal folding deckchairs which, we were often informed, were liable to collapse flat and amputate the limbs of the occupant without warning.

'It's good to see you looking so well,' Mum was saying to Aunty Barbara, whose face was half hidden by a giant pair of mirrored sunglasses.

'It's because I'm working again,' she replied. 'I know it's only a tiny job, this radio thing, but it's *work*. And I have to work.' She plugged another cigarette into the tortoiseshell holder and lit it, drawing deeply.

'There's always unpaid work, between whiles,' Mum suggested. 'You could do meals on wheels. Or prison visiting.'

'Prison visiting? Does that still go on? I thought it went out with the Victorians. Oh here's this gorgeous creature,' she went on, seizing one of my hands in hers and crushing it with her ringed fingers. Her flattery made me squirm: Mum wasn't given to praising our appearance: when pressed she might say that I looked perfectly acceptable, but that was as far as she'd go.

'Has she started ballet yet?' Aunty Barbara went on. 'I've still got all my old tutus in a trunk in the loft. I don't know what I'm saving them for.'

'Esther's not really a ballet girl,' Dad explained. 'She's more . . .'

'Outdoorsy,' Mum suggested.

'A tomboy, are you?' said Aunty Barbara. 'Well. Never mind.' She seemed to lose interest in me after that, though she kept my hand grasped in hers so that I was forced to squat on the grass beside her chair. Presently she turned to Mum and Dad. 'You've heard that Alan and his new wife have just had a baby girl, I suppose?'

'No, we hadn't. We're not in contact any more,' Dad replied. This seemed to please Aunty Barbara.

'I only found out because a letter came from Alan for Donovan while he was away and when I opened it a photo fell out,' she went on. 'I must say it gave me a jolt.'

'Well, that's what comes of opening other people's mail,' said Dad, affronted on Donovan's behalf.

'I thought it might be urgent,' Aunty Barbara replied, waving away his objection with a plume of smoke. 'She's ever so fair, even blonder than Donovan was.' She dropped my hand to reach for her handbag. 'I've got the photo here somewhere. Do you want to look?'

'Not especially,' said Mum.

Aunty Barbara produced it anyway and wafted it about, before dropping it back in the bag. 'A new baby. At his age. Well good luck to them,' she said, in a voice that suggested she wished them anything but.

'It must be difficult for you,' Mum said in a gentle voice.

Aunty Barbara shook her head and smoke streamed from her nostrils. 'I'm fine. Fine,' she insisted, mashing her cigarette into the lawn. 'Donovan doesn't know yet. I'm wondering how best to tell him.'

'He surely knows they were expecting?' said Mum.

'He never told me. And he hasn't seen them for five months. She might not have been showing much then. And he's not terribly observant,' said Aunty Barbara, untying and retying her plait. I wanted to ask who they were talking about, but I knew from experience that the minute you reminded grown-ups you were there listening, they invariably started talking about something less interesting. It was better to sit quietly and pretend to be away with the fairies.

'Perhaps you should sit him down when you get home and show him the letter and photo,' Mum advised. 'Maybe encourage him to send a little card or gift.'

'Yes,' Dad agreed. 'Try to present it as something positive. For his sake.'

Aunty Barbara nodded slowly as she digested this advice. There was a commotion from inside and Donovan and Christian came crashing through the kitchen door clutching a pair of chewed tennis rackets in wooden presses.

'Can we put a net up?' Christian asked as they approached.

'Not right where we're sitting,' Mum said. 'Over there.' She pointed to the wilderness beyond the oak tree, a sloping triangle of knee-length grass and nettles. Christian rolled his eyes.

'Why not just come and have a drink?' Dad suggested. 'We'll be having lunch in a moment.' He poured out two more glasses of iced coffee and the boys flopped down on the lawn beside me. In the stillness and silence that accompanied their drinking, Aunty Barbara twitched the photograph out of her bag and across to Donovan. 'You've got a new baby sister,' she said, in the tone of voice you might use to tell someone they had an earwig on their shirt.

Mum and Dad froze, their glasses halfway to their lips, in a pantomime of shock and dismay.

'What do you mean?' said Donovan, suspicious that he was the butt of some private joke. He picked up the photo and frowned. 'Who's this?'

'Your sister. Half-sister, I should say. Daddy and Suzie have had a little girl.'

Donovan looked from Aunty Barbara to Mum and Dad for confirmation that this was true. Their stricken faces cracked into reassuring smiles and Donovan's cheeks flared.

'That's jolly nice, isn't it,' said Dad at last.

'You'll be able to take her out in the pram when you go and stay,' Mum added. 'I'm sure you'll be a great help to them.'

'Oh, God, they won't want Donovan around yet,' said his mother. Donovan's eyes narrowed.

'Not right away, perhaps. But soon, surely?' said Mum. Her voice sounded unusually high and bright.

'Well, don't you want to know her name?' Aunty Barbara asked.

Donovan shrugged.

'It's Pippa.'

'Oh.' Donovan gave an indifferent grunt, then seemed to become absorbed in tightening the catch on the racket press, and the subject was dropped.

'He seemed to take the news okay,' Aunty Barbara hissed to Mum as we made our way in for lunch, but Mum's lips formed a tight, straight line and she said nothing.

WHEN LUNCH WAS OVER AND THE GROWN-UPS HAD DRUNK their coffee, it was time to say goodbye. Dad went upstairs to help Donovan bring Chewy down, and I followed to check that he hadn't left anything behind, or worse, packed something of mine by mistake.

They were standing by the window when I walked in, and Dad had one arm round Donovan's shoulder. 'Don't upset yourself, old fellow,' Dad was saying. 'You know you're welcome to come and stay any time. You've only got to ask.'

Donovan drew his sleeve across his eyes. 'Do you really mean that or are you just saying it?'

'Of course I mean it,' Dad laughed. 'Try me and see.'

'People always promise they're going to do things and they never do and when you remind them they just get cross and say, "Don't keep going on about it!"' He sniffed deeply, his green-glass eyes shining like wet stones, and then turned away, embarrassed when he saw me standing there.

'In this house a promise is a promise,' Dad said. He picked up the cage, the large sack of sawdust, and the smaller bag of hamster food and left Donovan to carry his case.

'We could write to each other,' I suggested. 'I can do joined-up.'

Donovan nodded, without much enthusiasm. From down below came the sound of Aunty Barbara revving up the car. 'People always say that,' he said morosely. 'But they never do.' And he clumped down the stairs, suitcase in hand, and out of the door without a backward glance.

Before the dust had even settled in the lane I was peeling off a sheet of Mum's Three Candlesticks, just to prove him wrong.

Dear Donovan
You see I am writing like I said I would and you didn't believe me.

I stopped, stuck. There wasn't anything to tell him as nothing had happened since his departure, so I left the sheet on my bedside table, intending to add further news as it occurred, over the coming days.

Then term started again and life seemed to change gear, and memories of Donovan and the summer holidays began to fade like the aftermath of a pleasant dream whose details can't quite be recalled. After a while I started to use the piece of paper as a bookmark to keep it flat, and then one day I came home to find that Mum had had a purge of overdue library books, and that Mrs Pepperpot and my unfinished letter were now back on a shelf somewhere in Junior Lending, and that was that.

10

THE NEXT OCCUPANT OF THE GUEST ROOM WAS A CLERGYMAN
called Mr Spragg, an old acquaintance of Dad's from theological college. He had a parish somewhere in the north of
England, but had come south on retreat. Who or what he
was retreating from was not explained at the time: Dad
hadn't been in contact with him since they were ordained,
but a mutual friend, knowing of Mr Spragg's situation and
my parents' generosity to the Less Fortunate, had put them
in touch again.

At first he kept to his room almost as much as Cindy,
only venturing out to attend Matins, mealtimes, or to take
long restorative walks on the common. Christian and I had
no particular desire for this arrangement to change, as he
was not of much interest to us, and was, besides, rather
alarming-looking. He was small and twitchy, with wild, wiry
eyebrows and still more of these fibres sprouting from his
ears and nostrils, and a perpetual fleck of mobile saliva on

his lower lip, which held us mesmerised as he spoke. Christian – always a master of the apt nickname – referred to him privately as Reverend Spitfire, and enlivened many dull afternoons imitating his twitch. Mum caught us laughing about him one day when he was out, and sprang to his defence.

'I don't know why you're so critical, Christian. He's done nothing to you.'

'He gobs at us every time he speaks.'

'Don't say that.'

'It's true.'

'Is it true? Is it kind? Is it necessary?' she demanded – her usual response to loose talk.

It was Reverend Spitfire who inadvertently set me on the road to becoming an illustrator. Mum and Dad had, of course, given my drawing every encouragement by displaying the best of my early scribbles and daubs on a large cork board in the kitchen. But they never took the old pictures down and replaced them, instead pinning fresh ones on top, layer after haphazard layer, until the whole structure became rather unstable and a gust of wind from the garden door could bring a flurry of pages down like autumn leaves. Sometimes the fallen pictures would lie on the floor for some days before being put back. Occasionally they would vanish altogether and, when questioned, Mum would grow vague.

One rainy Saturday in November when it was too wet for his walk, Mr Spragg took the unusual step of joining us in the sitting room. Perhaps he wanted company, or, more likely, a share of the coal fire, the only source of heat in the house. It was getting to the time of year when the toilet bowl froze over and ice formed on the inside of the windows, and we had to keep our clothes clean for twice as long because Mum couldn't get anything dry.

Dad was in the armchair doing the *Times* bridge problem. Mum was in the window seat darning a pair of knickers and I was doing a pencil sketch (from memory) of a fox that had been slinking across the garden that morning. Christian, oblivious to the cold, was up in his room playing darts, his favourite wet-weather activity. Overhead I could hear the thud, thud, as the points struck home.

When Mr Spragg came in Dad immediately laid aside his newspaper and challenged him to a game of backgammon. This was apparently how they had whiled away the long evenings at college when not studying. Mum put down her darning and went to make tea.

I watched Mr Spragg set out his counters on the board, his pointed nose quivering as though he was an animal following a trail. When I looked down at my sketch of the fox the resemblance was striking: it was something to do with the muzzle. I added a pair of shaggy eyebrows and tufts of hair at ears and nostrils. Then I did a stupid thing: I gave the fox a dog-collar, just like the one Mr Spragg had been wearing on his arrival. He had told Mum and Dad he always wore it on train journeys because it guaranteed him a compartment to himself, and they had laughed. I was so engrossed, shading in the body and drawing a bushy tail with hundreds of flicks of my sharp pencil, that I didn't notice Mr Spragg approaching the table until he was standing over me. Before I had a chance to cover the picture he said, 'May I?' and tweaked it from beneath my fingers. I cringed, waiting for the explosion: I knew, without needing to be told, that I had done something the adult world would see as rude, and that Mum and Dad would not be pleased. But Mr Spragg failed to explode.

'This is rather good,' he tittered, handing the picture to Dad. 'Look at that, Gordon. She's got some talent, this girl.'

Dad scrutinised the drawing for a second or two, taking in the likeness, and a frown gathered on his forehead. 'Esther, this is clever, but it's not very polite,' he said, but I could tell he wasn't really cross.

'Nonsense,' said Mr Spragg. 'I'm flattered. May I keep it?'

I hesitated, uncertain of the polite response, and appealed to Dad for a ruling.

Mr Spragg must have misinterpreted my hesitation as he whipped out his wallet and handed me a pound note before either of us could speak. 'Of course, artists must be paid for their work,' he said. 'Or how can they live?'

For the first time I started to warm to the man. After all, he couldn't help having an overactive salivary gland, as Mum had explained in his defence.

'You must put your signature in the corner,' he went on, 'so that future generations will know it is an original Fairchild.'

My first commercial transaction as an artist unfortunately proved to be my last for some while. Although, in the first surge of enthusiasm following that unexpected sale my output trebled overnight and I produced quality caricatures of the rest of the household, they were annoyingly reluctant to spend.

'I'm not doing this for fun, you know,' I complained to Dad when I had filled an entire pad with unsold sketches.

'In that case don't do it,' was his stern advice.

* * *

MY SUCCESS, HOWEVER SHORT-LIVED, SERVED AT LEAST TO inspire Christian to go out and make his fortune. Having lost the argument over pocket money, and failed to fleece Donovan at cards, Christian had been forced over the course of the year to consider other sources of revenue. All our parents' warnings and anxieties about the boys at Turton's were proving to be well founded. Christian's scholarship, far from being a badge of distinction, was a mark of poverty and therefore a source of shame. Every day brought fresh examples of his schoolmates' material advantages and his own humiliation.

His school uniform, now well into its second year, was starting to look shabby. The green wool blazer he wore every day was going bald at collar and cuffs and had a faded streak down the front where Mum had scrubbed at a spill rather than taking it to the cleaners as the label recommended. She had already sewn patches onto the holey elbows and had to be dissuaded from doing the same for the knees of his trousers. 'There's nothing wrong with wearing clothes that have been mended,' she said in response to his protests. 'I surely can't be the only mother who darns.'

Sports equipment was another source of conflict. The antiquated assortment of warped bats and home-strung rackets, which had served perfectly well in the privacy of our own garden, brought him a rather less welcome brand of notoriety at school.

The extent of his unhappiness only came to light when Mum and Dad received a letter from the deputy head. Christian had attempted to forge a note from Mum, in a script that would fool no one, asking for him to be excused from games. This had greatly surprised the sports teacher, who had considered Christian to be an honest boy, and one of his more able and enthusiastic pupils. It emerged, under interrogation, that Christian was hoping to dodge games in order to avoid suffering agonies of embarrassment in the changing rooms over the state of his underpants, which were off-white, reached almost to his armpits, and had probably once belonged to Grandpa Percy.

'The other boys laugh at me and go on about them *all the time*,' he complained, during the family conference that was held to resolve the affair. 'They call them my Mighty Whities.'

I could see Dad trying not to smile, but Mum looked mortified. 'I knew this sort of thing would happen,' she said, shaking her head. 'We should have sent him to Underwood.' Underwood was the nearest state school, a bleak grey building on the edge of a large housing estate.

After some more discussion it was agreed that there were two possible solutions to the predicament. One: Christian should embrace the opportunity to practise some character-building stoicism in the face of mockery. This option, though unpleasant, would serve him well in the long term. Two: the forces of materialism and conformity should be allowed to triumph and Mum should buy Christian some new underpants.

'What sort of pants do the other boys wear?' Mum wanted to know, when option two had emerged the victor by three votes to one.

'New ones,' said Christian. 'From a shop.'

AS A DIRECT RESULT OF THIS INCIDENT CHRISTIAN WAS ALLOWED to take up a paper round, with the proviso that his earnings should be used to defray the costs of any future 'luxuries'. It was argued that he would be less likely to fritter away money on inessentials like new underpants if he had earned it by the sweat of his brow. Christian was delighted with this arrangement: at last a whole world of commercial possibilities lay spread before him.

Naturally I accompanied him on his round, which took in most of the village and some of the outlying houses and covered a good couple of miles. At first Mum and Dad expressed some unease at my involvement. There had been several recent reports in the local paper of schoolgirls being troubled in the lanes by a 'flasher'. I imagined this to be some species of monster with blazing green eyes, but it turned out to be nothing of the kind, just a man with his trousers undone. We were instructed to keep together at all times and not to take the short cut down the lanes or across the common, but to keep to the roads, until he was caught. This point was hammered home with the threat that any breach of the rules would result in Christian's immediate return to the ranks of the unemployed. 'We're absolutely serious about this,' Dad said, looking from me to Christian for signs of rebellion. 'There are some funny people out there.'

The morning paper round became the highlight of my day: up before dawn and into my school uniform in the blue chill of a November morning. Mist trails on the common and the crunch of frosted leaves beneath our wheels as we cycled along, and Christian waiting for me, keeping together as he'd promised, with only occasional signs of impatience.

As an athlete and sportsman, Christian was forever looking to improve our performance and shave valuable minutes from the round. We had achieved our best time of fifty-five minutes door to door by abandoning my bike altogether so that I could sit on his crossbar and be tipped off into each driveway to post the paper. I could tell that this result wouldn't satisfy him for long.

'You know, if we split up we'd be finished in half the time,' he said wistfully, as we set off one December morning in a shower of sleet.

'What about the flasher?' I reminded him. 'Mum and Dad said you've got to stay with me.'

'No one goes flashing in weather like this,' Christian replied. 'He'd freeze his balls off.' We laughed so much at this that Christian nearly rode into the ditch, and for the rest of the round all he had to do to set me off was to call out, 'Hey, Frozenballs!' I was good for nothing after that, and we turned in one of our worst times on record and were very nearly late for school.

Christian was not to be deflected from his mission, though, and the following morning he once more suggested splitting up and taking half the papers each.

'Will you give me half the money?' I asked. So far my role as paperboy's assistant had only brought me the odd fifty pence here and there. This had never bothered me before: just being out with Christian was enough for me. But now he was proposing to send me off without him I thought it only fair to take a bigger cut of his earnings.

'Half?' Christian looked aggrieved. 'I hadn't really thought about the money side of things. Anyway, perhaps you're right about sticking together,' he said, backtracking hastily. 'I'll tell you what, though. We could take the short cut across the common. That'll be way quicker. At the moment we're doing two sides of a triangle.'

'Well . . .' I said doubtfully, remembering Dad's stern warnings.

'We'd be together. I'll look after you,' he wheedled. 'If

we see any old flasher I'll just yell out "Oy! Frozenballs!"
and ride off at top speed.' I started to giggle and he pressed
on, sensing victory. 'It means we could get up twenty
minutes later, or get back twenty minutes earlier and have
more time for toast.'

I wavered. The extra toast wasn't a huge incentive: Mum
always cut the bread so thin that it shattered into millions
of fragments as soon as you applied any margarine. But the
extra sleep appealed: I always hated that moment of emerging from body-warmed blankets into the icy clutch of the
sleeping house, and would defer it if I could.

'All right,' I said. 'As long as Mum and Dad don't find out.'
'Course they won't,' he said. 'They'll never know.'

THE NEW ROUTINE WORKED FINE: WE COULD GET UP AT TEN
to seven instead of half past six, and we returned home in
time for porridge and brittle toast, just as before, arousing
no suspicion. We didn't meet the flasher, or any other living
soul on the common – a matter of relief mixed with disappointment. I was half looking forward to hearing Christian's
war cry 'Frozenballs!' echoing through the trees.

On one occasion we thought we could hear footsteps in
the undergrowth beside us, and then an Alsatian came
crashing through the bushes and across our path, sending
us skidding into a pile of leaves in a tangle of limbs and
spinning pedals. When I got to school I discovered that I
had lost the book of matches that Donovan had given me
for rescuing Chewy. It went everywhere with me in my coat
pocket, wishing me welcome to Biarritz, and now it was
gone. Mum commented on my long face when I came home,
and when I told her about my lost treasure, she suggested
we retrace my paper round route until we found it. 'I've got

some envelopes to collect so we can kill two birds with one
stone,' she said, clipping her Oxfam identity card to the
front of her shaggy Oxfam coat. 'Why are you carrying
matches around anyway?' she asked as we set off, keeping
our eyes on the pavement.

'In case I need to light a fire in an emergency,' I explained.

'I should think you're more likely to cause the emergency,' she said mildly.

Our progress was slow because at every house we had to
ring the doorbell and wait while the owner hunted first for
the envelope and second for some cash to fill it. It was a
standing joke with Mother that the occupants of the row
of smart detached houses on the edge of the village were
the least likely to give, and the most inventive with excuses.
'A mercedes in the driveway and a miser in the house,' she
muttered as another door slammed in our faces.

The sun had disappeared below the trees by the time
Mum had called in the last of her envelopes, and I was
eager to check out the site of my encounter with the Alsatian
before it got even darker. I had an inkling that the match-
book might have fallen out of my pocket when the bike
had flipped over in the leaves. Without thinking, I turned
off the road along the forbidden path across the common,
and strode on for several yards before I realised that Mum
wasn't following.

I turned round and saw her standing at the verge, hands
on hips, a stony look on her face. 'So this is the way you
come, is it?' she asked. 'After everything we said.' I nodded
miserably. I could see she was building up to a big lecture,
and my heart sank. That would be the end of the paper
round. Christian would be angry with me for giving us away;
Dad would be, not angry, exactly, because he never got

angry, but disappointed and hurt. There would be no more fifty pences coming my way and no more early morning outings with Christian.

'It's all because I lost that stupid matchbook,' I burst out, lacerated by self-pity. And then, 'It's all Donovan's fault!'

Before the words had even dried in the air I spotted it, lying face down in the mound of mulched leaves at the side of the track. I snatched it up and wiped the dirt from its shiny cover. The cardboard felt spongy to the touch and the matches inside were soft and damp. It was in all probability useless as far as lighting fires in emergencies went, and I resolved to relegate it to the Germolene tin, where it would be unable to get me into further trouble.

'I blame Christian more than you,' Mum said, catching me up. 'He's older and he was supposed to be responsible. But you may as well learn this useful lesson: in this life you never get away with anything. Everything you do comes back and trips you up sooner or later. Just bear that in mind next time you feel tempted to do something wrong.'

And that was all she said to me on the subject, though Christian was treated to a rather lengthier disquisition and had to resign the paper round.

THE UNIVERSAL TRUTH OF MUM'S WARNING WAS PROVED ONLY a week or so later, when I arrived home from school to find a police car in the driveway. Mum intercepted me on the doorstep and ushered me up to my room with instructions to close the door and stay there until told otherwise. Something in her face told me it would be a mistake to challenge her.

'What's happened?' I asked, from halfway up the stairs.

'Nothing,' she whispered back. 'Nothing to worry about.'

Shut in my attic room I couldn't hear a word of what was taking place two storeys below, but the window overlooked the driveway, and from this vantage point I had a perfect view of the patrol car and the WPC who was leaning against it, biting her nails and spitting the pieces into the bushes. Presently her walkie-talkie spluttered into life and she leant down and spoke into it before resuming her nibbling. Then the front door slammed and Mr Spragg emerged, followed by a uniformed policeman, and the two of them climbed into the car and were driven away. I knocked on the window and gave Mr Spragg a wave, but he had his head down and didn't see me.

I waited for a few minutes to be summoned, and when no one called me I crept downstairs. Mum was sitting at the kitchen table, chin in hand, staring into space. Dinner had been abandoned, half-prepared on the sideboard. She jumped when she saw me.

'Can I come down now?' I asked.

'What? Yes, of course,' she said, vaguely, and put out one arm to draw me into her side for a hug. Her cardigan was fastened on the wrong buttons so that it gaped across her chest.

'Why has Mr Spragg gone with the police?' I asked.

'They want to talk to him.'

'Has he done something wrong?'

'That'll be for the court to decide.' She licked a finger and wiped a smudge from my cheek.

'Is he coming back?'

'No, not to this house.'

'Will we be getting someone else?'

'No,' said Mum emphatically. 'No more visitors.'

* * *

IT WAS SHORTLY AFTER THIS THAT DAD TOOK CHRISTIAN ASIDE and told him that he and Mum considered the whole match-book incident over and done with, and that he could resume his paper round if it was still available. And this time, strangely, there were no rules and regulations about short cuts across the common and down the lanes.

11

DAD USED TO SAY THAT THE ONLY LETTERS WORTH OPENING were ones with handwritten envelopes. Type seldom meant good news, and window envelopes were the worst of all. As someone who was only guaranteed to receive one piece of mail per year – a birthday card from Grandpa Percy – I found this attitude bizarre and ungrateful. It was just another example of the topsy-turvy values of the adult world, which claimed to prefer early mornings to late nights and giving to receiving.

One morning a letter arrived that made us all sit up. It was Christmas Eve, 1976 and I was eight years old. Mum was in the kitchen, reluctantly shelling chestnuts for stuffing. A rubbery ham was simmering in a preserving pan and a batch of mince pies was cooling on a wire rack. Christian was trying to light the sitting room fire using a base of fir cones, while Dad and I made crackers out of crepe paper and loo roll innards. I was trying to measure Christian's skull for a bespoke paper crown, and he was cuffing me out of the way, when the letter box clanged.

'Second post,' said Dad, abandoning his task and going out to investigate. He returned with a stack of cards, and proceeded to flip through them, apparently able to divine the identity of the senders without even opening the envelopes.

'Did we send a card to Doug and Betty?' he called.

'No,' came the reply.

'The Porters?'

'No.'

'Mrs Spiller?'

'I thought she was dead. I crossed her off.'

'Well, you'd better reinstate her. Oh, look at this.' He started to laugh. The last envelope was postmarked Bath and addressed as follows in chaotic handwriting:

> Mr and Mrs G Fairchild
> The big red brick schoolhouse with the bell on top
> Down a lane with brambles near a church
> Next to the common
> Not far from Biggin Hill airfield
> Kent, I think
> Sorry.

Within seconds of opening it and examining the contents – a scrap of paper torn from a school exercise book – he stopped laughing and strode out of the room, leaving the letter fluttering to the floor. From the kitchen came the sound of Mum and Dad in hurried conference, and then the front door slammed and we watched the car reverse erratically up the driveway with Dad at the wheel. A

moment later, Mum, still in apron and slippers, chased after
him, signalling urgently. She was carrying something – a
mince pie – which she passed through the car window before
waving Dad off.

Christian and I exchanged puzzled frowns before our eyes
fell simultaneously on the discarded letter, which Dad had
flung aside in his haste. We lunged with one movement,
clashing foreheads and ripping the page neatly in half. When
we had realigned the pieces, we read the following message,
written with the dying gasps of a red biro.

> *Dear Uncle Gordon and Aunty Pru*
> *I hope you get this. I don't know your proper address.*
> *Mum is ill again. Please come.*
>   *Love from Donovan.*
>   *P.S. You said if I ever wanted to stay I just had to ask.*

In the kitchen Mum was still pulverising a bag of chestnuts with a meat mallet. There were shells all over the floor.

'Is Donovan coming for Christmas?' I asked, waving the
letter. 'Has Dad gone to get him?'

Mum nodded. 'Which reminds me, I'll need your help
to get the spare room ready.'

'What's wrong with Aunty Barbara?' asked Christian,
hanging over the rack of mince pies.

'Good question,' Mum replied, deploying the mallet with
increased vigour. 'If it's not one thing it's another. Sometimes
I wonder if it's all in her head.' She abandoned the chestnut pulp and turned her attention to the ham, now steaming on a plate. 'Don't repeat that by the way.' Writhing with
distaste, she took out a sharp knife and cut away the layer
of white blubber, dropping it into the bin with a shudder.

'Why do we have turkey *and* ham?' I wondered aloud.

'You might well ask,' Mum replied. 'I'm glad it's only once a year' – a remark which struck me as another example of wrong-headed adult thinking.

She had always been disappointingly lukewarm about Christmas, viewing it as an occasion of unnecessary extravagance and greed. It made her feel physically sick to walk into toy shops packed to the rafters with expensive trash. Anything colourful and tempting would be dismissed as cheap and plasticky. This led me to the puzzling conclusion that two words I'd considered natural opposites in fact meant the same thing. Cheap = bad; expensive = bad.

IT WAS TEATIME BEFORE DAD RETURNED FROM BATH. THE journey home had taken twice as long because Donovan insisted on bringing his fish tank. It was the usual story: there was nobody who could be relied upon to feed them, and no telling how long he might be away. Dad had been forced to drive at the speed of a hearse to prevent the water sloshing about and dashing the fish against the sides of the tank. Beside him in the front seat sat Aunty Barbara, shrunken and shivering in her gerbil coat. She tottered into the house and collapsed into Mum's arms.

'I'm sorry to be a burden,' she said, as Mum led her upstairs to the guest room we had hastily prepared for Donovan, with clean bedding and a hot waterbottle to take the chill off the sheets.

'We're very glad to have you,' Mum said firmly, then glared at Christian and me as we stood there gawping.

'Don't just stand there, help your father with the cases. And put the kettle on,' she ordered.

Then Donovan appeared, duffel bag in hand, and there

was an awkward moment of mutual reappraisal while we said our hellos and fidgeted from foot to foot.

'You never wrote,' he accused me.

'Neither did you,' I retorted, and he laughed, showing two rows of even white teeth, now fully grown. I kept my lips tightly together: my teeth were still at different stages of development, some loose, some missing, some crooked, giving me a smile like a mouthful of broken biscuits.

'Where's Chewy?' I asked, making subconscious connections.

'He got mossy foot and died,' Donovan explained. 'I buried him in the garden but a fox dug him up. I've got two fish now. Starsky and Hutch.'

Christian and I looked blank.

'Off the telly.' He shook his head in disbelief. 'Don't you two know anything?'

IN THE EARLY HOURS OF CHRISTMAS MORNING A NOISE WOKE me. I thought it might be Santa Claus but it was just Aunty Barbara having a panic attack in the bathroom. Of course I had known for some while that he didn't exist, but the discovery had come as a relief rather than a disappointment. At last the fact that other children got Princess Pippa or Girlsworld while I got a shoe-cleaning kit made sense. Dad had taken me and Donovan to midnight communion at the parish church, while Mum stayed behind with Aunty Barbara to prepare the vegetables for the next day.

'That's what you need – simple, repetitive tasks,' Mum said cheerily, slitting open a net of sprouts.

'I don't know if I trust myself with a sharp knife,' came the mournful reply. We left them at the kitchen table, a growing pile of sprout peelings on Mum's side and a growing pile

of cigarette butts on Aunty Barbara's. She had only been with
us a few hours and already the whole house smelled of her
smoke.

Donovan had never been in a church before and didn't
know the drill. He couldn't follow the responses and kept
sitting when he should be kneeling and standing when he
should be sitting. His face fell when he flicked through the
green order-of-service booklet. 'Do we have to read it right
to the end?' he hissed as we took our places in the pew. I
nodded and he pulled a tortured, cross-eyed face that had
me snorting into my hymnbook. He cheered up when, inex-
plicably and without warning, we missed out the bits in
square brackets, or skipped four or five pages, and he gave
me an ostentatious thumbs-up each time. And he got quite
carried away exchanging a sign of the Peace – which he
interpreted as a Red Indian salute – with the complete
strangers in the pew behind, and eventually had to be tapped
on the shoulder by Dad and told to turn round. 'That's
enough Peace,' Dad whispered, and they grinned at each
other.

Mum had given us fifty pence each for the collection,
but when the sidesman brought the velvet bag round during
'The First Nowell' I noticed that Donovan put his hand in
and withdrew it still clenched. Through the gaps in his
fingers I could see silver. I gave him my sternest glare but
he just winked at me and sang louder. We said prayers for
the parish and the Queen and the whole world, remembering the Less Fortunate everywhere who wouldn't be having
turkey and presents tomorrow, and then it was 'Hark the
Herald' and out into the freezing night as the church clock
struck twelve.

There was a small, icy moon and a scatter of stardust

above us. Beneath our heels the cold pavement rang like metal. I said, as I did every year, 'It's Christmas already. Can we open our presents now?'

Dad replied, 'Oh, didn't we tell you? We're not doing presents this year,' and I laughed, but with an edge of fear, because although this had never yet proved true, it was the sort of thing that one day might.

'I'm getting a skateboard from my dad,' Donovan said. 'He's bringing me one back from America.'

Christian kicked a loose stone across the road and it hit the lamp post with a clang. He would have liked a skateboard.

Mum and Aunty Barbara were in bed when we arrived home, and the house was dark. On the kitchen stove peeled potatoes and sprouts floated palely in pans of cold water. The turkey sat on a roasting tin in its tent of foil. Mum was careful to keep it covered up ever since the time she'd found a mouse had crept into the body cavity overnight and died. Dad stealthily hunted through the larder until he found the tin of mince pies. He gave us one each and rearranged the others to disguise the gap. 'If anyone notices, blame Father Christmas,' he said, through a mouthful of gritty mincemeat. He always said that, of the seven deadly sins, gluttony was the most likely to claim him. But then gluttony had a powerful adversary in the form of Mother's cooking, so he would probably be all right.

When I was woken by footsteps on the landing below I naturally thought of Father Christmas, but then there came the faint sound of groaning, and I remembered we had real visitors instead. I crept down the attic stairs, carrying my stump of a candle in its saucer of water. A draught from the broken skylight above made the flame wobble, and I drew it a little closer to my highly inflammable brushed nylon pyjamas.

The bathroom door stood half-open, flooding the landing with yellowish light. Aunty Barbara was standing over the sink, flicking water up at herself. She turned round to reach the towel rail and there was a look of terror on her face even before she saw me standing there. 'Can you get someone?' she said, sinking down onto the side of the bath. 'I'm feeling awful.' The front of her satin dressing gown was soaked and transparent from all the splashing.

I scuttled back along the landing, my candle flame guttering and bending, and knocked on Mum and Dad's door before opening it far enough to poke my head round.

'Aunty Barbara's feeling awful in the bathroom,' I said, and Mum erupted from the bed as though driven by the force of a small explosion, and flew across the room towards me, ballooning white cotton from neck to ankle. 'She's feeling funny,' I said again, sensing myself an important player in this drama. 'She said to get you.'

'All right,' said Mum, patting my arm. 'You go back to bed. I'll see to it. And keep that candle at arm's length.'

I ignored the first part of this advice, and hovered unthanked in the doorway while Mum took charge. I needed the loo now, in any case, after having been vertical for some minutes.

'What's wrong?' Mum asked, kneeling beside Aunty Barbara, who had now sunk to the floor. As she squatted down I could see she was wearing a pair of Grandpa Percy's old long-johns under her nightdress. 'Have you been sick?'

'No. It's the pills. I keep having these panic attacks, one after the other. They come over me in waves. It's like dying, again and again.' Aunty Barbara shuddered in her peach satin.

'You're freezing,' Mum said. 'Come back to bed and I'll stay with you until you feel better.'

Aunty Barbara managed a mirthless laugh. 'God. How long have you got?'

Mum helped her up and supported her shaky progress along the corridor. 'I could refill your hot waterbottle?' Mum said, but not too persuasively. She was thinking of the kettle, whose shriek would raise the whole house.

'No, it just makes me perspire.' They had reached the bedroom now and the door swung closed, blocking me out and creating a gust that extinguished my precious flame.

WE OPENED OUR PRESENTS AFTER BREAKFAST ON CHRISTMAS morning before Dad went off to the prison to take Holy Communion.

There was a snake belt and some clay for me, a slide rule and swimming goggles for Christian, a wastepaper basket and some hand cream for Mum, and a watch strap for Dad.

'Goodness, how extravagant,' Mum said, squeezing a pearl of cream onto her rough, red hands, filling the room with the soapy scent of lilies. 'I shall feel pampered.'

Donovan was toying with the few parcels Dad had had the foresight to collect from his house the day before. They were mostly from family friends like us, or distant relatives; there was nothing from either of his parents. 'I am actually getting a skateboard,' he kept saying, as each freshly opened gift proved to be something less welcome.

'Poor Donovan,' said Aunty Barbara, who was lying on the couch, still in her dressing gown, her angular shoulders and collar bone jutting out like furniture under a dust sheet. 'Christmas got away from me this year. Perhaps I'll get you something in the sales.' Her own gift from us – a pair of sheepskin gloves – lay discarded, half-unwrapped, beside her. I don't think she really had the hang of presents. When I asked her what she wanted for Christmas, she said, 'Peace on earth, good will to men and a new agent.'

From Grandpa Percy there was a card with robins on the front and inside a perfect, unused, twenty-pound note. I had it in my hand – unimaginable wealth – for just a few seconds before Mum pounced. 'Twenty pounds!' she exclaimed, swiping it. 'That can't be right. His eyesight must be going. I'll have to send it back.' My cries of protest fell unheard and futile, mere snowflakes on the sea.

When the last of the presents had been opened and admired, and the serviceable paper salvaged for next year, Dad prepared to depart. We hated the fact that he had to go to work on this of all days, but he said it was the only time he got a decent-sized congregation, and he wouldn't miss it for the world. For some of the prisoners it might be the first time they ever set foot in a church, he explained. It was up to him to make sure they felt God's welcome.

'I think church would be better if it was a bit warmer, and a bit shorter,' said Donovan, who remained unconverted by last night's experience.

'You've got no stamina, Donovan,' sighed Aunty Barbara, supine on the couch. 'Just like your father.'

AFTER LUNCH, HARD POTATOES, SQUEAKY SPROUTS, AND those outermost slices of turkey furthest from the uncooked pink centre, we went for a walk on the common, leaving Aunty Barbara eating dates and listening to a play on the radio. It was a cold day with blank, grey skies and a bitter wind, whose sting made your eardrums burn. I was glad of my hand-knitted balaclava, even if it did make me look like

a garden gnome on a bank raid, as Christian was the first
to point out. Donovan had brought along a boomerang – a
gift from a friend in Tasmania – and we took turns throwing and fetching, throwing and fetching, since despite our
best efforts it never showed any inclination to return.

'There must be a knack to it,' said Dad, as the boomerang
described the gentlest of curves and fell to earth a hundred
and fifty feet away. 'Next time I meet an aborigine I'll make
a point of asking.'

The experiment came to an abrupt end when Donovan,
whose turn it was, spun round like a discus thrower so that
the boomerang flew out of his hand at an unplanned angle
and struck the trunk of a beech tree, shattering into half a
dozen pieces and sending up a cloud of startled magpies.

'Whoopsie,' said Mum. 'That's that, then.'

'Can it be glued?' Donovan said in a forlorn voice, when
the fragments had been retrieved and reassembled.

'I expect so,' said Dad, who was always more of an optimist than Mum, and felt it just as unchristian to despair of
things as of people. 'We'll do our best.'

No one felt inclined to prolong the outing any longer,
so we turned back towards home, heads down and arms
folded against the wind. We arrived at the Old Schoolhouse
to find Aunty Barbara in the front garden, gathering sticks.
She was still in her silky dressing gown and barefoot, apparently oblivious to the cold.

'What are you doing, Barbara?' Mum said, aghast.

'The fire was getting a bit low,' Aunty Barbara said
reproachfully. 'I didn't want it to go out, so I thought I'd
get some twigs.' She was already holding quite a sizeable
bundle.

'But we've got a cellar full of coal,' said Mum, taking her

arm. Even her notions of thrift didn't run to these extremes. 'Come in. You'll get pneumonia.'

Aunty Barbara shook her off. 'It's crazy to waste coal when there's all this wood lying around out here,' she said, continuing to forage. 'Come on Donovan, Esther, give me a hand.'

We both hesitated and then stooped down to reach the sticks at our feet, bowed down by the force of her will.

'Masses of stuff here. Save yourselves a fortune,' she muttered. In her satin robe with her long hair flying in the wind, and her bare feet, blue-tinged with cold she resembled some species of fairy – not necessarily benign.

Dad took charge. 'Let's take them in shall we?' he said, relieving Donovan and me of our modest collection, 'before the fire goes out altogether. And we'll have a nice cup of tea and some of those mince pies, and thaw out. And then I'll fix that boomerang.' He made for the front door with a decisive stride.

Aunty Barbara cast her eyes quickly around the garden, as if assessing how much wood she was being required to abandon, before giving a shrug and following Dad indoors. She had the springy, graceful walk of a dancer – back straight, feet turned out. Her other walk was an old lady's shuffle: there was nothing in between.

'Go and fill the coal scuttle,' Mum instructed Christian, who was the last in. She shut the front door and then her hand hovered for a moment over the key, which she turned quietly and put in her pocket.

In the living room the fire had collapsed into a pile of glowing ash.

'I've got a feeling that wood might be a bit damp to use right away,' Dad was saying. Not loudly enough, it seemed, since Aunty Barbara marched over to the fireplace and flung an armful of wet sticks into the grate, knocking the last gleam of life from the embers, which expired with a hiss, filling the room with acrid smoke.

12

AUNTY BARBARA MUST HAVE CAUGHT A CHILL OUT IN THE garden with no slippers, because she spent most of the next five days in bed. Sometimes Mum or I would take her turkey soup and toast on a tray. Once or twice she came down to eat with us. 'I've got no appetite,' she kept saying. 'I'm having to force this down.'

'That's all right,' Mum replied. 'It's not the first time that's been said of my cooking.'

There was one occasion when I came into the kitchen looking for scissors and found her leaning over the fish tank, adding pinch after pinch of fish food to the water and gazing in fascination as Starsky and Hutch gulped at the coloured flakes. She was dressed, for once, in outdoor clothes.

'I've already fed them today,' I said. Donovan was very strict about times, dosages, etc.

'They looked hungry,' she replied, tossing in another helping. 'Poor prisoners.'

Then Mum came in, buttoning her horse-blanket coat, and said they'd be late for the appointment if they didn't get a move on, and the surgery had been very good about fitting them in between Christmas and New Year, and they went off together in the car.

I went straight to Donovan and reported the offence. He swept down from the attic four stairs at a time, eyes blazing with fury. He scooped Starsky and Hutch and their shred of pondweed into Mum's measuring jug and then tipped the murky water and most of the gravel down the sink, spraying the crockery on the draining board in the process. I wondered at the time if anyone would notice that the cups tasted fishy, but nobody mentioned it. He refilled the tank with clean tap water and flopped the fish back in, and then took the much depleted tub of food back upstairs and hid it in his suitcase. 'She's just so . . . stupid,' he hissed, his teeth, fists, everything clenched.

The next morning there was the speckled one belly-up on the surface while the other still flickered to and fro in the shadow of his dead companion. Aunty Barbara wasn't to be disturbed, so Donovan wrote YOU'VE KILLED STARSKY! in furious capitals on a piece of paper and shoved it under her door.

She found the note when she emerged later that afternoon to empty her ashtray. 'I didn't kill him,' she said, tragically. 'I was just trying to jolly them up.' A thought struck her. 'In fact it was probably the change of water that killed him,' she said. 'Everyone knows you shouldn't put them in cold water straight from the tap.' She seemed greatly cheered by this hypothesis. Not so Donovan, who gave a sort of bellow, and rushed from the room. I found him on the stairs being comforted by Dad.

'She killed my fish, and now she says I did it by putting him in cold water, but I only did that to get rid of all the Guppy Flakes that *she'd* put in there,' he raved.

'Of course you didn't kill whatshisname. Spasski,' said Dad soothingly. 'And I'm sure Mummy didn't either. He probably just died of old age. In his sleep.'

'He wasn't old. We've only had him a year and a bit,' protested Donovan, who was not to be so easily appeased.

'Ah, but in fish years that's a long, long time. He may have been old, and ill and ready to die. Now he's probably in fish heaven,' Dad said. 'Whatever that may be,' he added, sensing himself on tricky theological terrain.

'Mum's always saying she wants to die,' said Donovan. 'But she never does.'

CHRISTIAN AND DONOVAN WERE BIG BUDDIES THIS TIME around and didn't want me in the way. They spent their time lighting fires down in the spinney, cycling over to Biggin Hill to look at aeroplanes, or knocking on doors to see if people wanted their cars cleaned for cash. There wasn't much uptake for their services. As Mum pointed out, their general appearance was unlikely to inspire confidence that they had ever had successful dealings with soap and water. I noticed that the two of them seemed to have built up this friendship without resorting to speech. Whenever I came across them they were either silently absorbed in some complex task – building a squirrel-proof bird-feeder, perhaps – or wrestling violently on the floor. According to Christian, conversation gave him a big fuzzy headache, and was 'mostly for girls'.

I didn't have much opportunity to be lonely. For some mysterious reason, Aunty Barbara seemed to take a liking to me and would often collar me for a chat when at large, or detain me in her room when I took up her meals or drinks. She had lots of silly names for me, such as her Gorgeous Girl, or the Divine Creature, and would gossip at me as if I was one of her old woman friends who understood.

The principal theme of her conversation was the Inferiority of Men, allowing for the odd exception such as my father. The weight of her argument rested on two exemplars who bore the brunt of her disdain. One was her agent, Clive, whose function remained obscure, but whom I pictured against a lamp post in a trench-coat with upturned collar.

'He always says I'm too old for this part or that part,' she complained to me one day, as I sat on her bed trying to peel a satsuma for her. She couldn't do it herself because the citrus juice got into the chewed skin around her nails and stung like hell. 'And then months later I find the part's gone to someone older than me, like Susannah York. He's got me nothing but piddly bits of radio work and voice-overs for years. I've a good mind to ditch him and get someone else. I told him that once, and do you know what he said? "Darling, that's like someone on the *Titanic* demanding a different deck-chair."' She gave a bitter laugh.

Most of her venom, however, was reserved for Donovan's father, Alan, who had announced his intention of leaving her by jumping out of the upstairs window of a Swiss hotel room during an argument. Fortunately for him he had landed in deep snow. Her complaints against him were numerous and contradictory: he kept them short of money; he spoiled Donovan with expensive presents; he was uncommunicative; she never wanted to speak to him again; he had deliberately cut off all links with the past; he was trying to win over their friends to his side; he had broken her heart; she had never loved him anyway . . . I found all this grown-up talk largely incomprehensible, but exhilarating. My parents never, ever spoke like this. They seldom discussed other people in front of me and Christian, and only in the blandest and most uncritical terms. True, Kind and Necessary were the three criteria which had to be met before a word was allowed through the gates of their teeth. I sensed that Mum was uneasy at the thought of my audiences with Aunty Barbara, as she often interrupted them to borrow me for some footling errand, but she couldn't bring herself to articulate her anxiety.

Finally she felt moved to intervene, precipitating a scene that very nearly wrecked New Year's Eve for all of us.

It was early evening and we were all in the sitting room except Mum and Dad, who were making cheese sandwiches for supper, there having been a revolt against turkey on the sixth day after Christmas. Christian and Donovan were lying in front of the fire, playing Scrabble, while I was working away at a piece of French knitting on a bobbin made from a wooden cotton reel with four brass screws in the top. I had become quite adept at this soothing, but senseless craft and had already turned out yards of multi-coloured woollen tubing, for which no purpose had yet presented itself.

Aunty Barbara was at full stretch on the couch. She had, unusually, discarded her nightwear in favour of one of Mum's dung-coloured corduroy skirts and a navy Shetland pullover. In her hurried departure from home she had not

packed sufficient warm clothing for the glacial tempera-
tures of the Old Schoolhouse and was now having
to borrow. She was playing with her long hair, plaiting
and then unplaiting it, while half-listening to a play
on the radio and chipping in with her comments on the
performance.

'Beryl Reid. I worked with her once. What a scream. I
wonder if she'd remember me . . . Joe Orton. What a tragedy.
All that talent wasted . . . Oh not *her* again, God, she's in
everything. Couldn't act her way out of, oh SHUT UP!'
Aunty Barbara slung a cushion at the radio set, narrowly
missing the Scrabble game and knocking the tuning button
so that the dialogue was swallowed up in a hailstorm of
interference and high-pitched whistling. She made no move
to restore the sound quality, or retrieve the cushion, but
slumped back to the horizontal again with her eyes clenched
shut.

After enduring this unfriendly noise for a minute or two
Donovan got up and gave the off switch a sharp twist. The
radio expired with a pop. Aunty Barbara opened one eye.
'Since you're up, go and fetch my bag, Donovan,' she said.
'It's in my room.'

He turned on his heel with a look of annoyance, and we
heard him clumping up the stairs with slow, emphatic tread.

I caught Christian's eye and he pulled a face – one of
those untranslatable grimaces which are perfectly understood by the recipient. Christian didn't like Aunty Barbara.
I could tell this because he answered her questions in mono-
syllables and without making eye contact. To be fair, she
didn't put him to this trouble often, considering the male
opinion of no great value. In private he confided that he
thought she was 'mad and scary' and 'not like a mum'. On

the last point I had to agree, but it's hard to dislike someone who seems bent on singling you out for praise and admiration.

Donovan returned with the bag, a hand-woven woollen sac which Aunty Barbara began to unpack onto the floor beside her. Presently she found what she was looking for – a round pocket mirror, in which she attempted to examine the top of her head.

'That's not a proper word,' Christian said suddenly. Donovan had laid down HORE on the triple word square and was totting up his score.

'It is,' Donovan retorted. 'I've heard it.'

'HORE isn't a word, is it?' Christian appealed to Aunty Barbara who had located a grey hair with the aid of her mirror, and was winding it around her finger.

'No. Ow.' The unwanted hair was plucked out at the root. 'Not spelled like that it isn't.' Her eyes narrowed. 'Anyway, where exactly did you hear it, Donovan?'

He looked uncomfortable. 'I don't know. I've forgotten.'

'I'm getting the dictionary,' Christian insisted. 'If you're wrong you miss a turn.' He strode out, nearly colliding with Mum, who was coming through the doorway with a plate of cheese sandwiches and a jar of mixed pickle. Dad was a few paces behind with the tea tray.

'God, listening to you two reminds me of arguments I used to have with Alan. Before the real arguments began, I mean,' said Aunty Barbara. 'He was a cheat, in Scrabble as in life.'

Mum put the sandwiches down and started to distribute plates.

'One time he got so annoyed because I said the word

"zoo" was an abbreviation that he tipped the whole table over and stormed out and didn't come back all night. You've never met such a bad loser. I should have read the warning signs then.'

Mum frowned and made throat-clearing noises.

'Right, who's for tea?' Dad said, with exaggerated cheeriness.

'He used to cheat at bridge too,' Aunty Barbara went on, undeflected. 'We had this code for how many aces, how many kings, depending on the way he was holding his cards. He always had to win at everything. Sometimes I'd deliberately overbid just to annoy him. I can't stand that male competitive stuff.'

At this point Christian reappeared holding the open dictionary, his finger planted on the crucial page. 'There. Told you. Horde. Horehound. Horizon. You lose.'

'Just because it's not in the dictionary doesn't mean it's not a word,' Donovan retorted, snatching the book.

'Course it does. Where do you think words come from, you div?'

'You're the div.'

'Listen to you, Donovan!' cried Aunty Barbara, reaching for a sandwich. 'You'll end up like your father if you don't watch out.'

Mum, who was holding the teapot, twitched, slopping scalding tea onto the tray. 'Barbara,' she said, in a low voice that silenced the room in an instant, 'I thought we'd agreed you wouldn't run Alan down in front of Donovan. It isn't fair.'

Aunty Barbara stopped, mouth open, sandwich halfway to her lips. 'Fair?' she said incredulously. 'You don't know the half of it. I'll tell you how fair Alan is: when we did the big carve-up we agreed to split everything equally. I went out and left him to it, and when I came back I found he'd taken one of every pair of curtains in the house. Just to spite me. That's the sort of person he is.'

'Nevertheless,' said Mum, who was looking as hot and uncomfortable as I'd ever seen her, 'I don't think it's especially helpful for Donovan to hear all this.'

Christian and I were riveted by this rare opportunity to witness grown-up conflict. Donovan, who was evidently accustomed to having people quarrel over him, was still thumbing through the dictionary, oblivious.

'Oh, don't worry about him,' Aunty Barbara gestured with her sandwich, scattering shreds of grated cheese. 'He's heard it all before. And worse. You should hear the choice language Alan's been teaching him for that matter,' she added, pointing at the game of Scrabble, now temporarily suspended.

Dad glanced over Christian's shoulder at the board and tutted. 'I expect you're thinking of HOAR,' he said to Donovan. 'It's a sort of frost.'

'I don't know why you're so keen to defend Alan all of a sudden.' Aunty Barbara's eyes narrowed. 'Actually I do know why. He's been onto you, hasn't he?'

'No,' Mum replied, taken aback by this turn the conversation was taking.

'He's trying to get all our friends onto his side by spreading lies about me. I knew it!' Her voice rose hysterically. 'What's he been saying?'

'Nothing. We've never . . .' Mum's attempt at reassurance was steamrollered by a fresh outburst of paranoia.

'He can't bear to think that anybody knows what he's really like. It's not enough that he's ruined my life. He wants

to ruin my reputation too. I bet he told you that I'm unstable and an unfit mother, and I drink and stuff like that.'

'No he . . .'

'The bastard won't rest till he's destroyed me,' she raved.

'Barbara,' Mum warned.

'Oh pardon my fucking French,' Aunty Barbara snapped,
subsiding unhappily into the sagging trench in the middle
of the couch.

The silence that greeted this remark was broken by the
gentle swishing sound of Donovan turning the pages of the
dictionary.

'Barbara.' Dad dropped to his knees in front of her and
grasped her by the elbows so that his face was level with
hers. 'I promise you we don't have any contact with Alan
whatsoever. The last time we heard from him was before
he . . . left. I think it's perfectly clear where our sympathies
lie.'

Aunty Barbara gave a violent tremble like a jumpy horse,
and then relaxed with a great sigh. 'I'm sorry,' she said. 'I
don't know why I get so . . .'

'It's all right,' Mum soothed. 'No need to apologise.'

'You've been so kind to us. And I'm just a crabby old
cow.'

Mum and Dad made polite demurring noises, while out
of the corner of my eye I saw Christian nodding solemnly.

'I wonder . . .' Aunty Barbara glanced at her watch. 'Do
you think anywhere will be open? I've run out of ciggies.'

Dad offered to drive down to the newsagent's for her, but
she said she needed the exercise, and in the end they left
together, on foot.

On the way Dad must have had one of his Kind Words,
because when they returned Aunty Barbara was more

cheerful, and even helped with the washing up. Her only other contribution to the running of the house was to suggest that Mum got a cleaner. 'Big house like this. You need some-one to come in and do for you.'

Mum dismissed the idea. She didn't see why someone else should clear up our dirt. 'Besides, how could we afford it?' she added.

'You could let out some of these rooms to paying guests,' Aunty Barbara said, scouring a dinner plate as though intent on removing the pattern as well as the remains of lunch.

'I have thought about it,' Mum said, rescuing the plate, 'but most of the time our spare rooms seem to be occupied by non-paying guests.'

Aunty Barbara failed to acknowledge this remark. 'I'd have a cleaner like a shot if I could,' she went on. 'But they take one look at my place and resign. The last one said, "I'm not working here, it's filthy!" I said, "Of course it's filthy. You don't think I'm going to pay you good money to clean a house that's already clean?" She didn't stay.'

FOR THE FIRST TIME I WAS ALLOWED TO STAY UP TO SEE IN the New Year, but in the end the grown-ups all fell asleep at about half past ten and had to be shaken awake in time for Auld Lang Syne. Christian was made to go out of the back door and come in at the front holding a lump of coal, for reasons no one could explain, and we toasted 1977 with Elderflower cordial, and made resolutions for the year to come. Christian and I promised not to go through shoes so fast, Donovan was going to eat vegetables, Dad would do something about the roof, Mum would sort out Grandpa Percy, and Aunty Barbara was going to put the whole damn thing behind her.

13

A FEW DAYS AFTER THE BANK HOLIDAY, AUNTY BARBARA
announced her intention of going to the sales, and offered
to take me with her.

'You can help me choose Donovan's Christmas present,'
she said.

Mum made no objection to this plan; in fact she was
quite happy for me to deputise for her in any confrontation
with the ugly forces of materialism. 'No, I certainly don't
feel left out,' she assured us. 'You know I can't stand shopping. I'd only spoil it for you.'

My enthusiasm was entirely mercenary. Aunty Barbara
had hinted that there might be something in it for me, and
I sensed that she was the sort of person who might spend,
as she did most other things, impulsively. The boys weren't
interested in accompanying us. 'We'll be looking at
ladieswear and shoes,' Aunty Barbara told them, by way of
deterrent.

'We'll have lunch out,' she said, as we set off for the bus stop in a buffeting wind. 'Perhaps you know somewhere nice we can go.' I didn't: we never ate out, except on holiday, as an absolute last resort. 'We're going to have a lovely time,' Aunty Barbara insisted. She had dressed up for the occasion in a black wool dress and high-heeled suede boots that zipped to the knee. Her hair had been teased and rolled into a cottage loaf shape on top of her head, and her face was fiercely painted – black for the eyes and red for the lips. As we walked along she crushed me to her side so that I was almost suffocated by the gerbil coat. While I fought for breath she instructed me to call her Barbara. 'I'm not a proper Aunty, and anyway it makes me feel old.'

She often returned to the subject of ageing and was full of advice and warnings. 'Neck and hands, Esther, they're the first to show.' 'Keep your face out of the sun, unless you want to end up looking like beef jerky.'

We sat on the top deck of the bus so that she could smoke, which she did with a curious grimacing expression to avoid growing pucker lines around her mouth. The wind had done its best to flatten the cottage loaf, and left streaky black tears at the corners of her eyes. When she opened her wallet to pay the conductor she caught sight of herself in the strip of mirror inside and gave a little scream.

'What a fright!' she exclaimed, dabbing at the smudges with a scrap of tissue.

The precinct was crowded with shoppers when we arrived, but Aunty Barbara showed the same steely resistance to obstruction as she had in the matter of wood-gathering.

'Hold tight,' she commanded, taking me by the wrist and elbowing a channel through the scrum that had formed around the entrance to Grantley's. 'Excuse us, excuse us,' she cried, oblivious to the reproachful mutters that attended our progress.

In ladieswear she thumbed through rails of beaded evening gowns, clamping one after another against her as though about to perform a tango. I sat outside the fitting room on a vinyl stool while she tried on the pick of them. Every few minutes she would emerge between the curtains in a different costume and strike a pose for my approval. 'What do you think?' she said, of a tissue-thin green dress with a pearl-crusted bodice.

'Beautiful,' I said, meaning the dress, and Aunty Barbara looked pleased. 'It's what Alan used to call a gownless evening strap,' she said with a laugh, and then her face darkened. She fingered the label, which was attached to a little bag of spare pearls. A nice touch that, I thought.

'It *is* half price,' she went on. 'The trouble is I don't go anywhere any more.' This melancholy thought seemed to spur her to a decision. 'Oh, what the hell, I'll take it.' And she swished behind the curtain to change.

At the till the assistant wrapped the dress in layers of white tissue and laid it in a box with gold lettering on the lid, a gesture so glamorous it brought a lump to my throat. *Bienvenu à Biarritz.* As we made our way back to the escalators through bridalwear I allowed my fingers to trail wistfully over the yards of bunched taffeta and silk. Aunty Barbara must have seen my hand lingering on the hem of a peach bridesmaid's dress, as she stopped and said, 'Oh, isn't that pretty? Do you like it?'

I nodded dumbly. It was the most beautiful, wondrous

creation, with gauzy sleeves, a wide satin sash, a ballooning skirt with a scalloped hem, covered buttons, and a heart-
shaped neckline decorated with tiny peach rosebuds. I would
never be able to wear it.

'Let's see if it fits,' she said, plucking it from the rail and
propelling me towards the cubicles once more. I struggled
out of my nylon trousers and skinny-rib sweater to reveal a
greyish vest and pants, while Aunty Barbara parted the petal
layers of the underskirt and lowered the dress over my head.
It rested on me as lightly as a cobweb, rustling and whis-
pering when I turned, like something alive. 'It does look
rather lovely,' Aunty Barbara admitted, when she had
finished tying the sash. 'Perhaps not with socks and sneak-
ers though.'

I gazed at my transformed reflection in the mirror with
frank admiration, bobbing up and down to make the skirt
puff up. 'Let's get it,' Aunty Barbara decided. 'That'll give
Mummy a surprise.'

Won't it, I thought, as Aunty Barbara wrote out another
cheque for a fantastic amount of money, far exceeding
Mum's annual expenditure on clothes. When the shop assistant produced another of those monogrammed boxes and
pressed it into my trembling hands I thought I would expire
with happiness.

'That was very expensive, wasn't it?' I said, to let her
know that her generosity wasn't lost on me. Aunty Barbara
nodded. 'You must have loads of money.'

'None at all,' she replied gaily. 'But I've got plenty of
cheques.'

We spent the next quarter of an hour in the millinery
department trying on picture hats, an enterprise which
finished the demolition job on the cottage loaf that the

wind had already begun. 'There were some sensational hats at our wedding,' Aunty Barbara said, selecting a white fedora with rhinestones. She pulled it down over one eye and pouted at herself in the mirror. 'They've fallen out of favour a bit nowadays. Like gloves. My mother had a drawer full of gloves: I don't think anyone outside the family ever saw the skin of her hands.' She laughed at this memory. 'I've still got her pair of ivory glove-stretchers at home. I use them as salad tongs.'

This mention of food led us to the fourth floor in search of the restaurant. We sat at a curious kidney-shaped table on a curved banquette of bright green vinyl, and ate prawn cocktail out of giant brandy glasses. Another first. At home prawns were held to be a delicacy enjoyed only by royalty and their like. We were on one occasion permitted tinned shrimps, which Christian said looked just like a cat's bottom, and thereafter they vanished from the menu.

The restaurant was crowded with other successful shoppers: I could see carrier bags bunched under every table. Columns of smoke rose from parked cigarettes, and all around us was the babble of female voices, like waves clattering on shingle.

Aunty Barbara had a black coffee while I ate a slab of cherry cheesecake. 'I'm off dairy products,' she said, and then proceeded to poach forkfuls from my plate. If she hadn't paid for it in the first place I would have been tempted to fend off these incursions. Left to myself I could have savoured it for hours, but now that we were in competition I had to rush.

After lunch we looked at shoes, but without trying any on. Aunty Barbara couldn't be bothered to keep unzipping

her boots, and besides she had atrocious feet, she said.
Ruined by ballet.

A sign for the toy department reminded her that it was
Donovan we had come for. She browsed the shelves helplessly, without a clue what he might like, whereas I could
see immediately half a dozen things that would have been
perfect. The pogo stick, indoor croquet set and stilts were
ruled out by Aunty Barbara as being too unwieldy to take
on the bus. In the end she settled on a crash helmet and
elbow and knee pads to compliment the phantom skateboard. 'I just hope Alan hasn't forgotten, or changed his
mind,' she muttered, as another cheque was torn off its
stub.

Now that lunch was over and I had my present I was
starting to weary of shopping, and Aunty Barbara's boots
were pinching, so we made our way onto the high street in
search of the bus stop. I had just spotted it in the distance
and was quickening my pace when Aunty Barbara noticed
a branch of Boots opposite and told me to wait outside with
the baggage while she made a few last-minute purchases. 'I
can't take all this clobber in with me,' she said, divesting
herself of bags. 'It'll hold me up.'

I stood on the pavement, guarding our purchases, my
monogrammed box safely under one arm. I felt a twinge of
anxiety at the thought of Mum's reaction to the peach satin
dress. She was not the sort to go into raptures over pretty
things. As for the price tag, I wondered whether I might be
able to remove it before we reached home. If Mum saw it
she would be bound to invoke the shades of the Less
Fortunate, and I didn't want those wraiths clutching at my
satin hem, staring up at me with their hungry eyes, when
I was trying to feel like a princess.

Aunty Barbara came out of Boots at a brisk walk and set off up the road, gesturing to me to follow. She was holding her gerbil coat together oddly, as though she had stomach ache.

'That's the wrong way,' I protested, struggling to gather up the bags. 'We need to cross back over.'

'Never mind,' she said over her shoulder. 'Just keep walking.' And she quickened her pace so that I had to run to catch up. In spite of her high heels and atrocious feet she could certainly step on it when required. I drew level with her just as our bus hove into view on the opposite side of the road.

'That's ours,' I said, and she grabbed my wrist with her free arm and we plunged through a gap in the traffic.

As we reached the kerb she caught her heel in the drain and stumbled, and from between the flaps of her coat slithered half a dozen packets of tights – fifteen denier, medium, mink – five packets of emery boards, six tubes of mascara and more eyeliner pencils than I could count. I'd never seen anyone buy so much of the same thing: you'd think she was stocking up for the rest of her life.

'They could have given you a bag,' I said indignantly, as I helped her to shovel it all in with Donovan's crash helmet and pads. 'How do they expect you to carry all this loose stuff?'

But Aunty Barbara didn't answer. She was inspecting the skinned heel of her boot. 'Serve me bloody well right,' she muttered. When she stood up I noticed she had grazed her knee and now had a huge hole and a racing ladder in her tights. Still, she had plenty of spares, I thought.

Some of the onlookers at the bus stop, seeing our

struggles, had held up the driver. The crowd parted to let us through, and Aunty Barbara gave them a regal smile as she climbed aboard and hobbled with great dignity down the aisle on her broken heel.

14

THE PEACH DRESS HAD A BETTER RECEPTION THAN I COULD have hoped for. Mum did not confiscate it or cut it up to make quilts for earthquake victims. Instead she said, 'Oh, Barbara, you shouldn't have,' and to me, 'Well, aren't you a lucky girl.'

Later that evening I put it on to show Dad when he came home from the prison, and he pretended not to recognise me. 'Good evening, madam,' he said, bowing slightly. 'Have you seen my daughter? She's about your height, but wild and scruffy-looking.' Mum smiled at this, though she couldn't do teasing herself. It was just the three of us. Aunty Barbara was having a lie-down on her bed and the boys were still out at the driving range, collecting up the golf balls for ten pence a bucket.

'Typical Barbara,' Mum said, shaking her head. 'Spending a fortune she hasn't got on something so frivolous.'

'The poor are always with us,' Dad reminded her.

'I know, I know,' sighed Mum. 'I never liked that story.'

AUNTY BARBARA'S RESOLUTION TO PUT IT ALL BEHIND HER proved no more successful than Donovan's to eat his greens. I knew that he had been spending his golf money at the Southern Fried Chicken shop on the way home because I found a serviette and a salt sachet in his bedroom when I went in looking for the fish flakes to feed Hutch. This was why he was able, when dinner appeared, to request only the smallest portions of everything, particularly Mum's par-boiled veg, which he would nibble and maul and hide under his knife and fork.

Aunty Barbara, it emerged, had also been enjoying alter-native refreshments. The experience with Mr Spragg had taught me to be suspicious of anyone who took long walks in the afternoon for no good reason, so when Aunty Barbara started going out for a breath of fresh air in the foulest weather imaginable I knew trouble was not far off.

It was January 6 and we were all sitting around the kitchen table for breakfast, apart from Aunty Barbara, who was doing something in the bathroom with wax. Dad was testing us on the feast of Epiphany.

'How many wise men?'

'Three,' we replied, in bored voices. *Too easy. Ask us another.*

He shook his head. A trick question. 'It doesn't actually say how many in the Gospels.'

'Why do they always put three on Christmas cards, then?' asked Christian.

'What about We Three Kings of Orien-tar?' Donovan wanted to know.

Dad shrugged. 'It's purely supposition that there were three. But we're not actually told. There were three *gifts*, but that doesn't necessarily mean there were three wise men.'

'They could have clubbed together,' Donovan said.

'Yeah,' I agreed. 'Especially for something expensive, like gold.'

'Gold, frankincense and myrrh – spazzy presents for a baby,' was Christian's verdict.

There followed a conversation about what gifts a modern messiah might expect. Premium bonds. An engraved pewter tankard. Cufflinks. A napkin ring.

We were still trying to top this last contribution for sheer uselessness, when the morning post hit the doormat. Donovan, who was nearest, went to fetch it: there was only one item, a postcard.

'It's Dad's writing,' he said, pausing to read the message aloud before handing it over. '*Thanks for all you're doing. So sorry you've been landed with B. If you've been put to any expense, please let me know. Yours ever, Alan.*'

Donovan's delivery of this message, in an uncomprehending monotone, unfortunately coincided with the entrance of Aunty Barbara, who froze in the doorway, nostrils dilated with fury. Before Mum and Dad, who looked equally paralysed, could intervene, she had recovered the use of her muscles sufficiently to snatch the card from Donovan's hand.

'What's he say?' she hissed, squinting at the card and holding it at arm's length to bring the writing into focus. She had reading glasses in her handbag, but never wore them because they put ten years on her. She'd told me she'd rather not read any more than look like a geriatric before her time. 'I knew it!' she said triumphantly. 'I knew there was something going on between you. *Landed*. The smug, patronising git. Go and get your things, Donovan. We're going.'

He hesitated, glancing at Dad for a ruling.

'NOW!' his mother shrilled, slamming her hand on the table and making the crockery rattle.

'Barbara, I've told you, there's nothing "going on" between us,' Dad protested as Donovan fled from the room. 'This is the first communication we've had from Alan.'

'Then how does he know we're here? Eh?'

Mum and Dad gave identical shrugs expressive of innocence and bafflement. 'Maybe Donovan's written to him.'

'He's been onto you, hasn't he? Telling you I'm off my trolley.'

'He honestly hasn't. We've not spoken a word since he ... went off.'

'I know what it's all about. I'm not stupid. He wants Donovan back. He's putting it about that I'm a bad mother, so he can get custody.'

'I really don't think . . .' Mum began, but her words of reassurance were bitten off by a fresh attack.

'Well, over my dead body is all I can say. And over his, too, for that matter.' She picked up the bread knife, which had a serrated blade divided into two sharp points at the end, and stabbed it through the heart of the uncut loaf with such force that it embedded itself in the chopping board beneath. Before any of us could speak she had stalked out of the room. The four of us exhaled as one. A minute later we heard her bedroom door slam with a terrific crash.

'I think we're out of our depth, here, Gordon,' Mum said. 'Once paranoia sets in . . .'

'She seemed to be getting better. After that little upset at New Year,' said Dad.

'The question is, what are we going to do?'

'If she's determined to go, we can't stop her.'

'Poor Donovan,' said Mum. 'Why don't you two go and see how he's getting on?' She was desperate to have us out of the way so they could talk. We'd already seen and heard too much of the strange, spiky adult world for one day.

We found him in his room, retrieving balled-up items of clothing from all four corners of the room and hurling them into his open suitcase. He tended to undress explosively, I'd noticed. A single sock was still lodged on the curtain rail, where it had landed the night before.

His Christmas presents had been more carefully packed in a single layer at the bottom of his case, apart from the helmet and knee-pads, which he was wearing – a sensible precaution in my view. There wasn't much for me and Christian to do, so we just stood around trying to look sympathetic. After all, it wasn't Donovan's fault that he had an angry, knife-wielding mother.

He had just snapped home the catches on the case when there came a tremendous racket of pounding and yelling from Aunty Barbara's room.

'Let me out of here!' she was shouting, almost drowning her own words with the frenzied clamour of fists on wood. 'Someone unlock this door!'

We ventured out onto the landing, in time to see Mum coming up the stairs at a run. 'It doesn't lock,' she called out, as the din subsided. 'It just sticks when it's slammed.' There was no reply from within the bedroom. 'Stand back!' Mum instructed, giving the handle a twist and launching her hip against the door, which resisted for the first inch or so and then flew open, smacking into the wall and chipping a lump out of the plaster. A blast of icy air whipped around our ankles. The window had been thrown up to its full extent and Aunty Barbara had one leg over the sill, a manoeuvre complicated by the fact that she was wearing a tight, straight skirt. The word HELP had been scrawled in lipstick on the glass.

'Oh my God,' said Mum, driven to blasphemy by this extremity. 'Be careful, the sash is broken.'

Christian and I had been brought up to think of our windows as so many primed guillotines, and tended to keep our distance, but of course occasional visitors didn't have our advantage. As Mum took a step into the room, Aunty Barbara, with a look of pure panic in her eyes, tried to swing her other leg up and over the sill. Inhibited by her tight skirt, she lost her balance, made a grab for the paintwork, which came away in her hand in great white flakes, and toppled backwards out of the window, with a shriek that raked the air like nails.

IT WAS VERY FORTUNATE, MUM SAID LATER, THAT AUNTY Barbara's window overlooked the flat roof of the kitchen so she hadn't too far to fall. Otherwise it might have been a different story.

Aunty Barbara didn't look like someone on whom fortune was smiling, as she went off in the ambulance with her neck in a brace. They had lowered her down from the roof on a stretcher, like the paralytic Jesus healed. But there was no Jesus at the bottom, with his kind, sad face, just a doctor in a hurry, who signed some papers, and went off in his car.

15

THE FOLLOWING DAY DONOVAN'S DAD ARRIVED TO TAKE HIM away in a blue Daimler with cream leather seats. He abandoned the car halfway up the drive because of the brambles. 'I must do something about those,' Dad murmured, tugging his eyebrow, but he never did. We were used to the swish and rattle of branches along the sides of our old Austin Princess. It was the sound of coming home.

I was interested to see Donovan's dad, Alan, because of what I'd heard about him, chiefly from Aunty Barbara. But he was disappointingly ordinary: nothing but a man in a smart suit, with thinning hair and a moustache, and not at all the sort you'd imagine throwing himself off Swiss balconies. The thought struck me: what a couple for jumping out of windows.

He and Dad shook hands awkwardly on the doorstep, and then there was one of those annoying scenes so common in the adult world, where Alan tried to give Dad some

money and Dad refused, and said, 'I don't want it,' but Alan
insisted, so Dad put his hands behind his back and the
whole shower of notes fluttered to the floor. 'Well, I don't
want it,' Alan said, and they both refused to pick it up, but
the moment Donovan and I made a dive for it they changed
their minds and back it all went in Alan's wallet.

'Did you get my skateboard?' was Donovan's first question after his Dad had greeted him with one of those man-
to-man sideways hugs.

For a moment it appeared that Alan hadn't heard him,
but then he said, 'Yes, of course. I've left it at the office.
We'll have to pick it up on the way home.' And he gave a
smile that made his moustache ripple like something alive.
'How have you been?' he asked.

'All right,' said Donovan. 'Except Starsky died. And
Mum fell out of the window.'

'I know,' said Alan. 'That's why I'm here.'

'She'll be all right, though, won't she?'

'Yes, of course.'

'Just a sprained wrist and some bruises,' said Mum. 'I rang
the hospital this morning.'

'They're not letting her out, though?' Alan asked.

'Oh no.'

'Right. Right.'

There was a pause, and then from around the bushes at
the edge of the driveway a woman appeared, dressed all in
white, with blonde hair and pale eyes – Aunty Barbara in
negative. She was stooping to hold both hands of a fat baby,
who hadn't quite mastered the art of walking unsupported.

'Pippa needs a nappy change,' said the woman in a
reproachful voice. Now that she mentioned it, the nappy
did look rather taut and low-slung.

'Oh, you haven't left Suzie in the car all this time!' Mum exclaimed. 'Come on in before you all freeze to death.'

We moved inside, leaving Suzie to complete her slow shuffle up the drive. There was no hurrying that bow-legged baby. I wondered why she didn't just pick it up. In the hallway there were more hugs and hellos, and some dithering over whether to remove coats.

'Are we staying?' Suzie asked Alan.

'I've put the kettle on,' Mum said, ushering mother and child towards the downstairs cloakroom to deal with that pungent nappy.

The rest of us adjourned to the sitting room, where the fire was alight. 'I love your house,' Suzie could be heard saying to Mum. 'It's so authentic.'

Dad was hunting around for something to use as a fire-guard to protect Pippa. In the end he tipped all the newspapers and chessmen and knitting and nutshells off the coffee table and turned it on its side to form a barrier, though on Suzie's return it was clear that she had no intention of putting Pippa down, especially now that the floor was covered with nutshells. Instead Pippa was passed around and made to kiss everyone – her latest trick – but before she got to me she took against the idea and buried her face in Suzie's neck. Attempts to cajole her in my direction were met with shrieks of rage. I didn't much want her moist lips and nose pressed up to my cheek anyway, but everyone else seemed to find her aversion to me hilarious.

'Ha ha,' said Donovan, tickling the fat folds of her neck to make her turn round. 'She doesn't like you, Esther.'

'Well, I don't like her,' I replied, and Suzie blinked at me, affronted.

Mum frowned. 'Go and get Pippa one of your dolls to

play with,' she said, as if I had loads to choose from. In fact I had only two: the Mary Quant doll and a Tiny Tears which had been done over with indelible red laundry marker years ago and now had an incurable case of measles. I settled on Mary Quant, somewhat against my instinct to preserve the nicer of the two, because I didn't want the marker pen lecture rehashed in front of a roomful of visitors. As I came down the stairs I could hear Alan on the telephone in the hallway.

'Don't worry about the price, just get one,' he was saying. 'You're an angel. We'll be along later to pick it up. Ta-ta.'

He hung up and turned round, giving a twitch of surprise to find me behind him. 'Hello,' he said, through another hairy smile. 'I didn't see you there. Ha ha. That's a nice dolly. Was she from Father Christmas?'

'No. Aunty Barbara gave her to me the time before.'

'Did she?' he said. 'Did she? Jolly good.'

In the sitting room no one had sat down. Suzie had Pippa on her hip, and Dad was too polite to take a seat while there was a woman still standing. Christian was bowling nutshells into the fire. Pippa accepted Mary Quant greedily, gave her a good shake and then threw her down on the floor. Everyone except me laughed. I wished Mum had been there to witness the result of her bright idea, but she was in the kitchen making tea. I could hear the clink of china and the scream of the kettle.

'Pippa. Naughty!' Suzie scolded, picking up the doll and immediately returning it to her for a second attempt.

Alan was inspecting a photograph on the crowded mantelpiece. It showed Christian and me in the dinghy in Pembrokeshire.

'Was that taken at the caravan?' he asked.

Dad nodded. 'Barbara very kindly gave us a key. We've had some good holidays there. The children love it.'

'We did too. We had some great times there when Donovan was small.' Then he glanced at Suzie and shut up, as if reminiscing was not allowed.

At the mention of his name Donovan disengaged himself from Christian, with whom he had started wrestling, and stood up. 'What? Where? When did we have great times?' He studied the photograph. 'There was a stone building with half a door, and a plastic toilet,' he said, screwing up his eyes with the effort of dredging his memory at such a distance of years. 'And a field with a bull. And sheep poo.'

'Like I said – great times,' Alan laughed.

'Can we go back there one day?'

'You'll have to ask your mother to take you. It's her caravan.'

'She won't take me. We never go on holiday. She doesn't like driving on motorways.'

'In that case, no then.'

'How come they can stay in our caravan but I can't?' Donovan demanded, indignantly. 'That's not fair.'

'We could stay in a different caravan somewhere else if you like,' Alan said, in an effort to appease.

'I'm not staying in any caravan,' Suzie retorted. 'Not with Pippa.'

This dispute was cut short by the arrival of Mum with the tea. She was looking slightly flustered: one of our 'authentic' light switches had given her a shock. 'Do sit down,' she said, putting the tray on the floor now that the coffee table was out of commission. Donovan threw himself into an armchair, releasing a puff of dust. Suzie glanced fearfully at her white suede skirt before perching reluctantly on the arm of the couch. I could see now why Mum never wore white, favouring instead shades of dung and porridge. 'White is for brides and babies,' she used to say. 'It wouldn't last two seconds in our house.'

She had dug out a bone china tea service that used to belong to Grandma Percy, who would never drink out of earthenware. I could see Mum checking the cups as she handed them round, to make sure Suzie and Alan didn't get the glued handles. Dad peeled Pippa from around Suzie's neck and took her off for a tour of the dining room so that Suzie could drink her tea.

'She's not very good with strangers,' Suzie warned, but Pippa's whining turned to giggles in Dad's arms as soon as they were out of the room.

'I don't know how to thank you for looking after Donovan,' Alan said to Mum. 'I feel so bad that we were away. If there's ever anything I can do for you . . . ' but Mum just laughed this suggestion away. In her view there were people in this world who gave help and people who took it, and precious little crossover between the parties.

When the time came to say goodbye, Pippa wound her fingers tightly into Mary Quant's hair and refused to give her up. 'Give it back, Pippa. It's not yours,' Suzie said mildly.

Even I could see mere suggestion would never work. Pippa wasn't going to let go unless someone got physical. I took Mary's ankles in one hand and Pippa's wrist in the other. 'Drop!' I said, sternly.

Pippa's face crumpled as she prepared for a good shriek, but her grip remained firm.

'Oh, goodness, don't upset her,' said Mum. 'Esther won't mind Pippa borrowing it – she's got dozens of toys upstairs.'

I opened my mouth to protest, but help came from an unexpected source.

'No she hasn't,' Donovan said stoutly. 'Pippa's got way more toys than Esther, and she's only one. Esther's hardly got any and they're mostly crap.'

'Oh. Well ...' It was the only time I'd ever known Mum to backtrack, and my eyes began to water with gratitude.

'That's not very polite, Donovan,' Alan said, firmly releasing Mary Quant from Pippa's iron grasp. All the same he was smiling. 'There you are sweetie,' he said, as he handed her back to me. 'Get your stuff together now, Donovan. Let's leave these good people in peace.' .

His smile faltered at the sight of the fish tank, its lone occupant stirring the murky water. He was thinking of his cream leather upholstery. 'Did you bring that all the way from home?' he asked incredulously. 'Good grief. I suppose it'll be all right on the floor.'

'You'll have to drive really, really slowly or he'll get seasick,' Donovan explained. 'About five miles an hour, like Uncle Gordon did.'

Dad gave Alan an apologetic shrug.

WHEN MUM CAME TO CLEAR OUT AUNTY BARBARA'S ROOM ready for its next occupant – as yet undeclared – she found a dozen empty miniature vodka bottles under the bed, along with all the packets of tights and make-up, still unopened. The cosmetics and tights went in a bring and buy sale for the Less Fortunate, but we kept the vodka bottles, and Christian showed me how to get a tune out of them by filling them with water to different levels and tapping them with a metal skewer. After some practice I managed to produce a recognisable rendition of 'Men of Harlech', but

Mum said it didn't look good for a girl of eight to have so many vodka bottles on her window sill, and she would buy me a proper xylophone instead. It was nowhere near my birthday, so she must still have been smarting from Donovan's remark about my 'mostly crap' toys.

16

WHEN I WAS TEN GRANDPA PERCY CAME TO STAY AND NEVER left. He'd lived on his own in a bungalow in King's Lynn since Grandma Percy died of pneumonia six years earlier. Her death had taken all the stuffing out of him, Mum said, and when you saw him you knew what she meant: his clothes hung from his shoulders and hips as though they'd been borrowed from a much bigger man.

According to legend he'd proposed to Grandma Percy seven times before she finally accepted, with the words: 'You be kind to me or I won't stay.' On their honeymoon she had taken a spare suitcase, packed with the essentials for a quick getaway, which she later kept in the back of the wardrobe at home, just in case. As far as we knew Grandpa's kindness never wavered throughout their marriage in the face of this ongoing threat. After her death, when Mum went to help sort out her belongings, she found the suitcase on top of the airing cupboard. Its contents had clearly been updated over the years as the accoutrements of a 1920s newlywed were accompanied by the paraphernalia of an older runaway: support tights, hot waterbottle, Rennies.

Relatives on Mum's side of the family always claimed to detect a resemblance between me and Grandma Percy. 'It's the chin,' they'd say, or 'the eyebrows', or 'that stubborn way she's got'. I didn't like this kind of talk: it's not fun being compared to a dead person you can't remember, who was only ever young in black and white.

Until now Grandpa Percy had seemed to be coping well on his own, grief aside. There were just a few lapses that were giving Mum some unease – that twenty pound note at Christmas, for example. Just recently he had let the gas man in to read the meter and noticed some time later that the tin of Old Holborn in which he kept a float of £100 for emergencies was missing from the window ledge. Later still he remembered that he didn't have gas.

Dad drove to King's Lynn and brought him back to the Old Schoolhouse for a week's holiday at Easter. He sat in an armchair by the French windows looking out over the garden, shouting abuse at any trespassing foxes. Occasionally he would advance to the doorway and pelt them with ice cubes from the freeze box. Christian and I liked having him around once we had grown used to the strange snoring sound he made even when awake. He had given up a lifetime of smoking only on Grandma Percy's death, replacing this with a tic-tac habit that had become equally obsessional. He always had at least one packet about his person, and would carefully decant one capsule every five minutes and lay it on the end of his tongue before rolling it around his mouth for maximum coverage. Although his teeth were yellow and crumbling his breath was always fresh and minty. He seemed delighted with everything we said or did, however trivial, and was forever winking at us and pressing pound notes into our hands when no one else was looking. When not persecuting foxes, he entertained himself by playing variants of patience on a tray on his lap. In spite of his ropey, old-man's hands, he was remarkably dextrous and could cut a pack of cards one-handed, a trick that always made me think of Donovan.

When the week was up Mum asked him if he'd like to stay longer – he was after all a far less demanding house guest than some of our previous visitors. He didn't take much persuading: it was lonely in the bungalow and apart from his cribbage team, and the Men's Afternoon Fellowship – who were a bunch of old women as far as he was concerned – he didn't have much of a social life. At the end of the fortnight he began to exhibit signs of anxiety: he remembered he had only cancelled the milk for a week; it would be piling up on the doorstep; the grass would be knee-high; the letterbox would be choked with free newspapers and leaflets.

Mum and Dad agreed to take him home. Naturally I was required to accompany them: Christian was unavailable as a babysitter as the cricket season had started, and Turton's reputation in the county depended on his presence at the crease.

While Grandpa worked through the pile of mail that had built up behind the front door, Dad whisked round performing various remedial chores: mowing the lawn; repairing a broken gutter and a sagging section of fence; removing furry cheese and liquefying vegetables from the fridge and desiccated plants from the window sills. The sort of things he never got around to at home. My job was to scour the

washbasin in the bathroom with Ajax, paying particular
attention to the streak of seaweed-coloured slime caused by
the perpetually dripping tap. Mum busied herself going
through Grandpa's wardrobe, sorting his clothes into two
piles: With and Without Blobs, then washing the former
pile in the kitchen sink and whizzing them to a blur in the
spin dryer.

Just as we came to say goodbye Grandpa flew into a panic:
he had hidden his pension book in a safe place before he
left and couldn't now remember where. It was somewhere,
he said, with a touch of pride, that no burglar would dream
of looking in a thousand years. Mum and Dad looked
dismayed: unfortunately this sort of ingenuity often went
hand in hand with total amnesia. A frustrating hour was
spent hunting in improbable places – the fridge, the oven,
inside the piano, while Grandpa paced and fretted. On the
one hand he wanted his pension book back: on the other,
its discovery would disprove the impregnability of his hiding
place. Our search, though unsuccessful in its main objec-
tive, turned up various other long-missing items: his gold
fob (taped under the kitchen table), passport (inside dress
shoe), and several old wallets full of cash (medicine cabinet, backs of drawers, under mattress, etc.).

It was only when we reconvened in the sitting room that
the hiding place revealed itself as if by divine intervention.
Mum was patiently lecturing Grandpa on the folly of keeping wads of notes in the house, when a clod of soot and loose
mortar came rattling down the chimney into the fireplace.
Newton himself could scarcely have been more grateful for
the providential fall of the apple. Grandpa smote his forehead. 'Of course,' he said. 'I put it in the fire.' Poking about
in the pyramid of anthracite he turned up an envelope

containing the pension book, a little streaky from the coal-dust, but perfectly serviceable.

Mum let out a sigh that ruffled the net curtains. 'What a place to choose. Honestly, Dad.'

'I know,' he said. 'A stroke of pure genius, that was.' Although he was relieved by the turn of events, I noticed that Grandpa's breathing was louder than usual. When he made to go out to the kitchen, he caught his foot against the leg of the coffee table and stumbled, falling against Dad, who caught him and returned him to the vertical.

'Whoopsy,' said Grandpa. 'Perhaps I'll sit down. You put the kettle on, Pru.'

In the kitchen the kettle stood neglected while Mum and Dad conferred in low voices. 'We can't leave him on his own,' Dad said. 'He's a liability.'

'He'll have to come back with us,' Mum said.

'He's not been coping here. Did you see the fridge?'

'I did.'

'And the bathroom?'

'Heaven knows I'm not houseproud, but ...'

'We've got the space.'

'How much of his stuff could we fit in the car, do you think?'

And so it was decided. 'You're coming to live with us,' Mum said, as we trooped back into the sitting room to deliver the verdict.

'Well, if you're sure,' said Grandpa, who wanted to give as little trouble as possible, even in the matter of polite resistance. 'It won't be for long.'

'Nonsense,' said Mum. 'You've got years.'

'I'll keep out of your way,' he promised. 'You just carry

on as if I'm not there.' And then the words that filled my ten-year-old heart with joy: 'Can I bring my television?'

GRANDPA WAS INSTALLED IN THE GUEST ROOM THE SAME DAY, with his black and white portable TV on a table at the end of his bed. Christian and I spent so much time in there, trying to catch up on years of deprivation, that the set was eventually brought down into the sitting room, a sign of parental resignation. Grandpa was not a terribly discriminating viewer: he just sat in his armchair and watched whatever was on. Sport, cartoons, old films, news, it made no difference to him. It was too much trouble to keep jumping up and down changing channels. Sometimes he'd tut and say, 'What a load of old rubbish,' but he watched it just the same.

Christian's favourite trick was to drag the cushions off the couch and lie on his stomach, propped on his elbows, a couple of feet from the screen. He'd watch anything too: horse racing, wrestling, *Scooby Doo*, *The Brady Bunch*, *The Muppet Show*. Nothing was too dull, nothing too childish.

'You'll go blind,' Mum would say. Or, 'You'll end up talking American,' but Christian just laughed, his response to all advice. She was full of these phrases: 'There'll be plenty of time for lying down when you're dead,' as she chivvied us out of bed on Saturday mornings. 'It's not fair,' I'd say, as we were hauled away from the TV on health grounds. 'Grandpa is allowed to watch it all day.'

'Grandpa's old. He's lived through two world wars, brought up a family, worked all his life, and now he's entitled to do as he pleases. In any case, he hasn't got your legs. Or your lungs. Don't you think he'd rather be out kicking a ball or rollerskating?' Then we both laughed at the notion of Grandpa on rollerskates.

CHRISTIAN, IN ANY CASE, HAD TOO MUCH GOING ON FOR TV to take over. During the cricket season he had trialled for the county under-18s. We had been to watch him in a few matches as far afield as Chichester and Brighton. It was a dull game, as far as I was concerned, with only about four of the twenty-two players having anything much to do. Dad, who seemed to find poetry even in the flight of a no-ball, explained its arcane scoring system to me time after time, yet was often unable to answer the simple question, 'Who's winning?' Mum, like me, was interested in Christian, not cricket, and took her knitting for those long interludes when he was in the pavilion.

In the winter he played rugby for Turton's and had lately discovered cross-country running. He still did his paper round in the morning, but on foot now, and alone, incorporating it into his pre-school five-mile jog. I tried to go with him one time but it was hopeless: even at full tilt I couldn't keep up with him. He'd shoot off into the distance, and, when he was nearly out of sight, turn and run back to meet me, laughing at my laboured progress. He couldn't keep alongside me, he explained apologetically. It wasn't physically possible for him to run that slowly.

Most evenings, between homework and dinner, he'd pull on his rugger shorts and green flash plimsolls and go out again, oblivious to rain, wind or darkness.

'He's got the legs, that boy,' Grandpa Percy would say, watching from the sitting room window as Christian set off with long, easy strides. He must have had different ways of running, because sometimes he'd come back gasping, drenched in sweat with a face like a whole edam, and collapse at full length on the couch, and other times he'd be scarcely short of breath, with not a hair out of place.

I couldn't understand the appeal myself, but Mum explained that boys of his age had all this energy surging around inside them, and if they didn't run it off regularly it would build up and up until eventually they'd explode. Not literally, of course, she reassured me: it was all more subtle than that. Boys like Christian were growing so fast they didn't even fit their own bodies any more. That was why he was always fixing himself bowls of Weetabix when everyone else was ready for bed, and why he couldn't even watch TV without fidgeting. We just had to be understanding.

Having been alerted to the phenomenon I watched Christian with greater interest, hoping to witness one of these non-literal explosions, and sure enough a few weeks later my patience was rewarded. It was all just as Mum had said.

Our nearest neighbour, Mrs Tapley, bearded widow, cat lover and rumoured practitioner of the Black Arts, was moving into sheltered accommodation and had offered Mum the pick of her leftover furniture and belongings for the charity shop. Thinking a van an extravagance for so short a distance, Mum had acquired a porter's trolley for the purpose of transporting the heavier items along the lane to our house, and volunteered Christian's services as removal man. She had mentioned this to him over breakfast on the appointed day and interpreted his answering grunt as a sign of assent – a mistake. I knew from experience that Christian grunted automatically at any mention of his name, and that it didn't necessarily signify agreement, or even comprehension. Lately the only way to be sure he had heard you was to secure and maintain eye contact, something Mum had failed to take into account.

She was therefore surprised and dismayed that evening to see Christian sitting on the doorstep in his jogging clothes, lacing up his plimsolls, five minutes before she was due at Mrs Tapley's.

'Where are you going?' she asked.

'Out for a run,' he answered, straightening up and retying the cord of his shorts. He had just washed his hair, and it hung in wet tassels to his shoulders. That was another funny thing. Sometimes he had a bath *before* he went for a run.

'No you're not. You're coming to help me,' Mum said. 'Had you forgotten?'

Christian frowned. 'How can I forget something I never knew?' He bent one leg and caught his foot behind his back, flexing his thigh muscle.

'I told you this morning. We're clearing out Mrs Tapley's.' She pointed at the porter's trolley, which had stood unremarked in the hallway for several days now. We were so used to having the house cluttered up with transient objects destined for the Less Fortunate that they no longer provoked any curiosity.

'Well, I've got to go out for a run,' Christian replied, continuing with his bending and stretching.

'Oh, don't worry, you'll get plenty of exercise at Mrs Tapley's. That I promise you.'

'It's not the same. Can't we do it later? Or tomorrow or something?'

'No,' said Mum, beginning to lose patience. 'She's expecting us now, and that generation doesn't like to be kept waiting. Anyway, it's got to be now: the house will be cleared out tomorrow.'

'I'll only be an hour. Can't I meet you there?' Christian suggested. He was standing on one leg, bringing his knee up to his chest now, squeeze, release, other leg, squeeze, release.

Mum clicked her tongue irritably. 'No. I can't shift furniture on my own, strong as I am. Esther and Grandpa can't do it. Mrs Tapley certainly can't. Your father's at work. It's got to be you. Now come on or we'll be late. You seem to forget that she's doing us the favour, and not the other way round.'

'She's not doing me any favour,' Christian snapped. 'You've no right to rope me into something without checking with me first. I might be busy. I *am* busy.'

I'd never heard him speak to Mum like this before. I closed my eyes and red sparks danced behind my eyelids.

'I think that school's given you an inflated sense of your own importance, my boy,' Mum said, in a dangerously quiet voice. 'It's about time you started thinking about other people instead of putting yourself first all the time.'

'I am thinking about someone else,' Christian retorted. 'Just not you.' And before Mum could stop him he was out of the door and off up the path at a run, without a backward glance.

Mum sat down hard on the settle and stared up at the ceiling, exhaling slowly.

'Don't worry, Mum,' I said, putting my arm round her shoulders. 'He didn't mean it. It's just all that energy whooshing around, like you said.'

When she smiled down at me her eyes were full of tears. 'I know,' she said, blinking hard. 'You're quite right.' Then she stood up and squeezed my shoulders, as if measuring me up for something. 'Could you manage some heavy lifting, do you think?' she said.

I nodded eagerly, glad to be the useful one for once. 'I'm strong,' I said. 'I can lift up Lisa Chick, and she's the fattest girl in the class.'

For some reason this made Mum laugh. 'It's good to be a strong girl,' she said, serious again. 'Because there are plenty of people out there who'd like girls to be weak and silly and easy to control, and we need a few strong ones like you to stand up to them.'

'Like that woman who ran in front of the King's horse and died?' I said. We'd had an assembly about it just that morning. There had been a gasp of sympathy for the horse, Anmer, who had turned a full somersault in the collision.

'Well, yes, sort of,' said Mum. 'Though I wasn't recommending martyrdom.' She hefted the porter's trolley over the threshold and down the front step. 'That's not for the likes of us.'

'I'VE BROUGHT ESTHER WITH ME INSTEAD OF CHRISTIAN,' MUM said to Mrs Tapley, without elucidating.

'So I see,' said Mrs Tapley, her jaws working as though at a piece of tough meat.

I looked at her, as I always did, with a combination of fascination and disgust: how could she have so many coarse, dark hairs sprouting from her chin and do nothing about them? She couldn't be entirely without vanity, because she went to the trouble of wearing a wig, a very obvious one of improbably regular, tight, brown curls. She wore it pulled down at the front, almost to her eyebrows, like a cap, exposing the white wisps at the nape of her neck. I knew she was immensely old, because just about every time we met she regaled us with the same story of how she and her parents had slept on the pavement overnight to secure a good

position along the route of Queen Victoria's funeral proces-
sion. And her own grandmother used to tell her that as a
young girl she had met the poet Wordsworth, then in his
seventies.

'How interesting,' Mum said when the story had its regular airing. 'Did your grandmother say what he was like?'

'Grey-haired and a trifle deaf,' was Mrs Tapley's scoop on
the great man.

I began to wonder what historical markers I would be
able to call up to bore my grandchildren with, but nothing
significant came to mind. I had witnessed no national spectacles, and met no famous people. Christian had had his
photograph in the *Advertiser* when Turton's won the South
East Cricket Cup, and he, I felt, represented my best chance
of brushing up against celebrity. Mr Spragg had also been
in the local paper when his case came to court. Christian
had shown me the cutting: Community Service for Sex Pest
Vicar. I'd wanted to take it to school for show and tell but
Mum said No with a capital N.

The pieces we could take, Mrs Tapley was telling Mum,
had been marked with a chalk cross. There were some
ladder-back chairs and carvers, a gateleg table, an oak bureau
and escritoire and numerous boxes of assorted junk. 'I don't
know how you'll manage, just the two of you,' she said,
shaking her head, so that the wig pitched to one side.
'There's more upstairs, but you'll need a man for that.'

'We'll do our best,' Mum replied, stacking two of the
chairs, seat to seat, onto the porter's trolley and strapping
them into place with an old skipping rope. It was the
thought of converting them into sacks of grain, vaccines,
bandages, penicillin, that put the necessary strength in her
arms.

On our fifth return journey, by which time we had cleared the chairs and boxes, leaving only the heavy stuff, we were met on her doorstep by Mrs Tapley. She was holding a bunch of flowers, culled, by the look of it, from front gardens or the fresher graves in the churchyard. 'Christian's here,' she said with a soppy smile. 'He brought me these. Sweet boy.'

Christian loitered in the shadows behind her, uneasy in his role as penitent, his hands thrust so deep into his pockets that they emerged beneath the hem of his shorts.

What a masterstroke, I thought, as I saw Mum's face bloom with pleasure. To think of bringing flowers, not for Mum herself, but for Mrs Tapley. That sort of subtle, sideways thinking was so unlike Christian, who came at everything head-on, that for an instant I hovered on the brink of enlightenment, as if a breeze blowing through my mind had lifted a curtain. Before I could understand what had been revealed, the moment passed, the curtain fell back, and the feeling of relief that the quarrel was over swept all other thoughts away.

17

NOT LONG AFTER THE INSTALLATION OF THE TELEVISION I WAS found to have developed a species of squint. Whether the TV was the cause of the problem, or an innocent diagnostic tool, remained a matter of fierce debate. The undisputed fact was that Mum had come into the sitting room one day to find me watching *The New Avengers* with my hand over one eye. My untroubled explanation that I would otherwise be seeing two images led us directly to the opticians and from there to hospital for tests. It was feared that fluid on the brain might be an underlying cause. Torches were shone into my eyes, stinging drops made my pupils dilate so that even dull daylight was unbearable, blood was siphoned from my veins and my brain was scanned for deformities, but these investigations uncovered nothing significant. Expert opinion concluded that I was suffering from nothing more than a 'lazy eye' – a label that was unnecessarily judgemental, to my mind. I preferred to call

it a squint. The doctor took the unusual step of recommending a patch for the unaffected eye – a treatment
commonly reserved for younger children, in whom success
was more likely. Still, it was felt that there was nothing
to be lost by the attempt, which might prevent a lifetime
of wearing corrective prismatic glasses. I was offered a
choice of patches.

'We do a flesh tint,' the doctor explained. 'It's a bit
less . . . piratical than black.'

I tried it on. From a distance it looked as though one
side of my face had melted. 'I want black,' I said.

There is never a good time to wear an eyepatch, but it
was especially unfortunate that this episode coincided with
my first term at secondary school, when inconspicuousness
would have served me better. Mum's attempts at home
tuition to prime me for grammar school or scholarships had
not worked this time around. I didn't have Christian's head
for figures. Talk of integers and denominators and percent-
ages caused a hot metal bolt of incomprehension to tighten
up behind my eyes.

'She's artistic,' was Mum's verdict.

'She's a dreamer,' said Grandpa Percy.

'She lacks concentration,' said my school report.

It was certainly true that I wasn't destined for exam
success. I couldn't seem to get the answers out of my head,
where they teemed, like shoals of slippery fish, and onto
the page. I would think for too long about each question,
my thoughts frequently taking off down byways of their own,
which though interesting were not in the least pertinent.
When some distraction would cause me to look down, half
the allotted time would have elapsed and I would have
produced nothing but a page of doodles.

So it was that I ended up at Underwood, the nearest school that required no proofs of intelligence or wealth; where in fact intelligence or wealth would have been serious impediments to survival. The school's motto was 'The Whole Child' – presumably to distinguish it from lesser establishments interested only in child portions. The phrase was printed on the headed notepaper, on the school gates, and on the embroidered crest, which had to be sewn onto our anoraks (held to be more practical and durable than blazers). This flexible approach to uniform was heartily approved by Mum, whose economies often fell foul of the more rigid regime at Turton's. In any case, incidents like the affair of the Mighty Whities had caused her to look less kindly on that institution. She didn't think it at all a bad thing for me to mix with ordinary, unpretentious people. 'Besides, if you go somewhere mediocre there's a better chance that you'll shine,' she said, by way of encouragement.

'FUCKINELL IT'S CAPTAIN PUGWASH,' SAID ONE OF THE ordinary, unpretentious people, whose influence Mum had so warmly recommended, on my first day at Underwood. At least, thanks to Grandpa Percy's TV I now knew who Captain Pugwash was. 'What's wrong with your eye?' she demanded, contacting my black patch with a fat finger.

'Nothing,' I said truthfully: it was the unpatched eye that was defective. Through it I examined my interrogator. She was above average height, and girth, with a barrel-shaped body and two flaps of fat where there would one day be proper breasts. Her hair had been scragged back into a stumpy ponytail with what seemed unnecessary severity, giving her the grim appearance of someone facing into a strong wind. Her cheeks were a sore shade of pink, and when she spoke I could see her teeth were imprisoned behind metal grilles. A group of her cronies gathered round us to see how the confrontation would develop.

'Watcher wearing it for then?' she wanted to know.

'Because I like it,' I said. 'I think it makes me look nice.' I'd learned this trick from Christian: if you're ever faced with a stupid remark, just say the exact opposite of what's expected and see what happens.

'You must be mad then,' she said. The onlookers laughed. 'She's mad.'

'I am,' I agreed. 'I went mad when I was six, and I've been like it ever since.'

'You're getting on my nerves,' the girl said. 'You'd better bring me fifty pence tomorrow.'

I looked at her, mystified. Did she need money to buy something that would calm her nerves? 'Why?' I asked.

'Don't get me angry,' came the reply, which sounded fairly angry already. 'Just bring it.'

'I NEED TO TAKE FIFTY PENCE TO SCHOOL TODAY,' I SAID OVER breakfast the following morning.

Christian had been for his run and was now trying to fit six Weetabix into a bowl that could comfortably accommodate two. I watched him stack them two by two to form a squat tower, and then trickle milk over them until they collapsed into a grey sludge, which he ate with great relish.

'It's not a good idea to take money to school,' Mum said. 'It might get taken.' In view of the circumstances I could hardly dispute this prediction. 'What do you need it for?'

'Nothing,' I said. 'I'll manage.'

* * *

SHE TRACKED ME DOWN TO THE FURTHEST CORNER OF THE playground at breaktime, where I was trying to blend into the fence. I wasn't the only one engaged in this attempt, I noticed. A little leadership, a little organisation, and we could have formed a marauding band of our own.

'Where's my money?' she said, arm out, palm uppermost.

This use of the possessive rankled. 'Wherever you keep it,' I replied. 'My money's in the bank.'

'Just give it. I've got other people to see after you,' she said.

'I haven't got it,' I said, shrugging. She looked from me to her two accomplices with an exaggerated expression of disbelief.

'What have you got then?' she demanded, removing my school bag from my shoulder and having a good rummage. She pocketed a foil pack of sandwiches and my banana before opening the lid of my thermos flask and tipping the contents out onto the floor. 'Fuckinell,' she said, as half a pint of Mum's chunky vegetable soup hit the deck. 'It looks like puke.'

'That's my lunch,' I protested, my unpatched eye watering with rage. No one, except me and Christian, was allowed to insult Mum's cooking, unappetising though it was.

'What are you going to do about it?' the girl wanted to know.

Do? I did what any right-thinking daughter of a Christian minister and a pacifist would do in the circumstances: I punched her in the mouth.

She was too taken aback to retaliate, and was in any case fully occupied with the business of trying to staunch the outwash of blood: I had forgotten about that brace.

'Sorry!' I said, horrified, and yet strangely elated. My fist still throbbed from the impact. I wouldn't be able to hold a pen steady for the rest of the day, an inconvenience I hadn't foreseen. I offered her a wad of cleanish tissues from my pocket to mop up the blood, but she applied them instead to her eyes, a gesture that made me feel doubly guilty.

'You didn't have to do that!' one of the cronies remonstrated. 'It was only a joke.' She put her arm round the victim and enquired tenderly, 'Are you all right, Dawn? Do you want me to get Miss?'

Dawn shook her head, fat-lipped. She would have a stupendous pout for the rest of the week.

The bell rang for lessons. 'I didn't mean it,' I said, still feeling that the defensive nature of my action was not being properly acknowledged. I tapped my head, remembering our conversation of the day before. 'It was the madness coming out,' I added, reclaiming my bag and flask, before making my way back to class. I didn't bother about the sandwiches and banana: I thought that might be pushing my luck. Besides, the sight of all that blood had taken the edge off my appetite.

I KEPT EXPECTING TO BE HAULED BEFORE THE HEADMASTER for the affray, and jumped every time there was a knock at the classroom door, expecting a summons. But none came. In school it was just as in Dad's prison: there was no form of life lower than a grass.

Outside school, of course, different rules applied. At seven o'clock that evening the doorbell rang. This wasn't an uncommon occurrence – word had got about that the occupants of the Old Schoolhouse were a soft touch as far as donations were concerned, and we were regularly troubled by people collecting for charities, genuine or otherwise. The traffic of funds was by no means always one-way, as Mum kept her own collecting tin on the hall table and would occasionally jangle it under the astonished caller's nose.

This time it was Dad who opened the door, while I hovered behind. We had been washing up and he was still wearing a Liberty print apron with a ruffled hem, over the top of his clerical garb. Mum was in the loft checking for squirrel damage; Grandpa was watching TV; Christian was working in his room.

The caller was a short, pigeon-chested man of about Dad's age. His fiery red arms and neck, revealed by a tight white T-shirt, implied a summer spent out of doors. He was shifting from foot to foot in an agitated manner, and seemed slightly thrown by the sight of Dad's dog-collar and floral pinny.

'You Mr Fairchild?' he demanded.

'I am,' said Dad politely, peeling off his rubber gloves with a snap and passing them back to me.

'Your kid thumped my kid in the mouth.' The man was still bobbing from side to side, as though preparing to throw, or possibly dodge, a punch himself.

Dad frowned. 'Goodness. I'd better see what he's got to say about it.' He moved to the foot of the stairs and called, 'Christian! Can you come here, please?'

A moment later Christian loped down, looking perplexed.

'Not him,' said the man, who had now caught sight of me lurking in the background. 'Her!'

The three of them stared at me incredulously. The anonymity of the headmaster's study would have been a treat in comparison.

'Is this true?' Dad asked, in a voice that seemed to plead for a denial.

'Well yes, but only after she nicked my lunch,' I replied. I was about to launch into a full account of my (relative) innocence, when I was saved by the complainant himself.

'Blimey, she's not very big,' he said, looking me over. I suppose the eyepatch might have contributed to an appearance of vulnerability. 'Oy, Dawn,' he summoned the victim, who had been standing out of sight behind the bramble hedge. 'Is this the girl you mean?'

Dawn emerged reluctantly from her hiding place. One side of her bottom lip still bulged, which made her look gormless as well as asymmetrical. I could see she wasn't nearly so hard now she was on our turf. She seemed to have lost all stomach for the confrontation, which had obviously been his idea, not hers. When she saw Christian, handsome in his Turton's uniform, with shirt collar unbuttoned and tie at half-mast, she even blushed. 'Yeah, it is, but ...'

'I thought it was one of the bigger girls who'd been picking on you,' said her father, looking thoroughly ill at ease now. 'You made out it was.'

'No I never,' Dawn muttered.

'But, I'm not being funny, you'd make two of her.'

I noticed that Dad and Christian had gradually moved closer to me, one on each side, and I was touched by this protective gesture.

'Nevertheless, Esther, I think an apology is in order,' Dad said, in his best 'severe' voice.

'I did apologise at the time,' I said. 'But I'll do it again if you insist. Sorry I hit you, Dawn.'

'Say you're sorry you nicked her lunch, or whatever,' said the man, nudging Dawn.

'Sorry I nicked your lunch,' she intoned listlessly. She was desperate to get away.

'That's it.' He nodded his approval. 'Kiss and make up.' He took a large, grey handkerchief from his jeans pocket and used it to wipe his neck.

'Would you like to come in and have a drink? We don't have to stand here discussing this on the doorstep,' said Dad politely, as if they were just a couple of regular parishioners wanting spiritual advice. It wouldn't have crossed his mind that the man had come here for a punch-up.

'No, no,' said Dawn's father hastily. 'We don't want to keep you. Just thought it was best to get this straightened out.'

'Absolutely.' Dad nodded emphatically. 'Very glad you did.' He thrust out his hand, which was still dusted with primrose lint from the inside of the rubber glove. Dawn's father automatically wiped his own palm on the side of his jeans before shaking.

'Girls, eh?' he said, with an exaggerated shake of the head.

'Yes, indeed,' said Dad, seeing the pair off with a cordial wave. Sometimes his manners made you want to cry.

As we resumed the washing up Dad remarked in his dry way that he hoped my thirst for violence had been fully slaked by the incident, and he needn't expect to find any more enraged fathers on the doorstep in future. I assured him it had, and the subject was never raised again.

18

IT WAS NOT LONG AFTER THIS THAT CHRISTIAN WENT AWAY for a week on an Outdoor Pursuits trip with the school. I know it must have been some time that term, because I was still wearing my eyepatch. I remember how it made a little reservoir for my tears. I never quite understood it, but the trip had something to do with the Duke of Edinburgh. After a year or so of performing good works and feats of skill and endurance, half a dozen boys and a teacher from Turton's were to go climbing in Snowdonia in the harshest possible conditions with the minimum of equipment. The survivors would get a medal at Buckingham Palace. Something like that.

Christian took Grandpa Percy's rucksack, which looked like a relic from the First World War. It was made of tubular steel and leather and thick green canvas, and was formidably heavy even when empty. Once it was stuffed with Christian's share of the camping equipment – tent pegs, mallet, groundsheet, sleeping bag, dried food, gas canister, maps, torch, billy-cans – it would have felled a donkey.

'Goodness,' Mum said, watching Christian's bent-backed progress around the garden. 'Do you seriously think you'll get to the top of Snowdon with that thing?'

'I'll be lucky to get to Paddington,' Christian gasped, legs buckling.

'It always was a blighter to carry,' Grandpa Percy conceded. I couldn't help feeling that this was a serious shortcoming for a piece of luggage.

'Is there nothing you can jettison?' Mum pleaded. She was starting to suffer from twingey cartilages herself, and was alert to the fragility of knee joints.

'We'll have a weigh-in at the station and even out the loads,' Christian reassured her. His fellow travellers – all Turton's fee-payers – would be roughing it with the very latest in outdoor survival gear and aluminium-framed nylon backpacks so lightweight that only the waist strap stopped them floating away.

He couldn't be persuaded to have a lift to the station, wanting to do the whole journey, door-to-tentflap, under his own steam.

'Will you send me a postcard?' I asked. It was the first time he'd been away for such a long stretch, and my anxiety at the prospect of a lonely week was only intensified by his eagerness to be gone: the yearning ran only one way.

'Yes, of course,' Christian replied. 'There's a pillar box on the summit of Snowdon. It's emptied twice a day.'

I pulled a face and he just laughed, maddeningly.

'Here's a pound for emergencies,' said Mum, taking the last note from her purse. 'I'd like it back if possible.' It occurred to me to wonder what species of mountain-top emergency could possibly be solved by a pound note, but Christian looked suitably grateful as he put it away. Mum didn't often wave money in his direction.

I handed over my own offering: a four-ounce bar of plain chocolate. It was something people in stories always seemed to have about their person, untouched, ready to produce in moments of extremity. This always struck me as unconvincing, but it gave me pleasure to imagine Christian awaiting rescue on some bleak crag, sustained only by dark chocolate and the memory of sisterly love. The gift was not made without sacrifice: it had cost me a sizeable part of my fortune, which consisted of the loose change culled from down the sides of our baggy armchairs. This was a useful, though unpredictable source of income. Experience had taught me that the collision between unwary male visitors with pockets full of coins and our slack and springless furniture produced the highest yields, and it was in this way that I had scraped together my modest fund.

'Thanks, Pest,' Christian said. He put the chocolate in the pocket of his parka, and gave me a kiss on the cheek – a pleasing variant of his usual embrace, which was to crush my head under his armpit.

Mum, who had been ransacking the broom cupboard, reappeared holding a scuffed shopping bag on wheels. 'If we get rid of the bag,' she said, starting to wrench the tartan vinyl, 'you can strap your rucksack onto the frame and wheel it along.'

Christian rolled his eyes. 'This is a wilderness trip, not the Women's Institute,' he said.

Mum had the decency to laugh at herself, and slung the half-demolished trolley back in the cupboard.

'Go on, then, Mr Wilderness,' she said. 'Enjoy your blisters.'

He shouldered his pack, and set off, whistling ostentatiously. I ran up to the attic to watch his progress along the lane. Before he had even reached the corner he had taken out my bar of emergency chocolate and disposed of it in three big bites.

THE WEEK PASSED MISERABLY WITHOUT HIM. THE HOUSE seemed too large, too quiet and too empty. I missed the sound of his homecoming each day, the clatter of his bike on the gravel, the slam of the door and the crash of his schoolbag on the hall floor. Watching TV wasn't nearly so much fun without him sprawled on a cushion in the middle of the carpet, laughing like a witch. Although he hadn't had so much time lately for pontoon and chess, with the rugby and the jogging, and the homework, it was his big, comforting presence that I was used to, and my own company was a poor substitute.

Grandpa Percy tried to fill the void by teaching me every two-handed card game in the canon, and Mum and Dad showered me with extra attention and kindness, but they, too, were finding Christian's absence strange. The weather had turned suddenly wet and cold, and we listened anxiously to the forecast for North Wales every evening.

One afternoon Dad went up into one of the lofts and came down with a wooden box containing some crumpled tubes of oil paint and balding brushes. Some of the colours were fossilised beyond redemption, but we managed to squeeze out a few threads of chrome yellow, white, ochre and ultramarine, and I produced what I considered a very passable still life, entitled Milk Jug, Egg and Banana.

I took it into school to show my art teacher, Mr Hatch, and he was very complimentary, and even gave me some hints on composition, suggesting, for example, that next time I didn't need to arrange the objects in a straight line, and could possibly put them on something, rather than have them floating in space.

Dad wanted to frame it, but once Mr Hatch had hinted at its flaws, I didn't feel it deserved to be displayed. I kept it anyway, as it represented a milestone: the beginning of a stormy relationship with oils.

On the day marked out for Christian's return, I decided to go and meet him at the station. It was a fair ride away, and I wasn't sure quite when in the afternoon to expect him, but I had nothing else to do, so I set off after lunch, taking a small sketch pad and pencil to help while away the time. My art teacher, in addition to his other advice, had recommended I carry these with me when I was out and about, and get into the habit of 'Sketching from Life'.

I chained my bike to the railings in the car park, found myself a seat at the end of the platform which commanded a view of trains arriving from London, opened my sketch pad, and began, rather self-consciously, to draw. My eyepatch seemed to be something of an asset in this endeavour, removing the troubling three-dimensional element from the matter of composition. Viewed through one eye the world already looked as flat as a picture. However, I was unprepared for the annoying reluctance of Life to keep still while I was drawing it, and several of my sketches had to be abandoned incomplete as the subjects wandered off to catch a train. After a while I began to appreciate the importance of speed in capturing the unposed human form, and to hanker for the relative compliance of my milk jug, egg and banana.

I eventually settled on a teenage girl who was sitting nice
and still on a bench further down the platform. She was at
too great a distance to suspect me of watching her, and was
in any case engrossed in a book, which gave me hope that
she might not be intending to move for a while. Her blonde
hair hung forward over her face, which saved me the bother
of tackling her profile. I had more or less caught her outline,
and was about to put in some light and shade, when she
stood up to examine the timetable board. A moment later
she sat back down in a fresh position, angled away from me,
at which point I gave up.

Half an hour passed. My pencil was blunt, my bottom
numb, and I had produced a dozen unfinished scribbles of
my surroundings, and one detailed drawing of my own foot,
clad in semi-perished plimsoll. I was growing tired of shielding my work from the stares of nosey parkers so I went in
search of a bin to deposit some pencil shavings, and immediately lost my seat. I don't know whether it was the cold
wind, or my great industry, but I suddenly had a fierce craving for sugar and spent some time debating whether to go
to the kiosk or risk my money in the machine on the platform, for the additional gambler's buzz, and the pleasure of
pressing buttons. The gamble won of course. I could almost
feel the hot breath of parental disapproval on the back of
my neck as I posted the coins in the slot. Mum had always
held vending machines to be instruments of Satan, and
would sooner starve than use one, with the result that they
now held a strange and terrible fascination for me. My feeling of guilt turned to dismay and rage as the dispensing
drawer refused to yield to gentle and then urgent tugs. I
could see my bar of Whole Nut, the nearside half-inch of
it at least, trapped in the bottom of the tray.

I was so engrossed in this futile struggle with the machine that I wasn't even aware of the arrival of a London train until the sound of slamming doors brought me to my senses. Beyond the other twenty or so passengers who had alighted, I caught sight of Christian at the far end of the platform, straining to lash himself back under his rucksack. I put my hand up in greeting and he gave a great, wild grin and waved back, but there was something not quite right about it. As I approached I realised what it was: the wave and the smile were not for me, but for someone ahead of me, to my right.

When comprehension finally comes to the chronically deluded it lands like a sledgehammer, and for a moment or two I stood reeling, as the blonde girl, whose likeness I had been attempting to capture with my pencil only minutes before, walked up to Christian and put her arms round his neck. I saw him stoop to kiss her, and then I shrank back behind the pillar where I had just been tussling with the chocolate machine, so that they wouldn't see me as they passed, hand in hand. I needn't have bothered, as they were entirely preoccupied with each other, but the desire to hide was instinctive.

I suppose it was disappointment at finding myself superfluous that caused a few tears to pool up behind my eyepatch, but it was a feeling more like grief that curdled in my blood as I watched them turn into the booking hall and vanish from sight. I aimed a final punch at the tin belly of the chocolate machine, and then trudged back to retrieve my bike for the long ride home, with the defeated attitude of someone twice robbed.

19

'CHRISTIAN'S GOT A GIRLFRIEND,' I ANNOUNCED OVER DINNER a few days later. I hadn't intended to say anything about it, but in spite of my broad hints in private, Christian had shown no signs of wanting to confide. There was nothing for it but to force his hand.

'Have you, Christian?' Mum enquired serenely. 'Is she nice?'

Christian shot me a look of pure hatred before saying, 'Yes', in a clipped tone that suggested further questions would not be welcome.

'Well, that's nice,' said Mum, fishing for seconds in the casserole.

'There was one of those urban foxes in the garden again today,' said Grandpa Percy, whose contributions to conversation tended not to relate to the prevailing topic. 'Skinny, emancipated creature,' he added with disgust.

'Are we allowed to know her name?' Mum asked,

dredging a ladleful of chicken bones from the pot and depositing them on Dad's plate with a clatter.

'Penny,' said Christian.

'He pretends to go jogging, but he's actually meeting her,' I explained. I'd burnt my boats as far as popularity went, so I thought I may as well make what I could of my hard-won knowledge. 'She's got blonde hair.'

'How do you know so much?' Christian demanded. 'Have you been following me?'

'No,' I replied, truthfully.

'I could probably have got a shot at him if I had an airgun,' said Grandpa Percy.

'I'm sure Christian would have told us about her if he'd wanted us to know,' Dad said to me with a frown, and it was so unlike him to offer me even the mildest rebuke that I felt myself shrivel.

Far from bringing Christian to order, my declaration had the opposite effect: legitimising his many absences from home. Instead of resorting to his former subterfuge and disguise to engineer his meetings, he now abandoned all pretence of jogging and sauntered out of the house each evening, smartly dressed, in a miasma of acrid antiperspirant. Penny lived in one of the houses at the very furthest extent of his paper round. They had met months ago in the driveway during a territorial dispute between Christian and her dachshund. This much information I had managed to wring from him.

'He's never here,' I complained to Mum. 'Doesn't he like us any more?'

Mum smiled indulgently. 'Of course he does.' The fact that nobody but me seemed to mind was just another provocation. 'You'll be exactly the same when you're sixteen.'

Yes, but what am I supposed to do with myself till then? I wanted to shout. It was so miserable being the younger of two: always the disciple, the bumbling apprentice, perpetually outstripped and outperformed.

Even when Christian was at home he was good for nothing. He was either busy with schoolwork, or lying in a daze on his bed, staring at the ceiling. Occasionally I would hear the thud of darts hitting their target, but by the time I'd made it up the stairs to challenge him to a game he'd have grown bored and fallen to mooching again. He had recently acquired a guitar on loan from Turton's music cupboard, and was trying to teach himself to play from a book. *A Tune a Day*, it was called, with fabulous optimism. Christian had been practising for many days and produced nothing more than a horrible discordant thrumming. No sooner did he reach a standard sufficient to pick out a recognisable tune – *Blackbird*, say, or *The House of the Rising Sun* – he would spoil it all by trying to sing along. Such was his distraction during this period that I managed to pull off my first and only victory at chess. He hadn't wanted to play, but I had nagged and nagged, and he put in at best only fifty per cent concentration, but still, it proved how deep the sickness had gone. He caught on to what I was doing just too late to rally. Before I could even say the words Check Mate, he had dragged one of the couch cushions down on top of me and sat on my head. I felt happier than I'd done for ages.

I didn't see it at the time, of course, but this was the beginning of Christian's gradual detachment from childhood. His boredom and irritation with home were just natural stages in his preparation to leave it behind and join the adult world, Mum explained. I wasn't to take it personally. Slowly, inexorably he was starting to cut the threads, so

that he would be ready, one day soon, to move on, out,
away. I found this idea hard to bear. To me the Old
Schoolhouse was still a sufficient world, and the only threat
was change. Whenever I thought about our family it was
always the same scene that came to mind: the four of us
playing table-tennis in the garden on Dad's knocked-
together table made of trestles and two sheets of blistered
plywood. The odd thing was we'd probably only played
together three or four times in my life, and yet this is what
I saw when I closed my eyes and imagined that entity: The
Fairchilds.

'I don't want to grow up if it makes me all moody like
Christian,' I said. 'I'm going to stay young for ever. Even
when I'm old I'll still like doing all the things I like now.'

Mum smiled. 'You sound like Aunty Barbara,' she said.
'She could never bear the idea of getting older.'

This use of the past tense made me suspicious. 'Is she
dead?' I asked. It was three years since we'd seen her, carried
off in an ambulance. There had been nothing since, not
even a belated birthday card or a plea for help.

'Oh, no, she's still alive as far as I know.'

'Why don't we ever see Donovan any more? I liked him.'

Mum grew evasive. 'It's such a difficult set-up. We've
rather lost touch.'

'But why?' I persisted. 'He used to come and stay for ages.'

'I did try to keep in contact, but . . . it's a funny thing
about human nature. If you've helped someone when they're
at their lowest, they don't want to be reminded.'

'You'd think they'd be grateful,' I said.

'You would,' said Mum. 'But sometimes it's more complicated than that. Barbara was very ill when she was with us,
and needed to go to hospital. But she was too ill to realise

she needed to go. So we had to make her go. She probably still resents that.'

'Perhaps it's better not to help people,' I decided.

'No, that's no good either. You have to help people, but don't expect any thanks.'

I NEVER DID GET TO MEET THIS PENNY. CHRISTIAN DIDN'T show the slightest inclination to bring her home, and Mum alluded to it only once. He replied with a cryptic laugh: his usual non-committal response to unwelcome suggestions, and the subject was dropped. Sometimes I couldn't help regretting Mum and Dad's policy of tact and tolerance. There were occasions when I felt some robust interference would have served.

Before I had a chance to accustom myself to this phantom presence it was all over: they had split up and Christian was back amongst us, for a while at least. I didn't allow myself to be too hopeful: there would be other Pennys, who would be able to tempt him away from us, with whatever mysterious attractions we lacked.

20

THE DAY MY EYEPATCH CAME OFF, THE WORLD ROSE UP TO
meet me. Houses and trees sprang to attention like the pages
of a pop-up book; the sharpness and solidity of things amazed
me and I started to draw again, inspired by this new insight.
'It's the artist's gift to make the familiar strange and the
strange familiar,' Mr Hatch said, and I saw at last what he
meant. He had been prompted to this remark by the sketch
of my plimsoll. It looked, he said, like something organic –
a species of cabbage, perhaps – and he put it up, properly
mounted, on the wall outside the head's office, where all
the best pictures went.

At school, being singled out for academic achievement
was an occasion of dread, as peer retribution was usually
swift and nasty. For some reason excellence at art or sport
did not provoke the same hostility, quite the reverse in fact:
most of the real hard-cases were themselves pillars of the
various sports teams. It was lucky for me that these were

the only two areas in which I had any chance of success. All those years of acting as Christian's ballboy, outfielder and sparring partner had paid off at last. Once I had lost the eyepatch and modified my accent, my assimilation would be complete. I had noticed that whereas at Turton's it was the way we looked rather than sounded that let us down, at Underwood the opposite was true. Everyone else there was as scruffy as we were, and we blended in beautifully, but the moment Mum spoke, in her fine-porcelain accent, from which years of elocution lessons had expunged the taint of Norfolk, heads would start to turn.

It didn't take me long to perfect the Underwood argot. It was simply a case of slurring words together, omitting consonants and slackening vowel sounds. It was easy to do, just as slouching comes more naturally than sitting bolt upright, but I sometimes felt the strain of switching between accents for home and school.

Friendship was another important area where unexpected improvement had occurred. Ever since the brawl with Dawn Clubb had been resolved by our dads' eccentric brand of doorstep diplomacy, she had been almost overpoweringly friendly, saving me a seat on the bus, offering me sweets and roaring at my jokes. I don't know why she should have been drawn to someone whose only recommendation was the ability to throw a punch, but in later years it would certainly inform her choice of boyfriend. It's hard to resist someone who is bent on befriending you, and, as I soon discovered, Dawn did have some useful qualities: she was widely feared, almost feudally loyal, and had experienced a side of life not much discussed at the Old Schoolhouse.

One day in spring she asked me to come back to her house after school. I knew where she lived because the bus

passed the end of her road each day on its slow, meander-
ing route through the council estate before it reached the
semi-rural outposts of the borough. She issued this invitation just as we reached her stop, so there wasn't much time
for deliberation. To help me make my mind up she seized
my school bag and flung it through the double doors, so I
was obliged to follow. The bus shuddered off, leaving us
standing on the pavement, laughing, amid the diamond
crusting of broken glass that formed the hinterland of most
of the bus stops on the estate. I wasn't cross – I had been
intending to accept anyway, as I knew the offer was a rare
privilege. We didn't have people back much in case they
were electrocuted by the faulty wiring, or beheaded by the
sash windows, or made disparaging remarks about the mess.

Dawn didn't have people back much on account of the
Old Bastard, as her father was known by the women of
the house. He worked nights as a packer in Fleet Street, and
days as a scaffolder, currently on the new supermarket
complex at the mouth of the estate. He slept as and when
he could, mostly in front of the TV, between shifts, and was
irascible if disturbed, forcing his wife and daughters to tiptoe
around him. He was not keen on strangers. Since I had
already been exposed to his charms, I would be immune
from attack, went Dawn's reasoning.

Her house was a tiny end-of-terrace of grey pebbledash,
like fossilised porridge. The front garden had been paved to
accommodate the carcass of an MG Midget whose innards
were mysteriously absent. My overriding impression of the
interior of the house was of plastic – a substance distrusted
by Mum as modern, and therefore corrupt. There was a
pimpled plastic runner across the middle of the living room
carpet from front door to kitchen, and the sofa, on which

the Old Bastard lay snoring, was still swagged in polythene.
Across the back door was a curtain made entirely of multi-
coloured plastic ribbons, which clattered and flapped in the
breeze. I spent hours communing with that curtain. I loved
its brazen colours, its soothing rustle, and the ecstasy of its
silky embrace. The kitchen itself was a shrine to hygiene,
with white, wipe-clean surfaces and laminated mats on top
of laminated tablecloths. Even the drink of squash Dawn's
mum offered me contained what looked like two floating
plastic golf balls. I didn't know what they were – disinfec-
tant, perhaps – but Dawn seemed unperturbed, and swished
them around the beaker, so I did the same.

Everything was so clean: there wasn't so much as a crumb,
a footprint or a hair to be seen. At our place great bales of
dust and fluff blew through the rooms like tumbleweed, and
it was not unknown to find dog hairs in the butter, even
though we'd never owned a dog. It was four years since
Aunty Barbara had visited, and I was still coming across
her discarded fag ends. It was one of those uncomfortable,
ground-shifting moments when you realise that your own
way of life, fondly assumed to be thoroughly mainstream, is
exceptional and very possibly deviant.

On my first visit I was introduced to what became my
principal motivation for all future visits: proper food. Dawn's
mum, when not taking on invisible dirt with a spray gun
and cloth, spent her time preparing meals for such members
of the family as were awake and receptive at any given
moment.

'Are you girls hungry?' she said, at four o'clock, and when
we nodded, she offered to 'rustle something up' – an expression that accurately described the sound of pillow-sized bags
of oven chips and diced mixed veg being dragged from the

chest freezer in the living room. The joy of those meals: meat cooked all the way through; vegetables which arrived on the plate hot, and yielded without exceptional force to pressure from cutlery and teeth; chips, fat, thin or crinkle-cut; gravy without clods of flour. Mrs Clubb had never before had anyone praise her cooking so warmly and sincerely. The Old Bastard wasn't given to compliments, Dawn just shov-elled the food in, oblivious, and her older sister, Pam, was trying to get down to a size twelve for her wedding and ate nothing but yoghurt and apples. My groans of pleasure and eye-rolling delighted Mrs Clubb so much that I was guar-anteed a man-sized meal every time I appeared. Her special-ity was batter – crisp, knobbly, honey-coloured explosions of grease – and she battered practically everything. Fish, sausages, spam, pineapple rings, bananas, cheddar: there was almost nothing outside her range.

Dawn's bedroom was about seven feet square and contained a bed, a chest of drawers and a beanbag. Its pink sandtex walls were decorated with pin-ups of the Hunk of the Month from *My Guy* and *Blue Jeans*, boys with shiny hair, perfect skin and straight white teeth – immaculate creatures who bore no resemblance to the scrofulous oiks at Underwood. Dawn's most precious possession was a radio cassette player, which she used to tape the Top Forty every Sunday. She had a chart on the wall on which to mark the weekly fluctuations: the new entries, the highest climbers and the non-movers were all meticulously recorded and colour-coded. When this was done she set about learning the words to all the songs by playing them over and over, at a low volume, naturally, so as not to rouse the Old Bastard from his slumber. Sometimes, having committed the lyrics of a song to memory, we would rehearse a dance routine, our movements somewhat inhibited by lack of space, and then perform it in front of Pam, who would offer encouragement and advice.

When not coaching us, Pam was generally occupied in one of three pursuits: going out with her fiancé Andy, getting herself ready to go out with Andy, or planning her wedding to Andy. Of these, the second was much the most arduous and time-consuming. Watching her preparations put me in mind of our former lodger, Cindy, with her arsenal of coloured potions. As well as mortifying her flesh with the apple and yoghurt diet, Pam was bent on denaturing her straight blonde hair with a succession of cruel electrical gadgets. She had a box of heated rollers, an electric red-hot poker, and a set of crimping irons. These last came to grief one day when Dawn and I borrowed them to heat up a crumpet and ruined the hotplates. Pam would spend hours in front of her mirror, curling, teasing and backcombing to achieve the vital extra volume, before fixing it all in place with a burst of lacquer. Gravity and damp weather were her sworn enemies. 'Oh no, it's gone all flat!' was a regular lament from the bedroom.

Sometimes Dawn would be summoned to help Pam on with her jeans, which were a skintight fit from waist to ankle. When they came out of the wash, stiff as bark, she would have to put them on lying on her back, with Dawn tugging the two halves of the fly together while Pam yanked on the zip.

If Andy was unavailable, Pam would stay in with flat hair and baggy track pants and read *Bride* magazine, making notes in the margin.

There were always stacks of magazines lying around at the Clubbs'. The Old Bastard picked them up from the

depots in Fleet Street, whole bales of them. He kept a pile
for himself in the toilet under the crocheted ballerina loo-
roll holder. I picked one up once and put it back pretty
quickly. It had a topless woman on the front with her hands
stuffed down her knickers. Someone had drawn smiley faces
around the nipples. When I flicked through there were more
breasts inside, all with biro faces. *One Hundred Genuine
Married Tits and Clits*, the cover promised. I gave Mr Clubb
a wide berth after that.

As well as teen magazines, which were full of photo-
stories about the perils of love, and hints on how to get and
keep a 'fella', Dawn had squirrelled away a collection of
American imports with titles like *True Confession!* These
were terrifyingly lurid first person accounts of rape and
molestation, interspersed with advertisements for sex aids
and kinky underwear. Dawn and I, bloated with batter and
chips, and worn out from disco practice, would lie on her
bed, side by side, poring over the pages together, trying to
make sense of it all. Of course I knew about the facts of
life: Mum had sat me down and explained them in unflinch-
ing detail, and I can't say I was impressed. It may well have
been 'perfectly natural' as she insisted, but she made the
whole business sound about as appealing as surgery without
anaesthetic, which was no doubt her intention.

'Do you think Pam and Andy have had it?' I asked one
day, when we were puzzling over an advert for *Chinese Love
Balls*, £4.99 plus p+p. 'All the pleasure you can stand!' the
promise went. Above the P.O. box number was a picture of
a non-Chinese woman in a pair of black camiknickers, with
a foxy expression on her face.

'I know they have,' Dawn replied. 'She told me. They
got carried away.'

'Did she say what it was like?' It was hard to imagine Pam getting carried away in those jeans of hers. You'd have thought it would take nothing less than grim determination.

'She said it's not like on telly, where the woman starts moaning and groaning the minute a bloke kisses her neck.'

'But was it nice?'

'She said it's all right if you love the person,' Dawn replied, chewing her lip with the effort of recalling these pearls. 'Andy enjoyed it, anyway.'

We both pulled a face at the notion of Andy's enjoyment. He was pale and lanky with spots and a slack mouth. I'd only ever heard him say one word: *awright*, which served as both question and answer in any exchange of views.

'What about Christian?' Dawn asked, blushing a deeper shade than usual. 'Do you think he's had it?'

'Oh no,' I said hurriedly. 'No way.' The thought of Christian having urges made me feel slightly queasy.

'Why not?' she asked.

'Well, he's only seventeen,' I replied – a thoughtless error of tact: Pam was not yet eighteen. 'And anyway,' I hurried on, 'he hasn't got a girlfriend.'

'Hasn't he?' said Dawn, wistfully. 'You'd think he would, being so good-looking.'

It had occurred to me some while ago that Dawn's effort to befriend me might not have been on my own account. She brought Christian's name into conversation on the flimsiest of pretexts, and on the few occasions she had come round to the Old Schoolhouse she had become fidgety and awkward in his presence.

'I suppose you don't notice his looks, being his sister,' she said. 'He probably looks like nothing to you.'

'No,' I reassured her. 'I notice.'

'By the time I'm old enough to be his girlfriend he'll have met someone else,' she sighed. 'Anyway, he'd never look at me that way, because I'm just your friend.'

I gave her a sympathetic smile. Privately I thought the matter of my friendship was not likely to be the chief obstacle, but I thought I'd check with Christian to make sure.

'WHAT DO YOU THINK OF DAWN?' I ASKED, MANAGING TO catch him in the larder one day between absences. 'Do you think she's pretty?'

Christian withdrew, carrying a packet of Ryvita and a slab of Cheshire cheese. 'Why are you talking in that stupid voice?' he enquired. 'Are you trying to sound thick?'

'Sorry,' I said, reverting to home-speak. The mention of Dawn's name had confused me into selecting the wrong accent. 'Forgot where I was for a moment.' I watched him build a tower of sandwiches, layer by crumbling layer. 'Well, do you?'

He looked at me incredulously. 'You mean that fat girl with the red face and metal teeth?'

I nodded slowly. 'Well, I guess that answers my question,' I said, and we both burst into noisy laughter, united for once, in a moment of clannish superiority.

21

A NEW PENNY ARRIVED IN THE SPRING, ALONG WITH WARMER weather, light evenings and Asian flu.

Christian was the only one of us to succumb, losing the use of his legs for three weeks as the virus ravaged his muscles. For a while it was feared he had something more serious. Terrible words like leukaemia were whispered behind closed doors and drifted through keyholes like wraiths. It was as if we were holding our breath for the five days he was in hospital having tests. One of the lifers at the prison said a special prayer for Christian's recovery at the Sunday morning Eucharist, an experience which moved Dad almost to tears. I couldn't help wondering how much clout the prayers of a convicted murderer were likely to have with God, but then I remembered the bit about there being more rejoicing in heaven over prodigal sons than stay-at-home sons, and decided it might be just the intercession we needed. Dad was reassuring on that point, alluding also to the significance of lost sheep and coins.

When the influenza B diagnosis was confirmed, Christian was brought home to convalesce. There was never a patient less suited to immobility: poor Christian, who couldn't conduct a conversation without fast bowling or practising his golf swing, was reduced to dragging himself around the floor by his arms, or sliding bumpity-bump down the stairs like Winnie-the-Pooh. Having reached the ground floor he would be stranded there all day until Dad came home to help him back up to bed, so he resorted to this measure as little as possible.

'When am I going to be able to play cricket?' was his regular refrain, once the fever had passed.

Although it wrung my heart to see him so low, there was a dark, selfish corner of me that was glad to have him house-bound. You're ours again, I thought. It was the Easter holi-days, so I was able to spend all my time ministering to him. I brought him damp flannels, hot waterbottles and parac-etamol, and then later, cups of tea and hot cross buns. I fetched and carried his books so that he could study for his A levels, and jumped up and down to plump his pillows and adjust the curtains. Sometimes I just sat with him while he dozed.

'Don't worry, Christian,' I said one morning, when he had had a disappointing session with the physiotherapist, where almost no progress seemed to have been made, 'I'll always look after you.' He had given me a wan smile in reply, and slumped a little further down the pillow.

It was during this stage of his recovery that Penny Two appeared. I had been tempted away from the invalid's bedside for the morning by the promise of an outing with

Dawn and Pam to look at bridesmaid's dresses, but when I arrived at the Clubbs' the house was in uproar. Andy had been seen out and about with the local tart, Pam was in hysterics, the wedding was off, and the Old Bastard was threatening to go and string Andy up from the scaffolding. There wasn't going to be any trip to Pronuptia, Dawn was busy comforting Pam, and Mrs Clubb was too overwrought to be bothered with batter, so I thought it was best to leave. It struck me that at times of crisis families tend to close up and repel outsiders: it had been just the same with us when Christian was in hospital. I thought about this idea on the bus home, and resolved to make a note of it, and any other insights that occurred to me.

As soon as I reached home I bounded up the stairs and into Christian's room without knocking, and then stopped short. Sitting on the bed, with her back to the door, was a girl. She had shoulder-length hair that had the colour and gloss of a fresh conker, and she was wearing a skirt that appeared to have been made of multicoloured silk scarves. Her jacket, and the pixie boots which protruded from the drapes of the scarf-skirt, were lilac suede. Christian was looking at her with a misty, adoring expression, which switched to impatience when he registered my presence.

'Can't you knock?' he said, not angrily, but politely, with no trace of warmth.

The stranger turned towards me and I found myself looking into the slate-grey eyes of a girl – young woman, I suppose – of such intimidating beauty that I couldn't hold her gaze without blushing. I was painfully conscious that I was wearing the first things that had fallen out of the wardrobe that morning – namely, brown socks, a denim skirt, tartan shirt, and a variegated tank top knitted by

Mum – and that I had no memory of the last time I'd washed my hair.

She smiled at my confusion, as though the effect was familiar to her. 'Hello,' she said. 'You must be the famous Esther.'

'I'm not famous,' I said. This was the best I could do.

'Oh well, I'm sure you will be one day. I've heard what a star you are.'

Christian rolled his eyes at this, to let me know that from him at least she had heard no such thing. 'You've been looking after Christian,' she went on, giving him a prod with the toe of her boot, 'and I bet he's been a really grumpy patient.'

He slung his pillow at her and they tussled for possession of it for a minute until she bought him off with a kiss. Feeling spare, I looked down at my feet, shod in a pair of beaten-up Clarks' Nature Trekkers. Perhaps not the thing with a skirt, I decided.

'Well,' the girl slid off the bed. 'I've got to take the dogs out. I don't suppose Captain Interesting wants to come.' She gave Christian another playful poke, and he just laughed. 'Hmm. Pity. Such a nice day, too. You don't fancy a walk in the park with a couple of mad dogs do you, Esther?'

'Three mad dogs,' said Christian, and received another kick.

'Oh ...' I was so surprised I didn't reply straight away, but looked to Christian.

'You don't need his permission,' the girl said, indignantly. 'Come on,' and she grabbed my arm and practically dragged me from the room.

'Men are the pits when they're ill,' she explained, as we made our way downstairs. 'They just want you to be Mummy.'

I grinned at her. It was strange hearing Christian come in for some criticism: uncomfortable but exhilarating. It was the same feeling I'd had when I was left all alone in the house while Mum took Grandpa Percy to the chiropodist, and I stood in the hall and shouted FUCK over and over again, at the top of my voice, just because I could. That sort of opportunity wasn't likely to arise again, as Grandpa hardly went out now, and I couldn't do it with him in the house, deaf as he was.

'I'd better say goodbye to your mum,' she went on, before putting her head in at the kitchen door. Mum was sitting at the table sorting through a stack of bills. A nimbus of hair had come adrift from its moorings, and there was a diagonal crack across one lens of her glasses, which gave her a slightly deranged appearance. She'd trodden on them months ago and still hadn't had them mended. 'Oh, it can wait till my birthday,' she'd said, when Dad chivvied her.

'Goodbye, Mrs Fairchild,' the girl called. 'I'm off now.'

'Goodbye, dear,' said Mum, pausing with her pencil pressed to the page, midway through some complicated arithmetic.

'I'm borrowing Esther, if that's all right with you,' my new friend added.

'Yes, fine,' Mum said, vaguely, her mind still turning on columns of figures. 'Drop these in the post box on your way, would you?' And she handed over a pile of reply-paid envelopes. Those that required stamps would be delivered later, by hand.

Out in the lane, safe from the bramble snare of the driveway, stood a bright yellow Mini. I had passed it on my way in without giving it a thought.

'I don't even know your name,' I said, as the girl unlocked

the doors and slung her handbag onto the back seat. For a second she seemed unsettled.

'Christian's never mentioned me?' she asked lightly.

'No, but that's because he's really secretive about that sort of thing,' I replied, eager to reassure her. 'We never even met the last one ...' That mouth of mine, I thought, as the troubled expression returned to her face.

'Who was that, then?' she asked, this time without any attempt at nonchalance.

'I don't know. Someone called Penny. I only saw her from a distance. She didn't last long,' I said. It was only later, as I ran through the conversation in my head, that it occurred to me my final remark might not have been as heartening as I'd intended.

'That's funny,' she said, snapping her seatbelt home. 'Because I'm called Penny too.'

'Penny Two,' I murmured. 'Well, that's easy to remember.'

She looked sideways at me and laughed. I think she was starting to find my lack of tact entertaining.

'I like your skirt,' I said, as we drove along. Now that I looked closely at the material I could see it was printed to resemble patchwork, but was in fact seamless, sliding over Penny's legs as she drove.

'Thank you,' she said. She glanced at my faded denim skirt, which had a dark patch where a pocket had fallen off, and a ridge around the bottom where the hem had been let down. She opened her mouth to speak and shut it again, and we both burst into giggles. 'I'm sorry,' she said, wiping her eyes. 'I was going to return the compliment, but that is a truly terrible outfit.'

'I know,' I said, still laughing, though not without a

twinge of pain, for even affectionate ridicule hurts when it's deserved. 'All my clothes look like this.'

'Is it some kind of political statement?' she asked.

'What do you mean?'

Penny explained, as she threaded the car down the lanes to the main road, that there was something almost heroic about my indifference to prevailing standards of taste.

'I haven't got any nice stuff,' I said. 'We get all our things from jumble sales. Mum gets first pick, because she organises them. She doesn't believe in spending money on new clothes.'

'God,' said Penny. 'My mum doesn't believe in anything else.'

WE WERE HEADING INTO THE SUBURBS NOW, AWAY FROM familiar territory. The streets grew wider, and the houses larger and further apart, until we finally turned through some gates into a private avenue of detached mansions, set in immaculately tended front gardens, which bled into the wide grass verges. Few of them were as big as the Old Schoolhouse, but they proclaimed Money, where the Old Schoolhouse whispered Neglect. In the driveways of most of the houses stood various vans, belonging to the legions of staff who arrived each day to service the inhabitants' needs. Swithin's Pool Care; Chislehurst Tree Surgeons; Green Fingers Garden Design; Molly Maids; Browns' Bespoke Bathrooms.

'I wonder if you'd fit into any of my stuff,' Penny was musing, as we pulled up outside one of the mansions. 'I'll have a look.'

I didn't think this was likely, given that I was an average-sized thirteen-year-old and she was a taller than aver-age eighteen-year-old, but I was enthusiastic in principle. Even

Mum could hardly disapprove of a fresh source of hand-me-downs, however luxurious they proved to be.

Penny put her key in the lock, setting off a frantic scuffling from within, and as she opened the front door two Old English Sheepdogs flung themselves on us, barking joyfully.

'All right, all right,' Penny commanded, fending off their slobbery advances. 'Don't drool on my jacket you little sod.' She waited until she had subdued them sufficiently for us to gain admittance, and shut the door. Once they were crouched, quivering at her feet she rewarded them with a vigorous rub behind the ears, which sent them springing up and down again, turning frenzied circles.

'They need a W-A-L-K,' she explained, shutting them in the kitchen. 'We'll take them to the park in a moment.' I followed her up the wide staircase, my Nature Trekkers leaving treadmarks in the blond carpet. From one of the rooms the sound of a Hoover issued. 'Hello Maria,' Penny called to the closed door. 'It's only me.'

Penny's bedroom was vast, and furnished with every necessity for a modern princess: thick, white carpet, four-poster bed with muslin drapes, a dressing table with lights around the mirror, writing desk and bookshelves, TV, music centre, even a corner with slipper chairs and a coffee table, for relaxation and grown-up talk. French windows led out onto a small balcony overlooking the garden. Another door was ajar to reveal the white tiles of a private bathroom.

'Now, let's see,' said Penny, approaching the built-in wardrobes and sliding the doors across to reveal a sweep of beautiful clothes, arranged by category and colour. Some were evidently unworn as cardboard tags still swung from the hangers. 'I wonder if any of these would fit.' She began to pluck dresses, skirts and blouses from the rail, slinging them onto the bed. 'Try them on,' she instructed. 'Take anything you fancy.'

'You can't just give me these,' I protested. 'Some of them are brand new.'

'Oh, those are just things Mum bought me. I never wear them. She's a compulsive shopper – it drives my dad insane. But it seems to appease her conscience if she buys stuff for other people as well as herself, so every time she goes out spending, I get something too. I wish she wouldn't.'

I wriggled out of my jumble sale bargains, feeling like a child given a free hand with the dressing-up box. Fortunately, ever since the affair of the Mighty Whities, Mum had relaxed her spending rules to allow for the purchase of new underwear from a cheap department store, so my bra and knickers, though plain, were not a source of further mortification.

Most of the skirts were too big, and swivelled freely around my hips, but after further rummaging Penny produced a black and orange kilt with an adjustable waist. Its original partner, a black angora sweater, was discovered at the back of the wardrobe, still in its bag. It was a roomy fit, but I was glad of that because it itched like crazy where it touched. Still, it looked great, according to Penny, to whose expert opinion I was only too happy to surrender.

'Now we can't have you covering it all up with some hideous old anorak,' she said, rolling back another door which concealed a row of coats and jackets. After some deliberation Penny pulled out a hacking jacket in black needle cord. 'This might work,' she said, then had second thoughts. 'Oh no, the lining's torn.'

I had to physically restrain her from throwing it out, explaining that I would consider myself fortunate indeed to own a garment with a lining, torn or not.

'As long as you're sure,' she said. 'I don't want you to think you've been fobbed off with the old tat.'

I assured her I didn't. Clothed in my new finery, and basking in the thousand-watt glare of her dressing table lights I felt a new warmth stealing over me. This was how spoilt girls felt every day.

Behind me Penny was stuffing jumpers, dresses, and silk shirts into a shopping bag. 'Take them home with you. You can chuck out anything that doesn't fit. I don't want them back.'

'Won't you get into trouble, giving all this away?' I asked.

Penny shook her head. 'Of course not. My older sister used to do the same for me when I was your age.'

'I wish you were my sister,' I said.

She gave a sly smile. 'Maybe I will be one day,' she said, and then looked horrified at this lapse. 'Don't ever tell Christian I said that,' she begged. 'Promise.' To cover her confusion she started rummaging again, presently emerging from the wardrobe with a black velvet beret. 'Here,' she said, tossing it over. 'This will look great on you. You're a hat person.'

A keeper of confidences and a hat person – all in one day! I put the beret on and allowed Penny to tweak it into position. 'It's not a pancake,' she reproved. Her final donation was a pair of pointed mock-croc stilettos. 'They're sheer torture to wear,' she promised, watching my pinched expression as I forced my feet, minus the woolly brown socks, as far as they would go down the rigid conical toes, until my eyes watered with the pain.

'Perhaps that's what they mean by crocodile tears,' I said, as I freed my crushed feet and massaged them back to life.

'They're not comfy,' Penny agreed. 'But there are some occasions,' and here she shot an unfriendly look at my Nature Trekkers, 'when comfy just won't do.'

I nodded, thinking of Pam and her bone-hugging jeans. I could see that elegance came at a price, and I wasn't sure if I was willing to pay, just yet.

'Well,' Penny was saying, adding the shoes to the bag. 'They'll do for parties.'

'I never go to any parties,' I said.

I offered this as a plain fact, but my tone must have been unintentionally woebegone because Penny said, 'Poor little Cinders,' in a tragic voice. 'What do you do with yourself, then?' she went on, more seriously. 'You must have some hobbies.'

I shrugged. 'I go round to my friend Dawn's and we make up dances to the Top Forty.'

For some reason this had Penny in convulsions. 'Oh God, Esther, you kill me,' she said.

THE DOGS, MATT AND GLOSS, ALMOST GARROTTING themselves on their choke chains, dragged us all the way to the park and then bolted for the trees the moment we released them. Penny and I followed at a more leisurely pace, swinging the empty leads. She had exchanged her lilac suede boots for black leather as a precaution against grass stains, and was carrying a zip-up nylon holdall, which she had taken from the boot of the Mini.

At the boundary of the field, between a cycle track and the trees was a wooden bench, which we headed for to await the dogs' return. Every so often they would come tearing out of the undergrowth, leaping from side to side as though the ground was scorching. Penny tutted at the carved graffiti on the bench, twitching her skirt away as she sat down. 'I don't know what's more annoying,' she said, 'the stuff you can read or the stuff you can't.'

I just grunted. I decided I wouldn't mention that Dawn was a compulsive gouger in case she thought I was similarly inclined. On our walk I'd told her about the Clubb household and I'd formed the impression she didn't approve. When I'd come to the bit about the Old Bastard and his magazines, she'd pulled a face and told me to make sure I always kept between him and the door. This showed amazing insight on her part, as the one time I had been on my own in a room with him he had done something so creepy I couldn't even mention it to Dawn. It had been a hot day and we'd been sunbathing in our bikinis. When I came in to get some more golf balls out of the freezer for our drinks Mr Clubb had come into the kitchen and run his finger down my bare back, to the top of my bikini pants, and I'd dropped the whole ice tray. I made sure I was never on my own or less than fully dressed in his presence again.

'Where did you and Christian meet?' I asked Penny at last, looking sideways at her. She was unzipping the holdall, from which she pulled a headscarf, a nylon overall, a packet of Raffles and a lighter.

'He was caddying up at the golf course one time when I was there for a lesson,' she said, throwing her hair forward and using the scarf to tie it all up in a turban. 'He offered to buy me a drink, but he couldn't go into the bar because he wasn't a member, and I couldn't go in because I wasn't a man. So we went to the pub instead. Being fellow outcasts brought us together.'

'What are you doing?' I asked, as she put on the overall
and buttoned it to the neck. She looked like a film star
pretending to be a charlady. Before answering she lit a cigarette and drew on it deeply, with profound relief. 'It's my
parents,' she explained. 'They're both reformed smokers, so
naturally they're total bigots. They've threatened to cut off
my allowance if I spend any of it on cigarettes, so I mustn't
go home smelling of smoke.'

'How much do they give you?' I asked. I was expecting
to be amazed, but even so wasn't prepared for the exorbitant sum she named. 'It goes nowhere,' she sighed, and then
looked ashamed. 'I'm not complaining. I'm very lucky.' She
leant back, enjoying the cigarette and the sunshine. Sitting
there, blinking through the smoke, dressed in that bizarre
outfit, she suddenly reminded me of Aunty Barbara: a
younger, prettier, saner Aunty Barbara. But then, I told
myself, Aunty Barbara had been young and pretty and sane
once too, as that brief piece of film footage had proved. It
wasn't her appearance, so much as her proprietorial attitude
towards me that rang a bell. They had both tried to dress
me up in pretty clothes, although Aunty Barbara's gift of
the bridesmaid's dress had more of unhinged defiance than
practical assistance about it, I now realised.

As if reading my thoughts, Penny said, 'I need a project.
Something to get my teeth into. I think you could be it.'
She smiled, and I looked at her straight, white teeth and
shivered inwardly with a mixture of excitement and trepi-
dation at what form this mauling might take. 'You've got a
lot of potential,' she went on, 'but at the moment it's buried
under . . . under . . .' she groped for the tactful word.

'Underwood?' I suggested, and she laughed. The school,
and the estate it served was infamous across the county, its

name a byword for social evils of every kind. Only my parents refused to view it in these terms: for them humanity was divided into the Fortunate and the Less Fortunate, and their life's aim was the more equitable spreading of that elusive commodity, Fortune.

'We could start with your hair,' Penny said, pinching a limp curl and examining the ends. 'I suppose you're going to tell me your mum cuts it.'

'Dad, actually,' I said.

Penny rolled her eyes. She had finished her cigarette by now and carefully removed her disguise and stowed it in the holdall. 'Come on. We'll go and do it now.' She put two fingers in her mouth and whistled for the dogs, who came bounding over, ready to play. They didn't like the sight of their leads in Penny's hand, and kept their distance so we were forced to throw sticks for them to fetch, in order to bring them close enough to be collared.

Back at the house Maria had finished the carpets and was polishing the parquet with a sort of throbbing dalek. She was wearing an overall from the same range as Penny's smoking jacket. 'Your mum's home,' she said to Penny. 'She's gone to bed.' Penny seemed unperturbed by this news, though it was only three in the afternoon.

'Is she ill?' I asked, as we shut the dogs in the conservatory.

'Oh no,' Penny replied. 'She often goes to bed early to try and lose weight. She thinks if she stays in bed drinking mint tea it'll stop her eating. Sometimes she stays up there all weekend.'

'Is she very fat?' I asked.

'God, no,' said Penny. 'She's as thin as a twig, the silly cow.'

Before we left she pressed a copy of *I Capture the Castle* into my hands. 'You must read this,' she instructed. 'It's my favourite book. I'll draw up a list of others.'

'I didn't realise I was going to have to do homework,' I grumbled, as we got back in the Mini. Suddenly being Penny's protégée wasn't looking so attractive. I hadn't read much fiction since graduating from children's books. In fact the only grown-up book I'd read all the way through was *The Lord of the Rings* because it was Christian's favourite, but I hadn't enjoyed the experience. I found I couldn't work up much enthusiasm for non-human predicaments, however well described.

Penny took me to her local hairdressing salon, a frightening place staffed by androgynes in boiler suits. Over the roar of hairdryers and pop music she managed to secure me an appointment, and told the genderless alien assigned to me to 'tidy it up a bit'.

After two shampoos and a 'treatment' my hair was as slippery as sealskin. It never felt this clean at home. I wondered if there might be something wrong with our water supply: deposits of lead or rust, or dead squirrels in the tank. While the alien combed and snipped, scuttling round me on a plastic stool-on-wheels, like a giant spider, Penny lounged in a cane armchair, browsing through *Harpers & Queen*. Every few minutes another member of staff would be over to offer her tea or coffee or more magazines. As I got to know her better I would become familiar with this phenomenon. Wherever Penny went people would spring to do her bidding. Doors would be opened, bags carried, obstacles removed, assistance offered, so that her path would always be smooth. It was just a way she had – nothing tangible that could be imitated – and she accepted it all with

perfect equanimity. Now she approached to supervise the
blow-drying, smiling encouragement at me in the mirror as
the hairdresser tried to subdue and straighten my curls.

'Do you think you'll be bothered to do this at home?' he
asked, dragging a section of hair taut with a fat brush and
blasting it from above with a jet of scorching air. I laughed
aloud at the idea. We did have a hairdryer at home – a
1950s model with a frayed flex and a rattling motor that
was just as likely to suck hair in and chew it up as blow it
dry. It lived in a box on top of the wardrobe along with a
rubber glove which had to be worn to protect against shocks.

When he was finished with me, he dusted my shoulders
and held up a hand mirror so I could inspect the back of
my head. I thought it might look vain to show too much
delight in my changed appearance, so I just nodded non-
commitally, then it occurred to me that not wishing to be
thought vain was itself a form of vanity. I decided to make
a note of this when I got home, in my book of interesting
observations, which was still largely blank.

Penny came to my rescue by telling me how nice I looked,
which allowed me to smile, showing some of the pleasure
I felt at my transformation. My hair swung, shiny and thick
to just above my shoulders, where it tipped up to tickle me
under the chin. I knew that as soon as I was outside the
damp air and gravity – Pam's old enemies – would flatten
the top and crinkle the ends, but for the moment it was
perfect.

WHEN PENNY DROPPED ME BACK HOME MUM WAS STILL AT
the kitchen table tussling with the household finances.
Something told me it wouldn't be a good time to flaunt my
change of image, however cheaply acquired, so I decided to

creep upstairs to my room. But ours wasn't the sort of house
where you could creep successfully: hinges squeaked and
floorboards jumped and banged and before I had crossed the
hall Mum had spotted me over the top of her cracked
spectacles.

'Goodness, look at you,' she said. 'Have you won the
Pools?' This was her idea of a joke. We never did the Pools,
of course. I shook my head.

'That's a pity,' she said, tapping her pencil on the topmost
of her papers.

'Penny paid,' I said. 'And she gave me all these clothes.
Cast-offs,' I wheedled. 'But really nice ones.'

'I suppose the hairdresser told you to come back every
three months for a trim,' Mum said.

'Six weeks,' I replied.

'Well, you've had that.' She looked down at the columns
of figures in front of her and sighed.

'You could get a job that actually pays,' I suggested.

'There aren't quite enough jobs to go around at the
moment,' she said. 'It wouldn't be right for our family to
have two when some families don't even have one. Besides,
it won't be long before Grandpa can't be left alone. He's so
forgetful.' This was true. Only the other day I had caught
him trying to leave the house in his pyjamas. He'd thanked
me and laughed at his own absent-mindedness, and gone
upstairs to dress, but half an hour later when I looked in
his room, he'd gone back to bed, even though it was midday.

'The trouble with never spending anything is that it
leaves you nowhere to make economies,' Mum said at last.

THAT DAY MARKED A RITE OF PASSAGE IN ANOTHER WAY TOO.
When I got undressed for bed I found a stain, like tar, in

my knickers. I went down to Mum, who had abandoned the accounts and was mending the broken strap of her hand-bag with duck tape.

'I've started my periods,' I said, suddenly embarrassed to be a conspirator with her in this dark, female mystery.

Her face fell for a second. *My little girl*, she was perhaps thinking. Or probably: *more expense*. She went to the cupboard under the sink and brought out a pile of old news-papers, and my heart quailed. Surely we're not that poor, I thought. Then, from the depths of another cupboard she produced a pink squashy packet of Dr Whites.

'See how you get on with these,' she said. 'Don't flush them down the loo or they'll bung up the drains. Wrap the used ones in newspaper and put them in the boiler.'

She must have seen my queasy expression and mistaken its cause, because she laid a hand on my abdomen and said, 'Does it hurt?' I said it didn't, but even as I was shaking my head I felt an unfamiliar ache, bone-deep and burning, spreading down the top of each leg, and I winced.

'Poor you,' said Mum. 'A hot waterbottle sometimes helps. I'll go and get it off Christian.'

And so I went to bed with the hot waterbottle that night, and Christian had to do without, because I had stepped through a doorway now, into a special female world of privilege and pain.

22

PENNY CALLED HER PARENTS DOUG AND HEATHER, OR THE Raving Tory and the Old Hag, depending on circumstances. The three of them played out a strange version of family life in which they doggedly pursued their own interests with the minimum of involvement from the others. Penny's dad ran his own company – something to do with reprographics, she said – and worked long hours. Even when he came home he carried on working in his study until after midnight. If he ever took a day off he spent it on the golf course, where he played off nine. Penny's mum put in equally long hours battling against advancing middle age and diminishing beauty, by means of shopping, surgery, and various fitness regimes. The rest of her time was spent in bed recovering from these exertions. Penny went to school, studied for her A levels, went out in her yellow Mini with Christian, or her girlfriends, or entertained them at home by making cheese fondues and discussing Art and Literature and the Meaning of Life.

Occasionally Penny and her parents coincided for exchanges of essential information, and what they called 'diary meetings', where important events would be timetabled. Sometimes they would book a Civilised Evening In, when the three of them would sit down to dinner together, and Penny would be offered a Dubonnet and lemonade as an aperitif, while Doug and Heather put away the best part of a bottle of gin. They often had lively discussions, Penny said, the sort that might be called blazing arguments in another household. Her mother had been known to throw things for emphasis, and Penny herself said she didn't feel properly alive unless she'd had four good rows in a year.

Naturally I looked up to Penny as a mentor, and came to worship her with the same uncritical devotion that I'd previously reserved for Christian. It was Penny, more than anyone, who rescued me from myself. Without her influence I would have become a clueless, greasy-haired, teenage misfit. She teased and cajoled and flattered me into shape, and offered the kind of brutal advice my parents wouldn't have presumed to utter, and which I would have ignored if they had. It was her example that made me think being a girl might actually be fun – an idea I would never have picked up from my mother, whose femininity took a more puritanical form. Years of trying to win Christian's approval by imitation had inevitably left me with reservations about the value of my own sex. Observing Penny, or rather the progress of Christian's infatuation with her, made me realise that girls were not defective versions of boys at all, but different creatures, deep and complex and fascinating, even to boys. Especially to boys. Suddenly just being a girl seemed to give me an edge over Christian. However much he loved Penny, and however well he thought he knew her, he would never fully understand the mystery of what it was to be female.

But Penny's intervention was practical as well as spiritual: I was her project, and she was accustomed to getting good grades. She had time and money to spend on me and she was generous with both. It was her support that gave me the confidence to develop my particular style of drawing, which Mr Hatch, my art teacher, was in the process of trying to undo. Whenever I did a picture, I always started with some small detail and worked out from there, using the sharpest pencil or the finest brush I could find, and proceeded minutely, rarely finishing. In life drawing classes, everyone but me managed to sketch a full figure in the allotted time, while I would have produced just one perfectly executed ear. My technique exasperated Mr Hatch, who favoured bold, sweeping strokes, and felt it his mission to liberate me from myself. He replaced my tiny brush and 4H pencil with palette knives, blunt stumps of charcoal and fan-shaped brushes, and gave me vast sheets of paper to fill. 'Draw from the shoulder, not the fingertips,' he commanded, watching my struggles to subdue these monstrous tools. 'Relax. You're all hunched up. Block it in. Don't worry about the detail. BIG GESTURES.' It wasn't sheer cruelty on his part: he had the exams to consider, and unless I could be persuaded to cover an A1 sheet within six hours I was certain to fail.

Penny's contribution to this battle was to tell me my own style was exquisite, and to buy me a set of Rotring pens, with nibs like needles, and a box of coloured inks. Generous soul, she knew that as well as praise and encouragement an artist needs materials. It was the best present I'd ever had, and I immediately reverted to my own method of stubborn miniaturism.

IT WAS THE ATTRACTION OF OPPOSITES THAT PULLED Christian and Penny together. One area in which this difference proclaimed itself was their attitude to conversation. Christian tended to favour long silences, punctuated by the delivery of strictly factual information. 'I'm going out.' 'I can't find my calculator.' 'God, it's cold in here.' Penny, on the other hand, liked nothing better than to talk, and had fluent and well-rehearsed opinions on a staggering range of subjects. She felt it her pressing duty to discover as much as possible about the world around her, why she was here, and what she should do about it. Her favourite topics for discussion were moral dilemmas, and she would often read out salient items from the newspaper and demand our views. Do the parents of an anorexic sixteen-year-old have the right to force-feed her? Should white couples be allowed to adopt mixed-race babies? Should Siamese twin A be sacrificed to save Siamese twin B? I think it was Dad who enjoyed these discussions more than anyone: they reminded him of being at theological college. I could usually predict what he was going to say. For weighty matters he advocated praying for guidance, and considering the examples set by Jesus. For dilemmas about personal behaviour, he said, the conscience was usually a reliable guide. 'Even when I think I'm torn between two courses of action, I find that after careful reflection I generally know what to do: and it's nearly always the thing I'm least inclined to.'

It was during one of these conversations at which Penny,

Christian and I were present, that Dad said something that amazed us all.

I'd wasted the morning messing about with lemons. A beauty tip in one of Dawn's magazines recommended rinsing mid-brown hair in lemon juice to bring out the natural highlights, so I'd bought a net of lemons from the market and done as advised. My hair didn't look any lighter for my efforts, in fact it looked slightly darker, where it was now stuck together in crispy clumps. Rather than waste the rest of the lemons, I trawled Mum's ancient, greasy recipe book for ideas. It had to be something simple which wouldn't tax me beyond my enthusiasm, or require exotic additional ingredients unavailable in our larder. At last I found something suitable: written on one of the many scraps of loose paper stuffed into the back of the book. *Barbara Fry's Real Lemonade*. I'd noticed that most of these handwritten recipes were attributed to some original inventor or donor. *Grandma Percy's Queen of Puddings; Aunty Molly's One-Egg Sponge; Mrs Tapley's Meatless Meatloaf.* It was as if they were part of some ancient female lore that even women like my mother, who hated cooking, had to guard and pass on. Aunty Barbara's lemonade recipe obviously dated from happier times, when she and Alan used to entertain: it even included instructions on how to frost the rims of the glasses with egg white and sugar – a touch of refinement I was determined to copy.

I remembered, as I was paring the lemons, that Penny had once let slip that her parents sometimes had the neighbours round for *cocktails on the terrace*, and I had a sudden impulse to recreate this experience in our own garden, with homemade lemonade and whatever snacks I could find in the larder: peanuts left over from Christmas, perhaps. Penny

was due to come round to pick up Christian at six. They
were spending the day apart, allegedly studying for their A
levels, which were looming, although the mournful strains
of acoustic guitar and the regular thud of darts issuing from
Christian's room led me to have grave doubts about his
commitment.

We didn't have a terrace, exactly, but while the lemons
and sugar were steeping in the boiling water, I swept the
dirt and shrivelled leaves from the brick paving outside the
French windows, and shaved off the clumps of moss and
sprouting weeds with the edge of a spade. It was late May,
and the afternoon sun was warm on my back as I worked.
Now that I bothered to look, I could see that the brickwork had been laid out in an intricate herringbone pattern,
with a hexagonal mosaic effect in the centre. It astonished
me that for all these years I'd walked back and forth across
it and never noticed. Then I fetched the wooden table,
which was parked, neglected in the long grass under the
apple tree, and scrubbed away the dead blossom, bird drop-
pings and snail slime. Some of the stains went deep into
the wood, which was grey and spongy from its untreated
exposure to the elements, so I covered it up with a once-
white tablecloth. The unfamiliar sounds of industry brought
Mum out to investigate.

'Goodness, you've been busy,' she said, with approval.
My general indolence – especially my habit of falling asleep
in the afternoons – had lately provided her with regular
material for her Little Talks. 'What's brought this on? Are
you expecting company?'

'When Penny comes to get Christian, we're all going to
sit out here and have lemonade,' I explained. 'We're going
to be civilised.' Civilised was my adjective of the moment:

it expressed my deepest yearnings for order, luxury, good taste – all those things which seemed to fall naturally to Penny, but which daily life at home made impossible. Purple suede boots were civilised: Nature Trekkers were not. Having a Portuguese cleaning lady was civilised: dirt was not. En suite bathrooms were civilised: wrapping used sanitary towels in newspaper and putting them in the boiler was not.

'What a good idea,' said Mum, clearly delighted that my bourgeois aspirations had at least raised me from my usual torpor. 'I'll find some decent glasses.'

By the time Penny arrived, car keys swinging from her middle finger, and Christian had emerged from his room, yawning and stretching and cracking his knuckles, as if from a long hibernation, my preparations were complete. In the course of searching through long-neglected cabinets and dressers, Mum had discovered six undamaged glasses and a large pitcher (civilised), and I had strained the cooled lemonade through a stocking (uncivilised). I had frosted the edges of the glasses and filled them with crushed ice (civilised) and Grandpa Percy had installed himself at the table, in a pair of trousers with a stain down the front (uncivilised).

There wasn't much in the larder that could serve as nibbles, but I did find an open packet of walnut pieces. They were soft and rather bitter, but I put them out anyway, along with a bowl of sugar in case the lemonade needed sweetening.

Everyone was very complimentary about my efforts, though the frosted rims had to be explained to Grandpa, who thought he'd got a dirty glass.

'It's certainly very refreshing,' said Dad, surreptitiously wiping his eyes.

'So much better than shop-bought,' said Mum. As if we'd ever had shop-bought lemonade!

Christian drained his glass at a gulp, then pretended to flail and claw at his throat. But he helped himself to seconds, which pleased me. There were no takers for the walnuts, I noticed, though the sugar was warmly appreciated.

'How homely,' said Penny, swilling ice around her glass. 'My family never does anything like this.'

But I got the idea from you! I wanted to protest.

'Have you been working hard?' Mum asked her. 'Your eyes look a bit bleary.'

Penny almost bridled at this, but collected herself with a laugh. 'Yes. All day. My head's full of Milton.' She shook it as if to dislodge him.

'How uncomfortable for you both,' said Dad, gravely. 'You probably deserve an evening off. Christian's been buried in his room all day, too.'

'Playing darts,' I said, and Christian gave me a disdainful look.

'Where are you youngsters off to tonight?' asked Grandpa. He always wanted to know, even though the possible answers: 'Izzy's', 'The Wire Mill', 'The Great American Disaster', 'The Old Turtonians', couldn't have meant much to him.

It was weird how we all seemed to live vicariously through Penny and Christian, as though they were our chosen emissaries to the world of fun, which we were too young or too old or too nervous to experience ourselves. There was a sort of wistfulness in Mum and Dad's directions to 'have a lovely time' and 'take care', and yet they never showed any inclination to follow suit. There was nothing to stop them going for a drive in the country, or out to a pub, but they never went. In fact, now I came to think about it, they hardly did anything that might be termed fun. All their activities were tied up with service to other people. One evening a week Dad went to play cards with Mrs Tapley, who had no other visitors. Mum made the tea at the mother and toddler group, knitted six inch squares for the Universal Quilt, and read books onto tapes for the blind. Sometimes, with a sort of puzzled detachment, they watched television, but that was just to keep Grandpa company, and not for their own pleasure. No wonder I was always being told what good people my parents were: they were a regular pair of doormats!

While Christian was explaining to Grandpa that he and Penny were going to an eighteenth birthday party in a room over a pub in Chislehurst, Penny picked up Dad's discarded newspaper and began browsing.

'Oh no, it's that girl,' I heard her say, while I was still tuning into Christian's conversation with Grandpa.

On the back page was a grainy black and white photograph of a girl's face at a window, partly obscured by shadow. The caption read: *Janine Fellowes, Britain's most notorious juvenile killer, celebrates her nineteenth birthday at the Young Offender's institution where she has spent the last eight years. In two years' time the Home Office must decide whether she will be released or transferred to an adult prison.* Below the article, which rehearsed the known details of the crime, was the now-famous picture of her as an eleven-year-old schoolgirl – long, dark hair, Alice band, stern, unsmiling gaze – and the equally famous image of the victim, Baby Claudia – blonde curls, dimples, laughter.

'That awful case,' Mum murmured, moving in to get a closer look. 'Why can't they leave her alone?'

'Surely they're not allowed to publish a picture of her as

she is now,' said Penny. 'What happens when she comes
out?'

'She'll never get out,' said Christian.

'I quite agree, Penny,' said Dad. 'These newspaper editors
are completely irresponsible. It's just pandering to the
public's morbid curiosity, with no thought for the future
safety of the poor girl – woman, I should say.'

'Well, we're all gawping at it,' Christian pointed out. He
leaned over Penny's shoulder. 'Mind you, she does look
pretty evil,' he added. 'It's the eyes.'

'No, it's the mouth,' I said. 'She's got a cruel mouth.'
Although the photo was fuzzy, I found that looking at it
through half-closed eyes brought it into sharper focus.

'I wonder if she's sorry for what she did,' said Penny. 'She
doesn't look very contrite.'

'Well, I can assure you she is,' said Dad sharply, and we
all stared at him.

'How do you know?' Christian asked. 'Have you met her?'

'Yes,' he said, already regretting his indiscretion. There
was no way we were going to let it go: our family never got
caught up with anything interesting.

'Well?'

'When? How come?'

'What was she like?'

Dad sighed, and Mum gave him a look that said, *you got
yourself into it.*

'I shouldn't really have said anything,' he said at last, 'but
I was driven to it by your inane remarks about evil eyes and
cruel mouths.' Christian and I looked suitably humbled. 'I've
visited her a few times over the years. It started when I wrote
a letter to the *Times*, criticising aspects of the trial. You might
remember the brick incident – it was probably related.'

'I remember. It could have killed me,' said Christian, with a belated attack of indignation. 'Didn't we ever follow it up?'

'I seem to recall a policeman came round and had a poke about in the bushes,' said Mum. 'We didn't really expect them to catch anyone.'

'Anyway,' I said, keen to get back to the main story. 'Janine's mother saw my letter and seemed to seize on me as a lone sympathetic voice. She asked me to go and visit Janine, and talk to her, so I did.'

'What was she like?' Penny wanted to know.

'I can't say she was *ordinary*, because she'd had such an odd upbringing, but she certainly didn't strike me as a monster. Her father left home when she was two, then five years later her mother met this Australian in the pub and married him almost immediately. He wanted to go back to Australia, so Janine's mother gave her and her older sister the choice: come to Australia with them or stay behind. Imagine giving a seven-year-old that choice. The girls decided to stay, so they were packed off to live with their father, who had remarried and had two more children by now. Then the father died horribly at work – I think he was crushed by a digger, or something appalling, anyway – and the stepmother brought them up for a while. But that didn't work terribly well, not surprisingly, so the mother, who had parted company from the Australian by now, came back home for a belated attempt at bringing up her own daughters. With disastrous results.'

'Did she ever explain why she killed the baby?' Penny wanted to know.

'That had all come out during the trial,' Dad explained. 'It was partly rage and frustration at being left alone to look after a baby while everyone else was out enjoying themselves. Claudia's mother, who lived in the same street, asked Janine's mother if she'd mind Claudia for the day, while she visited her husband. I think he was inside for something or other. So Janine's mother agreed, but she went out shopping and left the baby with the girls instead. Janine's sister, who was fifteen at the time, wasn't having any of that; she had arranged to meet her boyfriend at the cinema, so she went out as well. Which left poor Janine. The baby wouldn't stop crying. Janine was only eleven. She couldn't cope with the noise, and smothering her was the only way to shut her up. She had no normal feelings of love or sympathy for the child, whom she'd never met before, and no thought of the consequences. To Janine Claudia was just a nuisance, another obstacle between herself and her own pleasure.'

'Why did she get such a harsh sentence?' Christian asked. 'Plenty of people have got away with less for worse crimes than that.'

Dad shrugged. 'Because she was tried in an adult court. Because there's a mandatory life sentence for murder. Because of the way she behaved after the killing. To satisfy public outrage . . . lots of reasons.'

'What did she do that was so terrible?'

'She didn't tell anyone what she'd done. She just hid the body in a wardrobe and went to the cinema. That was what really got people: that a young girl could be so heartless.'

'But her mother and sister were as much to blame,' I said. 'Didn't they get into trouble too?'

'They certainly came in for a lot of abuse in the press. The sister came to stay here for a while, after the trial, because it wasn't safe at home. I don't suppose you remember her.'

'Cindy,' I said, trying to resurrect some memory of her that wasn't related to cosmetics.

'You said she was our au pair,' Christian protested.

'That's right. Fancy your remembering,' said Mum.

I didn't say that if I'd known at the time she was the sister of a famous murderess I'd have made a point of remembering more.

'First Cindy, then that vicar-pervert guy, then Aunty Barbara,' said Christian. 'What is this – open house for sociopaths?'

Grandpa Percy, who had been snoozing over his lemonade throughout this discussion, sat up sharply. 'Is it time for me to go?' he said.

23

'YOU SHOULDN'T SPEND SO MUCH TIME HANGING AROUND with Christian and Penny,' Mum admonished me from time to time. 'It's not right. You should be mixing with people your own age.' It was their privacy that concerned her, rather than my exposure to their corrupting influence. To them she said, 'Don't feel you have to entertain Esther. She has her own friends.' (This was an exaggeration: I had Dawn.) 'You go off and do your own thing.'

Christian took her very much at her word, as the following day he announced that he and Penny were going away to the Norfolk Broads for a week. There would be three other people in the party: two girls and a boy. The odd number was intended to reassure Mum and Dad that there would be no hanky-panky – a piece of flawed logic, to my mind, but it seemed to allay their suspicions. I knew Christian and Penny must have been having sex for ages, as Penny had confessed to me that she had lost her virginity at the age of fifteen to a friend of her father, a fact I found deeply disturbing. If I was to emulate my mentor in every respect I would have to get a move on: I still hadn't even been kissed. I think Mum was won over by the fact that the canal boat belonged to the parents of one of the girls and therefore the holiday wouldn't cost anything. We hadn't been able to go away ourselves since Aunty Barbara's estrangement had put the caravan out of bounds.

The day before they were due to leave, Dad took Christian aside and told him to remember that Penny was somebody's daughter, and somebody's sister, and should be treated with respect, and he wasn't going to say any more, but he hoped Christian knew what he was driving at. Christian, showing unusual self-control, managed to keep a straight face for the duration of the interview, and replied that he had every respect for Penny and all her ancestors, and could he please go and finish packing.

I caught up with him in his room, where he was still chortling over it hours later. 'In the unlikely event that you ever get a boyfriend, don't ever introduce him to Dad,' he advised. He was folding T-shirts, shorts and trousers and stowing them in a zip-up sports bag. On the bed was a pile of discarded clothes.

'Won't you be wanting these?' I asked, picking up his swimming trunks and slinging them across to him.

'No,' he said, chucking them back on the heap.

'Aren't you allowed to swim in the Norfolk Broads?' I asked. To me, that would have made for a very frustrating boat trip.

'Oh,' said Christian, nonplussed. 'I don't know. Probably. Oh, give them here, then.' He didn't seem the least bit

grateful for my intervention, but carried on packing with
his back to me.

WHILE HE AND PENNY WERE AWAY I TOOK THE OPPORTUNITY
to ingratiate myself with Dawn again. Since Penny's arrival
on the scene I had tended to neglect her, especially at weekends, when I had been in the habit of making myself available at home in case Christian and Penny decided to include
me in any of their jaunts. I had deliberately engineered it
so that although Penny and Dawn knew plenty about each
other, they had never actually met. For reasons that I hadn't
troubled to examine, I preferred not to let my friends cross-
pollinate. Perhaps I sensed that I presented a different face
to each of them, and to bring them together would involve
me in a tricky collision of roles. Although I was not prepared
to abandon my quest for all things civilised, in truth I did
still enjoy many aspects of my pre-civilised life: prancing
around to the Top Forty, Mrs Clubb's batter, *True
Confessions!*, and hanging around the garages on the estate
with Dawn, watching the gangs of boys squaring up.

  This particular free weekend I arranged to meet Dawn
in town. The plan was to spend the day according to our
usual fashion: loitering in the precinct; trying out the make-
up testers in Boots until the assistants shooed us away;
checking out the ethnic jewellery in the indoor market and
stalking any good-looking boys. The last of these schemes
got no further than our imaginations: good-looking boys
were a scarcity and those few who met our exacting
criteria were invariably attached to good-looking girls.

  By lunchtime Dawn and I had run through our usual
repertoire and spent nearly all our limited funds in the pound
store and the discount stalls in the indoor market. Now we

were sitting in Luigi's grill – the cheapest and least civilised
café in the precinct – picking over our bargains and making
two Cokes last an hour.

'Do you think these are real gold?' Dawn asked, finger-
ing her ten-pence bangles. As if in reply a tiny piece flaked
off against her nail. 'Bloody typical,' she grumbled. 'I've a
good mind to take it back.' Amongst her other lucky finds
were a make-up compact containing pressed rectangles of
eyeshadow and lipstick in various shades of bruise, and a
travel toothbrush, which made me laugh because, like me,
the furthest Dawn ever travelled was to school and back.

I had chosen vanilla joss-sticks, a floating candle, and a
set of 'Six Wives of Henry VIII' guest soaps. I thought it
might be civilised to put one of these in the bathroom to
replace the hairy slab of Camay next time visitors were
expected.

The waitress at Luigi's was the most miserable woman
alive, and her glowering presence in the doorway was a
deterrent to all but the most determined customers. She
had been over a couple of times to check the levels in
our glasses, and give the table a wipe with her greasy
cloth to encourage us to be on our way, not realising
that in matters of thrift I was my mother's child, and
unembarrassable.

Now she was back on sentry duty by the door, and Dawn
was busy tearing one corner off all the sugar sachets in the
dish, just to be petty, when the strangest thing happened.
Dawn dug me in the ribs and said, 'Hey, isn't that your
brother?'

I looked up and simultaneously saw and did not see
Christian, outside the window, peering in at the display of
cheesecakes and pastries, before moving off, out of sight. I

saw him, because he was there, but at the same time I didn't see him, because he was far away in Norfolk.

'Isn't he meant to be in Norfolk?' said Dawn, echoing my own thoughts.

'It wasn't him,' I said. 'It just looked like him.'

'It was him, I tell you,' Dawn insisted.

'I think I'd know my own brother,' I replied indignantly.

'Well, if it wasn't him it must have been his twin,' she retorted and, nettled by my intransigence, she raced to the doorway to call after him and prove me wrong. Old Cerberus must have thought she was doing a runner, because she stuck out her arm to bar the exit, and there followed a frank exchange of views between Dawn and the waitress, which was only halted by the intervention of Luigi himself, who told us to pay up and scram.

By the time we had extricated ourselves, Christian or his double had disappeared, of course, so the dispute couldn't be resolved. Our difference of opinion had only succeeded in souring the atmosphere, and as neither of us had the grace to climb down, and we had spent all our money, we decided to go our separate ways.

The journey home – a half-hour bus ride and a long walk – gave me ample time for reflection. I sat upstairs in a fog of exhaled smoke as the bus juddered its way out of town, through the suburban streets until it reached the semi-rural pick-your-own farms and scrubby common land that marked the boundaries of our 'village'. The roads grew narrower, pavements disappeared, and overhanging branches clattered and clawed at the windows of the upper deck as I sat there, chewing it all over. What did Christian's presence outside Luigi's signify? Why wasn't he in Norfolk as he'd led us to believe? In spite of my denials, it had certainly been him

I'd seen, for what I had not admitted to Dawn was that, in the split second before he had turned away, *he* had recognised *me*. What really hurt was the sense of betrayal, of being lied to, and lumped in with Mum and Dad as people who are in the way, who have to be deceived. It was this feeling that had led me in turn to lie to Dawn, an additional source of bitterness. 'I think I'd know my own brother,' I'd said, so confidently, even as events were proving, yet again, how little I really knew him.

As soon as I reached the Old Schoolhouse I rang Penny's number. The phone was picked up almost immediately and I heard a sharp intake of breath before it was put down again. It was the sort of sound you might make if you had inadvertently done something you weren't supposed to: like pick up a phone when you were supposed to be somewhere else. I redialled immediately, but this time there was no reply. While I was still standing in the hall, staring at the phone, I remembered something Penny had said months ago. She was looking forward to the beginning of July because the Raving Tory and the Old Hag were going to Greece to celebrate twenty years of marital torment, so she would have the house to herself, day and night.

I realised at last what a smarter, sharper person would have suspected straight away: there was no boat trip. Christian and Penny were staying in her empty house. *Living together as man and wife*, as Dad would have put it. Once I had worked this out I hardly needed any more confirmation, but as I was at a loose end, I decided to take Mum's bike and ride straight over to Penny's anyway.

The journey was a lot longer than it had seemed by car, and I had to keep stopping to read the A-Z, and reattach the chain, which had an annoying habit of jerking free whenever I changed gear. It really was the crappiest bike imaginable, with its rusted brakes and withered saddle, and I marvelled yet again at my mother's patient acceptance of dross. By the time I was halfway there, and committed to continuing, I was seriously regretting my decision, and wishing I'd opted instead for my usual afternoon nap.

Another complication occurred to me as I swung into the broad avenue leading to Penny's house. Suppose they were just arriving or leaving as I drew up? I had no wish to be caught spying, and didn't want to confront them. Something told me that wouldn't be civilised behaviour. I intended to deploy my hard-won knowledge with more finesse. These anxieties proved groundless, because as I approached the house neither Christian nor Penny appeared, but an upstairs window had been left open, and the yellow Mini stood on the horseshoe-shaped drive, proclaiming their occupancy like a royal pennant. With my object achieved there was nothing for it but to turn around and head for home, which I did with some regret. It was a hot July afternoon, and in other circumstances I would have been able to knock at the door and cadge some refreshment. That carefully eked out Coke from Luigi's had worn off long ago, and thanks to those Six Wives of Henry VIII guest soaps I had no money for another.

I rode home, dry-mouthed, the warm wind in my face, my right ankle skinned raw from the slipping bicycle chain, strangely uncomforted by having had my suspicions confirmed.

Back at the Old Schoolhouse Mum was on the telephone, and in a state of agitation. She wagged her hand to tell me to wait. 'She's just walked in. I'll ask her now,' she said into the receiver, and hung up with a crash. 'Grandpa's gone walkabout,' she explained breathlessly. 'I've only just come in to find him missing. I went to see if I could try and track him down on the bicycle but it's been stolen . . .' She stopped, seeing my guilty expression.

'Sorry,' I said, pointing out of the window to the drive where the bike lay, its front wheel still spinning. 'I just borrowed it. I didn't realise you'd be needing it.'

Mum blinked with astonishment. 'You? Whatever for?' My slothfulness was the cause of much nagging and sarcasm at home, a fact I decided to use to my own advantage.

'You're always telling me I need to get up and about more, and do some exercise,' I improvised. 'So I did. I would have asked, if you'd been here.'

Mum looked sceptical. 'Well, never mind that now. Was Grandpa still here when you left?'

'I don't know. I didn't look.'

'Oh, hell's teeth. He could have been gone hours.'

'The TV was on,' I remembered. I'd heard it in the background when I went to phone Penny.

'That doesn't mean anything. He wouldn't think to turn it off.' She was already dragging on her sandals. 'I'll ride around the lanes. Since you're so keen on exercise all of a sudden, you can run up to the paper shop and the pub – actually, you'd better not go in the pub – and ask if they've seen him. Your dad's on his way home. I'll meet you back here in half an hour.'

I helped myself to a glass of water and set off on foot as instructed. As I emerged from the paper shop I spotted Dad driving past the Fox and Pheasant, a serene and unrepentant Grandpa beside him, and was able to flag them down for a lift home. Dad had found Grandpa sitting on a bench in the churchyard, still in his pyjamas, talking to one of the churchwardens. All the way home he kept rattling his tic-tacs and saying, 'Are we nearly there?' just like a child on a long journey.

'WHAT'S THE MATTER WITH GRANDPA?' I ASKED MUM, LATER, when we were alone. As well as wandering off in his pyjamas, he occasionally went to bed in his clothes, accused Mum of stealing his false teeth, fished rubbish out of the wastepaper baskets and hid it in his room, and called me Kitty, which was Grandma Percy's name.

'He's got dementia, I'm afraid,' she replied. 'It's his age.'

She was sitting at the kitchen table writing the days of the week and other memory aids – MORNING, AFTERNOON, NIGHT-TIME, TEETH, PILLS – on large pieces of card to be posted in prominent places around the house. She shook her head.

'Will he get better?' I asked, not liking the sound of it. 'If he had some medicine or something?'

She shook her head. 'No. That's the trouble with getting old.' She automatically rubbed her knee, which was stiff and sore after that emergency bike ride. 'Things get worse rather than better. I'd advise you to stay young.' And she smiled to reassure me that it was her attempt at a joke. And I smiled back to let her know I appreciated the effort. At the same time I felt the slight chill I always did whenever anyone alluded to the distant future. 'When you have children of your own . . .' 'Wait till you have to pay the bills . . .' 'When you're working for a living . . .' These words never failed to provoke an angry buzzing deep in the channels of my ears: to imagine myself old was just as ludicrous and impossible as imagining my parents young.

MY CONFIDENCE IN MY POWERS OF DETECTION WAS momentarily shaken a couple of days later by the arrival of

a postcard from Norfolk. It showed a picture of river cruis-
ers moored on a stretch of unconvincingly turquoise water,
and was postmarked Thetford.

Hi Folks, it said, in Christian's unmistakably slanting
handwriting. *Having a great week. Weather's brill. No disas-
ters so far. Penny sends love. See you soon. Chris.*

There was something in the blandness of this message,
and its lack of detail, that persuaded me not to take it at
face value, and I decided to have some fun at Christian's
expense when he returned. Not to get him into trouble, of
course, but just so he would know I was Not A Fool.

There were plenty of books about Norfolk in the travel
section of the Central Library: local history; camping and
caravanning guides; *A Wildfowler's Norfolk; An Artist's
Norfolk*, and pretty soon I had found out everything I needed
to know. In fact the whole experience made me realise what
an amazing place the library was, and what a treasure house
it would be, if only I was the sort of person who liked reading books. But I had my own stern librarian in the shape
of Penny, who was now trying to steer me through the works
of Thomas Hardy – gloomy tales of catastrophic coinci-
dences and thwarted potential that made me vow never to
set foot in Dorset.

'YOU'RE NOT VERY BROWN,' MUM SAID, ON THE PRODIGAL'S
return. 'I wouldn't have thought there'd be much shade on
a boat. Wasn't it sunny?'

I couldn't help smirking. Christian's skin had the pallor
of someone who has spent a week under the duvet. 'Yes, it
was sunny,' said Christian smoothly. 'But I didn't lie around
sunbathing.'

'Very sensible,' said Dad, who was fair-skinned.

We were eating dinner together, just the family. Penny, though invited, had declined. My guess was she was putting the house back in order before her parents came home. As it was a special occasion Mum had exerted herself in the kitchen and produced a roast. A roast what, we couldn't be sure. We were sitting outside enjoying the evening sun, which came glancing over the tops of the beech trees. Since I'd cleaned up the old table for the lemonade experiment we often ate outdoors. Dad was fending off wasps with a rolled napkin.

'Did you see Berney Arms Mill?' I asked innocently. 'It's the biggest in Norfolk.'

Christian looked at me through narrowed eyes. 'How would you know? You've never been there.'

'It's famous,' I insisted. 'Didn't you see it?'

'Where are you going?' Grandpa Percy asked.

'Nowhere,' Christian replied, accepting the diversion gratefully. 'I've just come back.'

There was a thwack as Dad dispatched another wasp. 'We must have a nest,' he said. 'I must do something about it.'

'What about the bridge at Potter Heigham?' I asked. 'That's supposed to be worth a trip.'

Christian shot me a look of deep disgust.

'You're very well informed,' said Mum. 'Is this something you're doing at school?'

'Where's he going?' Grandpa asked Dad.

'Nowhere. He's just come back from Norfolk.'

'Norfolk!' The word seemed to penetrate the fog of confusion in Grandpa's brain, because he became suddenly animated. 'We used to go mackerel fishing at Great Yarmouth,' he said. 'Beautiful sandy beach. We had our own boat. Did you see the boats?'

'Or the thirteenth-century toll house?' I asked.

Christian stood up and picked up his plate. 'Do you mind if I finish this indoors? These wasps are driving me mad.' And he glared at me to let me know he considered me an equivalent pest.

IT WAS ONLY MUCH LATER, WHEN CHRISTIAN REALISED HIS secret was safe, and that my performance at dinner had been for my amusement alone, that he came clean. He and Penny had indeed spent the week at her place, and for the first few days had been afraid to leave the house in case they were spotted by someone who might give them away. On the day I had seen Christian outside Luigi's, claustrophobia had made him reckless, and he had gone into town to buy Penny a dress. That sighting of me, followed by Penny's slip in answering the phone, had sent them into a guilty panic, and the next day they had driven all the way to Thetford to consolidate their alibi with that postcard, and to ease their troubled consciences. Now they could say they'd been to Norfolk without actually lying.

When I asked him why he hadn't acknowledged me in Luigi's he said he wasn't absolutely certain I'd seen him. It was quite dark in the interior and he was hoping he'd got away with it.

'What did you do all day?' I asked. 'Was it like being married?'

'Oh, I dunno,' said Christian vaguely. 'Not a lot. Anyway, I never want to go through another week like that,' he added, which struck me as a curious thing to say about an experience of secret passion.

24

THE FIRST CHINKS IN PENNY AND CHRISTIAN'S RELATIONSHIP began to show during their second year of university. In order to be together they had, against parental advice on both sides, sacrificed their first choices of destination – at opposite ends of the country – and settled as a compromise on Exeter, their second choice. Penny was studying law, with a view to defending the innocent; Christian was study-ing maths and computing, with a view to making money.

In the first year Penny had been billeted in an all-female hall of residence, while Christian had a room in a tower block on campus. In their second year, when they were expected to make their own arrangements, they rented the top floor flat of a large house in Plymtree, a small village some miles from the university, with two of the girls from Penny's hall. It was Penny's generosity as chauffeuse that made this rural idyll possible: it inevitably fell to her to drive her housemates in to the campus in the morning and

home again at night. The ground floor of the accommodation was used as a vet's surgery – a detail that had seemed
picturesque on paper, but proved less so in life. *There is a
perpetual smell of wet dog about the place, and the traffic of sick
animals and whelping from the waiting room is not conducive
to study. The driveway and front garden are littered with diar-
rhoeic turds. You must come and stay,* as Penny put it in one
of her letters to me. If it hadn't been for her correspondence I would have heard no news of Christian whatsoever,
as he never made any effort to write himself. Every few
weeks on a Sunday morning Mum would telephone him to
reassure herself on three points. Was he well? Was he working? Was his grant lasting? There was no opportunity for
anything but the most superficial exchange of news as we
had always been given to understand that long-distance
calls, like prawns and rump steak, were strictly for
millionaires.

In fairness to Christian, he had never misled me about
the probability of receiving any post. When the morning
of his departure came, I'd watched with a lump in my throat
as he struggled to fit his one small suitcase and anglepoise
lamp into the back of the yellow Mini, which was already
crammed to the roof with Penny's belongings.

'You will write to me, won't you?' I said. It was September.
I was still in summer clothes and flip-flops. The sumac trees
hadn't even begun to turn red. The next time I saw him it
would be midwinter, cold and branchbare.

Christian looked flummoxed by this request. 'Write?' he
said slowly. 'I don't know about that. Unlikely, I'd say.' He
turned to Penny, who was hunched behind the steering
wheel, hemmed in by an advancing overhang of cushions,
duvets, pot plants, holdalls and lampshades. 'Writing letters,'

he said through the open window. 'That's more your sort of thing, isn't it?'

She gave an exaggerated sigh of impatience. 'Of course I'll write to you, Esther. Anyway, you must come and stay as soon as we're settled in.'

On the first point Penny kept her word, though it was another four terms before I had an official invitation to visit. I assumed that they hadn't forgotten, but that the business of settling in must be more subtle and protracted than I'd imagined.

Penny's favoured form of communication was the postcard. She obviously had a big box of them, depicting masterpieces of twentieth-century art. Sometimes, when she had plenty to recount, she would fill two or three, and fire them all off at once. When news was thin I might receive a simple exhortation to keep my pecker up, or a quotation intended to inspire, or possibly baffle. *We think in generalities, but we live in detail* (Whitehead). *It is a great art to saunter* (Thoreau). I kept these pinned to my bedroom wall, text side down, as I found the pictures – Kandinsky's spiky abstracts, and Rothko's throbbing abysses of red and black – more to my liking. My favourite card of all was the one that said: *Why don't you come down for the weekend of 24 Feb? Catch the 6.40 from Paddington on Friday night and I'll meet you at Exeter St David's. Bring warm clothes and something suitable for a party. P.*

I prepared a short speech in defence of the scheme before I showed the note to Mum, but to my surprise she agreed immediately. Perhaps she thought early exposure to the pleasures of university life might motivate me to work harder at school. (My latest report had alluded to my tendency to doze off in class, a revelation that had caused some raised eyebrows at home.)

'What about your paper round?' was her only objection. 'You can't let people down.' I had inherited the round from Christian when he had moved on to caddying and other more lucrative jobs. I was sure it was the six a.m. start that accounted for my doziness in the afternoons, but there was no alternative until I was old enough for a proper Saturday job in Boots – then the pinnacle of my ambitions.

'I'll get Dawn to stand in for me. She'll do it,' I said, with desperate optimism. It wouldn't have occurred to Mum that Dawn lived too far away to make this viable. In her view a five-mile walk before breakfast was just what teenagers needed. Dawn herself was not so easy to convince, and had to be brought round with exorbitant promises of future favours.

'Christian never once let me down,' the newsagent observed wistfully, when I explained the switch.

'I know,' I said. 'He is perfect.' And she gave me a sharp look, as if to say, *Don't get lippy with me, young lady.*

DAD RAN ME TO PADDINGTON. IT WAS DUSK, AND HE DIDN'T want me getting lost in the underground in the rush hour and missing the train.

'Make sure you're in a carriage with another woman,' he advised, as we said our farewells at the barrier. I don't think he'd set foot on a train since coming back from his National Service. As I opened my purse to show my ticket, he whipped out two ten-pound notes. 'One for you and one for Christian,' he said. 'Give him our love.' His lips skimmed my cheek. He still had hold of my overnight bag, which he'd insisted on carrying from the car, though it weighed next to nothing, and seemed unwilling to relinquish it.

'Well . . . goodbye. Thank you for the money,' I said, when

I'd repossessed the bag. We were in plenty of time, and
my seat was reserved, but the impulse to run for a train
is almost overpowering. All around us people were in a
hurry, rushing home from work and the city. This, and
the mingled roar of arriving and departing trains echoing
up into the great, blackened vaults above, seemed to infect
me with the same sense of urgency, and my feet were
almost twitching with impatience. But I remembered
Thoreau, and with a great effort of will, sauntered the
length of the platform, until I found my carriage, earning some curious looks from my fellow travellers, who
nevertheless appeared to slow down slightly as they passed
through my forcefield.

I gave Dad a last wave as I boarded, then the door
slammed shut behind me and I thought, Yes! I'm alone. My
seat was in a corner of a long carriage, with tables and a
central aisle running the length of the train, and nowhere
for Dad's imagined predators to hide. I put my coat and case
on the luggage rack and slid open the window 'for ventila-
tion without draughts' as the notice advised, with splendid
precision. I kept my handbag on the seat beside me to ward
off other passengers. It contained everything I needed for
the journey: purse, now twenty pounds fatter, palm-sized
sketch pad, pencil, rubber and sharpener, *The Mill on the
Floss* (the next volume on Penny's reading list), and a Mars
bar. There was something immensely comforting about a
well-stocked handbag.

At the first tug of the train's departure, I felt a sudden
surge of euphoria that made my face break into a grin. To
be setting off on a long-anticipated journey, with money in
my purse, and everything good still to come: this was perfect
happiness.

The Mill on the Floss and the sketch pad didn't get a look in until Reading. For the first half-hour I just sat gazing out into the darkness in a daze of contentment. Then I remembered that I ought to be making more of the experience, so I went to the loo, and then the buffet car, where I bought a cup of tea to go with my Mars bar.

Somewhere outside Taunton, while I was struggling to keep my eyes open over *The Mill on the Floss*, because Penny was sure to ask how far I'd got with it, I noticed someone walking up the central aisle. I didn't pay much attention, just enough to absorb that he was wearing a backpack and a Walkman, and holding an apple in his teeth. I put my head down for another assault on the long description of St Ogg's, flicking through the pages in dismay to see how much I'd have to read before I hit on any dialogue, and gradually became aware that the person in the Walkman had stopped beside my table.

Damn. He's after my spare seat, I thought, refusing to oblige him with eye contact, when he tapped me on the shoulder and said, 'Esther?'

I gave a twitch of surprise, bringing up one knee and smacking it on the metal bracket underneath the table, so it was through watering eyes that I recognised the face of our former house-guest, and not-quite-cousin.

'Donovan!' I exclaimed in astonishment. 'What are you doing here?'

Now that he'd taken the apple out of his mouth and I was looking at him properly I could see he hadn't really changed at all: those surprising green-glass eyes were the same, but his features had lost that slightly pretty look they'd had in childhood. He was taller than Christian now, and just as broad – a fully grown bloke, in fact.

'I thought it was you,' he said, dumping my bag on the table and sliding into the seat beside me. A strong smell of cigarettes came off him as he sloughed off his backpack. He pulled down his headphones and there was a loud metallic guzz of synthesisers while he fumbled for the off switch. He glanced around. 'Are you on your own?'

I nodded, nonchalantly. The seasoned traveller. 'I'm going to Exeter to see Christian. He's at the university.'

'Oh, that's nice. What's he up to, then?'

'I don't really know. He never says. He's studying maths and computers. I expect I'll find out more this weekend.'

'What about your mum and dad?'

'They're still the same. You know.'

'Yes.' He grinned at some memory, and then looked serious again. 'They were very kind to me, and I never thanked them properly,' he added. 'Give them my love, won't you?'

'Of course.'

'Actually, better not. It might eventually get back to Mum that you saw me. And then she'll want to know where I was going.'

'Where are you going?'

'To visit a friend near Taunton. I've been staying with Dad and Suzie for half term. Mum thinks I'm still there.' He took a bite of the apple.

'Oh. Why mustn't she know?'

'Because she doesn't *approve*,' he said, in a world-weary tone. I wondered just how degenerate this friend would have to be to deserve the disapproval of someone like Aunty Barbara.

'Is he a criminal?' I asked.

'It's a she, actually,' said Donovan. My eyebrows went up involuntarily. This put rather a different complexion on the matter. 'Mum doesn't like me seeing her, because she's ten years older than me, she's married and she's my teacher.'

'Ah.' I didn't know whether I was supposed to be sympathetic or shocked by this revelation, so instead I said, 'How is your mum?'

'She's all right, actually. When she's not moaning at me about something or other.' He offered me the clean face of his apple, but I shook my head. 'She had a cancer scare two years ago, and although it was really bad at the time, it seems to have completely cured her depression.'

Now I really was shocked. How could he mention his own mother and cancer − even a phantom cancer − in the same breath, with such composure. 'But she's okay now?' I pleaded, faintly.

'Oh yeah. It was nothing major. Just a dodgy mole. She has to keep out of the sun now. She just uses it as an excuse to wear ridiculous hats.'

I couldn't help laughing at this, then felt guilty. 'Does she still do acting?' I asked.

Donovan shook his head. 'Deep down I think she still dreams . . . But she has got a job. She does voice coaching at one of these private stage schools for performing brats. She seems to quite enjoy it.'

'That's good. Mum and Dad will be so pleased. Except I can't tell them I bumped into you,' I remembered.

'No. If you wouldn't mind.' Having finished the apple, core and all, he brought out a packet of ham sandwiches from the backpack and offered me one. It looked rather unappetising: a few moist membranes of translucent gristle in greasy white bread, but I accepted to be friendly. When he had disposed of his half with a few bites, he produced a crushed packet of cigarettes and took one out, twirling it and tapping it on the table, and finally putting it in his mouth unlit. Several passengers, including myself, stiffened visibly. The carriage was a non-smoker.

'It's all right, I'm not going to light it,' Donovan announced cheerfully to the company in general. 'I bet you wish I'd never sat here now, don't you?' he said to me, grinning. I returned his smile but didn't contradict him. 'I nearly didn't,' he went on. 'I had to walk up and down here a couple of times to check it was you because you always had your head in that book.' He picked up *The Mill on the Floss* and started to read the blurb. 'Is it any good?'

'No,' I replied. 'It's really dull. She's supposed to be a literary genius – George Eliot's a she.' For this I was treated to a withering look. 'Well, anyway,' I went on, flustered. 'I can't get into it at all. It's probably just me.'

Donovan opened the book and began to read, his forehead ploughed with concentration. After a minute or two, he slumped forward, snoring. 'No, it's not you. It's completely turgid,' he said, decisively, and before I could stop him he stood up and posted it through the open window, where it was instantly sucked away into the darkness.

He roared with laughter at my look of indignation. 'You can't do that,' I protested. 'That's a Penguin Classic.' This made him laugh all the more. 'And it's not even mine. It's Penny's,' I wailed.

'Who's Penny?'

'Christian's girlfriend. She's trying to civilise me.'

'Are you very uncivilised then?' said Donovan, looking at me with fresh interest.

'I suppose I must be. She has got very high standards.'

'She sounds like a bossy old cow.'

'No, no. She's more like a fairy godmother.' It was hard
to describe Penny's strange brand of perfectionism-by-proxy
to someone who hadn't experienced it.

The train slowed to a halt, and sat, still throbbing and
whining for a few moments before the engine cut out,
leaving us suddenly becalmed. In the blackness outside a
few distant points of light were reflected in the scatter of
raindrops on the window.

'How old are you now?' Donovan asked. I had already
calculated that he must be seventeen or thereabouts.

'Fourteen. Fifteen in June.'

'Hmm. You seem older.'

I expanded like a tulip, then it occurred to me that only
a child would be pleased by such a remark. I began to
consider at what age it might lose the force of a compliment. At twenty-one it would be neutral, I decided. The
tide would start to turn at twenty-four. By twenty-seven it
would be a downright insult. Twenty-seven. The age of
Donovan's still-married teacher 'friend'. This line of thought
led me directly to sex. An image of adulterous liaisons in
the school stock cupboards rose up before me. Perhaps she
was waiting for him now, on the marital counterpane, in
black satin camiknickers, Chinese love balls at the ready,
while her husband was conveniently absent – at a political
rally perhaps, or visiting an elderly aunt.

These reveries were cut short by a sudden exclamation of
annoyance from Donovan; he knelt on the seat and leant
right across me to peer out of the window, cupping his hands
against the glass to block out the light. One knee was pressing against my thigh and his shirt was trailing against my
cheek. Overlaid by the cigarette smoke was another, less
familiar smell: not sweat exactly, but something slightly feral.

'Sorry,' he said, clambering back again. 'Where are we, I wonder?'

The woman opposite lowered her *Catholic Herald*. 'Just outside Taunton,' she said. The lights in the carriage flickered off and on. People were starting to fidget. 'There must be a blockage up ahead. Someone's probably fallen on the track.' She raised her paper again, snapping it open.

Donovan and I exchanged a conspiratorial snigger at this unnecessarily gloomy prediction. He was growing impatient at the unexplained delay, drumming a three-two rhythm on the table-top with his fingertips, shifting about in his seat, and tapping the table leg with one foot. This aimless fiddling led him to my depleted store of amusements. He flipped open my sketch pad and began to browse through the contents. There was a series of drawings of my left hand, a three-pin plug, a bunch of keys, an onion and an apple core, all executed in my obsessively representational style.

'Hey, Esther, these are pretty good,' he said, when he'd finished his examination. 'Are they yours?'

'Yes.'

He nodded, impressed. 'They're brilliant actually. I couldn't do anything like that.'

'My art teacher doesn't think so,' I said, closing the book firmly, experiencing the curious clash of pleasure and anguish that accompanied any appraisal of my artwork, however favourable. 'He says they're too draughstmanlike. They look too much like the object.'

'I thought that was the idea.'

'He wants me to be more free. To put more emotion into them.'

'How emotional can you get about a plug?' he wanted to know.

'I don't know. Sometimes he makes me draw things blind-fold, to stop me getting fixated by detail.'

'Kinky,' said Donovan. 'I'd keep an eye on him if I were you.'

Around us people were becoming restive. A deputation marched up to the front of the train on a quest for information, and returned some minutes later, shrugging shoulders, unenlightened. 'I might as well jump out here and go cross country,' Donovan said, peering again into the rain-lashed darkness. As he said this a ticket inspector appeared at the far end of the carriage, and was immediately besieged by indignant passengers. 'In fact I definitely will,' Donovan said, hastily shouldering his pack. 'Nice meeting you again, Esther. Take care.' He thrust out his hand, and as I went to shake it, a great bolt of static snapped between us and we flinched apart, shaking our fingers and laughing. 'Bloody nylon carpets,' he complained.

'First you throw my book out of the window, then you try to electrocute me,' I grumbled. I watched him open the door a fraction, to check that it was safe to jump; he hesitated for a second, and then he seemed to drop out of sight. Under the disapproving eye of my fellow travellers, I walked across and pulled the door shut, implicated now in his unorthodox departure. I caught sight of him then, scrambling down the embankment and making off across the fields, the orange tip of his cigarette weaving and swaying. The Frys had always been a family for dramatic exits, I remembered.

A moment later the train revived with a whine and a shudder and continued on its way without further incident. I spent the rest of the journey thinking over that encounter with Donovan. I would have liked to tell Christian about it, but at fourteen I held a pledge of secrecy to be sacred.

25

PENNY WAS WAITING FOR ME ON THE PLATFORM AT EXETER St David's. She was wearing an ankle-length Cossack's coat, a knitted hat and a scarf whose fringes skimmed the floor. She fended off my attempt at a hug.

'Don't come near me; I've got a disgusting cold. I've had it for about four months.' Even as she said this she broke into a wheezy cough. Her nose was as red as a radish. It was the first time I had ever seen her looking unglamorous. The rain was still falling as we made our way to the car park.

'Where's Christian?' I asked, disappointed that he hadn't turned out to meet me.

'At home with a hangover,' she replied crisply. 'But don't worry about him. *We're* going to have a lovely time. I hope you've brought plenty of thick jumpers,' she warned, as we set off. 'The flat's like an igloo.'

'I'm used to a cold house,' I reminded her.

'Well, that's true enough,' said Penny, who could seldom

be persuaded to remove her coat in the Old Schoolhouse. She lapsed into a preoccupied silence as she drove us, somewhat erratically, through the city streets. She hasn't even asked about my journey, I thought, glancing at her determined profile. Conversation was, in any case, inhibited by an imposing orchestra of sound from the wipers and fan heater, which were both going at full pelt. In spite of their efforts the windscreen kept steaming up, and every so often Penny would lean forward and scrub a peephole in the glass with one end of her scarf.

In a few minutes we had left the terraced cottages of the suburbs behind, and were into open countryside. The headlights combed the dripping hedgerows through a glitter of raindust.

Presently Penny burst out: 'Oh, Christian's such an arsehole!'

'Why? What's he done?' I said, completely taken aback.

'It's too complicated to explain,' she replied, taking the deep breath required for such an explanation nevertheless. 'It goes back to, oh, I don't know, your mum probably.'

'Mum? What's she got to do with it?'

'It's his attitude to money, to everything. He's such a bad *planner*. I keep having to bail him out. I shouldn't be saying this to you – I know you won't hear a word against him – but it's all come to a head this weekend, and you've arrived in the thick of it, and it can't be helped.' And then she slewed the car into a passing place and burst into tears.

'Don't cry, Penny,' I pleaded, handing her a clump of tissues from the dashboard. 'It'll be all right.' It's an unsettling experience, comforting your mentor. I didn't enjoy it at all. Suddenly the prospects for the weekend ahead looked grim. I was there not as a guest now, but a potential mediator in some simmering dispute. The contents of my stomach began to coagulate with anxiety. I swallowed hard. 'You're not going to split up, are you?' I asked.

Penny applied the tissue to her eyes and then nose, and shook her head. 'I shouldn't think so. It's just a hiccup.'

'Would it be better if I went home?' This was an offer without much substance. I knew she wouldn't pack me back off to London on my own, but I wanted some reassurance that they weren't planning a marathon row in my presence.

'No, of course you can't go,' she sniffed. 'This was going to be your special weekend. I've got us tickets for Tom Robinson at the Union tonight, but I don't feel like it now. Do you?'

'Not if you don't,' I said. Whoever he was.

'Mind you, I don't particularly want to go home either. It's too cold. Shall we find a nice pub with a log fire, just the two of us?'

'Okay,' I said. The idea seemed to cheer her up so I didn't dare oppose it. I couldn't help wondering what Christian would make of our non-arrival. Would he mind, or even notice? How, come to that, did he manage to be nursing a hangover at seven o'clock in the evening? Was this evidence of the fabled debauchery of undergraduates, or just a fib on Penny's part to excuse his absence? I didn't have the courage to probe while we were skidding along waterlogged country lanes in a blackout. I thought anything contentious had better wait.

About half a mile further on the headlights picked out a painted sign propped against a tree at the roadside. *The Wheatsheaf – 100yds. Real Ale. Bar Meals.* An arrow pointed through a gap in the hedge not much wider than the car. At the end of the narrow track was the welcoming sight of a squat stone pub with thatched roof and golden lights in every window. In spite of its location it was fairly busy, but I'd noticed before that Penny had a gift for being served. The crowd around the bar seemed to fall away to let her through, and within minutes of her arrival we had secured a corner table beside the inglenook, and the barman had made her up a hot toddy to her exact specifications: juice of one lemon, one measure of single malt, one tablespoon of clear honey, water just off the boil.

As she unswaddled herself from her scarf and coat, she began to lay out her case against Christian.

'It started with this idea that we'd go to the States this summer,' she said, removing her woolly hat to reveal hair ravaged by static. 'We both applied to go and work in one of these summer camps. I got all the forms and did all the research, tarted up my CV a bit, you know. We thought we'd do two months at one of the camps and then go travelling for a month. Well, last week the letters came: I've got an interview; Christian hasn't. I don't know what to do. It's causing so much bad feeling between us.'

'Why didn't they want him?' It was the first time Christian had failed at anything: it was inexplicable.

'I don't know. I thought they'd snap him up, with all his sporting achievements. He'd make a great athletics coach, or whatever. I've got a feeling he didn't do a very good application. You see, he's a bit lazy about some things. I spent ages on my personal statement.' She gave a guilty laugh. 'I had to embroider a little, but they allow for that. I think Christian wanted me to do his application for him, and when I wouldn't, he just dashed it off in a hurry. I refuse to mother him. I can't stand men when they go all helpless.'

There was a pause as a waitress brought over the two bowls of treacle sponge and custard that Penny had ordered as an antidote to despondency and foul weather. 'Pudding's so comforting isn't it?' she said, taking up her spoon. 'I can face almost anything on a full stomach.'

'Christian can't really blame you for being selected,' I said, when we'd fortified ourselves with a few mouthfuls of the elixir. 'I mean, it's not really your fault.' Here I was, taking sides already.

'Exactly,' Penny agreed. 'But Christian's now hinting that he doesn't want me to go. He says if it had been the other way round he wouldn't go without me.'

'Didn't you ever discuss the possibility that only one of you might be chosen?' I asked.

Penny shook her head. 'I'm such an eternal optimist. I never even considered failure.'

'Wouldn't you miss him if you were apart for two months?' This, after all, had been the basis of their decision to forgo their first choices of university.

'Yes, of course. But I'm in an impossible situation. If I go, he'll probably take up with someone else, and if I don't, I'll feel all bitter and resentful. And come the summer, I'll say let's go to France or something, and Christian will say he can't because he hasn't got any money – he's permanently broke – so he'll spend all summer working to pay off his overdraft and I'll hardly see him anyway.' She threw down her spoon. 'I can't eat this, it's too sickly.'

'Oh dear,' I said. If even pudding had failed to console then the outlook was bleak indeed. I started to eat faster: I had a feeling Penny might suddenly decide it was time to leave. 'I'm sure you'll think of a solution,' I said, encouragingly.

'There is no solution,' the eternal optimist replied. 'It's one of those situations where a compromise doesn't exist. One of us will have to back down.'

As I disposed of my last mouthful of custard, she stood up. 'Come on. Let's go back to the igloo. Don't look so scared. We won't start shouting and throwing things at each other. Not in front of a visitor.'

TWENTY MINUTES LATER WE PULLED UP ON THE PAVED forecourt of a large Edwardian house, which stood by itself at the edge of a village. The ground floor was disfigured by a glass and aluminium porch, topped by an illuminated sign saying: VETERINARY PRACTICE. Apart from a dull glow from the curtained dormer windows the house was in darkness. The top flat was reached by a wobbly wooden fire escape at the back of the building.

'Mind the turds,' Penny instructed, as we picked our way across the wet grass. The rain had stopped while we were in the pub and all but a few shreds of cloud had blown away. Above us the sky was a velvety black, undimmed by the pollution of street lamps, and a hail of brilliant stars hung as if just out of reach.

The fire door at the top of the steps led directly into a shabby kitchen, semi-lit by a bare pendant bulb. There was unwashed crockery on the table and in the sink, and the lino was tacky underfoot. I instantly felt at home. A tall, skinny girl in jeans and leg-warmers and a long, hairy pullover stood at the gas stove, stirring something in a saucepan. She turned as we came in. She had long feathery hair and dark shadows under her eyes. 'Oh, you're back,' she said neutrally. Although her voice and movements were languid I could detect tension.

'Yes, we went to the Wheatsheaf. It's quite nice. Have you ever been there?' said Penny, taking off her coat and throwing it over a chair.

'No, I haven't got a car,' the girl said pointedly.

'This is Esther,' said Penny, refusing to acknowledge the last remark. 'This is Martina.'

'Oh hullo,' said Martina, dismissing me with a glance. 'What happened to Tom Robinson?'

'I didn't feel like it.'

'I would have gone,' said Martina, turning back to the stove.

'Well, go then,' said Penny, dropping her keys on the worktop. 'Take the car.'

'It's too late now,' Martina replied. She stopped stirring and inverted the saucepan over a plate. A clod of scrambled egg flopped out. She cleared a space on the table amidst the debris of former meals and began to eat, slowly and without relish.

'No it isn't,' Penny persisted, looking at her watch. 'Bands never start on time.'

Martina shrugged. 'By the time I've got ready.'

'It's up to you,' said Penny, and recognising that she was not to be persuaded, changed the subject. 'Is Christian in?'

'Yes.' This through a mouthful of egg. 'Wart's here again.'

'Oh? Well he can't stay. The sofa's taken.' Penny propelled me towards the doorway through which I could see a narrow hall, obstructed by a wooden drying frame hung with clothes. 'She'd no intention of going out,' Penny whispered, when we were through the door. 'She just wanted to make a point.' As we passed the washing, she gave one of the socks a squeeze. 'I think it's wetter than when I put it there,' she said.

She certainly hadn't exaggerated about the gnawing coldness in the flat. Eddies of icy air swirled up through gaps in the floorboards to add an extra dimension to the frigid atmosphere; the wallpaper was clammy to the touch. I couldn't envisage getting undressed for bed: I still didn't feel tempted to take my coat off.

Penny took my bag and deposited it in one of the rooms off the hallway beside a double bed, which appeared to have been only recently vacated: the duvet and blankets were flung back to reveal a body-shaped depression in the sheet. I couldn't help noticing that without the ministrations of Maria, the Portuguese home help, Penny's living conditions were considerably less civilised, and took some comfort from the fact.

In the sitting room, which was no less seedy than the rest of the flat, Christian and (presumably) Wart were sitting cross-legged on the world's baldest carpet, playing cards. In the corner a paraffin heater was pumping out its nauseous perfume along with a welcome measure of warmth. The room's furnishings consisted of sofa, one hardbacked chair, a wicker armchair, hi-fi, tile-topped coffee table, and a few sickly pot plants. A collection of books and records sat on an arrangement of brick and plank shelving.

When he saw me Christian leapt up and gave me a kiss. Wart stayed put. 'We're here,' Penny said superfluously.

They both stood awkwardly: two people in the middle of a quarrel that has lost its momentum but not yet been resolved. After what seemed, to an embarrassed observer like me, a long time, Christian put out one arm and Penny went to him for a hug. A truce.

'Hello, Wart, what are you doing here?' said Penny, when they had disengaged.

'Hello, Princess. Just being sociable. Aren't you going to introduce me?' He nodded in my direction. Even though he was on the floor I could see that he was tall, with big shoulders and arms, like a rugby player. He had a slight gut, which hung over the top of his jeans and rested against his shirt. His hair was short – aggressively so in my view. There was nothing attractive about him. And yet.

'This is my little sister, Esther,' Christian obliged. 'So just watch your filthy mouth when she's around.'

Wart held out a hand which turned out to be surprisingly soft when I reluctantly shook it. 'Welcome to our humble abode,' he said, baring his teeth at me.

'This isn't your humble abode,' Penny reminded him. 'How are you getting back?'

'I thought I'd just crash here on the sofa. I can't cycle home because I haven't got any lights on my bike.'

'Well you can't,' said Penny. 'We need the sofa tonight. We've got a visitor.'

'Esther can have Lynn's room. She's gone home for the weekend,' said Christian.

'That's settled then.' Wart beamed.

'Hmph,' said Penny, outmanoeuvred.

Christian turned to me. 'How are you anyway, Pest? Look, make yourself at home.'

I took my coat off and sat down with a jolt. What I had taken to be a sofa was in fact a park bench with a carpet thrown over it. Christian sat beside me. 'What have you been doing since I last saw you?'

'Nothing.'

'Oh. Okay. How are Mum and Dad?'

'Mum's going frantic looking after Grandpa. He keeps

escaping. Dad's doing loads of extra stuff at church because
of the interregnum. He's been doing a lot of funerals.'

'Nice,' said Christian.

'I didn't know your dad was a vicar,' said Wart.

'He's not. He's a chaplain at one of Her Majesty's prisons,' Christian replied. 'You'll probably get to meet him in
his professional capacity one day.'

'Ha ha,' said Wart.

I suddenly remembered the tenner. 'A present from Dad,'
I said, handing it over. Christian took it from me and gave
it a wistful look before passing it solemnly to Wart, who
put it in his back pocket.

Penny raised her eyes to heaven. 'I think I'll go to bed
if that's all right,' she said. 'Today is the one hundred and
twentieth day of my cold, if anybody's interested.' No one
was. 'Shall I show you where you're sleeping, Esther?'

I was reluctant to leave the warmth of the sitting room
for the more bracing climate of the bedrooms, but the heady
fumes of the paraffin heater were making me feel queasy so
I followed her out.

'Goodnight,' called Christian.

'Goodnight Bruv,' I replied. I don't know why. I never
called him Bruv at home. I suppose I was trying to claim
some rights of kinship in these alien surroundings.

In the enduring chaos of the kitchen, Penny made me a
hot waterbottle, which she wrapped in a pillowcase. This
maternal gesture gave me the courage to ask her to leave
the bathroom light on overnight. I knew the darkness here
would be absolute.

Lynn's bedroom, a wedge-shaped nook under the eaves,
had an uncurtained skylight and a narrow bed, which let
out twangs of protest whenever I made the minutest adjust-

ment to my position. Someone, presumably the landlord, had attempted to redecorate the room without bothering to move the furniture: the gloss on the skirting board stopped where the bed began.

I had lagged myself for sleep in pants, socks, pyjamas, sweatshirt, and Lynn's dressing gown, and burrowed down into Christian's Snowdon survivor's sleeping-bag, clutching the hot waterbottle to my chest like a life jacket. Through the wall I could hear the murmur of Martina's radio. I lay there for what seemed like hours, afraid to go to sleep in case someone switched the bathroom light off, gazing at the cold stars through the skylight, and thinking, If this is university, thank God I'm thick. In truth I felt a little home-sick, though at home I only wanted to be with Christian. At some point I remember realising that apart from my face I was actually warm, and then it was morning, and Penny was standing over me with tea and toast.

'I'VE SAID I WON'T GO TO AMERICA,' PENNY SAID, AS WE crunched across the shingle on Sidmouth beach. It only struck me later that this didn't have quite the same force as, 'I won't go to America'. Down on the red sand, beyond which a rusty sea boiled and churned, Christian and Wart, who had somehow managed to inveigle his way into the outing, were playing Frisbee. Every so often Christian would skim it in our direction, and Penny would deflect it with a gloved hand, sending it clattering across the stones.

'So is everything back to normal with you and Christian?' I asked. There had certainly been no repeat of the strained atmosphere on my arrival.

'I suppose so. We've kissed and made up, if that's what you mean.'

'Good. I knew you would.' As if Christian had heard us, he came charging up the beach, floundering over the stones, and hoisted Penny over his shoulder in a fireman's lift. He went running back towards the water's edge, ignoring her shrieks, and pretended to throw her in, urged on by Wart, before depositing her back on the sand. She rejoined me, brushing herself down and removing and pocketing one of the brass buttons from her Cossack's coat, which had come loose in the affray. She didn't enjoy horseplay of any kind. It wasn't civilised.

'I don't like Wart,' I said, when I'd allowed her a moment or two to convalesce. I had bumped into him coming out of the bathroom that morning. He was wearing nothing but a pair of briefs – a piece of wilful exhibitionism, given the temperature – and was, in my view, unnecessarily hairy.

'He's an acquired taste,' said Penny. 'He grows on you.'

'Perhaps that's why he's called Wart.'

Penny tittered at this. 'No, it's short for John Wharton-Smith. It just happens to suit.'

'Christian seems to like him.' The two of them were still larking about on the sand, chucking the Frisbee nearer and nearer to the incoming waves. Presently, Christian executed a fiendish throw, which curved gently out to sea at shoulder height, just out of Wart's reach. He lunged for the catch, missed, and landed ankle deep in water, swearing lavishly.

'Oh, Christian's so easy going, he likes everybody,' said Penny, as though this was a serious flaw. 'Mind you, he owes Wart so much money, he has to be nice to him.'

This sort of information about Christian, so casually delivered, always made me uncomfortable. It was like yesterday's allusion to hangovers. There was so much I didn't know about him. I immediately began to worry. Why did he borrow so much?' In Mum and Dad's moral universe, poverty was a virtue, but debt was definitely a vice.

'What does he spend it all on?' I wondered aloud.

'Food, drink, me, going out,' said Penny, unaware of the anxiety she'd caused. 'The pool table in the Union must account for a fair few quid.'

'Mum and Dad will be horrified.'

'Well, don't tell them. It's not their problem; it's his. He's a big boy now. He'll have to sort it out.'

IN THE AFTERNOON PENNY HAD A CRAVING FOR SOMETHING sweet, so she drove us to Newton Poppleford, where there was reputed to be a tea shop serving unlimited clotted cream. We sat at a table by the window and ate warm scones and home-made jam with our bottomless crock of cream. We drank Earl Grey out of bone china, like a vicarage tea party, and Penny and I laughed at the sight of Wart holding the dainty cup and saucer in his huge hands.

When it was time to leave I whipped out my purse to stop Christian paying, but Wart insisted it was his treat, and no one offered any resistance. He's not so bad after all, I thought, though I had to revise my opinion on the way home, when he fell asleep next to me in the back and kept keeling over onto my lap. When I had pushed him off for the third time I began to suspect him of shamming, so I gave him a sharp prod in the side, and he sat up, grunting and twitching in a pantomime of rude awakening. I glared at him to let him know I wasn't fooled, and he replied with a wink.

'What's that smell?' Penny demanded, as we neared Plymtree. We all sniffed experimentally. She was right: there was a certain pungency in the air. It was soon traced to

Wart's wet socks and shoes, now beginning to steam in the heat of the car.

'I'll drop you home shall I, Wart?' Penny offered.

'It's a bit out of your way.'

'That's no problem,' said Penny, taking the Exeter turning.

'Only I've left my bike at your place,' Wart remembered. 'I'd better come back with you and pick it up.'

Penny swung the car round without comment. I couldn't work out whether she liked or loathed him.

Of course when we arrived at the flat Wart made no move to depart, but trooped up the fire exit behind us. Once indoors, he took off his shoes and socks and balanced them on top of the paraffin heater, then settled down in the wicker armchair with a can of Guinness and was soon asleep.

It was left to the rest of us – me, Penny, Martina and Christian – to make the place presentable for the party planned for the evening. Even the rattle of grit going up the Hoover failed to rouse Wart from his slumbers. It was only when Christian, who was trying to shift furniture from the sitting room into the bedrooms, bellowed in his ear that he got up, complaining about his cold feet, and shambled off to the bathroom.

His popularity took a further dive an hour later when Penny discovered that he had hogged all the hot water. She and Martina, tired and filthy from their recent skirmish with the kitchen, were incoherent with rage. It was decided that they would drive all the way into Exeter and use the showers on campus rather than endure the torture of cold baths, so they collected towels and washbags and flounced out of the flat, taking me with them.

26

MY FIRST PARTY: THE EVENT FOR WHICH I HAD SPENT YEARS memorising the complete lyrics of Kool and the Gang, rehearsing dance routines to the Top Forty in front of Dawn's mirror, and experimenting with the eyeshadow testers in Boots.

Now, as I stood in the stripped and cheerless sitting room, looking at the relief work of ripples in the carpet, and the patches of unpainted wall revealed by the furniture removals, waiting for it to begin, I suddenly started to doubt the relevance of my preparations.

Christian and Wart were tinkering with the amplifier, which was misbehaving; Penny was distributing bowls of peanuts and dishes of gold-tipped cocktail cigarettes in shades of turquoise and pink, while Martina chopped up carrots and celery for the dip – a salty concoction of tinned cream and onion soup powder. They had originally planned a more ambitious menu, but this had become a casualty of the protracted bathing arrangements.

The dress I had brought from home, I now saw, was all wrong. It was a red velvet shift, one of Penny's unworn castoffs, which made me look as shapely as a pillar box, and was far too dressy for the occasion. Both Penny and Martina were in jeans and knee-length chunky knits. Fortunately Penny came to my rescue and lent me a long black mohair sweater, which offered me some protection from hypothermia and ridicule.

Every so often the speakers would give a loud crackle and a burst of Bruce Springsteen would erupt into the flat, making the windows tremble in their frames. It was ten o' clock and there was no sign of any guests. I wandered into the kitchen to see if I could help. Martina was warming her hands at the hob: all four gas rings blazed blue. Through the glass of the back door I could see a few grey flakes beginning to fall.

'Snow,' Penny groaned. 'I hope that doesn't put people off.'

As she said this there was the clubbing of feet on the fire escape and half a dozen people erupted noisily through the door, followed by a flurry of snowflakes. They deposited plastic carrier bags of drink on the table before joining Martina at the hob to thaw out. With the confidence of an established group they seemed to take command of the place, and their smoke and shouted conversation soon filled the room. No one remarked on my presence.

'This is Christian's little sister, Esther,' Penny announced to the backs of the closed circle. A few heads turned, politely, before their attention was claimed again by the kitchen door opening to admit fresh arrivals. For the first time it occurred to me that just being Christian's sister

wasn't the guarantee of social triumph that I'd always
supposed.

From the sitting room came an explosion of music: the
amplifier was fixed. Martina was handing out polystyrene
cups, urging people to help themselves to drink. Apart
from slimline tonic, an accompaniment to the bottle of
vodka donated by Wart, there wasn't much provision for
non-drinkers. I tried some white wine, which smelled like
the chemistry lab at school, medicinal and sour, and some
red wine, which was worse. It was a mystery to me how
the sweet and inoffensive grape could have been responsible. To take the taste away I had some of Martina's onion
dip: it was surprisingly nice, and reminded me that I hadn't
eaten since Newton Poppleford. Mealtimes here tended
not to be observed. Since my arrival I'd only had that
bowl of treacle pudding in the pub, toast and marmalade,
and a cream scone. Craving salt, I went into the sitting
room, ate a handful of peanuts, and felt much better. Bruce
Springsteen was roaring, pertinently, about hungry hearts.
Beneath my feet the floor throbbed in time to the bass.
I felt myself gripped by the heightened self-awareness that
often comes from feeling lonely in a crowd. I used to get
it in the playground at Underwood. It's a sensation of
separateness that, if unchecked, develops into a complete
defamiliarisation with your own body. My hands were
strange, awkward appendages; my legs twitched as though
I'd forgotten how to stand comfortably. I had realised that
I wasn't going to enjoy myself at the simple, immediate
level, but I'd hoped to derive some pleasure from the
detached observation of an unenjoyable experience. This
strategy wasn't working either.

Christian must have seen me looking pained, as he came

over and put a brotherly arm around my shoulder. 'Are you
okay?' he shouted in my ear. I nodded. 'Enjoying yourself?'
The smile I gave him in response must have been transpar-
ently false, as he laughed and said, 'You're bored,' shaking
his head at my half-hearted denials. 'Sorry,' he said. 'Parties
are no fun when you're sober. I'll make it up to you.
Tomorrow we'll do whatever you like.' And he ruffled my
hair. This scrap of human sympathy worked to break the
spell, and I was all right again, inhabiting my body with
only average awkwardness.

Penny, besieged by admirers, waved me over and
performed bellowed introductions, but the music proved too
loud to sustain anything but the most elementary conversation. One of the girls, whose hair was the colour of burnt
sienna straight from the tube, took pity on me and drew me
aside into the hall, where it was quieter. She was short and
fat, and wore a long tasselled skirt and smock top. Her feet
were small and planted well apart for balance, and her ankles,
just visible between the tassels, were slim. It didn't seem
feasible that they could meet up with that great bulk of flesh
around her middle. 'Is this your first visit?' she shouted, staring at me with smoky eyes. I nodded. 'I expect it's a bit over-
whelming,' she went on. 'It's probably put you off university
for good.'

'Yes it has,' I agreed, and she blinked, affronted. I couldn't
be bothered to explain that on the contrary I was under-
whelmed. I'd formed a romantic view, no doubt from television, that universities were rather like castles, with log
fires, oak panelling and sun-dappled quads. Reality, as usual,
had a more dismal cast.

She asked me if I knew the area, and if I had been taken
to this or that beauty spot, to all of which I answered no.

I sensed my interviewer's stamina beginning to evaporate, and was about to release her when she was rescued by one of her friends and rejoined her crowd with relief. '. . . blood out of a stone,' I heard her say during a break in the music, and felt betrayed.

There was no sign of Christian anywhere, and Penny was locked in an intense conversation with a bearded man in a denim jacket, who turned out to be her tutor, so I took refuge in Lynn's room for a while. Christian had used it as a repository for some of the sitting room furniture, and the park bench was now stacked on the bed. I sat on this precarious structure for a while listening to the distant thump of the music, and wondered if Christian would notice my absence, but ten minutes passed and no one came looking. I thought I might chase away one form of boredom with another and knock off a chapter of *The Mill on the Floss*, then I remembered that Donovan had thrown it out of the train window. There was nothing for it but to rejoin the party. In the sitting room, Penny was still being talked at very earnestly by the bearded man, her face wearing the pinched expression of someone straining to lip-read.

As I stepped into the hallway Martina's door opened and Christian emerged, followed a moment or two later by Martina, whose make-up was smudged, from crying perhaps, or some other interference. He gave the back of her neck a reassuring squeeze and they parted.

'What were you doing in there?' I asked, catching him up in the kitchen, where he was helping himself to bitter from a cask.

He frowned and shook his head, indicating that I should keep my voice down. 'Comforting her. She's a mess.'

'What's wrong with her?'

'Oh, everything. She's anorexic for a start. Hadn't you noticed?' I had of course noticed that the frame on which those whiskery sweaters hung was abnormally thin, but hadn't thought to give the condition its name.

'Why did she get like that?'

'I don't know. She's had it for years, off and on. She had this boyfriend she was really keen on, and he dumped her about six months ago and she's just found out that his new girlfriend's up the duff. She's a bit of a depressive actually. I feel sorry for her.'

'Penny doesn't like her,' I said, with a sudden flash of insight.

Christian took a swig of beer, leaving a crescent of foam on his upper lip. 'They used to be good friends last year,' he said. 'But they've had a bit of a falling out lately.'

'Why?'

'This and that. Penny's not very sympathetic to other people's weaknesses. She thinks Martina's trying it on. Which she probably is. Anyway, shh,' he added, as we were joined at the kitchen table by Wart and someone in a gorilla mask.

'He thought it was fancy dress,' Wart explained, and then pointed at the polystyrene cup I was still clutching and burst out laughing. There was a large bite-shaped piece missing from the rim. Could I conceivably have swallowed it?

'Hungry, were you?' he asked.

'Yes, starving,' I said. 'If I don't get some proper food soon I'll start on the furniture.'

Christian and the gorilla had departed to rescue Penny. 'I could make you some toast,' Wart suggested. 'I don't suppose there'll be anything much in here,' he went on, yanking open the fridge door to release a gust of sour, fishy air. On Martina's (labelled) shelf were a couple of natural yoghurts and a stick of floppy celery. The remaining contents were three cartons of milk, a cup of congealed fat with a piece of bacon rind sticking out like a drowned hand, and several open tins of tuna. Wart slammed the door in disgust. 'Toast or nothing,' he said, producing the two ends of a wholemeal loaf from the bread bin and posting them into the mouth of the toaster. 'You were after a drink, too, weren't you? Try this,' he went on, handing me a fresh cup of what looked like Coke. I took a tentative sip. It was Coke all right, but with a warm aftertaste.

'What's in it?' I asked suspiciously.

'Vodka,' Wart admitted. 'Just a trace. Not enough to pickle a flea.'

That onion dip had given me a violent thirst, so I took a few remedial gulps and immediately felt fantastically light-headed and cheerful. Some of the other guests were starting to take an interest in my toast, which had sprung up, a little charred around the edges, but smelling malty and delicious.

'Actually, I could do with some food,' one girl said, advancing.

'Well, you should have eaten before you came, then, shouldn't you?' said Wart, spreading the margarine in two swift strokes and stacking the slices on a plate. 'Come on,' he said, steering me through the crowd. 'Let's find somewhere to sit down.'

We ended up in Lynn's room, balanced on the park bench, with the plate of toast between us. It seemed much wobblier this time, since that Coke-with-a-trace-of-Vodka, and much funnier too. Just above our heads the skylight was scattered with frilly snow.

'I didn't like you earlier,' I said. 'But I do now.'

'I grow on people,' he replied.

'That's what Penny said.'

'Did she? Did she say that?' Wart seemed genuinely delighted. He started to tell me a long, involved story about some local scandal concerning a yachtswoman and her transsexual lover who were accused of trying to bump off the husband. His arm was along the back of the bench, and he kept reaching out to tuck my hair behind my ear to stop it screening my face. 'There were pictures in the paper of the two of them wearing long cloaks and boots, like a pair of witches. It was all as kinky as hell.' Stroke, stroke, went his fingertips in my hair. It wasn't a pleasant feeling: I wanted to give my scalp a good scratch.

'I suppose you've got a boyfriend back home,' he suddenly said, squinting at me with bloodshot eyes.

'Yes,' I said, marvelling at how shamelessly the lie slid out.

'Oh yeah. What's he called?'

'Donovan.' Before I could stop myself I'd blurted out the first name that came into my head. I froze, appalled. Where had that come from? Why hadn't I stuck to something plain? Matthew, Mark, Luke and John. Bill and Ben the Flowerpot Men. What was I thinking of? To invent a boyfriend was one thing, but to cast a real person in the role was quite another. Suppose Wart dropped his name into the conversation in Christian's hearing. What an amateur I was in the art of deceit. Two lies in and I was already squirming.

'Unusual name,' Wart was saying. He hummed a few bars of 'Catch the Wind'. He had at least stopped fiddling with my ear.

'You're a nice girl, Esther,' he said, yawning extravagantly. I realised he was completely drunk. 'You're natural, and that's nice. You don't bother about making an impression.'

'I do bother,' I protested. 'I'm just no good at it.'

The door opened, coming to rest against the back of the wicker chair, and Christian stood there, swaying slightly. Or perhaps it was me that was swaying. He looked rather disconcerted to see me and Wart installed on our perch under the eaves.

'Oh *there* you are. He hasn't been trying any funny business, has he?' he asked, frowning at Wart.

Wart held up his hands, a picture of aggrieved innocence.

'Would you challenge him to a duel if he had?' I asked.

'No, but I'd kick his arse,' Christian replied. The image of Christian getting physical on my behalf was so appealing that I almost wished some 'funny business' had occurred.

'I made her some toast,' Wart said, reproachfully. 'Since you neglected to feed her.'

'We've been having a nice cosy chat,' I added.

'Yes, Esther's been telling me about—'

'I think I'd like to go to bed now,' I said, hastily. 'But my room seems to be full of furniture.'

'You can sleep in our bed,' Christian offered. 'With Penny.'

'Where will you sleep?'

'I'll be all right. When everyone's gone I'll shift the stuff out of here and crash on Lynn's bed. Don't worry about me.'

I thought of messed-up Martina on the other side of the wall, who needed comforting behind closed doors. Christian and I faced each other, tipsily. 'No, it's all right,' I said. 'I'm not tired any more.'

* * *

WHEN I AWOKE, IN LYNN'S BED, I COULD TELL JUST FROM THE
smothered quality of the silence, even before I had looked
up at the blind white skylight, that there would be thick
snow outside. I was the first up – a legacy of the paper round.
I knew there would be nothing to do but clearing up party
wreckage, so I had a bath, dressed, and got back into bed
until I heard sounds of stirring.

After a breakfast of coffee, Christian and I took a tray
and a couple of bin bags and walked up to the woods, where
there was a good slope for sledging. The girls had opted to
stay behind and tidy up. Penny was planning to give Martina
some counselling while they worked, and had in any case
a limited appetite for the sort of childish fun that might
lead to dishevelment. Martina, whose condition made her
extra-sensitive to the cold, couldn't be tempted outdoors,
but lent me her boots instead. Wart was still asleep on the
park bench, wrapped in the piece of carpet, like a tramp.

Christian and I waded across the field, carving deep
furrows as we went. The sky was a clear, Alpine blue; fat
globes of snow hung from the trees' bare branches, and the
sunlight was hard and bright. Christian, who was looking
less than handsome with a woolly skull-cap, red eyes and
day-old stubble, began to whistle through his teeth – his
normal silence-filler. Instead of climbing the stile he tried
to vault the wire fence, catching his foot in the top strand
and pitching himself into the drift on the other side. He
staggered to his feet, laughing and spitting. 'Perfect hangover cure,' he said, shaking himself like a dog.

'Alan Fry chucked himself off a balcony into a snowdrift
once, to get away from Aunty Barbara,' I remembered. The
image had stayed with me over the years. Every so often,
as now, it surfaced.

'I don't blame him,' said Christian. 'I'd have done the same.'

'Why?'

'She's one of those women who have to make a drama out of everything. They can't just get on with things normally. They have to turn everything into some sort of emotional banquet. A lot of women are like that. Especially round here.'

'I'm not,' I said. 'And neither's Mum.'

'No, but she's insane in other ways. Penny has occasional tendencies. Martina – she's a ravenous emotional cannibal.' This made me laugh. 'I'm starting to get hungry,' added Christian, quick to tire of female psychology. He packed a snowball in his gloved hands and bowled it into the trees, where it detonated an explosion of snow and startled magpies. 'We'll go to the Wheel for lunch. They do this awesome beef and Guinness pie.'

'Won't that be expensive?'

Christian shrugged carelessly.

'Penny says you owe Wart a fortune.'

'He might let me off,' said Christian. 'His parents are loaded. The bank, on the other hand, probably won't . . .' He grinned at my stricken face. 'I'm not worried. I'll pay it off one day. In the meantime, we've got to live.'

We'd reached the top of the slope by now; some kids with proper toboggans must have beaten us to it as the snow there was already disfigured with tracks. We chose an unspoilt section, free from hazards like tree stumps, and took it in turns to ride the tray to the bottom. The bin bags proved faster, but less comfortable, offering no protection against protruding twigs, and were soon in shreds.

The sight of Christian, age twenty, five foot ten,

bombing downhill crouched on a plastic tray, was to me both hilarious and poignant. We'll never do this again, I thought. Already my enjoyment was tainted by nostalgia.

'Don't mention the money business to Mum and Dad,' Christian said to me, at one of our changeovers. He'd obviously been thinking about it, in spite of his professed indifference. 'You know they're completely weird about money. It's a generation thing.'

'I don't think it is. It's just them.' By way of example I told him about the latest eccentricities at the Old Schoolhouse. Just after Christmas Grandpa Percy had opened the front door to two men claiming to be buying antiques. With his blessing they had loaded the mahogany card table, an oak Bible box, and a walnut writing desk into their van, along with a number of non-antique items: camera, jewellery and radio, and driven off, waving cheerfully, never to be seen again. Mum and Dad had decided that most of these items couldn't or needn't be replaced, and then had qualms that the generous insurance payout had therefore been dishonestly acquired, and promptly donated it to Oxfam.

'I wish they'd donated it in my direction,' Christian grumbled. 'Isn't charity supposed to begin at home?'

'I don't think it actually says that in the Bible,' I said. It struck me that for children of a chaplain we weren't especially religious. Since Dad was conducting services at the prison on Sundays and was not around to supervise our church-going, we seldom went. And Mum, with her unique relationship with God, would only enter a church when it was empty. In fact, now that I came to think of it, I didn't know whether Christian even believed in God any more. I thought I'd ask him some time. Not now, though, as I didn't want to be accused of getting heavy. Besides, in these surroundings, where it was possible to see the hand of a Creator, you might get a false reading.

Suddenly from the woods behind us came a terrific crashing, and almost before we'd realised what was happening, a riderless horse erupted from between the trees, ears back, stirrups flying, not ten yards from where we'd been standing, and galloped away down the slope, churning the snow under its hooves. Christian and I were still recovering from the shock of this apparition, when a woman in jodhpurs and boots and a padded anorak came half-jogging, half-limping out of the woods and, giving us a polite nod, set off in pursuit of the horse, which had skittered to a halt in the corner of the field.

To add to the unreality of the scene, Christian now pointed in the direction we had come: there, in the distance, floundering towards us and waving frantically, was the figure of Wart, absurdly underdressed in jeans and a shirt.

'Why hasn't he got a coat on?' Christian said, and then it dawned on us, rather belatedly, that he was not coming to join in the fun, but rather to summon us to the scene of an emergency, and we began to run to meet him, in great leaps and strides.

'Martina's set fire to herself,' Wart said, panting, as we came to a standstill a few feet apart. 'She's all right, but Penny thinks she needs to go to Casualty.'

'What – you mean deliberately?' Christian asked.

'I don't think so. She was just standing too close to the hob.'

It seemed that Martina had been warming her hands over the gas jets when the trailing whiskers of her mohair sleeves had caught fire. Her panicked attempts to beat out the flames had only spread them, and in trying to strip off the now melting jumper, she had managed to set light to her hair. Penny, hearing her shrieks, had rushed in and smothered her with the nearest suitable item to hand, which happened to be Wart's coat.

When we arrived back at the flat Martina was sitting on a kitchen chair in her bra and knickers, wrapped in a duvet and shivering violently. One side of her long hair had perished to shoulder level. Even now, as she fingered the scorched ends, more of it crumbled away. The longer, undamaged side was dripping wet. Penny had made her stand in the bath while she hosed her down with cold water from the shower. 'To take the heat out of the burns,' Penny explained, deaf to her screams.

'I'm all right really,' Martina said, through chattering teeth. 'It's just my hair.'

'What about burns?' Christian asked, kneeling down and taking one of her long skinny hands in his. Martina allowed the duvet to slip down to allow for inspection of her injuries. There was a collective intake of breath, which had to be passed off as anxiety over her burns – few and not too alarming – but which in fact was a response to the sight of her bony torso, with its jutting collarbone and well-defined ribs.

'Not too bad,' said Penny, with forced brightness.

'Painful as hell, though, I bet,' said Wart.

'I think she should go to Casualty anyway, just in case,' Penny suggested. Martina flinched. 'I don't want to go to hospital,' she said. 'I hate hospitals. They freak me out.' As she fumbled to gather the duvet back around her, I caught sight of the inside of her arm. It was criss-crossed with pink lines like cuts or deep scratches, some fresh, some faded, as if she'd been regularly attacked by a cat over a period of years. A very neat and methodical cat. Suddenly a day that had begun full of light and promise seemed to have turned dark.

'We'll come with you,' Penny was saying. 'At least, some-one will. I've got to put Esther on her train this afternoon, so if you haven't been seen by then I'll have to leave you there.'

'I can wait with her,' said Christian. He slapped her duvet-wrapped knee. 'Don't worry, Marty, I'll look after you.'

She gazed up at him with grateful, doggy eyes. I remem-bered what Christian had said earlier about emotional cannibals, and for the second time that day I thought of Aunty Barbara, another woman who wielded her helpless-ness with considerable force.

WHEN I GOT HOME I GAVE MUM AND DAD AN EDITED ACCOUNT of my stay, omitting any mention of vodka, debt and hang-overs, and concentrating instead on our trip to Sidmouth, tobogganing, and Martina's near incineration. They laughed at my description of the state of the flat, and then stopped when I added, 'Even this place looks clean by comparison.'

Mum wanted to know if Christian had appeared to be well and happy, and I was able to report truthfully that he had. She also asked if he was eating 'proper food', but since her view of what constituted proper food had always been highly individual, I couldn't offer much reassurance on that point. We had ended up buying instant soup from the hospi-tal vending machine for our Sunday lunch while we waited for Martina to be seen.

Penny and I had left her and Christian behind while she ran me to the station. I'd tried to give Christian my unspent tenner as a parting gift, but he refused to take it. In the car I asked Penny about her 'falling out' with Martina. I was trying to lead the conversation round to my suspicion that Martina was overfond of Christian, without implicating him in any bad behaviour.

Penny said that she and Martina had been best friends last year. Martina had been a different person then, confident and fun, though her anorexic tendencies dated from her early teens. Christian had got along well with Ian, Martina's then boyfriend, and they had gone around together in a foursome. Things had started to deteriorate when Ian ditched Martina quite unexpectedly and began very publicly seeing someone else, the girl who was now pregnant. 'We tried to look after her as much as we could,' Penny explained, 'and still included her in everything. But a threesome isn't quite the same. It's unbalanced, and after a while someone else's misery becomes very draining.' She sighed. 'I always seem fated to attract these lame ducks.'

'She seems a bit keen on Christian, don't you think?' I ventured.

'What makes you say that?'

'Oh, nothing special. Just a feeling.'

'I think she's probably a bit jealous of our relationship. I suppose it's only natural. Anyway, everyone loves Christian because he always acts so kind and caring.'

I nodded slowly, weighing the word 'acts'.

'I don't regard Martina as a serious threat. I don't think vulnerability is attractive when it's taken to that extent.'

It was only as I ran through this conversation in my mind on the train journey home that it occurred to me to wonder whether she regarded me as one of those lame ducks with whom she had been lumbered by fate.

27

IT WAS MADNESS THAT DROVE AUNTY BARBARA AWAY FROM US all those years before and it was murder that brought her back.

The communication came in one of those handwritten envelopes regarded by Dad as the only sort worth opening. I remember its arrival particularly because it was the only piece of post to be delivered on my fifteenth birthday – confirmation of the indifference of the outside world to my continued existence. Penny and Christian, down in Exeter, marked the occasion by telephoning to let me know that a present too fragile to post would be with me on their return home next week.

'It's Barbara,' Dad exclaimed, on at last deciphering the signature. Her administrative skills had not improved over time: the letter was written with a series of expiring ball-points on the back of an estate agent's flyer. The hand-writing, which began as neat, horizontal lines, then succumbed to lack of space and careered twice round the border before straying over the page into illegible proximity to the small print of the advertisement.

'She must want a favour,' said Mum, cynic and shrewd judge of character.

Dad gave her a reproving look and we all crowded round to read the letter.

Dearest Gordon, Pru, Christian and Emily (that stung: I'd thought myself her favourite at one time)

I know I haven't been in touch for ages, but it doesn't mean you haven't been in my thoughts, because you have all of y (new biro)

The fact is, we're in a bit of a predicament over accommodation for a few weeks this summer, and you are the only people I can think of with room in their hearts and homes for a stray, namely Donov (new biro)

Alan has fixed him up with a job in some estate agent's office in the city over the summer holidays and he needs somewhere to stay within commuting distance. He'll be out at work all day, and I've told him to make himself scarce at weekends. He's completely self-sufficient about food and so on.

'I bet he is,' Mum said.

I promise you won't even know he's there. I'd feel so much happier if he was with friends rather than in some hostel. This whole situation has arisen because our house will be unavailable – I'm renting it out while I go to America to visit my pen-friend, Roy. He's been given a date for his execution, so I'm going over there to try and make some noise on his behalf.

I've written rather than rung, to give you time to discuss
this and marshall your excuses if necessary, but I'll call
soon for your verdict, as time is marching on.
    Fondest love
    Barbara
    P.S. I wonder if— (illegible)

THE RICH SILENCE THAT FOLLOWED THIS WAS BROKEN BY THE
ringing of the telephone. Dad was the first to recover.
Through the open door to the hallway we could hear him
say, 'Hello . . . Barbara, how lovely to hear from you . . .
Yes we did . . . yes of course we'd love to have him.' I gave
Mum a rueful smile and she replied by making throttling
motions in Dad's direction. I was beginning to see, as Mum
saw, that there was something slightly maverick in Dad's
hospitality. It wouldn't occur to him to consult before throwing our doors open for the whole summer. Applied
Christianity, he called it, when challenged.

Mum had sympathy enough for mankind, but she sometimes found its individual representatives a source of exas-
peration. She remembered our manners and pushed the door
shut on the conversation.

'Somehow I knew Barbara would resurface one day,' she
said. 'On her terms, of course.' She picked up the letter
again. *'He's just been given a date for his execution.* Ye gods!'

A moment later, Dad reappeared, smiling broadly. 'Well,
that's all settled. They'll be here in a fortnight.'

'They?' said Mum warily.

'Barbara's coming to spend the night so I can run her to
Gatwick the next morning, and then Donovan will stay on
for the summer. That's okay isn't it?'

'I suppose it'll have to be,' Mum replied. A lack of warmth

in her tone alerted Dad that his unilateral decision-making was not appreciated.

'Do you think I did wrong?' he asked. 'I thought it would be all right. Donovan was rather nice, I seem to remember.'

'Yes, but he was only eleven then. Anything could have happened in the last six years. He could be a drug addict for all we know.'

'All the more reason for him to be here instead of fending for himself.'

Mum grunted. She had her misgivings about Barbara and wanted them acknowledged. 'What's all this about an execution? Has she seriously been corresponding with someone on death row?'

'Very much so.'

Mum rolled her eyes. 'I can't think of anyone less suited to the job. I suppose it gives her some sort of morbid thrill.'

'Apparently she got the idea from you,' Dad said.

'From me?' Mum's face was a picture of astonishment.

'She says you once had a conversation with her about getting involved in prison visiting. She sort of took it from there.'

'I was thinking of something more local,' Mum protested. 'Trust Barbara to go to extremes.'

'Oh, I don't know,' said Dad. 'Maybe a crusade like this was just what she needed. She certainly sounded very cheerful.'

'We'll see.'

THE DAY BEFORE THE PAIR WERE DUE TO ARRIVE I WAS UP A ladder trying to hack away some of the ivy engulfing the front of the house. Its march was so relentless that some of the upstairs windows were completely smothered: the room

Mum had cleaned out for Donovan was particularly badly affected and received almost no natural light.

I was dressed for this job in a pair of men's dungarees and checked shirt, borrowed from one of Mum's jumble bags, and a plastic shower cap, to prevent creepy-crawlies dropping out of the ivy into my hair. I was saving my best outfit for tomorrow to impress the visitors. Only Grandpa Percy was in, watching *Pebble Mill*: Dad was at work and Mum was out, buying provisions.

It was a gusty July day with a busy, changing sky – not ideal weather to be up a ladder. To help the chore pass off more enjoyably I was singing along to The Jam on my new Sony Walkman, the late birthday present from Penny and Christian, who had arrived back for the summer vacation a few days earlier. At the foot of the ladder was a growing pile of severed strands of ivy. I had cleared one window when, over the music, I became aware of the slamming of car doors. Penny and Christian were back from some outing, and from the way they stalked into the house separately, without bothering to acknowledge me I could tell they'd been quarrelling.

For the next five minutes or so I carried on pruning, singing uninhibitedly and snapping the shears in time to the music. I was wondering whether it might look better to leave a few tendrils hanging over the top of the window rather than a blunt fringe, when I felt someone shaking the ladder. I looked down and saw Donovan, squinting up at me.

'Excuse me,' he began, breathlessly. 'Do you know if there's anyone at home? Oh my God, it's you,' he exclaimed, as I snatched off my shower cap, sending the earphones spinning. How long had he been standing there? How loudly had I been singing?

There is no such thing as graceful descent where ladders are concerned. I clumped down towards him, stepping on the trailing legs of my dungarees. 'We weren't expecting you till tomorrow,' I said – not the politest welcome, it later occurred to me.

'Ah, well, that'll be Mum getting the dates wrong,' he said in the untroubled tone of one used to this phenomenon. He took in my costume with an amused expression.

'Where is she?' I said, looking round for Aunty Barbara. The fact that he was alone, on foot and out of breath, was only just beginning to ring alarm bells.

'She's in the car in a ditch about half a mile down the lane. We were cut up on a bend by a yellow Mini and went into a skid.' Our eyes slid in the direction of Penny's car, standing on the driveway not ten yards away. Donovan refrained from commenting.

'Oh dear. How awful. Is she okay?' It must have been embarrassment or nerves or something, but for a second I had the most overpowering urge to laugh. It took all my concentration to subdue it.

'Yes, she's fine. She just decided to sit and listen to the radio while I sorted it out. Have you got a tow-rope?'

'I expect so. Let me see.' The only rope I could think of was the one suspended from the oak tree with the tyre on the end. I supposed in the circumstances it would have to be sacrificed. 'Come, in,' I said, pushing open the front door and kicking aside some bags of clobber. 'Christian and Penny are here. They'll give you a tow.'

'CHRISTIAN!' I yelled up the stairs. 'DONOVAN'S HERE AND HE'S IN A BIT OF A FIX.'

There was a pause and then Christian appeared, taking the stairs in four strides. 'Hello, Donovan, how are you, mate?' he said, in that hearty, blokeish way that serves men for best friends and strangers alike.

'All right, mate. Good to see you,' Donovan replied. They pumped hands enthusiastically, seven years of estrangement dusted off in a second.

'Donovan's car's just been run off the road by a yellow Mini,' I explained brightly.

Christian looked aghast, then turned to Penny, who had reached the top of the stairs just in time to hear my last remark. 'I told you you'd taken that corner too fast, you stupid tart,' he said.

Penny covered her mouth with one hand. 'Oh God, I'm so sorry. I knew I was over your side a bit, but I'd no idea I'd forced you off the road. I'll pay for any damage.'

I left her babbling apologies and went off to fetch the rope, wondering how best to retrieve it from the oak tree. It was some years since I had clambered up to sit in the branches, but I was pretty sure I could still manage it. Unpicking the knots would be another matter. Stepping through the French windows onto the brick paving I was brought up short: the swing had gone. Only a chafed groove in the bark of the ancient branch and a patch of bald earth directly below marked its passing. I felt a rising sense of indignation wholly at odds with my own intentions of a moment before. It was my swing. I had spent many happy hours riding the tyre, cheating death as the recipient of Christian's notorious 'up and rounds'. No one had asked me if I would mind.

'Someone's taken down the swing,' I said, as I rejoined the group in the hallway.

All three looked at me in bewilderment. I suppose without any accompanying explanation my remark might not have seemed entirely germane. Then Christian laughed. 'That's been gone nearly two years. Where have you been, Esther?'

'Oh.' For a moment I thought he must be winding me up. How could I not have noticed a thing like that?

Then Penny said, 'I've got a rope in the boot. Come on, let's go and rescue your car, Donovan.'

The three of them went off in the Mini, Penny's part in the accident apparently forgiven. I took the opportunity provided by their absence to change out of my dungarees into something more presentable, and organise some tea and biscuits with which to revive Aunty Barbara after her ordeal.

I had been looking forward to this visit ever since it had been confirmed. I felt somehow connected to Donovan after that meeting on the train, and my pledge of silence. I had been carrying the secret clasped to me like a precious vase all this time. On several occasions it had nearly slipped out of my grasp. When Mum said, casually, 'I wonder how Donovan's turned out. He's probably a punk rocker,' I almost lost it, CRASH, but fortunately Mum put my snorts of laughter down to her regal pronunciation. For another thing, I always associated the Frys with drama, and I was now at an age where it was starting to seem much more important to be interesting than to be nice.

Even in the manner of their arrival they didn't disappoint. From the front doorstep I watched the cavalcade approach at a crawl: first, the yellow Mini, with Penny and Christian in the front; second, the recovered Fiat, with its scraped wing, Donovan steering, Aunty Barbara in the passenger seat; finally, Mum on her bicycle, French loaves balanced in the basket like pencils in a pot.

'That was a piece of luck your being around, Penny,' said Mum, as everyone emerged from the cars. She had cycled up just in time to see the Fiat being dragged from the ditch, and hadn't heard the history of the accident.

'You could say that,' said Christian. 'On the other hand...' There was general laughter. Mum looked puzzled.

'I've made tea,' I said. 'In a teapot.'

Aunty Barbara was standing on the driveway, staring up at the house, one hand shading her eyes. Perhaps she was remembering her last view of it, from the back of an ambulance. She was dressed in a long red skirt and a ruffle-fronted blouse, deeply unbuttoned. Her black hair was divided into two short, stiff plaits, either side of a chalk-white parting. Her face was a mask of make-up, most of which came off on my cheek as she moved in for a kiss. Christian and Penny must have been similarly done over at the roadside: their faces bore matching scarlet smears.

'Hello, darling girl. You're looking wonderful. So slim.' I yelped as she tried to enclose my waist with her hands. I'd forgotten that intimidating way she had of talking straight in your face. The heavy, spicy smell of her scent made my eyeballs smart. 'You're lucky, you know. Most skinny girls have no bosoms,' she added behind her hand, in what she imagined to be a whisper.

'Hello Barbara,' said Mum, coming to my rescue. 'You look very well. You've put on weight.'

'I've actually lost half a stone,' Aunty Barbara corrected her.

'Oh. Perhaps you're just a bit fatter in the face,' said Mum, undaunted. She led the way indoors. 'I expect you'd like a cup of tea after your little adventure.'

'I'd rather have something stronger,' said Aunty Barbara,

who had always refused to acknowledge my parents' status
as teetotallers. 'There's a bottle of fizzy in one of the bags.
I wrapped it in newspaper to keep it cold. If Donovan had
been any longer fetching help I'd have drunk it.'

'I ran all the way here and we drove straight back,'
Donovan protested. 'It can't have been ten minutes.'

'You mustn't mind Donovan if he gets moody,' Aunty
Barbara advised Mum in another of her loud whispers. 'He's
nursing a broken heart.' Donovan gave her a murderous
look.

'THIS PLACE HASN'T CHANGED AT ALL,' SAID DONOVAN IN A
kind of wonderment, as he carried the bags up to the
bedrooms. It was certainly true that the house had seen no
improvement in its general condition over the years. The
bogus antique dealers had made off with one or two pieces
of furniture, but other than that, everything remained much
the same, allowing for the slight deterioration wrought by
our occupancy.

He went into every room, shaking his head at the weird
familiarity of it all. 'It's like the museum of my childhood,'
he said at last, looking at the pattern of dart-holes in
Christian's bedroom door. On an impulse he went across to
the wardrobes and gave one of the brass handles an experimental twist. In immemorial fashion it came away in his
hand. 'Fantastic,' he murmured, slotting it back.
'Unbelievable.'

Over the next few weeks I would often come upon
Donovan in the act of surreptitiously fixing things: loose
switches, wobbly handles, dripping taps. It was only when
I saw how easily such problems were remedied that it
occurred to me to wonder why no one had thought to tackle

them before. I couldn't help inferring some criticism of our habits and standards from his behaviour, and my gratitude was often extinguished by gusts of self-consciousness and shame. There was no need for any polite subterfuge where Mum and Dad were concerned: they were delighted with his initiative and skill, and took no offence whatsoever. When he changed a fuse in the Hillman, a job that would have had Dad scratching his head and dithering for weeks, his conquest of them was complete.

AFTER TESTING AND REJECTING THE OTHERS, AUNTY BARBARA installed herself in the least uncomfortable of our chairs and picked up a copy of *Lady Chatterley's Lover*, which was lying open across the arm. 'Who's reading this?' she wanted to know. Penny raised her hand. Aunty Barbara pulled a face. 'It completely spoilt it for me when she went off to her tryst in rubber tennis shoes,' she sniffed. Having dismissed D.H. Lawrence for ever, she rummaged in her carrier bag and produced a velvet pouch, which she passed across to me. It contained a teardrop crystal pendant the size of a plum. For a piece of jewellery it was monstrous, but I dutifully thanked her and hung it round my neck, so that it sat like a great pebble on the shelf of my chest.

'No, you clown, it's not a necklace,' she said. 'You hang it in the window and it catches the light.' She took it off me and spun it in a shaft of furry sunshine, spraying the walls with rainbows.

The next item was a bottle of Veuve Cliquot. 'Champagne to my real friends: real pain to my sham friends, as Francis Bacon would say,' she announced, handing it over to Christian. 'Open it will you, there's a dear.'

Christian rather heavy-handedly thumbed the cork free

and a creamy plume rose from the neck of the bottle and trickled over his hands onto the carpet. He hadn't thought to have a glass ready.

'Hmm. I can see you haven't had much practice in the art of opening champagne,' Aunty Barbara observed. 'I'd better send you a crate for your twenty-first.'

Christian refused to look grateful in advance. His last ten birthdays had passed her by unacknowledged, and she had been known to forget her own son's Christmas present, so there were no real grounds for optimism. However, even he had to admit that this time around Aunty Barbara was an altogether more solid presence than the wraith who had tottered in through the door and out through the window all those years ago. Now she had a job, a salary, and most significant of all, a mission.

It was Dad who brought up the subject of the impending execution while we were all sitting round the dining table eating Penny's special cheese fondue. Aunty Barbara, it emerged, had joined a charitable organisation called Letters for Lifers, which had put her in touch with Roy Kapper, a prisoner who had been on death row in Georgia for over a decade. The last of his many crimes was a bungled robbery at a gas station in which the Vietnamese proprietor was shot. Kapper and his accomplice had both denied pulling the trigger, each pointing the finger at the other. The accomplice's lawyer was marginally more persuasive: his client was only given life.

'Do you have any grounds for an appeal?' Mum asked. She had seen too much suffering at the mission hospital to hold sacred the lives of individual criminals. Dad, on the other hand, thought Satan himself could be rehabilitated with a proper programme of education and counselling.

'If it fails I shall appeal to President Reagan as a fellow actor,' she replied.

'Does your man show any remorse?' Dad wanted to know.

'He certainly regrets getting involved with Gyle – that's his partner in crime,' said Aunty Barbara, spearing a chunk of bread and stirring it through the hot cheese. 'He says he wouldn't mind dying so much if he knew Gyle was going too.'

'Does that sound like the view of an innocent man?' Dad wondered aloud.

'What do you find to write about?' Penny asked. 'I wouldn't have a clue.'

Aunty Barbara withdrew her bread cube, trailing strings of molten cheese. 'At first I wasn't sure what to say. I started off with these heartfelt expressions of sympathy, but I thought that would probably make rather dull reading, so then I just told him all about me, who I am, a typical day – that sort of thing.'

'What are his letters to you like?' Mum asked, wincing as a strand of cheese stuck to her chin.

'For someone who's had almost no education they're reasonably coherent. I've got one here.' She produced a piece of folded, lined paper and handed it across to Mum. I could see the handwriting, a random mixture of upper and lower case letters. Donovan, at the other end of the table from me, was looking bored. He's heard all this a thousand times before, I thought. Everyone who comes to the house wants to hear about Barbara's murderer friend.

'He calls you "dear lady",' said Mum, skimming the page before handing it back. 'That's nice.'

'He writes very movingly about his childhood, which was miserable, and prison routine, and facing death. I was thinking of trying to get our correspondence published,' Aunty Barbara went on.

'Like *84 Charing Cross Road?*' Mum suggested.

'Hardly,' said Dad.

I could see Christian starting to squirm in his seat. He hated this sort of talk, which he regarded as 'arty-farty'.

'Will you be allowed to watch the execution?' he asked, to bring the conversation back on track.

'Oh no,' said Aunty Barbara. 'I wouldn't want to. I'll be holding a vigil outside. There'll be protesters like me on one side, and the pro-death penalty lobby on the other with their barbecues and frying pans. Apparently it's the same old ghouls who show up at these executions. They go from state to state.'

'There are no shortage of ghouls over here,' Dad murmured.

'Oh yes, I read about your girl in the paper.'

'What girl?' I asked.

'Janine Fellowes,' Dad replied. 'The Home Secretary is wringing his hands over it now. She's twenty-one, so they've got to decide whether to release her or transfer her to an adult prison.'

'There'll be an outcry if she's freed, surely?' said Aunty Barbara.

'I must say the force of public opinion has surprised me. I don't think anyone except me and the Home Secretary wants to let her out.'

'That's because the gutter press have completely demonised her,' said Mum. 'Anything to sell papers.'

'The broadsheets are no better,' said Dad. 'I haven't seen a single sympathetic editorial.'

'It's because she's an affront to people's ideas about

childhood innocence,' said Penny. This sort of discussion was right up her street. Christian and Donovan were jousting for the same cube of bread, which had fallen into the cheese.

'Especially female innocence,' said Mum. Aunty Barbara and Penny nodded vigorously.

'The irony is that she is more fully rehabilitated than any prisoner I've ever met,' said Dad.

'Have you got involved with any public pronouncements, Gordon?' Aunty Barbara asked.

'I was hoping not to this time,' said Dad. 'But I probably will.'

'More bricks,' Mum sighed.

'She'd be lynched if she was let out anyway,' said Christian. 'She's safer inside.'

'That's another consideration,' Dad agreed. 'She'd have to assume a new identity, move to a new place, cut all ties with her family. That's quite a tall order.'

'Oh, I don't know,' said Aunty Barbara, dividing the last of the Veuve Cliquot between herself and Penny. 'Donovan threatens to do it regularly.'

The accused smiled at her. 'I still might.'

'I remember that time you ran away from here,' said Mum. 'I nearly had kittens.'

'I'm afraid that's one habit he hasn't grown out of. He's quite likely to take off at a moment's notice.'

'Perhaps you could leave us a little note this time, Donovan,' Mum suggested. 'Then I'll know not to worry.'

Donovan nodded placidly.

'Where do you go when you take off?' Penny asked.

'Nowhere special,' said Donovan. 'I just wander.'

* * *

DAD LEFT FOR THE AIRPORT WITH AUNTY BARBARA BEFORE
the rest of the house was awake, allowing plenty of time for
queues, breakdowns and all manner of delays. He was always
inclined to be early for things, and was overcompensating
for Aunty Barbara's tendency to become embroiled in last-
minute emergencies.

She had tried to give Mum some money for Donovan's
keep, but there had been the usual to-ing and fro-ing and
stubborn refusals to give in on both sides.

'It's no use leaving it behind,' I said to Aunty Barbara,
as she put the bundle of notes on the mantelpiece. 'It'll
only go to the Less Fortunate.'

'Oh, bugger the Less Fortunate,' she said, retrieving it.
'What have they ever done for us?' She entrusted the money
to Donovan with the proviso that he use it for household
expenses and not his own idle gratification.

Her other parting instructions were that he should not
smoke in the house (a courtesy she only observed herself
now that she had given up smoking) and should make sure
he ate heartily at work instead of raiding our fridge. To all
of this he listened with an attitude of deep concentration
and when she'd finished, said, 'Can I offer some advice in
return?'

'Of course you can,' said his mother.

'Don't marry him.'

Aunty Barbara replied to this with a peal of merry laughter but no promises.

28

ON DONOVAN'S FIRST DAY AT WORK I WATCHED FROM MY bedroom window as he set off for the city, stiff and self-conscious in his suit. Evidently he'd misjudged the dress code, as on day two he'd abandoned the jacket and tie and by day three he was in jeans.

Normally I would have been on my paper round at that hour, but since turning fifteen I'd felt the job to be beneath me and had quit. To replace the lost earnings I had set myself up as a babysitter. A new breed of professional couple had started moving into the Victorian cottages near the Fox and Pheasant, and were happy to pay stupid money to escape from their own children for a few hours. I'd stuck a card in the newsagent's window:

> *Reliable, friendly, local girl (15) available*
> *for babysitting (evenings). Reasonable rates.*
> *References on request.*

I had put that last line in at Penny's suggestion, and she
had agreed to act as a satisfied customer and vouch for my
character if required. Since then, I'd had a call at least once
a week, and was building up a list of regular clients. It was
a beautiful arrangement: the children were usually asleep,
or at least in bed out of my way, the parents were delirious
with gratitude, and as well as paying me, left me treats and
snacks and the freedom of the fridge. I could lie at full
stretch on the couch and watch colour TV all evening,
uninterrupted by Grandpa's noisy breathing and anxious
commentary.

During that first week of Donovan's residency I had
several bookings, so I hadn't seen much of him in the
evenings. According to Mum it was his habit to arrive home
from work towards 6.30 and disappear upstairs, closing his
bedroom door behind him. Taking Aunty Barbara's parting
injunction to heart, or perhaps remembering Mum's cooking from previous visits, he couldn't be persuaded to share
our supper, but ate alone, or fasted, in his room.

Then one evening that week I'd been babysitting for the
Conways, my favourite clients, and because it was a warm
summer night and I had the fidgets I declined their offer of
a lift home and decided to walk instead. Once I'd left the
pub and the green behind there were no more streetlamps,
but there was a crooked old moon hanging just above the
trees to light my way, and, besides, I knew every curve and
crater of those lanes and could have negotiated them blind-
folded. Although it was after midnight the air was still sultry,
heavy with the scent of crushed petals, woodsmoke and
sweating foliage. There was no breeze, but the hedgerows
seemed to seethe and rustle as I passed. As I reached the

bend where Penny had run Aunty Barbara off the road and where there was almost no moonlight, I stopped to enjoy the stillness and darkness and silence. In that moment of sensory deprivation, I suddenly experienced a blissful feeling of calm, contentment, the perfect rightness of the universe. I suppose I was having what is crudely described as an out-of-body experience, and yet it was more as if my body was dissolving into the darkness.

Presently, a twig cracked, and I picked up the distant crunch of footsteps. This roused me from my dreamlike state and I set off again. As I penetrated the bramble snare of the driveway I saw the orange glow of a cigarette tip between the rhododendrons, and Donovan loomed out of the shadows.

'What are you doing, skulking in the bushes?' I asked.

'I'm having a smoke. What are you doing?'

'I've been babysitting in the village. I walked home for a change.'

'Oh, that's where you go in the evenings, is it? I thought you were just avoiding me,' he said, squinting at me through the smoke.

'Why would I want to do that?'

'I don't know. Because your mum and dad have warned you that I'm a bit dodgy, and you mustn't get tangled up with me,' he suggested.

An indignant noise, somewhere between a laugh and a cough, escaped me. Indignant because although I knew he was only winding me up, the idea of some sort of entanglement had in fact occurred to me from time to time since his arrival, most often as I was dropping off to sleep at night.

'But I never had any intention of getting tangled up with you,' I said primly.

Donovan laughed. 'You're a bit young for me, anyway. I go for older women.'

It's impossible to put up any defence against a slur like that. My ego was still reeling when the porch light came on and Mum appeared in her dressing gown and slippers, holding a rinsed milkbottle for the doorstep.

'Is that you, Donovan?' She peered at us, blind without her glasses. 'Have you seen Esther? Oh, there you are. I wondered where you were.'

'I'm here,' I confirmed.

'Righto. Lock up when you come in. Night night.' She withdrew, leaving the porch light on, the bulb, in its death throes, flickering madly.

'You see. Mum doesn't think you're the least bit dodgy, Donovan. She thinks you're completely normal.' This was intended, and received, as an insult. Having delivered it I was about to suggest going in, then realised Donovan still had an inch or so of cigarette left, so instead I sat down on the edge of a stone planter in which nasturtiums and chick-weed fought for space. 'Besides,' I added, 'if anyone's doing the avoiding, it's you. You never come out of your room.'

'The reason I don't come out of my room is that I know the moment I do, someone is going to ask me how the job's going.'

'How's the job going?' I asked.

Donovan pulled a face at me. 'It's awful. It's the total pits. I don't even want to talk about it,' he said, and then proceeded to do just that for the next ten minutes. He was working for a big estate agent and surveyor near Cannon Street, he said, but instead of being up in the office doing the exciting stuff like valuations, he was stuck down in a windowless vault all day long by himself, filing maps. Every so often the phone would ring and someone upstairs would request a particular map. He would have to locate it amongst the thousands of files, put it in a tube, and send it up this chute. At other times a whole batch of used maps would be returned for re-filing. That was it, all day. There wasn't even a chair, just a desk. 'I thought there would be people to talk to,' he said. 'But the only time I've actually seen a human being is when I lit up a fag and set off the smoke alarm and someone came down to switch it off and have a go at me. There isn't even a window to look out of. It's like a tomb.'

'Can't you listen to your Walkman?'

'I tried that, but then I can't hear the phone. I tell you, Esther, it's so tedious, I go off into this trance of boredom for hours on end, and then I look at my watch and only five minutes have gone past.' He glanced automatically at his watch. 'Only nine hours till it all starts again.'

'Why don't you just leave if you hate it so much?'

'I can't. It's a friend of Dad's who got me the job, and Dad made such a big deal of it – what a favour this guy was doing me and how lucky I was to be earning money, etc. etc. I can't just leave. Anyway, what else could I do? I can't go home. The house is let all summer.'

'Maybe one of your older women could look after you?' I suggested evenly. Later I thought this was rather a mean remark, in view of his recently broken heart, but I was still smarting from that dig about my tender age.

Donovan smiled. 'The fact is, I'm between older women at the moment.' He sighed. 'No, I'll just have to grin and bear it.' He bared his teeth in an experimental grin, then an idea seemed to strike him. 'What do you do around here all day?'

I shrugged. 'I sort of mooch about. Sometimes I go and hang around the precinct with my mate, Dawn. Or I might go over to Penny's to walk the dogs. Mostly I just mooch about,' I conceded.

'You could come up and meet me for lunch tomorrow,' he suggested. 'If you're not too busy mooching.'

I said I could probably spare a few hours from my packed schedule. 'If you're sure you can put up with my extreme youth,' I couldn't resist adding.

Donovan flung his cigarette butt into the bushes, laughing remorselessly.

WE HAD ARRANGED TO MEET ON THE STEPS OF ST PAUL'S Cathedral at five past one. This precision timing was important as Donovan had exactly one hour for lunch and couldn't afford to waste a minute of it. I wasn't used to making my own way around London, but reckoned that even I ought to be able to find something the size of St Paul's without too much trouble.

I was rather hot and flustered when I arrived, after my experience in the underground. The automatic barrier had swallowed my ticket, and one of the men on duty had practically stripped the machine down to retrieve it, eating into those valuable extra minutes I had allowed myself for getting lost. As it happened I was still early, so I went into the cathedral to cool off. As I stepped inside, the roar and hum of the London traffic was replaced by a purer sound: the reverential hush of large numbers of people trying to keep silence. Then over the top of that came the angel voices of the choristers, rising in perfect unison, clear and true. I stood, spellbound for a while, and then looked at my watch and discovered it was six minutes past one. I emerged, blinking, into the noise and sunlight, and saw Donovan sitting on the steps. He was in black jeans and a T-shirt and the soft leather cap he always wore, which made him look like a Russian peasant. Dad had christened it his Raskolnikov hat.

'You're late,' he accused, but he looked pleased to see me, nevertheless. One side of his face was red and crumpled as though he'd been lying on something patterned. I refrained from mentioning it, but he must have caught me staring as he rubbed his cheek and said, 'I fell asleep. I was only woken by the phone. If it hadn't rung I'd have slept through the whole lunch hour.' He seemed horrified by this thought. 'Where shall we eat?'

'There's a coffee shop in the crypt here, I think,' I said, remembering a sign I'd passed, but he shook his head.

'I've been in a crypt all morning. I need fresh air.' We walked down Ludgate Hill towards Fleet Street until we found a café that had a couple of wobbly aluminium tables outside on the street. Exhaust fumes competed with the smell of garbage and drains rising from the vents in the pavement. It was a relief when Donovan lit up. Over two 'all-day breakfasts' he told me his working conditions had dramatically improved since he had borrowed a chair from the lobby, and located the Klix coffee machine on the third floor. Now he could lounge around in comfort, reading John Updike between interruptions. I said I'd never come across any of his stuff. (He wasn't on Penny's reading list.)

'It's probably just as well,' Donovan replied, keeping a very straight face. 'It's not really suitable for girls as young as you.' I refused to rise: this joke was going to run and run, I could tell.

When it was time to pay, Donovan brushed aside my
offers, producing a roll of notes from his jeans pocket. 'This
is the money Mum left me,' he explained. 'Might as well
use it.'

'I thought it was supposed to be for household expenses,'
I reminded him.

'That's right. Consider yourself a necessary household
expense.'

As we walked back up Ludgate Hill Donovan suggested
that I come back to the office to check out his tomb.

'Will I be allowed to walk in off the street?' I asked,
doubtfully.

'No one will even notice,' he promised.

His building was a squat, ugly, concrete and glass block
in a side road off Cannon Street. Various other workers were
scurrying up the steps to the glass doors as we arrived, trying
to make the two o'clock deadline.

Inside the meanly lit lobby, with its zig-zag carpet of
competing colours that jumped and receded dizzily before
my eyes, Donovan handed his time card to a girl behind
a high kidney-shaped desk, and we passed on to the lift,
unremarked. In the corner, starved of natural light, stood
a flourishing fig tree in a terracotta urn.

'Plastic,' said Donovan. 'All plastic. Even the gravel is
fake.'

We took the lift to Basement Two, and stepped out into
a narrow corridor, partially blocked by cardboard boxes and
broken filing cabinet drawers, where the air was subter-
ranean and cool. 'You need a canary down here,' I said.
'There might be firedamp.'

Donovan gave me a quick grin. 'Look at that. Health
and Safety,' he said, pointing to the boxes. 'I could get

this whole place closed down.' Instead, he showed me his quarters: a twenty-foot square bunker lit by a whining neon strip, and furnished with rows of grey filing cabinets. In one corner was a vinyl bucket seat, recently filched from the lobby, and a desk on which sat a phone. To the untrained eye the filing system seemed not to be arranged according to sound alphabetical or numerical principles: drawers would be labelled X0005932-ZA8 or similar, but Donovan had evidently mastered these strange and complex encryptions.

It was a thoroughly depressing place, and I couldn't wait to get away, though I felt almost guilty abandoning him there.

'What do you think?' he asked, throwing out both arms in fake pride.

I walked to one of the blank, porridge-coloured walls, where a window might have been expected to sit, and tried to peer out. 'It's got no prospects, Donovan,' I said, making a move to go.

'You're not going to leave me mouldering down here?' he said, indignantly. 'I was just going to get us a coffee from the machine. Sit down.' He put his hands on my shoulders and pushed me firmly into the chair. 'Don't answer the phone,' he instructed as he left. A minute later I heard the lift door ping and then there was silence. Not the awe-inspiring hush of St Paul's, but an oppressive, crushing nothingness, maddeningly overlaid by the whine of that overhead light. A few minutes passed. I began to wonder whether Donovan had deliberately abandoned me, just so I'd know how it felt. The phone rang. I ignored it. After a few rings it stopped, then started again, more insistently, it seemed to me. I picked it up.

'It's me,' said Donovan. 'I forgot to ask if you take milk and sugar.'

I said I did.

'Anyway,' he added sternly, 'I thought I told you not to pick up the phone.'

I think it was at this point that I decided falling in love with Donovan might be as pleasant a way as any to pass the summer.

29

AFTER THAT DAY I OFTEN MET DONOVAN FOR LUNCH, AT least twice a week, and always at his invitation. These invitations were casually delivered, as if it was a matter of complete indifference to him whether or not I came, and were accepted in the same vein. In fact I made sure to keep my afternoons free, just in case he should ask, and on one occasion cancelled an outing with Dawn at short notice, using Grandpa as an excuse – a shabby trick, but infatuation can make traitors of us all.

We were supposed to be going to help Pam and Andy decorate their spare room in preparation for the imminent arrival of twins. They had recovered from their falling out and were married now, and living in a two-bedroomed place on the same estate as the Clubbs.

'Why do you have to stay in with your Grandpa?' Dawn wanted to know when I rang up to cry off. 'He'll be okay for an hour or two, won't he?'

'He's a bit doo-lally,' I replied. 'He wanders off, or lets
burglars in. It would be just my luck if I popped out and he
chose today to burn the house down.'

'Can't Christian do it?'

'He's working.' As Penny had predicted, Christian was
too broke to consider travelling, and had taken a job as a
plasterer's labourer – just one source of friction between the
two of them.

'I could come to you instead,' Dawn suggested.

'No, no,' I said, hastily. 'You go to Pam's. I'll come another
day.' I was glad that exchange took place over the telephone
because my face was burning by the time I'd finished. I
suppose I should have felt ashamed of myself, but Penny
had always insisted that fibs were a necessary emollient to
relationships and not to be despised.

Generally, after having lunch at our favourite café, I would
accompany Donovan back to the tomb, and we would while
away the afternoon playing cards: knockout whist, demon
patience and box rummy – all the games Christian had taught
him during those childhood visits to the Old Schoolhouse.
His general mode of address could only be described as affectionate scorn, and I seemed to provide him with endless
material. Chief amongst my deficiencies was my dress sense.
In spite of Penny's coaching I still suffered occasional lapses
when she wasn't on hand to intervene. A pair of smart grey
trousers with a belted jacket had seemed fine to me until
Donovan said they made me look like a bus conductor, and
at the other extreme, a white ruffled skirt, which I had
thought pretty and romantic, had elicited a raised eyebrow
and the enquiry, 'Are you off to a barn dance?'

In spite of this mockery he was otherwise very generous,
always paying for my lunch (from Aunty Barbara's funds, of

course), and from his first pay packet he bought me an enamel hair slide from a stall in Covent Garden. He had left the price on the box, in case I wanted to take it back, he said, but I think it was to let me know that it was more expensive than it looked. Anyway, it was an unusual and thoughtful gift, and it occurred to me that Donovan had had past experience of buying presents for women.

Penny took great interest in this development. 'He must be quite keen on you, Esther,' she said.

'He's never said anything keen,' I replied, pleased all the same. She had come over one Thursday morning so that I could do her hair in dozens of tiny braids. She had a page from Cosmo which showed you exactly how to do it with beads and cotton. It was going to take hours, but we had nothing else to do.

'Ah, but the giving of gifts is a sure sign,' she said. 'Christian bought me a pair of gold earrings when we started going out. I had to go and get my ears pierced so I could wear them.'

She wasn't wearing them now, I noticed.

'He was always bringing me little presents. He doesn't any more,' she added. 'He'd have to borrow the money off me first.'

'He told me this plastering job pays quite well, so maybe he'll get back into the habit,' I said, making a mental note to take him aside and suggest it. At the same time I couldn't help thinking it typical of Penny to expect the tide of generosity to flow only one way – in her direction.

She rolled her eyes at the mention of the plastering job. 'Didn't I tell you how it would be back in February? I turned down the America trip so we could go somewhere together, and now he's got to work all summer just to pay off his debts. I've a good mind to go to France with Wart instead. His parents have got a place in the Loire. A whole group of people are going down there.'

'I didn't realise you liked Wart,' I said.

'Oh, he's all right,' she said, blushing slightly. 'He pays me a lot of attention, and it's hard not to like someone who does that.'

The phone rang, so I left Penny pinching a half-finished braid between finger and thumb while I went to answer it. It was the garage, saying Donovan's car was fixed and ready for collection. As I hung up the ringing began again. I snatched up the receiver.

'Is Donovan there?' said a female voice. Not Aunty Barbara.

'No, he's at work.'

'Oh. Have you got his number?'

I hadn't. I couldn't even remember the name of the office, despite my frequent visits to its vaults. 'It's got two names – two surnames, you know, like Clayton Fortescue, or Taylor Chadwell, but that's not it.'

'Oh.' The voice was sounding bothered. 'Could you tell him to ring me tomorrow evening at home. It's got to be tomorrow. That's very important. He mustn't ring at any other time. He'll understand.' I was taking such care to remember this curious detail that I put down the phone without asking her name. He'll know, I thought, with a slight stirring of jealousy.

Penny was standing at my bedroom window when I went to resume my hairdressing duties. 'Speak of the devil,' she said putting a finger to the glass. It was Wart. He had driven right up to the house and was now exam-ining the dark green paintwork of his MG for scratches.

The bench seat was occupied by a wooden rocking-horse and a bouquet of flowers.

'God almighty, it's a bit overgrown here,' he protested, when we had joined him in the driveway. 'What are you? Sleeping Beauty or something?'

'It dies back in winter,' I said. I would have to get those shears out again.

'What brings you here?' Penny asked. 'You're a long way from home.'

'I'm going to visit my sister in Sevenoaks. She's just had her first sprog. I thought I'd take a little detour to see Christian. Where is he?'

'Helping to plaster the Holiday Inn,' said Penny.

'Oh good, he's got a job, has he? Because he still owes me a few pennies. And I was hoping to get my hands on some of them before I go to France.' He spat a gobbet of chewing gum into the bushes and grinned at me, his mirrored sunglasses obscuring the direction of his gaze, making him look more than usually sinister. I felt the same odd mixture of repulsion and mesmerism that I'd experienced at our first meeting. He was wearing very tight jeans and a sweatshirt with the sleeves torn off to reveal his muscly shoulders and plenty of underarm hair. There was something belligerent about his masculinity that made me uncomfortable.

Penny seemed unintimidated. 'What have you been doing with yourself since the end of term?' she asked.

'Just rattling around at home. I knocked down a couple of outhouses that were about to collapse. I went to see Martina in Clapham one day. She was in a pretty bad way.'

'What was wrong with her?'

'Same old stuff. Really low, not eating again. She said you hadn't been returning her calls.'

A guilty blush spread over Penny's cheeks. 'I did try once, but she was out,' she said defensively. 'Anyway, it's not me she wants to see. It's Christian. I'm not stupid.'

'She just needs someone to take her out of herself. Stop her getting all introspective. I'll try and go again before I go to France.'

'When are you off?' asked Penny, a touch wistfully to my mind.

'Next week. Why don't you come? I've got room.' He nodded towards the MG.

'Oh, I don't know. Next week's a bit soon.'

'I could delay it,' Wart replied, too quickly.

'We'll see. I don't know about Christian . . .'

'Do you want a cup of tea?' I asked him, remembering my manners. It occurred to me that if Penny hadn't been here I'd have had to entertain him alone.

'No. Something stronger. Is there a pub around here?'

'There's the Fox and Pheasant on the green,' I said, pointing in the direction of the village.

'Anyone want to come?' he offered, climbing behind the wheel of the MG. All three of us glanced at the one empty seat. Penny won't go, I thought. Not with half her hair done. 'I can't,' I said. 'I've got to give Grandpa his lunch.'

'Oh, well, if you can't I might as well,' said Penny, jumping in beside him.

'What about your hair?' I reminded her.

Her hand strayed to the half-dozen completed braids that swung like so many fancy bell-pulls on one side of her head. 'Oh.' There was a moment's hesitation while she weighed this state of asymmetry against other considerations. 'It doesn't matter what I look like,' she said, laying her hand on Wart's hairy arm. 'It's only Wart.'

He gave her a sickly smile, before flipping on the ignition and reversing the car back down the driveway, treating its bodywork to a second ordeal by flail.

30

I WONDERED WHETHER DONOVAN MIGHT OFFER TO TAKE ME
for a drive at the weekend now that his car was back in service. I had a hankering to do something civilised, like take
a picnic of strawberries to Hever Castle and do some sketching. What Donovan was supposed to do with himself while
I sketched hadn't quite emerged from the fog of egotism that
tended to shroud the awkward details of my daydreams. In
any case, when I got up on Saturday morning I found his
room empty and the car gone. I knew it was something to
do with that phone message I'd given him, because on Friday
evening as I was on my way to the Conways to babysit, I
saw him in the call box on the green. He had his back to
me and didn't see me approach, so I was able to creep up
alongside and rap on the glass, making him jump. He must
have been in the middle of an absorbing conversation as he
shook his head irritably and waved me off. I slunk away,
mortified, feeling more than ever like a silly child.

By Saturday evening he had still not returned, so I gave Dawn a call. She was rather cool with me on account of my recent neglect, but she soon thawed when I offered to buy her a shandy and chips with my babysitting money. We sat on the wall outside Ozzie's Fishbar in the precinct, catching up. She told me Pam was due to have her twins any day now, and was so enormous she couldn't get down the stairs, but sat in bed all day eating digestives and rubbing baby oil into her stretch marks. 'I'm really looking forward to being an Aunty,' Dawn said. 'I can't wait to give the babies their bottles.'

A group of lads arrived on their 50cc motorbikes and started buzzing round us like mosquitoes, revving loudly and showing off. We recognised one as a former inmate of Underwood, recently expelled. He persuaded Dawn onto the back of his bike and took her for a ride up and down the long, straight road that formed the main artery of the estate. As they disappeared one of the other lads rode over and offered to take me round the back of the garages 'to show me something interesting'. I declined his offer without much regret. 'Do you want to sit on my face?' he asked. I told him it looked like somebody already had, which caused so much hilarity amongst his mates that he ended up swinging a punch and knocking one of them off balance into another, whose bike fell over, taking a scratch on its new paintwork. By the time Dawn returned, her face a mask of exhilaration and fear, quite an impressive brawl had developed, so we sloped off to the bus stop.

'Don't call me next week because I won't be at home,' Dawn said, as we sat waiting in the shelter. 'We're going to Minehead.'

'Where's that?'

'Dunno. Mum doesn't even want to go in case the twins come early.' And she uncapped a black pen she'd been carrying in her bag and drew a little row of babies' bottles on the bench between us.

THERE WAS STILL NO SIGN OF DONOVAN ON SUNDAY morning. I went into the kitchen where Mum was adding up the takings from last night's inter-church Top of the Pew Quiz between St Mungo's and Holy Trinity, which she had helped to organise. She was wearing a rubber thimble and peeling through a pile of notes, counting under her breath.

'It looks like Donovan's done his disappearing act again,' I said, lightly. 'I don't think he came back last night.'

'No, he told me he was going away for the weekend,' Mum said, snapping an elastic band round the roll of notes and posting it into the charity jar along with a handful of coppers.

'Oh, really? I wonder where?' I said.

'I didn't ask. To see some friend, I think,' said Mum, with typical vagueness. Her lack of curiosity, though it occasionally worked in my favour, could be maddening. 'I must say,' she went on, climbing on to a stool to put the money jar on the topmost shelf of the dresser, 'he's much the easiest house-guest we've ever had. I take back all my cynical predictions about drugs and punk rock. It's extraordinary that he's turned out so well, given what he had to contend with. And he's so helpful too.'

'He fixed the porch light,' I said.

'Was that him, too?' said Mum. 'He put a new brake cable on my bicycle the other day. I can't tell you the difference it's made, being able to stop.'

* * *

I WAS A LITTLE HURT THAT DONOVAN HADN'T BOTHERED TO mention to me that he was going away, and I was still smarting from that brush-off at the phone box, so I decided to keep out of his way on his return. Let him seek me out if he wanted.

Resolutions of this sort are easy to make, but the execution is another matter. It took all my determination not to engineer accidental meetings on the landing, or leave myself lying about where I knew he would have to acknowledge me. Fortunately circumstances came to the aid of my faltering willpower in the form of a series of evening babysitting engagements in the village, which kept me out of the house at the critical time. By staying in bed until after Donovan had left for work in the mornings (which was no hardship to me as I was generally fast asleep) and leaving for my evening appointments before he came home, I managed to maintain my unavailability until the following Thursday without any appearance of effort.

On that morning I was brutally awoken just after nine thirty by a tremendous mechanical buzzing, like a chain-saw, coming from the front garden. Heart hammering, I clawed back the curtain and peered down through my open window to see Donovan taking on the brambles with a motorised strimmer, which he was wielding waist-high like a machine gun, with considerable relish. He was wearing protective earphones, DMs and a pair of jeans, amputated at the knees and fraying. I was about to withdraw, pulling the window shut while I found something suitable to pelt him with, when he glanced up and saw me. His satisfaction at my dishevelment was obvious.

'I hope I didn't disturb you,' he called, over the roar of the strimmer.

I opened my mouth to reply, but he turned his back on me and continued to blast the bushes. Thoroughly awake now, I washed and dressed quickly in shorts and a sleeveless yellow shirt with mother-of-pearl poppers down the front, raked my hair into position with a comb, and went down to pursue the conversation face to face.

He had moved on to the wilderness alongside the driveway, felling the shoulder-high tangle of nettles and brambles in swinging strokes.

'Why aren't you at work?' I demanded, a parody of a hectoring wife.

He turned towards me, spraying my bare legs with shredded vegetation before he managed to subdue the machine. It gave a last few shudders and died.

'Because I couldn't stand being down in that tomb any longer. I don't know how I stuck it as long as I did.'

It emerged, under closer questioning, that his departure hadn't been nearly so high-minded. He had in fact stuffed the smoke alarm with paper towels so that he could enjoy a peaceful fag in his bunker, and set off the sprinkler system, destroying most of the maps in his care.

'What's your dad going to say?'

He shrugged. 'It won't change his opinion of me. He thinks I'm a useless layabout already.' I thought this could hardly be the case, but I didn't bother to contradict him. 'Anyway, it wasn't a complete waste of time: now I know I'm never going to work in an office.'

'Oh, everyone says that,' I retorted. 'But they all end up in offices just the same.'

He looked at me sternly. 'You've been avoiding me. Why?'

I laughed dismissively. 'You accused me of that before. You're paranoid, Donovan—'

'I'd just like to know what it is I've done.'

'—and very probably delusional.'

'If you say so.'

'I've just been busy,' I said, revelling in my own aloofness. I'd never realised the power of indifference. I felt I could ignore him for the rest of my life if it produced this sense of advantage.

'Is it because I went away at the weekend without telling you?'

'Oh, were you away?' I said.

'Oh, fuck off, Esther, you know I was. I had to go and see my teacher – the married one I told you about – and tell her it was all over. I thought I'd already done it, but apparently I hadn't made myself clear enough. I don't know why I'm telling you this. You're not the least bit interested.'

This was ecstasy. I had been gazing serenely about me as he spoke, taking in the extent of the defoliation. 'That's our blackberry crop you've just destroyed,' I said. 'Now what are we going to put on our toast all winter?'

He gave a sort of hiss of annoyance. 'If someone doesn't do it soon, that path will be completely blocked. Are you trying to seal yourselves off in here?'

'Where did you get that thing, anyway?' I said, pointing at the strimmer.

'I hired it from a shop in Biggin Hill. It's really quite ingenious, Esther. If there's a little job that needs doing, you ask yourself, "Now, what tools will I need?" and if you don't happen to have them, you go to these special shops, and for a small sum—'

'All right, all right, I get the picture,' I interrupted.

Mum came round the side of the house wheeling her newly restored bike. 'Oh Donovan,' she twittered, when she saw the evidence of his labours. 'You're clearing those briars. What a terrific idea. Esther, why don't you get the wheelbarrow and give him a hand?' And she pedalled off, humming delightedly.

I stood there for a minute, watching him work, wondering how men could be so unselfconscious about their hairy legs, until at last he turned round.

'Are you going to stand there staring all day, or are you going to help?' he asked. 'I suppose you're worried about breaking a fingernail.'

I spun on my heel and strode off down the side of the house to fetch the wheelbarrow. It was parked behind the disused greenhouse, full of a foul-smelling mulch of rotted grass-cuttings. When I tipped them out I found the bottom of the barrow had practically rusted through. The front tyre was completely flat. I was about to start pushing it up the garden nevertheless, when I remembered Donovan's earlier remarks. What tools do I need for this job? I asked myself. A pump! came the answer, quick as a flash. I found what I was looking for in a box of spanners in the woodshed, and with only mild exertion on my part the tyre was soon full of air and fixed. I felt quite immoderately pleased with myself for this accomplishment, and rejoined Donovan in the front garden, ready to demonstrate further resourcefulness if required.

'You'll be needing those.' He pointed to a pair of cracked leather gardening gloves on the stone planter, as I dithered beside a heap of slayed nettles. He had laid to waste one entire border and was about to start on the opposite side, refilling the strimmer's fuel chamber from a dented tin of two-stroke.

It was only ten o'clock in the morning, but the sun was

already high. There was no breeze and the air was treacly with trapped heat. Clouds of gnats fizzed above the rhodo-dendrons. The black metal handles of the wheelbarrow were hot to the touch. He'll burn, I thought, looking at Donovan's bare back. Serve him right.

The strimmer's noise made conversation impossible, so we worked without talking. While Donovan continued his massacre in the driveway, I raked and gathered, clearing the beds and transporting barrowloads of wilting vegetation to the mound behind the greenhouse in the furthest corner of the back garden. In spite of the gloves and my careful handling, the brambles had a way of springing back to snag me with their spikes. They seemed possessed by a devilish spirit, and my inner arms were soon scored with deep scratches.

Once the worst of the weeds had been hewn to ground level, Donovan began to dig over the soil to get at the roots, now and then going in with his bare hands for a tug of war. Even through the silence I could still hear the phantom wail of the strimmer ringing in my ears. Occasionally amidst the fallen debris I would come across something worth saving – a wild strawberry plant, or some flowering nastur-tiums – and work carefully around them, marvelling at their survival in that choking darkness.

One victim of Donovan's indiscriminate slaughter was a single raspberry cane, hung with fruit. 'Whoops,' he said, retrieving it from the barrow. 'Casualty of war.' He stripped off the berries and offered them to me in a hand ingrained with soil. I wasn't sure whether he meant me to take them indoors to be washed or eat them then and there. But a little dirt was nothing to me, who was used to snail shells in the blackberry crumble, and besides, I thought intimations of hygiene might detract from the spontaneity of the gesture. I helped myself, fumbling in my oversize leather gloves, and ended up squashing a soft raspberry against the front of my yellow shirt, leaving a streak of red, like a knife-wound in my chest. Donovan laughed. My hand itched to slap him, but I was interrupted by an apparition in pyjamas, trilby and anorak, walking unsteadily around the side of the house, tic-tacs rattling.

'Grandpa,' I said, intercepting him in the driveway. 'Where are you going?'

'I've got to go and meet Roland.' (His brother – long dead.) 'I must go or I'll be late.' He stared, perplexed, at his watchless wrist for a moment or two. 'Where's the Norton?'

'We haven't got one,' I said. I hated it when he got like this. It always seemed to happen when I was in charge. 'Roland's dead,' I added, for good measure.

'What?' He gave me a hard look. 'Who the hell are you?'

'I'm Esther,' I said, as he set off again, doddery but determined.

Donovan, who had been leaning on his fork, watching this, came over and took Grandpa's arm, and gently but firmly turned him round.

'I don't think it's time to go yet,' he said.

'Not time?' said Grandpa. 'Am I early?'

'Yes. And if you go, there'll be no one to keep an eye on the foxes.'

'Those foxes, yes. Have they been giving you any trouble? They're vermin, you know.'

'Yes. They need watching.'

Grandpa relaxed for a moment, then a thought struck him. 'Is it time to go now?'

'No.' Donovan led him back into the house, and soon had him installed in a chair overlooking the garden, where he could guard us from the depredations of vermin.

'You're a good lad, Christian,' Grandpa said, patting Donovan's arm. 'But that ladyfriend of yours,' he added in a confidential tone, 'is a trollop.'

'What on earth did he mean by that?' I said, when we were in the kitchen, enjoying long drinks of water. We were still laughing about it half an hour later. Every time I composed myself, Donovan would rasp 'trollop!' in a menacing voice, and that would set me off again.

By mid-afternoon, the front garden was transformed. The driveway was cleared and wide enough to admit a truck unscathed. The weed beds were dug over, and the whole area was bright and open. I could have done with a rest, but Donovan had the bit between his teeth now. While I forced the rotary mower over the patch of overgrown lawn between the rhododendrons and the gravel sweep, its blunt blades gnawing at the long grass and scalping the bumps, Donovan disappeared with the barrow on another errand. He returned with it laden with old bricks. 'There's a whole pile of these behind the shed,' he said. 'Do you think they're being saved for anything?' He had taken the opportunity to stick his head under the outdoor tap, and his wet hair clung together in spikes, dripping clean trails through the dust and grime on his chest.

I gave a snort. 'I doubt it. They've probably been lying there since whatever they used to be fell down.'

'Good. I'm going to use them to edge the flowerbeds. You can go and get another barrowful when you've finished that, if you like.' And he started unloading them in a neat criss-cross stack.

A moment later we heard the sound of a car engine, and the yellow Mini came bouncing up the drive towards us, raising clouds of dust. Penny jumped out, looking pristine in a mint-green halter dress and white sandals. She had the sort of even strapless tan that results from regular devotions on a sunbed. Someone else had completed the braiding job I'd begun on her hair: the beads clattered like distant applause as she walked. 'Wow!' she said, surveying the results of our labour. 'What a transformation.' We fell back, grubby serfs, to let her pass. 'I'm just going to pick up some things of Christian's,' she explained, heading for the house. 'Don't let me interrupt.'

'A goddess has come amongst us,' I observed, not entirely ironically.

'Trollop!' Donovan hissed, rolling his eyes wrathfully, and I had only just mastered my giggles by the time Penny reappeared, carrying Christian's swimming gear and a change of clothing.

'God, I don't know how you can work in this heat,' she said, watching my exertions with the lawnmower. 'I'm good for nothing when it's over eighty.' She got back in the Mini, yelping as her bare legs contacted the simmering vinyl. She solved the problem by sitting on Christian's shirt, and drove off, spraying gravel.

I fetched the rest of the bricks from the back of the shed as instructed, and while Donovan laid them out end to end along the borders, I combed the lawn clippings into a pile with a spindly leaf rake and transported them in the barrow to the now-towering mound behind the greenhouse.

The garden shimmered and sweltered in the heat of the afternoon. The bushes seemed to hiss with invisible insect life, and everywhere I looked filaments of silver spider silk caught the sunlight as they drifted in the breezeless air. I eased off my plimsolls and allowed my crumpled feet to expand, enjoying the scratchiness of the parched grass against my skin. High above me an aeroplane gouged its chalk trail in the blue. I put my head back and watched its progress dizzily. It occurred to me that, apart from those raspberries, I hadn't eaten all day, which probably accounted for my feeling of lightheadedness.

I flung the last armful of grass onto the heap and leant the empty barrow against the side of the greenhouse, catching sight of my reflection as I did so. My arms and legs were covered in scratches and weals from my tussles with the brambles and giant stingers, there was that raspberry wound on my shirt, in the midst of other grime, my face was streaked with dirt and there were bits of twig in my hair. To make matters worse I could feel an unmistakable prickling sensation at my neckline, and when I pulled open my shirt to inspect the damage I could see a burnt pink triangle pointing down my cleavage. 'Look at the state of you,' I said in disgust.

Something moved in the reflection and I spun round to find Donovan standing behind me. For a second those cold, green eyes of his stared into mine with an intensity that unnerved me, and then before I could collect myself, he launched himself at me – that's the only way to describe it – and kissed me. I felt it right through me, a swooping, sinking feeling of pleasure and fear. Somehow our arms had got round each other, and we swayed and staggered, still kissing, and I slammed hard back against the rotten frame of the greenhouse. There was a crack, and a sheet of glass like the blade of a guillotine came scything down off the roof inches from my cheek and exploded in pieces at our feet.

31

IF THE ONLY TWO WITNESSES TO AN EVENT REFUSE TO acknowledge that it took place, and refuse even to acknowledge their refusal, then for as long as that equilibrium is maintained *it never happened.*

At the sound of shattering glass, Donovan and I broke apart and looked at each other with matching expressions of shock, and something else – dismay, I think. There was just a moment when salvage might have been possible, when one of us might have thought of the right word or gesture to carry us forward from the shame of self-revelation to a safer harbour, but the moment passed. The remaining poppers of my shirt had burst open in the collision to display my sunburnt cleavage and a once-white bra. It was Donovan who looked away first, and I stepped around him, buttoning myself up, and walked up the garden and into the house. When I looked back from the safety of the kitchen's dark interior, I could see him sweeping up the broken glass.

I went upstairs and lay on my bed for a long time, look-ing at all the familiar things in my room that spoke so clearly of childhood, and felt utterly alienated from them. There were my shelves containing all the books I'd ever owned, from Enid Blyton and *Jennings* right up to *Tess of the D'Urbevilles*, my trinket dish, a charcoal drawing of Christian that I'd copied from a school photo, my glass-topped dressing table, dusted with joss-stick ash, a turquoise candle – too pretty ever to be lit. In spite of the heat I felt shivery, so I wrapped myself in my knitted counterpane, a poor relation of the Universal Quilt that had been on my bed since I was tiny. I knew every square of it, every pulled thread, every dropped stitch. It had a reas-suring, doggy smell, like one of Mum's Shetland pullovers, which reminded me of the bristly cuddles she used to give me. This memory of mother love was oddly comforting.

Why did I feel so agitated? Why wasn't I laughing and dancing around the room, enjoying this moment of epiphany? It was because I had let myself go and kissed him back with such fury. I had abandoned all reserve, all detach-ment, all dignity, and I knew without a whisper of doubt that if it hadn't been for that providential pane of glass we would have kept right on and I would have let him go

All
The
Way.

After lying in the foetal position for some time I ran myself a bath and washed all traces of the garden from my skin and hair. I put on a long white skirt and T-shirt, and went downstairs to face Donovan down with a display of complete normality.

He was nowhere to be seen, but Penny, Christian and Wart were in the kitchen making margaritas. Penny and Wart had met Christian from work and been for a swim at the Old Turtonians'. From the way they were all laughing and fooling about it seemed likely that they'd been at the tequila already. Wart kept putting his head back, blowing an ice cube high into the air and catching it in a glass. He checked me over with his usual carnivorous gaze. 'You're looking very virginal,' he said. I replied with a frigid stare.

'Front garden's a bit different,' said Christian approvingly.

'I'll say. Christ!' Wart said with feeling. He still hadn't forgiven it for the assault on his MG.

'Was that your doing?' Christian asked. He was pounding a bag of ice cubes with a meat mallet.

I nodded. 'Donovan started it. I just sort of joined in.'

At that moment in he walked.

'I can't believe what you just did out there,' said Christian. Donovan looked wary. 'What a transformation.'

Donovan relaxed. 'I quite enjoyed it,' he replied.

'Oh so *you're* the famous Donovan,' said Wart significantly, to the mystification of everyone else. Please, Wart, choke on an ice cube, drop down dead, spontaneously combust, I prayed.

Penny, who had been rooting in the larder, backed out carrying a jar of fine white crystals, and a lemon-squeezer with the snout chipped off. 'Do you suppose this is salt or rat poison?' she asked. 'Here, Wart, try it and see.'

He dipped his finger in and licked it obligingly. 'Salt,' he said, then, 'No, wait a minute,' and he threw himself on the floor and lay there twitching, while Christian and Penny went into convulsions of laughter.

Donovan and I, on the sober fringes of all this hilarity, were forced to exchange a careful, neutral smile.

Penny held up the broken lemon-squeezer for our inspection. 'I don't know what it is about this house,' she said, 'but I don't think I've ever drunk out of a teacup or glass here that wasn't chipped or cracked or held together with glue.'

I thought of my recent brush with broken glass and stared at the floor.

Wart, who had stood up and dusted himself off, having picked up quite a coating of fluff and grit, began halving lemons. 'Right. Who's for margaritas?' he said, pointing the knife at each of us in turn. 'You drinking, Donovan?'

'All right,' said Donovan, who still hadn't committed himself to the conversation and was only just inside the doorway.

'You can't, Esther,' said Wart. 'You're underage.'

'I don't want anything,' I said.

'Sour lemons,' said Wart.

There came the creak and jingle of a bicycle from outside and a moment later Mum appeared at the back door, carrying a newspaper. She raised her eyebrows to find the kitchen so crowded with people and bottles.

'Goodness, a party,' she said, removing a moulting straw hat and impaling it on a hook. She was pink in the face and perspiring freely. 'What are you making?'

'Margaritas,' said Christian, measuring tequila into the cocktail shaker.

'That sounds alcoholic,' said Mum. She climbed on a chair and deposited a fistful of loose change in the charity jar on the dresser.

'We could do you a non-alcoholic version,' Penny offered. She checked the recipe on the bottle. 'It would be just lemon juice, by the look of it.'

'Lovely,' said Mum. She snapped open the newspaper and

spread it on the table for our inspection. 'Apparently your father's got a letter in. Oh, hell's teeth! He's given our home address. I told him to do it from work.'

We crowded round and read the following:

Dear Sir

The Home Secretary is to be applauded for his bravery in taking the unpopular but nonetheless proper and necessary decision to release Janine Fellowes.

If the prison system cannot rehabilitate an eleven-year-old girl, it may as well admit publicly that all rehabilitation is beyond its power.

Those who feel ten years' imprisonment to be an insufficient punishment should remember that the ten-year stretch from eleven to twenty-one is indeed a life sentence.

Furthermore, Janine Fellowes has acknowledged her guilt, reflected at length on the effects of her crime, and expressed profound remorse. There are many convicted killers released from our prisons without a public outcry in whom this process is far from complete.

Obviously, to point out that society is in no way served by the indefinite incarceration of Janine Fellowes is not to condone her crime.

Yours faithfully
Rev Gordon Fairchild

The Old Schoolhouse
Knots Lane
Knot
Kent.

Mum chewed her lip thoughtfully. I could see she was bothered about the address. This was uncharacteristic: she wasn't generally a worrier. 'There'll be trouble,' she said.

'He's not saying anything especially controversial,' said Christian.

'No one could take offence at that, surely?' Penny agreed.

'Unfortunately it's one of those subjects that inflame people,' said Mum. 'Particularly the family of the victim.'

'They may not read *The Times*,' Donovan pointed out.

'I'm quite sure they don't,' Mum said. 'I'd be amazed if they can read at all. But once you've linked your name to a cause, news gets around. And Gordon has been outspoken on the subject before, during the trial.'

'I don't suppose there'll be the same intensity of feeling after so many years,' said Penny, soothingly.

'No, I'm probably worrying unnecessarily,' Mum said, but she didn't sound especially convinced.

The conversation moved on to plans for Penny's forthcoming birthday. She had left it too late to organise a party, and, besides, the Old Hag and the Raving Tory had made it clear they wouldn't welcome an invasion of drunken undergraduates dropping beer and cigarette ash on the blond carpets. Christian would have to take her out for a meal instead. Somewhere special. Christian rolled his eyes at this: he knew enough of Penny's tastes and expectations to deduce what this would cost him.

Acting normally is harder than it sounds when you are suffering from the impaired concentration of the newly kissed, and I could feel the old, familiar awkwardness begin to affect my limbs. I was glad when Donovan sat down at the table, apparently absorbed in the foreign news pages of the paper, and I could escape unnoticed.

In my bedroom I found a note had been pushed under the door. I scanned it as quickly as possible to see whether it contained good or bad news, before reading it properly and committing it to memory (providently, as it turned out).

> Dear Esther
> I'm sorry if I offended you just now. I didn't mean to do that. Perhaps it was the sun. If you want to go back to how we were before, that's fine. You are special to me. I can't explain.
>   D.
> Please let me know if you forgive me.

I spent a long time analysing this message, and picked it over and pulled it apart so mercilessly that pretty soon all the meaning had drained away and I couldn't work out if he was glad or sorry. It wasn't clear whether it was kissing me he regretted, or just the possibility of giving offence, but one word leapt out at me again and again. Special. You are special: the mere fact of his writing it made it true.

Everything depended on my reply.

The letter I composed, with this in mind, was very short, though long in the composition.

> Dear Donovan
> No need to apologise, there's nothing to forgive.
> You are special to me too. You always will be. So what now?
>   E.

I didn't push this under his door, like Tess of the D'Urbevilles. Not for fear of the malign influence of carpet – there was no carpet – but because I couldn't risk its being read by anyone else. I waited for Donovan to go outdoors for his night-time smoke, and when I could safely see the tip of his cigarette glowing in the front garden, I let myself into his room.

I wasn't intending to snoop: the place was in any case monastically bare. He had brought only one small bag from home, and it sat open on the floor, deputising for a wardrobe and disgorging crumpled garments. His suit – hardly worn – drooped, round-shouldered, on a sagging wire hanger on the back of the door, a symbol of his failed attempt at office life. The rest of his belongings were laid out on the table beside the unmade bed: an alarm clock, sunglasses, notebook and pen, loose change, a splayed paperback copy of *Rabbit, Run*. There was his Walkman and half a dozen tapes – Thomas Dolby, Heaven 17, Jean-Michel Jarre, and some compilations called 'synth' – and a miniature TV set with a four-inch screen. So that was what he did in his room all evening!

I cast around for a safe place to leave my note: somewhere it would be immediately found, but only by Donovan. I thought if I slipped it inside *Rabbit, Run*, marking the page, and slightly protruding, and then left the book on his pillow, he would know instantly that it had been moved, and be prompted to investigate.

As I picked up the book an envelope slid out onto the bed. It was open – in fact it must have been opened and shut many times, because the flap had started to come adrift at the crease – and a triangle of photograph was just visible. I shouldn't have looked. I wish I hadn't. But I'd seen enough by sheer accident for my curiosity to be provoked beyond the point of no return, and before my conscience could intercept I'd pulled the picture out of the envelope.

It was a colour photo of a woman lying on a bed. She wasn't naked, exactly, but the only clothes she had on – a black skirt, rucked up to the waist, and a school tie – somehow made her look more exposed than mere nudity ever could. She seemed to be laughing, but at the same time had one arm shielding her eyes from the camera. The fact that she troubled to cover her face but left her body uncovered, was another disturbing aspect of the picture. What made it more bizarre was the homeliness of the surroundings – a flowery bedspread, a reading light with a scalloped shade, a bedside table crowded with knick-knacks and clutter. There was even a pair of slippers on the floor!

I thought of Mr Clubb's magazines in the toilet – *One Hundred Genuine Married Tits and Clits* – and felt the same churning in my stomach: a curdled mixture of loathing for men, disgust at those women who gave up their secrets so easily, and shame at being made in their form.

I knew that Donovan had taken the photograph – it was so amateurish – and I guessed the woman must be his teacher. The skirt and tie was their little joke. I went to put it back in the envelope and saw someone had written a message on the back:

It's been an education!
  E.

The coincidence of that shared initial was another slap in the face, and it reminded me of my original errand, the delivery of my letter, which now struck me as ludicrously romantic and naïve. My hand closed around it and crushed it into a tight ball: I would never send it now. All the feelings of optimism stirred up by Donovan's message had evaporated. He didn't love me: he was just an incipient pervert, in the same mould as Mr Clubb, who would one day spend his leisure reading porn in the toilet and touching up his daughter's friends in the kitchen.

The slam of the front door made me jump. Using his own notepad and pen I quickly scribbled: *Donovan, Forget it. It was nothing. E.* and put it on the pillow. I replaced the photo and book as I'd found them, and dashed back to my room, closing the door just as he reached the top of the stairs. Then I tore my unsent letter into pieces and burnt them to ash using the Biarritz matchbook, which he had given me all those years ago as a token of eternal friendship.

32

WHENEVER I LOOK BACK ON THE EVENTS THAT FOLLOWED that strange day, I'm always appalled by the thought of how little it would have taken for catastrophe to have been averted. With only minute adjustments to the behaviour of any one of us, the future might have unrolled quite differently. This line of thinking can lead to madness, of course, so I don't indulge in it too often. What bothers me most, I suppose, is that we didn't realise then how happy we were. It's as if happiness is something we can only experience in retrospect, as a contrast to present misery.

The telephone calls started a few days later. No threats, or abuse, just silence, several times a day and during the night. Somehow those night calls felt much more intimidating, so we got into the habit of taking the phone off the hook after dark, in spite of Mum's misgivings that someone from overseas – Aunty Barbara, for example – might be trying to make contact. I nursed a secret ambition to intercept one of these calls and hear that sinister silence for myself. But the one time I managed to beat Mum to the phone it was just Martina, wanting to reach Christian.

'Is that you, Esther?' she asked in her uninflected drawl.

'Yes.'

'It's Martina. I'm trying to get hold of Christian. No one returns my calls nowadays.'

'He's at work.'

'Can you give me his work number?'

'He hasn't got one. It's a sort of building site.'

'Oh. Well, when you see him can you tell him to call me as soon as possible?'

'Have you tried Penny? She's not at work.'

'I've left her loads of messages and she never rings back. Anyway, it's Christian I'm after.'

The conversation ended there, and it slipped from my mind so thoroughly that I omitted to mention it to Christian when I next saw him. People say there's no such thing as forgetting; that it's all a matter of acting out subconscious desires. With that in mind, I've tried to examine my conscience since for any signs that I deliberately failed to pass on Martina's message. All I can say with certainty is that it wasn't planned.

One night, soon after this, Dad came back from visiting Mrs Tapley and said he'd seen a car parked, without lights, at the end of the lane leading to our driveway. It had sped off as he approached, before he had a chance to distinguish its make or registration. As a precaution it was decided that I should be picked up from any late babysitting appointments, and Donovan was advised to curtail his moonlight rambles, and stay close to the house when he had his last smoke of the evening. In fact he was invited, repeatedly, to smoke in the house, but couldn't be persuaded.

Christian was in favour of rounding up some of his fellow labourers from the Holiday Inn and staking out the area after dark. This was, he assured us, just the sort of job they would enjoy and excel at, some of them having already done long stretches inside for taking an overly physical approach to resolving grievances. Dad vetoed this suggestion in the strongest possible terms. 'I'm sure if we're sensible it will all blow over. A confrontation is the last thing we want.'

All this excitement provided a welcome diversion from my uneasy relationship with Donovan, which was characterised by electric awkwardness dressed up as perfect civility. I suppose he might have been taken aback by the dismissive tone of my reply. I hoped so. He certainly hadn't felt inspired to continue the correspondence. In any case, there was now a distance between us, which I felt, stubbornly, it was not up to me to bridge, though of course he was ignorant of its cause. I don't know how long I planned to sustain this impasse. There were times when I thought I'd behaved stupidly, and wasted a precious opportunity to advance our relationship. But then I thought of the photograph, and that woman, with her genuine-married-tits-and-clit, and my calcified heart hardened all over again.

THEN THE MONEY FROM THE CHARITY JAR DISAPPEARED, AND that gave me something new to think about. Mum had taken the earthenware pot down from the top of the dresser, with the intention of bagging up her year's collection of coins and taking them to the bank along with the Top of the Pew proceeds and converting the lot into a cheque for Christian Aid, and found the roll of notes – over £400 – missing.

Once the plausible explanation – that Dad, newly security-conscious in the wake of those phone calls, had taken the cash to the bank himself – had been discounted, Mum had turned the kitchen over, pulling everything out of cupboards and upending drawers. She seemed to be clinging to the hope that she might have sleepwalked one night, and removed the money to a safer place herself, without retaining any memory of the event. She said she'd once read something similar by Wilkie Collins, but Dad said nonsense, there was laudanum involved. I think she was clutching at straws, frankly. She didn't seem in the least surprised when her searches produced nothing.

The uncomfortable conclusion, reached privately but never articulated, was that one of the household must have stolen the £400. Mum and Dad, who would never accuse, or even suspect anyone of theft without proof, remained publicly wedded to the view that there must be some innocent explanation, as yet obscure to our limited human wisdom, which would eventually, with prayer and patience, be divinely revealed. What they thought and discussed behind their bedroom door I never knew. In the meantime, Dad would have to make good the loss from his Death Fund – earnings he had put by from taking local funeral services when the rector was unavailable, with the aim of accumulating enough to cover the cost of his own burial, whenever required.

It was Penny who whispered the unthinkable. We were in the very same department store café where Aunty Barbara had treated me to prawn cocktail during our assault on the sales, taking a break from the arduous job of choosing Penny something to wear on her birthday. She had brought me along as a sounding board – God only knew why, given her views on my fashion sense. Only recently she had said, 'It's incredible that you're brilliant at art, Esther. Anyone looking at what you're wearing would naturally assume you were colour blind.' I suppose my role was just to second her opinions, admire the things she liked, and disparage the things she didn't, and this I was happy to do. Then, over chocolate fudge cake, the conversation came around to the missing money.

'I hardly dare say this,' Penny said, combing ripples in the fudge with her fork, 'especially to you. But I keep having this horrible, nagging thought at the back of my mind that it was Christian.'

'Why?'

'Because he's the one who needs it most.'

'He'd never steal from Mum and Dad,' I protested. 'Or anyone, I mean.'

'Maybe he was only borrowing it, unofficially, until he got paid, not thinking it'd be missed.'

'So why didn't he just own up?'

'Because he doesn't want your parents to know he's in debt.'

'Or put it back secretly, then? Instead of sitting back and watching Dad pay up.'

'I don't know. Maybe he's got a perverted sense that he's entitled to it because your mum and dad have kept him short over the years.'

'That doesn't sound a bit like Christian,' I said. 'He's not devious like that. He's really kind – he'd do anything for anyone.'

'Yes, you're right,' said Penny, shaking her head as if to dislodge these ungenerous thoughts. Maybe she felt a little chastened by my robust defence. Then she said quietly, 'He has been known to do a little too much for some people.'

'What do you mean?' I had just taken a mouthful of cake, which I swallowed hastily. It seemed to land heavily and whole in my stomach, like a stone down a well.

'I know you think he's perfect. It's only natural. But he isn't: no one is, and you do people a disservice to imagine that they are. It means they're bound to disappoint you.'

'What has he done that's "too much"?'

'Well, he's so sympathetic and friendly, everyone comes to him with their problems. Women, I mean. And sometimes he does a rather thorough job of consoling them, if you know what I mean.'

'Oh.' I did know, and all of a sudden Penny's reluctance to return Martina's calls or go to America without him made perfect sense. Poor Penny. At last I had discovered the advantage of being Christian's sister: he could never be unfaithful to me. In fact, the more unfaithful he was to other women, the more enviable my position became. Even if Penny's revelation could not shatter my image of Christian as perfect, it did nothing for my sense of the reliability of his sex, already fatally undermined.

'Men are so horrible,' I burst out, throwing down my fork so that it bounced off the plate and cartwheeled across the table, leaving a trail of chocolate crumbs on the white table-top. 'Why are they so horrible?'

'What's brought this on?'

I could have confided in her then about Donovan. She might have given me some good advice and saved me from my own ignorance. But it was only secrecy that made it possible for me to behave normally in front of Donovan, something that would be impossible in the presence of a knowing witness. So instead I just said, 'They don't have real feelings, do they? Not like us.'

'Well,' said Penny, 'it's certainly true that they're different. But they're not all horrible all the time. I shouldn't have said any of that about Christian. I'm sorry if I've upset you. Forget I ever said it.' She had cleared her plate and was gathering herself up for another onslaught on the dress department.

'You don't really think he could have stolen the money?' I said.

'No, no. I never did. Not really. It was just my overheated imagination.'

'I would have said it's more likely that Wart might think he's entitled to the money. He was in the kitchen that day when Mum put some cash in the jar. He might have felt he was just recovering a debt.'

This seemed to strike Penny with some force. Then she shook her head. 'No. Wart wouldn't stoop to that,' she said, and I wished she could have expressed that sort of confidence in Christian.

I didn't contradict her though, because I knew it wasn't Wart. I knew very well who had taken the money, and I was just waiting to see whether, given the right occasion, he had any intention of confessing.

33

THE OPPORTUNITY AROSE QUITE SOON AND WITHOUT ANY contrivance on my part. The next time I babysat for the Conway twins it was, to my surprise, Donovan who arrived to fetch me home.

'Where's Dad?' I asked. Not ungratefully, I hoped, but as a point of information. Anything out of the ordinary was now a cause for concern.

'His car wouldn't start. Battery's flat.'

'I'm sorry you've had to come out.'

'I don't mind.' With great formality he opened the passenger door first and held it open for me. The inside of the car smelled of upholstery saturated with ancient smoke, like the saloon bar of the Fox and Pheasant.

'I used to like walking home by myself at night before all this Janine Fellowes business started up,' I said, making myself comfortable. 'It's such a pain.'

'I thought you were scared of the dark,' he said as we set off. 'You still sleep with the landing light on.'

'That's different,' I said, nonplussed to think that a habit I'd long ceased to think about had attracted his notice. 'I've got this thing about waking up in a blackout. It started at the caravan when I was little. You know how dark it is there at night.'

'The caravan,' Donovan repeated. 'I haven't thought of it for years. I wonder if it's still there.'

'I don't see why not. We used to go there every summer, until Grandpa moved in. The key's still on a hook in the cloakroom.'

'That was the last place I can remember Mum and Dad being happy. Before all the rows started.'

'Did it affect you badly when your dad left? We were never allowed to mention it at the time. Divorce was one of those words, like cancer, that you could never say out loud.'

Donovan shrugged. 'It wasn't much fun when Mum was ill. I used to stay out later and later just to avoid going home. I remember once I got locked in the park, so I stayed there all night, playing on the swings by myself. I went to sleep on a bench in the bandstand like a tramp. The funny thing was I didn't feel at all frightened or lonely. When I got home Mum hadn't even noticed I was missing. That's how bad she was. After that I did it again whenever I felt a bit low. I think I'd make a good tramp.'

'It's amazing you've turned out as normal as you have,' I said, echoing Mum's sentiments, and he acknowledged this faint praise with raised eyebrows.

'It's amazing I survived at all, considering some of the food I used to eat. I tried to cook for myself, but I hadn't got a clue. I thought everything had to be boiled – sausages, pork chops, mince, you name it. I couldn't understand why they never went brown.'

We had pulled into the driveway by now, but neither of us made any move to get out. Huge moths wheeled blurrily in the beam of the headlights, so Donovan flicked the switch off and we sat there in darkness. We were being so natural and friendly with each other that I almost forgot the electric fence of embarrassment between us.

'You laugh about it now, but it must have been horrible at the time,' I said, not wanting to bring the conversation to an end just yet.

'There were some awkward moments when Mum was really out of it. One time when I was at primary school she'd been in bed for about a week and I couldn't find any clean uniform for school, so I wore jeans and a football shirt with my tie. I was convinced I was going to get sent home or caned, but of course my teacher could see there was something going on at home, and I didn't get into trouble at all. In fact it was the kids who dared to point out that I was wearing the wrong stuff who got told off instead, which was really weird. My teacher called round after school to talk to Mum, and Mum wouldn't come out from under the bedclothes. So this teacher took all my dirty uniform home with her and washed and ironed it and brought it round at the crack of dawn so I'd have something to wear. I was so grateful, because that was all I wanted – just to come to school and not stand out.'

As someone who had never worn quite the correct uniform, but only its closest jumble sale equivalents, I could readily sympathise.

'I'm surprised she didn't get a doctor or someone in to help your mum,' I said.

'She may have done. I can only remember the bits that happened to me.'

Inside the house the front room light went off and a face appeared between the curtains, peering out, and then withdrew again. Not yet, I pleaded silently. Don't come looking for us yet. A moment or two later the bathroom light went on upstairs and I breathed again.

'Perhaps you'd have been better off living with your dad,' I said. He had always been the one with the big car and the big presents and the big wallet.

'I did for a while when Mum was taken into hospital. But I never got on that well with Suzie, not surprisingly. I know there's no one culprit in a divorce and all that, but Dad was the one who left, so naturally I blamed him. And I think he felt so guilty at the mess he'd made of everything that he was really uncomfortable in my company. He just got stuck into work and making pots of money, as if he could buy his way out of trouble.'

'Christian and I always envied you all your flash toys. We'd probably have been a bit kinder if we'd known what a miserable time you were having.'

'You weren't unkind,' Donovan said. 'I suppose I was pretty unhappy,' he went on. 'But a happy childhood's a terrible start in life: you'd never get over it. We all need a little disappointment.' And he gave me a sideways grimace that was almost a smile.

'I wonder if Mum and Dad knew all the details,' I said. 'You were always "poor Donovan" to them. Whereas you were always "rich Donovan" to us.'

'I think they did. They were fantastic to me, better than

my own parents. Your dad is such a good person. He'd give someone the shirt off his back if they asked. Before they asked, in fact.'

'It's his religion,' I replied. 'Love your neighbour as yourself, bless those that curse you, do good to them that hate you, and all that. Only he really believes it.'

'Shh!' Donovan put a finger to his lips. A fox had come slinking around the side of the house. It was a handsome, healthy-looking creature, with a lush, white-tipped tail, not one of those stringy, urban foxes with a mangy bit of rope for a brush. It must have detected movement from the car, as it stood very still and gave us a long, insolent stare. Donovan snapped the lights on and its eyes blazed yellow, then it shot across the lawn and away through a loose plank in the fence.

I'd never had such a serious and heartfelt conversation with Donovan: anything real was usually headed off by sarcasm. It was such a shame to spoil it, but I couldn't afford to waste this confessional mood. I knew what I'd seen. I hadn't imagined it, but I wanted to hear it from him.

IT HAD BEEN THE DAY AFTER THE KISS, THE NOTE, THE PHOTO. I had my period, and I came downstairs to put one of my newspaper parcels in the boiler. This was a ritual that had to be performed in private, naturally, and I was in the habit of lurking in the kitchen doorway to make sure the coast was clear, then dashing in, checking that the boiler was alight, dropping the vile thing onto the burning coals, slamming the lid, and standing guard until it was reduced to ash. On this occasion I could hear someone in the kitchen. I peeped round the door and saw Donovan standing on a chair at the dresser. There was a roll of money in his hand.

As I ducked into the cloakroom, I heard the scrape of the jar being put back on the shelf and the slap of Donovan's feet on the tiled floor as he jumped off the chair, and then the back door opened and shut and there was silence. I gave it a minute or two before venturing back to perform the rite at the boiler. With characteristic self-absorption I didn't give any thought to what Donovan was actually doing there: it was only later, when the money went missing, that the significance of the incident came back to me. At the time I experienced it quite differently, as a narrow escape from a double dose of embarrassment.

I LOOKED OUT AT THE NIGHT SKY, AND THE PROUD AND LONELY face of the moon above the treetops gave me courage. Donovan's hand moved to retrieve the keys that still dangled from the ignition.

'Why did you take the money?' I said.

Donovan looked at me blankly. 'What?' He gave a nervous laugh, as if waiting for the joke to develop, and when it didn't, he said, 'You think I stole that money. From your mum and dad?'

Deflecting a question with another question is not quite the same thing as a denial, I thought.

'Well, did you?'

'How can you come out and say that? How can you even think it? After what we've been talking about. Don't you know me at all?'

This wasn't going quite the way I'd planned. I hadn't allowed for counter-accusations in any of my mental rehearsals. I thought there might have been some pressing reason for him taking the money and I just wanted to hear it and understand.

'Apparently not,' I said. 'I would never have thought you'd steal from us. And I would never have thought you'd deny it to my face.' I risked a glance at him. He stared back at me with those acid green eyes full of hatred, the whole of his body tensed, and I thought of that other night-wanderer, the fox, standing there, not knowing whether to fight or run.

'Well, I've certainly been wrong about you, Esther,' he said in a hard voice that I'd never heard him use before. 'I used to think you were about the nicest person I'd ever met. Maybe I was a bit rough with you in the garden, but, Jesus, it was hardly more than a kiss, and you enjoyed it, I know you did. And I wrote and apologised, quite nicely, I thought, and you sent me that cold, tight-arsed note and have been avoiding me ever since like I'm a leper. Fair enough, that's up to you. But how you can sit there and accuse me of nicking four hundred quid from your mum and dad, who've taken me in again and again when they've got nothing and my own dad's practically a millionaire . . . If I had four hundred quid of my own I'd give it to them.' He was in such a spitting rage now I thought he might hit me and I flinched away, but he was just struggling to get his wallet out of his pocket. 'Here,' he scrabbled through it, pulling out notes. 'Ten, twenty, thirty, fifty. There you are, have the bloody lot.' And he threw them at me and jumped out of the car, banging the door so hard that the radio burst into life, the manic screech of bluegrass violins erupting like a coven of scrapping foxes. He strode off, not in the direction of the house, but back down the driveway into the lane, where he broke into a run. Off to find some ditch to sleep in, like a tramp, I thought spitefully.

I switched the music off and sat there, stunned, my heart

galloping in my ribs. Donovan's rant had left me completely winded. 'Men don't have feelings,' I'd complained to Penny. I was inclined to prefer them that way, now that I had been on the receiving end of a tirade of masculine 'feeling'. My legs shook as I walked towards the house. I closed the front door as quietly as possible, realising, with a fresh upsurge of indignation, that I would have to leave it unbolted in case he returned, and that there was nothing between us and our phantom enemy but a puny Yale lock.

I crept up to bed, dodging the creakier boards, and lay sleepless and agitated for hours, wondering how I would ever face him again. I think in some unexamined corner of my mind I must have known it wouldn't come to that.

34

MY SUBCONSCIOUS MUST HAVE NO SENSE OF OCCASION. When I finally fell asleep, I slept soundly until mid-morning and awoke refreshed from a series of pleasant, rosy dreams. The quarrel of the night before seemed a distant event, trivial and easily remedied – an impression that wore off with the narcotic effect of the dreams. By the time I had showered and dressed I was fretting about my mishandling of the whole business again and wondering how it could possibly be resolved. Perhaps my remarks would have made some impression on his conscience and the money would, as if magically, reappear. But he had been so emphatic, so furious in his denials. Perhaps I should have told him bluntly what I'd seen. But I hadn't wanted him to confess because he had no alternative. I'd wanted him to tell me because he wanted to tell me. Perhaps – a dark thought spread like spilt ink – I had made a terrible mistake.

I tapped on his bedroom door but there was no reply,

and when I looked inside it was clear the bed hadn't been slept in. His car was still in the driveway where we had left it. He must have stayed out all night.

I couldn't hang around at home all day waiting for him to come back, so I borrowed Mum's bike – Donovan's restoration job a fresh reproach – and cycled over to Dawn's. There was no one at home, so I rode right across the estate to Pam and Andy's, remembering as I rang the bell that the family had gone to Minehead for the week. Andy's car was not out front: I wondered if he had taken Pam to hospital. I was about to swing the bike round when Pam's face appeared at the upstairs window, and she gestured frantically for me to wait while she scrabbled with the catch.

'Oh, Esther, thank God someone's come,' she said, just her head and shoulders visible over the sill. My heart lurched. I'm going to have to deliver the twins! I thought.

'You're not in labour, are you?' I quailed.

'No,' she said impatiently. 'I've run out of biscuits.' She disappeared from view and a moment later bobbed up again and said 'Catch!' and threw a small beaded purse down to me. Inside was a door-key and some change. 'I can't come down the stairs, or I'll never get up again. Can you nip round the corner and get me a packet of digestives? Better make it two. And a bottle of Tizer.'

I waved my assent, delighted to be of any assistance that was not obstetrical.

'She's not had the babies then?' said the shopkeeper as she appraised my purchases.

I shook my head. 'Any time now,' I improvised, pleased to be at the cutting edge of local gossip.

'Oh, Esther, you've saved my life,' Pam called out as I let myself in and climbed the stairs to the flat, which was identified even at some distance by the astringent smell of fresh paint. Through an open doorway I could see the nursery, newly decorated in shades of yellow with a border of rabbits running round the wall.

Pam was propped on her bed against a bank of pillows, legs splayed, her once-pretty face set on top of a vast pyramid of flesh clad in grey jersey. An electric fan whirred in the corner, its head turning slowly from side to side in a disappointed fashion. As the breeze caught the hem of her T-shirt at each revolution, it lifted slightly to reveal a taut, shiny belly, strafed with red marks. Her navel bulged like an acorn. She received the bag of provisions with something close to rapture, tearing into the biscuits with urgent, clumsy fingers. 'Big, aren't I?' she said cheerfully. This was the Pam who had lived on apples and yoghurt to fit into her wedding dress. 'It's all water,' she went on, raising a puffy foot for my inspection.

'Are you having the babies at home?' I asked. I had serious doubts about her ability to get through the doorway.

'No, it's too risky for a first-timer. Especially with twins.' She lifted her T-shirt and scratched her belly violently. 'Excuse me,' she said. 'It itches like hell.'

'You poor thing,' I said helplessly. I was conscious as never before of my twenty-four-inch waist, and resolved to make more of it in future. 'It must be awful, just waiting.'

'It's not too bad,' said Pam, taking a swig of Tizer. 'I've got everything I need.' She waved a hand at the comforts of her confinement: a pile of Danielle Steel paperbacks on the bedside table, a small TV on a bracket on the opposite wall, and a telephone.

'It won't be long now,' I said, encouragingly.

'Yeah. I've had a few twinges today actually.'

I jumped up. 'Shall I phone Andy?'

'No, no.' She laughed at my anxiety. 'It's nothing major. You could give me a hand getting off this bed if you like. I'm dying for the loo.' She tried to shuffle towards the edge of the bed, but ended up stranded on her back like an upturned insect. I had to roll her onto her side and hoist her into a sitting position before bracing myself against the bedstead so she could use me as a crutch. In the course of this clumsy manoeuvre I brushed against her belly and recoiled from its unexpected solidity. I had imagined it to be soft and doughy, but it was hard as a sack of rocks. By the time Pam was vertical we were both giggling and panting from our exertions. 'You wait,' she grumbled, hobbling towards the door on her bloated feet. 'This'll be you one day.'

I just laughed, appreciating perhaps for the first time the many blessings of inexperience. Pam was someone whose independence and maturity Dawn and I had always envied: look at her now. I vowed I would never allow such an outrage to be perpetrated against me as long as I lived. If having children was compulsory, which I didn't admit, I would adopt them fully formed.

A while later Pam returned, looking calmer, and allowed herself to be repositioned on the bed. I had taken advantage of her absence to straighten the covers, brush biscuit crumbs out of the creases, and beat some air back into her crushed pillows. I took a couple of mouldering coffee cups to the kitchen and dumped them in the sink for Andy to deal with. For some reason I felt a simmering resentment against the man.

Pam seemed overcome by these minute attentions. 'Oh, Esther, it's so nice to have some company,' she said, grabbing my hand. 'Will you come again tomorrow, if you're not too busy? Only if you're not too busy. I get so lonely with Andy out all day and Mum and Dawn away.'

'Okay,' I shrugged, unused to finding myself in demand.

'Just ring the bell and I'll throw the key down,' she said. 'Don't worry if something comes up and you can't make it.'

'Nothing will come up,' I assured her. 'Nothing ever does.' Prophecy was never one of my gifts.

ON MY WAY HOME I TOOK A DETOUR TO THE CRAFT FAIR AT the church hall to find a present for Penny, whose birthday it was that day. She was coming round in the evening to receive due homage before Christian took her out to a Greek restaurant in Fitzrovia where they smashed plates for fun, a notion that appalled Mum, who considered it roughly equivalent to the excesses associated with the Fall of Rome.

I had amassed plenty of babysitting money now, and wanted to get her something special, but most of the stalls offered nothing but pointless domestic fripperies that seemed to date from the remotest periods of antiquity. Crocheted antimacassars, quilted tissue-box covers and padded coat hangers were unthinkable, even as a joke.

At one of the tables, Mrs Probert, one of Mum's old adversaries from the Mothers' Union, was selling hand-knitted baby clothes, so I bought two pairs of bootees for Pam's twins – primrose yellow to match the nursery walls. Mrs Probert raised her crayoned eyebrows as I handed over the money, and I replied with a mysterious smile. It would be all over the parish by tomorrow.

I was beginning to regret leaving my errand until the last minute, as there was clearly nothing suitable amongst this selection of chutney and old lace, when I noticed, stuck in

the furthest corner, a man of about Dad's age selling pieces
of turned wood and polished stones, as well as chunks of
rose quartz and amethyst. This was more like it. It didn't
take me long to settle on a dark green agate egg, which sat
heavily in the palm of my hand, cold and smooth and reassuring. The sensation was so pleasant that I was tempted
to buy one for myself, but to do that would somehow
cheapen the gift itself, so I gave myself a good stern talking to, and found I could do without one pretty well. The
man, who seemed delighted to have made a sale, put the
egg in a sturdy oval box wadded with packing straw, as
though there was a chance of it hatching, and I went on
my way thoroughly satisfied.

All these tasks had done an excellent job of filling up
the day and distracting me from the matter of Donovan.
The knowledge that he remained to be faced had been there
in the background, ticking away with the insistence of a
clock in an otherwise silent room. Nevertheless, as I rode
home with the sun on my back, flying down Knots Lane at
full tilt on the strength of those new brakes, I felt suddenly
optimistic. Maybe it was the weather, or that buying presents really does confer benefits on the giver, or perhaps I
was simply appreciating my freedom in contrast to Pam's
confinement: whatever the reason, I found myself laughing
out loud. It may as well be recorded. It would be a long,
long time before I was that happy again.

DONOVAN'S CAR WAS NOT IN THE DRIVEWAY. REPRIEVE! I
thought, and then moments later, Damn! If I was going to
have to endure another scene, or even dredge up an apology, it had better be sooner rather than later. It was only
as I was stowing my presents in the wardrobe that I was

struck by a bolt of belated intuition. I tore down the attic stairs to the landing and wrenched Donovan's door open without knocking. The sound of my footsteps echoed in the empty room. He had gone properly this time. Barely a trace remained of his occupancy; even the bed was stripped, the sheets and blankets neatly folded. Only a faint pattern in the dust on the bedside table, discernible to my fanatical eye, described the former position of his few possessions. The clock, the notepad, the book-with-photo. I opened the top drawer of the chest, and for the first time the handle stayed put. Another thing he'd fixed. I'm not sure what I was hoping to find. Some clue, perhaps, that he intended to return. But everything I saw suggested otherwise. I dropped to my knees and peered under the bed. A dark shape squatted in the fluff: the Raskolnikov hat. I dusted it and hung it on the doorhandle, just in case.

I found Mum in the dining room trying to wrap Penny's present — a cast-iron bootscraper — in a small piece of much-recycled paper. 'I didn't know what to get,' she said, nipping off a length of Sellotape with her teeth. 'Do you think it'll do?' Poor Mum. She didn't have a clue about presents. Not a clue. And poor Penny, who wore the sort of boots that required specialist dry cleaning, rather than scraping.

I looked at my watch. It was well past closing time. 'It'll have to, won't it,' I said. It wasn't her fault that she'd been left behind by the modern world of consumerism. If she had her way we'd still be bartering chickens. 'Donovan's gone. Did you know?'

'Yes, of course,' said Mum. 'He went off at lunchtime.'

'Did he say why?'

'I think he'd probably had enough of us. There wasn't much point his being here once he'd lost his job. It's a pity:

he was such a good handyman, but I couldn't very well keep him here against his will.'

'I wonder where he'll go,' I said, fishing for information. 'He can't go back to Bath, can he? There are tenants.'

'He said accommodation wasn't a problem. And he gave me a lovely fuchsia for the front garden as a thank you. I hope I don't kill it.'

'That was kind.'

'Yes, it was. You know, I'm surprised he didn't tell you he was going,' Mum said. She peered at my face as though trying to read small print. 'I thought you two were friends.'

I shrugged. 'We were. But not that friendly, evidently.'

'Ah well.'

I could have blurted everything out then: it might have given me some relief. But Mum, although sympathetic after a fashion, tended to face down displays of turbulent teenage emotion with a bracing pragmatism that left you strangely unconsoled. Besides, I was reluctant to admit my part in Donovan's exit. I knew that Dad, especially, would not look kindly on my accusation of theft, however well-founded.

Mum had given up trying to make the ends of the wrapping paper meet. The gaps were bridged by a weft of Sellotape. 'There we are. That's the best I can do. What did you get her?'

I fetched the agate egg and unveiled it with pride. Mum looked at it, perplexed. 'Whatever is it for?'

'It's not *for* anything. It's just a pleasing object,' I explained.

'How much did it cost?' she asked, and blenched at the answer. 'Good Lord. I didn't know you even had that much money. I suppose you know the sort of thing young women like better than I do. Penny's a complete enigma to me.'

'What do you mean?' Mum seldom ventured opinions about other people, but even so I had formed the impression that she didn't much care for Penny. I'd put it down to standard-issue maternal jealousy.

'Well, she has all these theories about social justice and equality and what-have-you. But in practice she's an out-and-out hedonist. I can't quite reconcile the two Pennys.'

'What's a hedonist?'

'How can I put it? A pleasure-seeker. Someone who likes the finer things in life.'

'Oh, Mum,' I said, exasperated. 'Only you could make that sound like a crime.' Mum acknowledged the truth of this with a laugh. 'Anyway, you'll have to get to like her,' I went on, 'because she's probably going to end up as your daughter-in-law.'

Mum looked wary. 'Is this prediction based on any particular information?'

'No,' I admitted. 'But it just seems likely. Sooner or later.'

Mum gave me one of those eyes-closed smiles, expressive of superior wisdom. 'I'm sure I'd feel very affectionate to anyone Christian chose to marry,' she said. 'But I don't think for one moment that it will be Penny.'

This potentially interesting conversation was cut short by the arrival of Christian, straight from his labouring job at the new Holiday Inn. He clumped into the kitchen, shedding clods of dried plaster and a nimbus of fine brown dust, in his habitual quest for food.

'You're eating out later,' Mum reminded him, as we watched him dispose of the end of a cottage loaf and a slab of Emmenthal. He stood at the fridge, still browsing. 'And Penny's due any moment. Shouldn't you get changed?'

Christian glanced at his watch. 'Ten minutes,' he said.

'Plenty of time to get ready.' He took the rest of the Emmenthal and went upstairs, humming, and presently we heard water thundering into the bath, as pipes all over the house began to knock and groan.

The next to arrive was Dad. He was supposed to have stopped off at a bakery on the way home to pick up a birth-day cake for Penny, but had predictably forgotten, and was immediately turned round to be re-dispatched. 'You're looking all preoccupied,' Mum said, as Dad stood on the threshold, patting his pockets and chuntering to himself. 'What's the matter?'

'Bit of an upsetting day,' Dad said. 'One of my prisoners tried to hang himself. We got him down in time, but it still leaves you feeling rather shaken. I hadn't even picked up that he was depressed. More depressed than anyone else, I mean. And then there was something this morning. I wasn't going to mention it. But when I went out to the car there was a dead fox on the bonnet. More than dead – mangled, in fact. I had to wash the windscreen, and then bury the poor thing.'

'Oh dear,' Mum exclaimed. 'Poor you. Never mind the cake, we'll find something else to put the candles in. Penny won't mind. You go and sit down.' She steered him back into the sitting room and pressed him into an armchair, where he sat looking thoroughly unrelaxed. I made him a cup of tea while Mum hunted in the larder for a cake-substitute.

Christian sauntered in, preceded by a spicy gust of cologne. He was wearing a salmon pink shirt, snakeskin boots with Cuban heels, and smart trousers. The fabric had a blue-black sheen, like birds' feathers. In one hand he carried the Raskolnikov hat. 'Where's Donovan?' he said. 'His room's empty.'

'Gone,' I said. 'Packed up and gone.'

'Oh bummer,' Christian replied. 'We were going to play squash tomorrow. I'd booked a court. Why did he go so suddenly?'

'Did you say Donovan's gone home?' asked Dad, catching up.

'Yes. He left today.'

'What a pity. It wasn't anything we did, was it?'

'I don't know,' I said, snappishly. 'I don't know why you all think I'm the expert on Donovan.'

'Touchy,' said Christian, pretending to quake.

I glared at him but he replied with a stagey wink. He had put the Raskolnikov hat on by now and it rather suited him.

Grandpa Percy, who had been asleep on the couch all this time, woke up suddenly and stared around in alarm. 'Who's that pansy?' he said, pointing at Christian. He looked affronted at our burst of laughter.

A silver Jaguar, registration DOU9, pulled up in the driveway. 'Oh-oh, it's the whole tribe,' said Christian, hoiking up his trousers, and tucking in the salmon pink shirt, as if to try and make less of it, before going to open the door.

I was still chortling over the wit of Grandpa, when he leant towards me and whispered, 'He's trouble, that boy. But don't worry: I've fixed him.' And he sat back, arms folded, in an attitude of deep satisfaction. I didn't have time to ponder this comment – in any case, Grandpa's remarks were seldom as apposite as his earlier one-liner – because at that moment Christian ushered in Penny's parents and began making introductions.

The Raving Tory and the Old Hag fell disappointingly

short of their epithets in the flesh. Mrs Ridyard was tall and
slim with an immaculate tan, and could have passed for
under forty. She wore her strawberry blonde hair in a French
plait, topped by a little tuft, and her dress, shoes and bag
were all in the same shade of green that must have been
plucked from a colour-chart to match her eyes. Only the
hand with which she shook mine betrayed her, and I remembered Aunty Barbara's oracular utterance on the horrors of
ageing. 'Neck and hands, Esther. They're the first to show.'
I glanced at Heather's neck: it was hidden by the sheerest
wisp of chiffon scarf.

Doug was over six feet tall and presented a massive, double-
breasted front to the world. He had regular features, a full
head of hair, greying from the front, and decent teeth: enough
to earn the accolade 'good looking' from women of Mum's
age and over. For a self-made man he was surprisingly diffi-
dent, and offered me the daintiest handshake imaginable.

Behind them stood Penny, looking elegant in a dark blue
crepe and velvet cocktail dress and velvet choker with a
diamond clasp. She seemed to find the collision of her two
worlds an uncomfortable experience, as a blush swept over
her face and neck as she entered the room.

'We're on our way out ourselves,' Heather was explaining to Dad. 'So we thought we might as well drop Penny
off on the way. And she insisted we stop off and say hello.
I hope we're not interrupting anything.'

'Not at all,' Dad replied. 'We're about to have some cake,
I think.' At which point Mum came in, carrying a tray and
singing Happy Birthday, so we all joined in, and if Doug
and Heather were surprised to see twenty candles impaled
in a round of Stilton, they were too polite to show it.

Christian re-did the introductions for Mum's benefit, and

there were more handshakes and polite expressions of pleasure at having met at last, having heard so much, etc, etc.
The formality of the scene struck me as highly significant.
The parents of the bride meet the parents of the groom. I
looked at Penny's flushed face. Perhaps she thinks he's going
to ask her to marry him tonight, I thought. Perhaps he is!
A weighty silence settled over the room. I felt as though
the cheese required some explanation, and I was worried
that Grandpa Percy might come out with another remark
about pansies or worse, so I said, 'We were going to have a
proper bought cake, but one of Dad's prisoners tried to hang
himself—' but Mum cut me off.

'I nearly forgot the most important thing,' she said, and
produced her present from behind the door, which it was
helping to prop open. Christian and I then fetched our gifts
and Penny was forced to open them in front of us all like
a child, an experience I knew she would be hating.

'Oh. A boot-scraper,' she said, liberating it from its snare
of Sellotape. 'How unusual. Thank you.' She said this with
real warmth, and I realised she didn't hold it against my
parents. It was only innocence, not malice, that informed
their lousy taste.

Maybe I imagined the blink of disappointment that
passed across her face when she saw that the box Christian
handed her was far too large to contain jewellery of any
kind. But I certainly didn't imagine the pause before the
ambiguous word 'Well!' when she found that it contained
a yoghurt-maker. She recovered her composure instantly.
'Thank you, Christian,' she said, laying a hand lightly on
his arm. 'Are you trying to domesticate me?'

'No. I prefer you wild,' he replied, and Mr Ridyard
guffawed.

'A yoghurt-maker,' Mum said enthusiastically, putting on her glasses to read the blurb on the box. 'That's useful. I wouldn't mind one of those myself.' I cringed. That was exactly the sort of endorsement that would consign it to the back of Penny's wardrobe for ever.

Penny was now lifting the lid on the agate egg. 'Oh Esther, it's beautiful,' she enthused, transferring it from hand to hand to feel its weight and smoothness, just as I had done. 'Look, everyone.' Her delight was so sincere, and contrasted so blatantly with her measured responses to the other gifts that I felt a little uncomfortable and almost wished I'd got her one of those antimacassars instead. The egg was passed around the company for general admiration.

'What a lot of thought has gone into these presents,' said Heather, regular recipient of measly old diamonds.

'I'll have you know I put a lot of thought into that cheque I wrote out,' Doug told his daughter. 'I thought: I wonder how quickly she'll get through that. And: I hope to God it doesn't bounce, among other things.' We all chortled politely.

'Are you sure we can't offer you some refreshments?' Dad said again, clapping his hands together and adopting the hearty vicar persona he often resorts to when at a loss. 'What have we got, Pru?' he said helplessly.

'Tea, coffee, milk, water ...' said Mum.

'Stilton,' said Christian.

'No, we must be on our way, thanks all the same,' said Doug, glancing at his watch. 'Some friends of Heather's are opening a restaurant tonight, so we're going along to be guinea pigs. Aren't we, darling?'

Heather grimaced. 'We could do without it, frankly. It's right down in Canterbury.'

'I hope they don't go in for breaking plates, like this place Christian's so keen on,' said Mum, for whom the issue still rankled. 'I wouldn't have thought that was any way to run a business.'

'They're only cheapo plates,' said Christian. 'It's not Wedgwood or anything.' Mum refused to be mollified.

'It was very nice to meet at last,' said Heather, and there was another round of criss-crossing handshakes, and Grandpa, who always took any signs of departure as a personal invitation, had to be persuaded that it wasn't time for him to go anywhere. The rest of us filed out onto the driveway to wave them off. Doug opened the passenger door for Heather and allowed her to arrange herself in a position likely to minimise creasing, before shutting her in. He gave a last wave through the open window as they drove off.

'Wasn't that a nice surprise?' said Dad.

'I must say, your parents are very charming, Penny,' said Mum.

'That was just for show,' Penny replied. 'They were at each other's throats in the car before we arrived.'

'You're not serious,' said Mum, affronted to have been so easily deceived by appearances. 'They looked perfectly devoted.'

'Oh, they can turn it on for an audience, but they actually can't stand each other. Dad's wanted a divorce for years, but Mum won't give him the satisfaction.'

Christian laughed at our parents' matching expressions of consternation. 'I'm very sorry to hear that,' said Dad, recovering. 'If it's true. But the fact is, Penny, a marriage is a sacred mystery that no one outside it can claim to understand. So it's safest not to speculate.' Penny blushed, rebuked.

The minicab that was due to take them up to town was booked for seven but by quarter past had not arrived. Christian was starting to pace, irritably: the restaurant had made it clear that they wouldn't hold the table for late-comers. Penny and I were playing backgammon on the coffee table. She, too, had remarked on Donovan's absence, and shot me an enquiring look when Christian said he had 'done a runner', but I had answered with a shake of the head. I knew what would happen: I'd get two sentences into my story and the cab would arrive and carry her off before she had a chance to commiserate. From the hallway came the trilling of the telephone.

'That'll be the cab company,' said Christian, beating me to the door. 'The driver's got lost. Or broken down.'

Then Dad's voice called, 'Christian. A young lady for you. Martina,' and I sensed Penny stiffen.

'I forgot to tell you, she rang a few days ago,' I called after Christian. 'You were supposed to ring her. Sorry.' He gave me a withering look.

In the sitting room Penny and I resumed our game, but I could tell her heart wasn't in it. Tuning in was taking all her concentration. I could practically see her hair standing on end to receive signals.

'What does she want, I wonder?' Penny said finally. 'She's not ringing to wish me a happy birthday, that's for sure.'

'Christian's not doing much of the talking,' I whispered. His contribution seemed to be confined to monosyllabic expressions of concern, and those reassuring grunts intended to convey unflagging attention. Then, after a longish silence at our end, we heard him say, 'Don't say that, Martina. You've got everything to live for,' at which point we abandoned any pretence of interest in backgammon and sat eavesdropping unashamedly.

'I never got that message...I would have rung back... of course I haven't been avoiding you...isn't your mum there?...of course you're not a burden...'

A black saloon car came bouncing over the potholes in the driveway, its waving aerials giving it the appearance of a giant beetle. The driver flicked a cigarette out of the window into the flowerbed and leaned on the horn.

'Christian, your chauffeur's here,' called Mum, for whom minicabs signified a profligacy that was all of a piece with snakeskin boots and plate-breaking. Penny jumped up, grabbing her handbag.

There was a pause. 'Penny, tell him to wait,' came the peremptory reply.

Penny bridled at being given an order, but obliged by signalling to the driver through the window that they'd be five minutes.

'On second thoughts tell him to go,' Christian called.

'What do you mean? Go without us?'

Christian had apparently finished his telephone conversation, as a moment later he appeared at the front of the house making placatory gestures to the minicab driver, who was starting to rant.

'What the hell is he doing?' asked Penny in bewilderment, as Christian produced a note from his wallet and handed it to the driver, who took it with a very bad grace, and drove off making V signs out of the window. 'What's going on?' she said, intercepting Christian as he came back indoors. Mum and Dad had also convened in the hallway, alarmed by the commotion outside.

'That was Martina on the phone,' said Christian. 'She's

seriously suicidal. I think I'm going to have to go and sort her out.'

Penny's face flamed, her prospects for a pleasant evening in ruins. 'How can you be sure it's not just emotional black-mail? She's done this sort of thing before, ' she said, appeal-ing to us.

'I don't know. She sounded very depressed. Much worse than usual. Sort of resigned to not getting better.'

'Where are her parents?' Dad asked. 'Is she by herself?'

'She hasn't got a dad. Her mum is away for the night, and she can't get hold of her.'

'She's doing it deliberately,' Penny said. The fact that her cynicism was partly motivated by selfishness was adding an extra dimension to her impatience. I knew what she was thinking but didn't dare say: *on my birthday!*

'Do you think she's likely to harm herself?' Dad asked, very serious now.

'It's possible,' said Christian. 'I don't know, I'm not a psychiatrist. She certainly threatened to.'

'Well, there you are,' said Penny. 'People who genuinely intend to kill themselves just go ahead and do it. They don't start advertising it.'

'That's not a safe assumption,' said Dad.

'If you really think she's in danger can't you call the police, or a doctor? Why do you have to get involved?' Penny pleaded.

'I can't just ignore her. It would be on my conscience for ever if something happened. Anyway, how can you be so callous? She used to be your friend.'

'Yes, she did. Until you slept with her.'

There was a bristly silence. 'Look, can we not talk about this now,' Christian said, sensing the moral high ground crumbling underfoot. 'My main concern at the moment is to prevent a tragedy. I'm sorry it's buggered up your special day. I'll make it up to you.'

'Go on, you go,' said Penny. 'But don't expect me to be here when you get back.'

'What's that supposed to mean?'

'Just what I say. I won't sit here twiddling my thumbs while you swan off playing the Good Samaritan to your admirers. You encouraged her dependence on you: now you solve it. But I'm not waiting for you. You've humiliated me enough.'

'What do you think I should do?' Christian appealed to Mum and Dad who were looking somewhat buffeted by this exchange.

Dad gave one of his eyebrows a desperate tug. 'If you feel there's a chance she might harm herself, and there's no one closer to her who might be able to help, then I think your instinct to go is probably right. As to the rest...' he shook his head to express his utter perplexity at the not-so-sacred mysteries of their relationship.

Penny's eyes bulged with the effort of not shedding tears. Her face was so red I could feel the heat coming off her cheeks. She sat down on the settle, fingers laced across her ribcage, gazing into space and making no further intervention. She knew the decision was made. The only question now was how to comport herself.

'You could come with me,' was Christian's last, desperate bid. 'We could have it all sorted out in an hour and go on somewhere from there.'

Penny replied to this with a slow lowering of her eyelids. She would never look on him again.

'Well, if I'm going I'd better go,' he said, to no one in particular, patting his pocket to check his wallet. Of course – it was full of cash to pay for the meal.

'Do you want to take the car?' Dad suggested.

Christian shook his head. 'She lives in Clapham. It'll be quicker by train. I wouldn't mind a lift to the station, though.'

'Is it a good idea to wear that shirt on public transport?' said Mum, without any comic intent. 'I should have thought it's asking for trouble.'

Christian laughed dismissively, but he obviously thought the better of it, as he went upstairs and came down a moment later in jeans and a T-shirt. He was still wearing the Raskolnikov hat, which he seemed to have claimed as his own.

'Righto then,' he said, looking expectantly at Dad, who plucked his car keys from the hall table and flung open the front door. Christian threw a last, supplicating glance at Penny, whose gaze remained averted, before following Dad out and slamming the door behind him.

There was a moment or two as we adjusted to their absence, then Penny opened her eyes.

'May I use your phone?' she said, with perfect composure.

'Of course, dear,' said Mum. 'You're very welcome to stay if you like. Or Gordon will run you home when he gets back. Whichever you prefer. I'm sorry your birthday's been spoilt, but there will be other opportunities...'

Penny gave a thin-lipped smile.

Mum and I withdrew as she picked up the phone, but eavesdropping was second nature to me now, and I felt somehow entitled to know the outcome of the drama.

'Hello Wart. Thank God you're there,' I heard her say, in a voice that took no pains over privacy. 'I thought you might be in France already. Can you come and get me?... Yes, right this minute...I'm at the Fairchilds'...I'll tell you about it later. Tomorrow?...I suppose I could pack tonight...Okay, see you soon.'

She returned to the sitting room, much comforted to find that in some quarters at least she still had the power to command.

'Are you going to France?' I asked, making no attempt to conceal what I'd heard.

Penny nodded. 'First thing in the morning.'

'Are you going to tell Christian?'

'You can tell him,' she said, indifferently. 'If he asks.'

'I thought you didn't like Wart that much,' I said, but even as I spoke I couldn't actually remember any specific instance where she'd expressed dislike. Perhaps I had just projected my own aversion onto her, when there was none.

'I never said that,' Penny replied. 'And anyway, he's crazy about me. Which can be quite persuasive.' She had positioned herself on the arm of the sofa, looking out of the front window. The backgammon set lay abandoned on the coffee table, mid-game. It would still be there days, weeks later, marking the moment like a stopped clock.

Wart arrived within the hour. He must have driven with his foot to the floor in case Penny changed her mind. Unable to judge the mood indoors, he stayed in the car, a proprietorial arm along the back of the passenger seat, while Penny called a goodbye to Mum and gave me a hug that had an air of finality about it. She ran out to the car and was back a moment later to retrieve the agate egg, which in her haste she had forgotten. She didn't bother to take the boot-scraper or the yoghurt machine, I noticed.

'I'm not offended,' Mum said firmly. 'The poor girl was overwrought.' She put the boot-scraper out on the doorstep in case Penny changed her mind and came back for it, and

there it would stay, unclaimed, until autumn, when it began
to acquire smears of mud and dead leaves from passing boots,
and was thereafter in daily use.

WHEN I TOOK MYSELF UP TO BED MY MIND WAS SPINNING LIKE
the plate trick in the unvisited Greek restaurant, except
that I couldn't keep my thoughts under control. Donovan:
crash, Pam: *crash*, the hanging man: *crash*, Martina,
Christian, Penny: *crash, crash, crash*. Even when I lay back
on the bed it seemed to tilt.

To cheer myself up I decided to re-read Donovan's note,
the only thing of his I had left. I knew it by heart anyway,
but somehow seeing his handwriting intensified the effect.
When I took it from its place of safe-keeping, tucked into
the frame of my dressing-table mirror, another horrible jolt
awaited me.

Esther
I have taken back my first letter because I retract what I
wrote. I said you were special to me. You are not.
     Donovan

It wasn't so much the contents of the note that floored
me as the method of delivery, which relied on the accurate,
mortifying assumption that I intended to re-read the original, and also allowed no opportunity for retaliation. Short
of dancing round the room, shaking my fist and slamming
a foot through the floorboards like Rumpelstiltskin, I had
no outlet for my rage. Nothing chases sleep away like this
sort of unspent indignation, so I pulled up a chair to the
window and watched the tatters of cloud racing across the
moon, and the trees jerking and diving in the copse. I could

hear the low growl of an aeroplane somewhere far above, the church bell tolling, and in the far distance, the mournful wail of an ambulance.

I suppose I must eventually have fallen asleep where I was sitting, because the next thing I knew Mum was standing over me, a ghost of herself, with her white nightdress and floating hair, shaking my shoulder and saying, 'Esther, Esther, wake up. Something terrible's happened.' And with those words the picturebook of my childhood fluttered before me, page by page, in all its strange and wonderful detail, and slammed shut for ever.

35

THE TWELVE MONTHS THAT FOLLOWED THE ACCIDENT WERE the worst of our lives. I use the word 'accident' grudgingly: only a pedant or a lawyer would deny that Christian was the victim of a crime.

Although he was the one paralysed, it's no exaggeration to say that what happened to him shattered us all. Only Grandpa Percy, adrift and unreachable in his dementia, remained untouched.

Dad underwent a spiritual crisis that took him years to resolve, and ultimately cost him his job: in the crucible of suffering, he found his faith melted away, leaving him prone to fits of crushing guilt and nihilistic despair. He saw the fault as his alone. If only he hadn't sent that letter to the papers supporting Janine Fellowes' release, and giving our home address in black and white. He was prepared for hostile criticism, and even some personal danger, but he had never dreamed that anyone would hunt down his son. I couldn't help remembering that they'd nearly got Christian the first time, with that brick through the window. I'm sure Dad remembered it too.

'You feel abandoned,' said his spiritual adviser, Canon Fogle. 'You think: how can a loving God have visited this tragedy upon my innocent son? Why, in my hour of need, is He so remote?'

'No,' said Dad. 'I think: there is no God. I've been wrong all along. My whole life has been based on a mistake.'

He lost interest in his work at the prison: he had no sympathy any more for criminals, those casual, remorseless wreckers of lives, and no message of divine salvation to redeem them. He tried to resign but they wouldn't let him. They gave him compassionate leave, and then sick leave, and then extended sick leave, until in the end he obliged and became sick. I remember coming home from school each day to find him sitting in the same chair in the dining room, absorbed, to the point of autism, in sorting the pieces of some vast jigsaw onto trays, by shape and colour, while the picture made a slow, ragged advance across the table. When it was finished he took a photograph of it, which struck me as highly peculiar. This was hardly an episode he'd want any reminder of, I thought. Not that there was much chance of a print ever surfacing: in our house films sat around in drawers undeveloped for years.

Mum's sympathies and energies were focused on Christian: there wasn't much left over for Dad. 'I've got two genuine invalids to care for here,' I once heard her snap. 'Don't waste my time with your bogus afflictions.' She coped better than him, publicly at least, but how much of it was a performance for Christian's benefit I never knew. Hers had always been a more wrathful God, and her opinion of mankind more pessimistic: it could be said that the disaster confirmed rather than undermined her view of the world as a vale of injustice and tears. Perhaps women are just stronger. I know she aged about ten years in as many months, and her hair fell out in handfuls. I used to find slimy skeins of it choking up the plughole in the bath. Where once it had been so lush, twisted and coiled and pinned, it now sat like cobwebs, revealing the pink of her scalp underneath. She didn't make any attempt to disguise it (if, indeed, she'd even noticed: she'd never had any personal vanity), until Christian asked if she was having chemotherapy without telling us. After that she combed the whole lot forward and chopped it into a fringe, and wore a headscarf to cover the back.

Just as I can't remember when I first learned that we all have to die, I don't think there was a specific moment when I was told that Christian would never walk again. The bad news seemed to come piece by piece, anticipated, delivered, withdrawn, rephrased and hedged about with uncertainties. Christian knew he'd broken his back from the moment he hit the ground, but some stubborn streak of optimism convinced him that the combination of modern medicine and his own invincible willpower would prevail. It was a long time before he was prepared to make any accommodation with his condition that was anything other than short term. 'Just until I'm back on my feet,' he'd say, as though he'd sprained his ankle.

Perhaps we were to blame for colluding in his self-deception. But we could see how close to despair he was, and none of us had the courage to extinguish that faint glimmer of false hope with a cold draught of truth. Sometimes honest comfort isn't well received. There was

one occasion early on, while Christian was still in hospital, before he was moved to the specialist unit at Hither
Green. I was sitting with him, watching him eat his lunch
– some sort of fish and potato gloop with peas: real invalid's
food. His legs, on top of the covers, were still tanned from
the summer; his catheter tube emerged from the hem of
his pyjama shorts and vanished over the far side of the bed.
He was propped up on a bank of pillows against the
adjustable backrest, but not quite upright enough, so he
couldn't always manage to convey the fork to his mouth
without dropping lumps of food. I didn't know whether to
pretend I hadn't noticed, or offer to try and shift him, but
after the third or fourth spill he started swearing, so not
noticing was no longer an option.

'You need to be sitting up more,' I said. And I had to
push him forwards off the backrest, so I could crank it up
a notch, and then haul him back against it. Even with
Christian using his arms for support, his lower body was
such a dead weight it was a real struggle. It struck me that
if it hadn't been so awful, it was just the sort of situation
that would have had us falling about with laughter. But we
weren't laughing; we were just sweating and cursing. When
I'd finally sorted him out, he let out a sigh and said, 'I can't
stand this much longer. How am I ever going to get my life
back to normal if I need help all the time?'

'Oh, Christian!' I said, slipping into that tone of mournful sympathy he hated. 'Don't worry. Whatever happens I'll
always be there to look after you.'

It was the wrong thing to say. He looked at me with
something like hatred and then turned his face to the wall.
Before I could think how to salvage the situation, he
snatched up the fork he had just been using and jammed it

into his thigh. He laughed in surprise as four, deep, pain-less puncture marks in his inert limb welled up with blood.

The nurse who came to clean it up and give him a tetanus jab was not impressed. 'Please don't do that again,' she said, mildly. They all loved Christian. 'You might have severed an artery. And as for using a dirty fork ...'

'I might have had to have the whole leg off, and then where would I be?' Christian retorted, and I could smile at last. Black humour was always preferable to black despair.

One of the many specialists who saw Christian in those early days made an unguarded (and, as it turned out, completely fanciful) remark along the lines that in his view they were only ten years away from a cure. I could see Christian latching onto this as though it was a cast-iron guarantee, accurate to the day. 'I'm going to be walking by the time I'm thirty,' he'd say, in the way that equally deluded souls proclaim they're going to be millionaires.

'I don't know what to do,' Mum said to the clinical psychologist. 'He sits there listening and nodding while the consultant explains that the damage to the spinal cord is irreversible, and then half an hour later he's off again, talk-ing about having physio to strengthen his leg muscles.'

'Well,' said the psychologist, clasping her hands in her lap. 'It's probably not a good idea to endorse anything that's plainly not true. But optimism should be encouraged: it just needs to be channelled towards achievable goals, if you see what I mean.'

'So when Christian says: "I am going to walk again, and I don't care how long it takes or what I have to do", what should I reply?' Mum asked.

'Oh, something like: "Your self-belief and strength of

character are two qualities that will help you to live a fulfilled life.'" Mum looked thoroughly sceptical.

THE DAY HE CAME HOME IN HIS WHEELCHAIR WAS THE SADDEST day of my life. The dining room had been converted into a bedroom for him, with all his belongings brought down and arranged in their former layout. Only the dartboard remained upstairs. Dad couldn't bring himself to nail it up at half-mast.

Christian wheeled himself over to the French windows and sat looking out over the garden. It was late autumn now and the trees in the spinney were in their usual fiery death throes, a blaze of copper and gold against a hard white sky. The apples had gone ungathered this year and lay rotting where they fell. Unpruned bushes sagged over the leaf-spattered lawn, steaming from recent rain. Beside the greenhouse something glittered in the grass. A fragment of broken pane: debris from another lifetime.

Mum had collected together all the cards that had arrived from well-wishers during his absence and put them in a pile for him to read. There were dozens and dozens. I would never have believed we knew so many people: the congregation at Holy Trinity, Old Turtonians, people from the golf club, and the Fox and Pheasant, friends from Exeter, Mrs Tapley, Martina. Many cards bore the shamelessly inappropriate message 'Get Well Soon'. At the other end of the spectrum, a few offered 'Deepest Sympathy'. Christian's predicament clearly represented a gap in the market that was not being addressed.

He ran his eyes over them listlessly, in the manner of someone exposed to other people's holiday photos, and laid them aside with relief.

Two squirrels were playing chase on the grass, scrambling up and down the fence, tumbling and clowning. At last Christian broke the silence.

'Mary Lennox,' he said.

'What?'

'Mary Lennox. I've been racking my brain trying to remember the name of the girl in that book we read when we were little. She goes to live with some old uncle and there's this cripple hidden in the attic or somewhere.'

'*The Secret Garden*,' I said, the memory clawing its way into the light.

'That's right. What was his name?'

'Colin.'

'*Colin*,' he repeated, with something like delight.

'Yes, he learns to walk again,' I said, without any forethought.

'Does he?' said Christian, suddenly alert. 'I'd forgotten that. Yes, you're right!' And the way he seized on this detail from what was, after all, just a story, wrenched at my heart, and the endless horror of it all swept over me again. My face must have betrayed me, because Christian's expression darkened. 'Don't look at me like that,' he snapped, and he turned away and stared out of the window until I slunk away.

NO ONE MINDS A LITTLE SYMPATHY, BUT WHAT CHRISTIAN couldn't bear was to be an object of pity *for ever*. That was why he didn't want, and refused to see, any visitors in hospital. He'd asked for Penny on the first or second day, and when I told him she'd gone to France he didn't even need me to elaborate. 'They didn't waste much time,' he said. 'He always was a shitty, conniving little bastard.'

By the time she came back home and heard the news his resolve was as hard as steel. I wasn't there the day she turned up at the hospital: it was left to Mum to turn her away. She had brought a bunch of white roses, still in bud, which Mum promised to pass on, but Christian dropped them unopened into the rubbish bag on the door of his bedside cabinet. A nurse, not knowing their history, retrieved them and put them in a plastic vase, where they hung their heads and withered without ever coming into bloom.

'Do you think you'll ever see her again?' I asked him, when I heard about the failed visit. He shook his head with slow deliberation. 'No. He can have her,' he said.

I wondered if she'd try again, or make some effort to use me as an intermediary, but she never did: I suppose she had her pride, too.

There was no likelihood of his ever bumping into her. He seldom left the house, and had no intention of returning to Exeter to finish his degree. He'd already missed one whole term of his final year. Mum offered to move down there with him and act as nurse, chauffeur, cook, amanuensis, whatever it took so he could study, but he decided he didn't want to be a student on those terms. He said he'd be better off doing a correspondence course, an idea he brought up from time to time to head off motivational peptalks from Mum, but never pursued with any vigour. I think he was reluctant to face those friends who'd known him as he was. It was that everlasting sympathy he dreaded. 'I don't want anyone coming over to gawp at me, or getting all emotional, so I end up having to comfort them.' On the other hand he was no keener to mix with other disabled people, and flatly refused to attend the Spinal Injuries

Support Group. 'Waste an afternoon sitting around in a circle with a bunch of other cripples? No way!'

He had been warned he might put on weight, and, in this respect at least, he was happy to conform. He'd always had a prodigious appetite, even given the disincentive of Mum's cooking, but now his only exercise was bouncing a tennis ball against the floor and catching it off the wall. *Ker-thunk, ker-thunk*, it went, hour after hour in exactly the same spot, so that it left a grey, shiny patch on the wall-paper.

'There's loads of sports you can do in a wheelchair,' I said to him one day. I'd been looking through all the leaflets about keeping fit that the physio at the spinal unit had given him, and which he'd left unread in their folder. 'You could do basketball, hockey, even tennis. You'd be brilliant at it.'

He looked at me as though I'd suggested joining the Brownies. 'That's not proper sport,' was his bitter riposte. 'It's like...*women's rugby*,' he said, managing to denigrate two sectors of the population for the price of one.

The best times were when he asked for help, and there was something I could do for him. Occasionally, last thing at night, as I was about to go up to bed, he'd say, 'Hey, Esther, take us out for a push, will you?' He could manage the wheelchair perfectly well by himself on the flat, but the gravel in the driveway was deep and slushy in places, and there was nothing that maddened him more than getting beached. Also, I don't think he liked being out on his own any more, though he would never admit to a weakness like fear. I'd wheel him round the lanes – always, and without discussion avoiding the churchyard – up to the green, past the Fox and Pheasant, Mrs Tapley's old house (now flats),

the Victorian cottages where the Conways lived, and back
along the stretch of road where Aunty Barbara had skidded
into the ditch. On one of these walks he said to me,
unprompted by anything we'd been discussing, 'You know
something, Esther? You're the only person I know who
doesn't totally wind me up.'

Here was the recognition I'd been striving for all my life,
but it brought me no pleasure, because for him to appreciate me at last had taken the wreck of all his hopes.

WHEN I SAY THAT MY OWN FEELINGS WERE NEVER
acknowledged, it is a matter of record, not of complaint.
My own trivial heartaches about the loss of Donovan, and
then Penny, had been engulfed, quite understandably, by
the larger sorrow, and my grieving had to be done in private.
There wasn't enough sympathy left over: it was all drawn
into the black hole of Christian's pain. I thought about
Donovan often, with a sense of regret and helplessness.
Occasionally, when I was out, I would catch a glimpse of
someone who, after pursuit and proper scrutiny, turned out
to bear no more than a feeble resemblance. I looked
forward to going to bed each night, because it gave me the
chance to relive that stupid, bungled kiss before I dropped
off to sleep, in the hope that I would dream a fitting sequel,
but I never did. At first it took some willpower not to bring
his name up in conversation, or when it did arise naturally,
not to pounce.

When a six-page letter of condolence arrived from Aunty
Barbara, written, as a mark of respect, on actual notepaper,
I skimmed directly to the reference to Donovan. . . .
Donovan has decamped to the caravan and shows no sign of
returning. He seems to be intent on turning into one of these

travellers. (This struck me as bizarre, since the very last thing anyone could do in that bog-bound caravan was travel.) *I'm not sure what he's living on. He says he does odd jobs – no doubt a euphemism for pilfering. I await a call from the Dyfed constabulary.*

The main body of the letter was peppered with emphatic capitals and underlinings. I could practically hear her roars of sympathy coming off the page.

I was absolutely DEVASTATED to hear your APPALLING news. I can only imagine the HORROR you must be going through . . . Poor Christian! . . . Poor all of you! What a LOATHSOME world we live in. I hope your faith and your goodness and your great love for each other will sustain you, as it must.

She signed off 'Barbara Fry-Kapper' – a detail whose significance was missed by everyone but me, who recalled perfectly Donovan's parting advice to her, as I recalled all his words.

CHRONIC MISERY HAS A NUMBING EFFECT, THANKFULLY. IT blunts the sharp edges of experience, until you reach a curious state of immunity to extremes of joy or sorrow. Months after Christian's accident I found that graphic news reports of famine or child abuse left me quite unharrowed, and I remember contemplating the possibility of my parents' death with complete detachment – something previously unthinkable.

It was the year of my O levels. My teachers knew what was happening at home and made no attempt to pressurise me, and the prevailing culture of underachievement meant that my apathy and lack of concentration were well-camouflaged. Art was the only subject at which I exerted

myself. For my exam piece I did a series of pen and ink
studies and a large portrait of Christian. When I asked
him if he'd mind modelling for me, he gave me a dour
smile and said, 'I might as well. Sitting still is the one
thing I really excel at.'

Mr Hatch asked me if he'd consider coming in to sit for
the whole class, but I thought twenty-four pairs of eyes
might be interpreted as gawping, so I declined on his behalf.

When my results came – a mixture of flukey passes and
unclassifieds, crowned by that one A grade in art, no one
knew whether to congratulate me or commiserate. Mum
and Dad had rather lost track of my potential, and perhaps
felt guilty at their lack of involvement. I think they were
waiting for some cue from me, and were lost when it failed
to materialise.

'Are you pleased with your results, Esther?' Mum asked
me in a carefully non-committal tone. She'd cornered me
in my bedroom, where I was putting navy blue polish on
my toenails.

'Not really,' I replied.

'So you're a bit disappointed, then?'

'Not really.'

'Oh. So you're just, sort of... satisfied.'

'Not really, no. I'm not anything.' I was thinking how
furry her face had become. In the bright sunlight the downy
hairs made her cheeks look like a tiny field of silver grass.

'You must feel something,' said Mum, who was beginning to find my serenity unnerving.

'But O levels just lead to A levels, which lead to university, which leads to a career. So what's the point? I mean,
my career is going to be looking after Christian, and I don't
need exams for that.'

Mum's face crumpled. 'Oh, Esther, don't be silly,' she cried, clutching my shoulders with her strong, knobbly hands. 'You don't have to give up the rest of your life for Christian. You've got work of your own to do.'

She must have gone up to the school soon after that to have a word, because when I went back in September to do re-sits Mr Hatch took me aside and gave me a long, rambling lecture – a sort of secular parable of the talents – which was only curtailed by my agreeing to do A levels, with a view to art college.

'It'd have to be somewhere near, though,' I said. 'I'm not going away.'

'You wouldn't have to. There are excellent places in London – Slade, Saint Martin's: they're the best in the country.'

'Which is the nearest?' I asked, and he made strangling gestures in my direction.

I don't think I appreciated the effort he put into me at the time: all the chivvying and chasing to help me build up my portfolio, and the phone calls and favours called in to secure me interviews. I thought it was just nagging, and refused to be flattered. He'd given up trying to loosen my draughtsmanlike style, and decided to make a virtue of my fanatical precision. It was so contrary to the predominant fashion among art school students for boldness and expressionism that he thought one of the professors might take me on out of sheer curiosity – and so it proved.

When my first illustrated book was published I sent him a copy, inscribed with appropriate expressions of gratitude. Almost by return of post I received a long letter saying that he was delighted to hear of my success, and that I was the best pupil he'd ever had, and the most rewarding to teach, etc. Really, it was so full of compliments and praise that I couldn't help wondering if he was remembering somebody else.

A FEW POINTS OF BRIGHTNESS FROM THAT DARK YEAR. WHEN Christian's colleagues from the building site heard about the accident they turned up at the house one weekend with a concrete mixer and built a ramp up to the front door, and another leading from the old dining room into the garden, and wouldn't accept any payment.

Another time, very early on, while Christian was still in hospital, Pam came over with her newborn twins and a sausage casserole from Mrs Clubb. It was the first proper meal we'd had in weeks: we'd almost given up eating as an irrelevance. Mum and I sat on the couch and held the tiny palm-sized miracles, trussed up in identical marshmallow-pink strip: bibs, bootees, mittens and bonnets, while Pam, who looked scarcely less pregnant than before, prattled on about her caesarean and centile charts and what a devoted dad Andy was, as long as he got his eight hours sleep, minimum.

I gazed at the babies' little froggy legs and puny, inadequate necks and the diamond-shaped patch of unjoined skull pulsing on the scalp, and wondered how it was any of us survived the perilous journey to adulthood intact.

Strangest and most marvellous of all was the gift that arrived with so little fanfare in the morning post, in a pile of bills and fliers. A cheque for £200,000 – a fantastic, mythical amount of money back then – was accompanied by the briefest letter from a solicitor, whose name itself was straight from a fairytale.

Dear Mr Fairchild
My client, who wishes to remain anonymous, has heard
of your plight, and would like you to accept the enclosed.
There are no conditions attached to its use.
  Yours sincerely
  A. Weazlewort

THERE HAD, OF COURSE, BEEN OTHER, SMALLER DONATIONS before, from local businessmen and church groups, and generous individuals who'd read about Christian's predicament in the local paper. There had been editorial outrage that the ambiguous circumstances of his injury made him ineligible for a payout from the Criminal Injuries Compensation Board, and the resulting whip-round had paid for the conversion of the downstairs cloakroom into a bathroom, and a hoist for getting him in and out of bed.

But this was something different. Anyone who says money can't buy happiness has obviously never felt the transforming touch of sudden wealth. It wasn't love or faith or counselling or pills that raised Christian from the trough of depression into which he'd sunk: it was money. And the fact that it came unasked for and unearned was a double blessing. It was as if all the pennies and pounds that Mum had scraped together and sent off to the Less Fortunate over the years had now come back to us a hundredfold.

Mum and Dad had been quietly formulating a plan to sell the Old Schoolhouse to the developer who had turned over Mrs Tapley's place and buy back one of the converted apartments. With the released capital they intended to buy or build a place where Christian could live with as much independence as possible. Unfortunately this scheme depended on the death of Grandpa Percy, or his removal to a nursing home, whichever came sooner, and therefore serious discussion of it had to be indefinitely postponed on humanitarian grounds. The dreamlike arrival of the windfall removed all the obstacles from the planning of Christian's ideal home. It started life as a sketch on the back of my O level history file, and grew, over three years, into the house we live in today.

Christian was involved in every aspect of its design, and became so absorbed in the minutiae of architectural drawings and building regulations that I began to wonder how he would ever fill the void once the job was done. He made regular visits to the site – a half-acre plot inside the M25 at Caterham that met all his criteria: secluded but not isolated; close enough to Mum and Dad to allow support rather than indiscriminate dropping-in; somewhere new, but not alien – and watched the creeping progress with a fanatical eye. The team of builders, once they'd met Christian and knew his story, seemed to view the project as something of a crusade themselves, and were painstaking in their pursuit of perfection.

'Oh, that'll do,' Christian would say, as they agonised over some infinitesimal flaw, and the site manager would fix him with a stern gaze and reply, '"That'll do" won't do!'

Having begun to entertain the possibility of selling the Old Schoolhouse, Mum and Dad couldn't quite let it drop, and when Grandpa Percy finally died much later – I was twenty-one and doing my Master's degree at the time – they revived the idea. It was in clearing out his room for the move that they discovered, behind a plug of loose plaster in the wall, the missing £400 from the jar on the kitchen dresser.

36

WHAT FOLLOWS IS CHRISTIAN'S ACCOUNT OF THE NIGHT HE broke his back, written up from notes he dictated to me in hospital, and part of which formed the basis of his statement to the police.

WHEN I ARRIVED AT MARTINA'S AT ABOUT TEN PAST EIGHT she had already taken the overdose. (I only slept with her once, by the way, and regretted it immediately: it was the worst thing I could have done.) Her aunt opened the door to me. I thought maybe she was a doctor and she thought I was the ambulanceman, and it took us a moment or two to clear up the misunderstanding. She'd come home to find an incoherent message from Martina on her answerphone, and had driven over straight away to find Martina drowsy but still conscious enough to tell her what she'd taken. The aunt had dialled 999 and then made Martina drink salt water till she was sick. She said she didn't know if this was the right thing to do. I said I thought it probably was as long as she hadn't drunk bleach or anything.

All this information was delivered as we ran upstairs to the sitting room, where Martina was curled up in an armchair, shivering. She had threads of watery vomit from her chin to her T-shirt, and her face was slack and putty-coloured, but she was lucid enough to force the corners of her mouth into a smile for my benefit, and say 'sorry'. The blanket she'd been wrapped in had slipped to the floor and she hadn't bothered or been able to retrieve it. I tucked the blanket round her again and held her hand, and tried to think of comforting things to say – you know how crap I am at that – to keep her awake and alert while her aunt went out to move her car so there'd be a space for the ambulance. It was one of those roads of redbrick, Victorian terraces, completely parked up both sides. By the time she'd driven round the corner and found a spot someone was already indicating to pull in. I was torn between going down there to explain, and staying with Martina, who in any case had hold of my hand so tightly I couldn't have got away if I'd wanted to.

Through the window I saw the aunt sprinting along the road, waving at the driver, who had now reversed into the space and was opening the door. Just a few polite words of explanation would have done the trick, but the aunt was obviously fired up for a confrontation, because she started shouting and gesticulating, completely ruining any chance that the other woman would go quietly. Now she was getting out of the car I could see she was one of those hatchet-faced upper-class types who don't take orders from anybody, but I felt reassured that she wasn't likely to throw a punch. I didn't have a clue how

I'd break up a scrap between two women. It was a double
relief when the whoop of the siren heralded the approach
of the ambulance, and hatchet-face yielded to a higher
authority and drove off.

I was so grateful when the two paramedics came
clumping up the stairs and took over. They were calm,
businesslike blokes, completely impervious to the chaos
of female emotions around them. Martina and the aunt
deferred to them immediately. I couldn't help thanking
God I wasn't a woman, pitched from crisis to crisis by
feelings.

Martina went off in the ambulance and the aunt said
she'd follow in her car. She asked me if I wanted to come
too. I had a horrible feeling she thought I was Martina's
boyfriend, and I was quite keen to clear up any confusion
on that score, but I couldn't get the conversation round
to it. We went along to the hospital and I sat in Casualty
for an hour or so, listening to the sighs of the waiting
wounded, while the aunt filled in forms at the desk, and
Martina was taken off somewhere. Once the experts were
in control and Martina was part of some vast system,
which would process her without any help from me, I was
able to relax a little. I wanted to phone Penny, but the
aunt had borrowed all my loose change to ring round
trying to find Martina's mum. Once she'd got hold of her
she calmed down. Like me, she didn't want the responsibility.

It was about half ten before they'd finished with Martina
and shifted her onto a ward. While I was saying goodbye
her mum arrived in a great fluster, and sort of fell on Marty,
weeping. I thought, yeah, well done, that's just what she
needs.

I said cheerio to the aunt, and turned down her offer of a lift. She shook my hand and said thank you, and because it was my last chance, I blurted out: 'I'm not Martina's boyfriend, by the way.' She looked at me as much to say, 'What's your point?' and I felt such a prick I couldn't get away fast enough. When I got out on the street I realised I was actually quite dizzy with hunger and the stress of it all, so I went into a pub and had a Guinness and some peanuts. I tried Penny's number again from a call box but there was no one in.

I fell asleep on the night bus and overshot the stop, but it wasn't raining so I decided to walk home. I was the only passenger left on board, and I wasn't aware of being followed. I'd forgotten about the precautions we were supposed to take when coming back after dark: I hadn't ever taken it very seriously and, besides, I was preoccupied with the events of the evening: I still had Martina's dried vomit on my T-shirt. I didn't pay much attention to the car parked and unlit in Knots Lane, but as I drew level I did notice that there was someone sitting very low down in the driver's seat, which struck me as odd, because the lane doesn't lead anywhere except the church, and eventually the turning to the Old Schoolhouse. When I'd gone past I heard the door click, very softly, and that was when I first thought I might be in trouble. I didn't look round, or start running, I just kept walking at the same pace, but tense and super-alert to any sound. As soon as I heard the scuff of shoes I was off at a sprint. If I'd just kept going I could probably have outrun him and reached home safely – I had a head start after all – but I stupidly ran into the churchyard. I thought I could lose him, or cut straight through and up over the wall. Anyway, I didn't

know if he had a gun or what. I knew it was me he was
after though, because I could hear running feet behind
me.

As soon as I was in the churchyard I knew I was cornered.
There was no gate in the far wall, which was too high and
sheer for me to climb in a hurry, and it wasn't easy to stray
off the path without tripping over protruding gravestones
in the dark. The clouds were blowing so fast across the sky
that the moon was coming and going like a strobe. I ran
round the far side of the church, locked at that time of
night because of vandals, and did the only thing I could
think of – something I'd always done as a child when I
wanted to get away from someone – I climbed a tree. Just
inside the flint wall was an old chestnut tree. I took a flying
leap and swung myself up onto the lowest branch and then
it was easy. I kept on scrambling up until I saw the beam
of his torch come swinging around the side of the church,
combing the gravestones to find me. I didn't get a good
look at him – the angle of the beam meant he was never
lit up, but I could see what he was carrying. A cricket bat.
It was the one detail that kept coming back to me. If I
hadn't been at such an extremity of fear, cowering in a tree,
I'd have found it funny: death stalking me with a cricket
bat.

I don't know how long I stayed in the tree – time probably gets distorted by terror, and it was no longer than
minutes – but I could see the cone of torchlight still
moving methodically below, searching. I had frozen in an
awkward position with my neck cricked, and the muscles
were burning with pain: I knew it would only require a
fractional adjustment to bring me relief, but as I moved
my head the brim of the Raskolnikov hat snagged on a

twig and peeled back off my head. I knew that if it hit the ground the noise would give me away, but of course there was no time to formulate this or any other coherent thought – I acted entirely on instinct and lunged to catch it.

I didn't feel the impact as I landed, but I did hear it, as a loud crump, like a nearby explosion, and I seemed to see myself, as if from above, lying half across the tomb of Walter James Traill, only son of Cuthbert Traill and Caroline Traill, died 4 August 1917, aged 26. Then I drifted down and rejoined my body, which was something separate, without sensation. I knew I had broken my back because when the torchlight shone in my face and his black shape stood over me I tried to roll into a ball, but nothing happened. One arm was trapped underneath me. I covered my eyes with the other because I didn't want to watch myself being killed. It was very peaceful wait-ing for Death. Once it was certain there was no fear at all, just a sliding surrender.

But he didn't kill me: he snapped off the torch and took off at a run as if I was after him. The terror came crowding back then, because now I still had my life I had something to lose. And with fear came pain from that trapped arm. I tried to call for help, but the fall had knocked all the voice out of me. I heard the car start up in the lane and the whirr of the engine growing fainter until it was swallowed up by the wind shaking the leaves. I must have gone into a kind of faint to protect me from the sparking pain in my arm and shoulder, because I wasn't aware of anything more until I was roused by the church clock striking one, and the beautiful, raucous sound of an ambulance, racing to my salvation.

PART THREE

37

'SO CHRISTIAN WANTS TO MARRY THIS GIRL,' SAID DAD, AS
we stopped to tread water in the deep end of the Holiday
Inn pool. We meet there every Tuesday morning for thirty
lengths and a chat during the Evergreen session for the over-
sixties. They let me in because I'm accompanying Dad. At
least I hope that's the reasoning.

'Hardly a girl,' I replied. 'She's forty-seven.'

'As old as that? I didn't realise. Has she been married
before?'

I nodded. 'She separated from her husband when they
were in their twenties, but they never formally divorced.
Then when he got ill last year she went back and nursed
him till he died. So I suppose she's widowed, technically.'

'Any children?'

'No. They'd fallen out before they ever got round to it.'
I'd had all this from Elaine herself, but in greater detail.
Since her status as Christian's girlfriend was now official,

she'd taken every opportunity to collar me for what she no doubt regarded as bonding sessions, in the face of which I remained resolutely non-stick.

'I really want to get to know you, Esther,' she said, cornering me in the utility room one day while I was rinsing out some tights. 'It's quite hard to cross that boundary between being a paid helper and a friend. It's something we need to work on.'

I refrained from commenting that she hadn't had any trouble vaulting the boundary where Christian was concerned. 'I don't think there are any shortcuts when it comes to getting to know someone,' I said, giving the tights a final squeeze. I draped them over the airer, where they hung, repulsive, withered legs. 'In fact,' I added with sudden inspiration, 'I don't think you can know someone properly unless you knew them as a child.' I haven't a clue where this came from, but it felt irrefutable.

Elaine thought about this for a second. 'There's nobody left who remembers me as a child,' she said. This seemed to me a tragedy that might bear investigating, but I didn't have the chance. She was off again: 'I'll tell you what you should do with tights. Pop them in a pillowcase and stick them in the machine on your wool cycle. That's what I do. Saves you doing them by hand.'

'I'VE ONLY MET HER A COUPLE OF TIMES,' DAD WAS SAYING, as he struck out for another length on his back. 'And I confess I didn't pay her anything like the attention I would have if I'd known she was going to be my daughter-in-law.' His arms circled lazily. He was wearing a pair of black Nike swimming shorts, a recent extravagance. I had made it clear that I wouldn't be accompanying him any longer if he persisted in turning up in knitted trunks.

'She's rather bossy,' I said, catching up.

'Maybe Christian wants someone to take him in hand,' said Dad.

'She'll do that all right,' I muttered. An overweight elderly man overtook us in a fast, splashy crawl. We paused in our strokes for a second to ride the choppy wash.

'It's you I feel sorry for,' said Dad. 'Where will you go?'

'I thought I might move back with you initially. If that's okay?'

'Of course. Love to have you. If that's what you want. Though it seems a dismal life for a young woman.'

'Anyway, he hasn't proposed yet, and she hasn't accepted,' I reminded him. 'So let's not be hasty.'

'But we are agreed it would be a good thing? For Christian.' Dad was beginning to register my lack of enthusiasm with concern.

'What? You mean marriage?'

'Yes. Love, marriage, and all that it entails. I'm rather glad to think of Christian having a companion in his old age.'

'Well, he had me for companionship,' I pointed out.

'I was thinking of those comforts you can't give him,' Dad said, not looking directly at me. 'There's more to marriage than sharing a house.'

'Yes, I suppose so.' I thought of Mum and Dad, living thousands of miles apart, and yet still married, still apparently devoted. Once Christian and I were completely settled in our adult life Mum had felt a calling once again to use her medical training, and was now working as a volunteer in a health centre in Eastern Nepal. She came home for four weeks each year. Dad didn't want to go with her: his calling was to stay near Christian, and so they'd ended up in this curious state of loving separation, communicating by phone and letter, each obedient to their own calling and respectful of each other's. It was a modern marriage, all right, and had very little to do with sharing a house.

We'd done our thirty lengths by now, and the top of my head was still dry. Dad hauled himself out and hobbled across the pimpled, non-slip tiles to the changing rooms while I had a quick steep in the hot tub. Since Mum went away, Dad has discovered he can cook, rather well in fact, and so I generally go back to the flat (formerly the ground floor of the Old Schoolhouse) for lunch on Tuesdays. Bread is his speciality. He does all sorts of interesting variations: rosemary and onion or bay and vanilla, but he'll happily get a recipe book out of the library and work through it methodically and without fear. Another consequence of Mum's absence, and the sale of the Old Schoolhouse, is a slackening of the purse-strings, of which those Nike trunks were just the latest manifestation.

Today it was minestrone soup with goat's cheese bread. I watched him frisking round the kitchen, laying the table, humming along to the lunchtime requests on Classic FM. As always, he hadn't bothered to comb his hair out after swimming, so it had dried in a great white thatch (his eyebrows and nose-hair had retained their ginger coloration). I noticed he'd bought a piece of parmesan the size of a house-brick, and one of those battery-operated graters – further evidence of this newfound frivolity. I gave the machine an experimental squeeze and it whirred into life, showering the table with shreds of cheese. 'It tastes so much nicer fresh,' he explained. 'I don't think that dried stuff is cheese at all. I think it's dandruff.'

On the poster-sized calendar stuck to the side of the fridge he'd written ESTHER – SWIM in every Tuesday slot for the whole year. Given that our arrangement is cast in iron I found this, like so much about Dad, touching, but completely daft.

'If Christian and Elaine do get married,' he said, as we ate our soup, 'your mother might come back for the wedding.'

'Ah, that's why you're so in favour,' I said, and he smiled. I told him about my visit to the primary school and my encounter with the living ghost-child of Penny. 'I thought I might follow it up,' I said, helping myself to another handful of loaf. 'I'd be curious to find out what she's doing now.'

Dad looked dubious. 'Do you think that's a good idea?'

'Yes. Why shouldn't it be?'

'Well...I don't know. It seems rather unfortunate timing. Just when Christian's finally fallen in love. Has it occurred to you he might not want any reminders of that time?'

'He doesn't have to meet her if he doesn't want to. She was my friend too.'

'I'm not sure that curiosity always needs to be satisfied.'

'But without it we'd all still believe in a flat earth,' I protested.

'I don't like to think of anyone getting hurt,' he said, clearing away the plates and the subject. 'Speaking of the flat earth, I've got a puzzle for you.' He pointed to a diamond-shaped pencil outline on the wallpaper above the kitchen table. I'd noticed it before but never remarked on it. 'You see that piece of stained glass above the back door? Well, at noon on the longest day every year the sun falls on it so that a blue diamond of light lands just there. You can see where I've drawn round the shape. Now last year it had moved by about a centimetre. How do you account for that? Is the earth shifting on its axis?'

I didn't have an answer off pat, but I promised I'd look into it. He often sends me off with some brain-teaser that needs solving. When I got home I asked Christian for his scientific view of the matter and he tittered at Dad's suggestion.

'The door frame's probably warped,' was his unromantic suggestion. 'Or the house is subsiding.'

On reflection I had to agree that this was the more likely explanation, though it was rather an anticlimax: the earth hadn't moved at all, just our small corner of it.

38

I MET GEOFF, AS USUAL, IN THE BAR OF THE GEORGE AND Dragon at Westerham. We're there every second and fourth Wednesday of the month. It's easy to remember because the council recycling lorry, which comes to collect our old news-papers and empties, works on exactly the same timetable. I have to drag the black and green boxes to 'the edge of the curtilage', as the leaflet put it, by 7 a.m., or they're left to fester for another fortnight.

We always sit in the same place if it's free: a pair of old brown armchairs by the fire, the best imitation of hearth and home that we can manage. We fixed on Westerham because it's well outside the catchment area of the surgery and a good distance from Geoff's house, so there's less chance of bumping into patients or friends of his wife. Although he has to pass fairly near the end of my road to get there we still take the precaution of trav-elling separately. Geoff's alibi for these encounters is a wholly fictitious 'peer review committee', about which his wife appears to exhibit no curiosity. She once commented on the fact that he smelled of cigarettes, after which he was forced to invent a colleague on the panel who's a heavy smoker. Neither of us derives any pleasure from these deceptions, and we don't make a habit of discussing them.

Tonight I could tell that my news about Christian had unsettled him. Routine is the calm water on which this strange relationship is kept afloat: any intimations of change are like a rock thrown in the pool.

'I wonder why we never foresaw something like this happening,' said Geoff, swilling ice round in his vodka. One of our founding principles was that we would never leave our partners. We hadn't allowed for the possibility that one of them might leave us.

'Because Christian is such a recluse. He never met anyone till now. He works from home; he's got a few friends, but they're blokes or married couples. He hardly ever puts himself in situations where single women are available.'

'But you must have female friends. Didn't you ever introduce any of them to him?'

'He's met Rowena, but she's totally unsuitable. She's a compulsive divorcee. Anyway, he's never asked me to introduce anyone.'

'How has he managed all this time without female company?'

'I'm female company, aren't I?'

'That wasn't what I meant.'

'Oh, I see. Mike, the carer before last, used to bring girls round to give Christian a massage. I used to think they were friends of his, but I'm coming round to the idea that they were prostitutes. It would be odd for one man to know so many physiotherapists, don't you think?'

Geoff laughed. 'Your naivety has a charm all of its own. Anyway, it's not Christian I'm worried about. It's you. Where will you live?'

'Oh, I'll be all right.'

'You don't own any of the equity in the house?'

'None at all. It was all paid for by Christian's mystery benefactor. I've lived there rent free. I'm just a sponger,' I said cheerfully.

'And I don't suppose you've set aside any money for a rainy day?' Geoff said.

'Well I put all my tips in a big jar, and then at the end of the year—' I tailed off. I could tell Geoff was finding the informality of my financial arrangements unnerving.

'You'll never be able to buy a place round here on what Rowena pays you. How much did you earn last year?'

'Oh, last year was a good year. Twelve thousand pounds.' Geoff looked aghast. 'But that includes the money I got for that book prize. I can't expect that much every year.'

'Esther, have you any idea how much it costs to rent a flat, or even a hovel, in this part of the world?'

'Yes.' Only that morning Elaine had left the local *Property News* lying open at the Lettings page for me to see. 'I'll probably have to move to Glasgow or Salford, or somewhere.' I said this in the same breezy tone, without thinking how it would be interpreted.

Geoff went quiet. He was chewing the inside of his mouth: a sign of anxiety. 'How would we ever see each other?' He had drawn away from me fractionally and his face had that hurt look that he sometimes wears when I've said something that appears to disparage the quality of our relationship.

'I was joking,' I said. 'Of *course* I'm not going to move miles away. I couldn't leave Christian, or Dad. Or you,' I added, but he wasn't listening; his mind was already racing ahead, trying to formulate solutions.

'I wish I could think of some way to help you out. I ought to be able to – I earn enough. But Mary does all the finances: she'd notice if large amounts of money started vanishing from the account.'

Now it was my turn to look affronted. 'Set me up in a little flat, you mean? That's a repulsive idea. I might as well go on the game.' *Splash.* Another rock for the pool.

'I didn't mean that. I wasn't trying to suggest... oh, Christ.'

'I've never taken any money from you,' I went on. 'We've always been equals. I can't stand the thought of being "kept" like a pet poodle.' My voice tends to turn shrill when I'm indignant: I can hear myself sounding like a drag artist's idea of a battleaxe. At the bar several heads turned in our direction.

'Look, I'm sorry,' Geoff whispered, trying to head off a scene. We never quarrel: it's another founding principle. 'I only want to help you. I love you and I don't want to see you struggling. It's only natural. Why shouldn't I give you money? I've got plenty: you haven't. I've just got to work out a way to do it discreetly.'

'I don't know why you're making such a drama out of this,' I said, lowering my voice to match. 'It's my problem, not yours. Anyway, it's emotional support I want from you, not strategies. You're as bad as Elaine.'

Geoff shook his head and went up to the bar for more

drinks. I thought that would bring an end to the subject and we could get back to familiar territory: his kids' progress at school and university, the antics of his more eccentric patients (anonymous). But as soon as he sat down again he said in a great rush, as though he'd been rehearsing while at the bar, 'You say we've always been equals, and that's the strength of our relationship, but that's just my point: we're not going to be equals any more and that's what worries me.'

'Why aren't we?'

'Because you're free and I'm not. And pretty soon you'll realise that the little I can offer you isn't enough.'

'I've always known how much of you I could have. And I've never asked for more, have I?'

'No. But when your circumstances change and you don't have Christian to look after or to keep you company any more, maybe you will.' Geoff is what you might call a predictive worrier. He believes that foreseeing problems that will in all likelihood never happen somehow arms him against them. I think it gives him gastritis.

'So what you want is some assurance from me that I'm not going to start making demands?' I said. The drinks sat on the table between us untasted. This was the closest to a disagreement we'd ever come.

He reached for my hand and gave it a squeeze. 'I don't want anything, darling. I'm sorry: you know what a pessimistic old git I am. Don't take any notice of me.'

'Okay, let's talk about something else,' I said, returning his squeeze. 'We're wasting our precious evening.' I only realised as I spoke that this last remark might, in the current climate, be construed as demanding. 'Better still,' I went on hurriedly, 'let's go back to mine.' I stood up and pulled him to his feet, and we walked out of the heat and smoke of the pub into the dark and chill of the March night, towards our separate cars.

39

I PARKED AT THE END OF PENNY'S ROAD AND SWITCHED OFF the engine. I was ten minutes early. I'd brought the Lettings section of the local paper along as a time-filler, and began working through it methodically, crossing out ineligible properties with a red pen. Too big, too expensive, way too expensive, too far away *and* too expensive. *Slash, slash.* Geoff had not exaggerated the cost of renting in the commuter belt. After ten minutes the only ad to be spared the red pen was for one room in a shared flat above a dry cleaner's on the main road. I could imagine the toxic fumes drifting up through the open windows on summer evenings, the perpetual thrum of machines and traffic.

I got out and checked my appearance in the shine on the car door. Penny had said that she had an enduring memory of my delinquent fashion sense, so I had made an effort to conform today, and was clad in long, high-heeled boots, a suede skirt with a tasselled belt, and a white shirt.

I knew it went together okay, because I'd seen it on a store dummy in Marks & Spencer's window, and bought the whole rig. The boots were killers, though.

The house was large, 1930s Tudorbethan, and set back from a wide, straight road flanked by grass verges and naked trees. There was a truck in the driveway containing various garden equipment, including a giant shredder. As I approached a white Appliance Care van pulled up and a man jumped out carrying a case of tools. I hung back out of sight until he'd been admitted, so as not to have to share my moment of reunion with the plumber, or whoever he was, and then I teetered down the driveway, carrying a bottle of Chablis and some lilies, and rang the bell.

After some time the door opened, and she stood before me, unmistakably Penny and yet utterly changed. She had put on weight, especially round the bust and hips; her hair was now very short, with a feathery fringe and grey highlights, and her skin had acquired that crinkled effect of habitual sunbathers. She wore a tiny pair of oblong rimless spectacles, but within this altered setting her features were the same.

'Esther. At last!' she said, although I was in fact dead on time, and we leant towards each other and clunked jaws across my armful of wine and flowers.

DAD WAS RIGHT OF COURSE: SOMEONE DID GET HURT, BUT not the person he had in mind. Once I'd made up my mind to find Penny – and Dad's disapproval gave me just the impetus I needed – it was amazingly easy, thanks to the internet. Christian would have been an ideal recruit for this task as he is on the computer all day, either refining a new game, or surfing spinal injury websites for the latest research, but of course he was the one person I couldn't enlist. I'm ashamed to say I had never mastered anything other than simple word-processing. My excuse is that the computer is never free for me to use, but it's also something to do with being a novice in the shadow of an expert. It's like living with someone who can programme the video recorder, or speak a foreign language: you never bother to learn because it's pointless duplicating skills.

Fortunately, at Rowena's prompting, one of the chefs, Daniel, offered to help me out, and the night after I'd provided him with what little information I had concerning Cassie and Penny, he had produced an address and phone number.

'Did it take long?' I asked him, watching as he chopped an onion to a fine tilth with what seemed to me reckless haste.

'Nah,' he said. 'I could probably have found out her work address, bra size and credit rating if you'd wanted it.'

'Really?'

'Yeah.' He pointed the knife at me. 'I looked you up while I was online. You've got about sixty mentions on Google.'

'Me?' I said, thinking, What the hell's Google?

'All about your illustrating stuff. All the books you've done. Winning that prize. Basically every time your name's been in a newspaper. I'm like, wow, she's more interesting than she looks.'

'Thank you so much, Daniel,' I said, wilting.

I considered turning up on Penny's doorstep unannounced, but common sense prevailed. Weybridge was that bit too far to drive on the off-chance that she'd be at home. A letter would require more patience than I possessed. It would have to be the phone. I preferred to make the call when I had the house to myself, and I didn't have to wait long: Christian and Elaine were off out on little jaunts at every opportunity. Today they were going to Tate Modern. Christian's an art-lover all of a sudden!

I didn't plan what I was going to say. I thought it would be better to crash in and be spontaneous, so as soon as I'd waved Christian and Elaine off I snatched up the receiver and dialled without giving myself any time to rehearse.

The phone was picked up after half a dozen rings, and a curt female voice said, 'Hi.' This monosyllable wasn't quite enough for me to make a positive identification, so I said, 'Is that Penny?'

'Hello Esther.' The reply came back instantly, with all her old warmth, but without any trace of the surprise that I would have thought the breaking of a nineteen-year silence deserved. From her tone you would think I was just return-ing a call.

'Yes, it's me,' I ploughed on, trying not to be derailed by her composure. 'I got your number off the internet. I hope you don't mind. I thought I'd get in touch and see how you are and what you're doing and all that.' I found myself revert-ing under her influence to teenage levels of inarticulacy.

'Well, I'm so delighted that you have, Esther. Shall we meet? I'd love to see you.'

It was as easy as that.

IN THE KITCHEN PENNY PREPARED LUNCH OF MUSHROOM omelettes while the man from Appliance Care dismantled the washing machine. 'I'm sorry about the chaos,' she said, 'but when you work full-time you have to get everything done on your day off.'

Already someone had come in to take the computer away to be fixed, and a crate of groceries had been delivered and unpacked. At the bottom of the garden a man was braced halfway up the largest of three tall poplars, a buzz saw swinging from a rope around his waist.

'I'm having them lopped,' Penny explained, uncorking the wine with a curious plunger. 'Cassie has worked out using Pythagoras that if they fall this way they'll demolish the house.'

Just beyond the trees was a railway cutting. What seemed like every few minutes an express train went screaming past, making the whole house quake. I found myself tensing up, waiting for the next onslaught. Penny didn't turn a hair. I suppose you get used to anything.

'Where do you work?' I asked her.

'For the Crown Prosecution Service. As a solicitor.'

'That sounds high-powered.'

She pulled a face. 'It's the civil service.' As if that explained everything. 'Whereas you,' she went on, fluffing up some salad leaves with a pair of wooden claws, 'are a successful illustrator of children's books. I've read all about you in the *Guardian*.'

I launched into my usual litany of denials. 'Oh, no, I'm not successful at all. I mean, I don't make a living. Almost nobody does, unless they sell TV and merchandising rights.'

She dismissed this talk as mere modesty. 'I always knew you'd be an artist of some sort. You were the only one who didn't realise what a talent you had.'

'There's your problem,' said the Appliance Care man, holding up a piece of semi-circular wire. 'That's what was making the noise. It had gone right through the drum.'

'Oh,' said Penny. 'I wonder where that came from.'

The man's face assumed the arch expression of one who has privileged information to impart. 'Shall I tell you what it is?' he said.

'Yes, do,' said Penny. 'We're on tenterhooks.'

'Put it this way,' he said, twiddling it round between finger and thumb, 'one of your bras is not giving you the support it should.' Penny was speechless. I roared with disloyal laughter. 'We get this all the time,' he said, laying the exhibit down on the kitchen table and shaking his head. 'You ladies.'

While he reassembled the machine and packed away his tools, we ladies ate our omelettes in the sunny, white-walled dining room, which looked onto the garden. The tree-man had moved on to the second of the poplars: the lawn below was six feet deep in fallen branches.

I explained the chain of circumstances that had led me to her, making no mention of Christian. 'I couldn't believe it when I saw Cassie. I knew she had to be yours. And then I read the name on her exercise book and that settled it. I just had to follow it up – it was such a monumental coincidence.'

'You surely don't think it was a coincidence, do you?' Penny said, with an enigmatic smile.

'What else would you call it?'

'Well, suppose I had read about you in the *Guardian*, and suggested to the literacy coordinator at Cassie's school that they invite you in to speak at Book Week.'

'Oh. Why would you do that?'

'Because I knew you'd recognise Cassie, and if you were interested in a reunion, you'd pursue it, and if you weren't you wouldn't.'

'Oh.' This was unsettling. I had considered myself to be

the manipulator of events. Penny was part of my plan. Instead, it seemed, I was part of hers.

'I'm not saying there's no such thing as coincidence,' she said, enjoying my mystification. 'I'm just saying that nothing that happens here today can be called a coincidence.'

In the doorway the Appliance Care man coughed discreetly. When Penny had paid him off she made a pot of sludgy Turkish coffee and we moved into the sitting room, which was large and slightly underfurnished, with dents in the carpet where the missing pieces had once stood. There were photos on the piano, studio portraits of Penny and Wart and Cassie, arms around each other, the united family.

'So you married Wart,' I said.

'Yes.' Penny's smile vanished. 'And then two years ago he left me for someone else.'

'Oh dear. I'm sorry to hear that.'

'I never thought I'd end up divorced. Even my parents are still together, and they can't stand each other.'

'How long were you married?' I asked her.

'Twelve years. And we were together for five years before that. That's what's so unfair. People assume the relationship was a failure, but it wasn't. It was successful for at least fourteen years, which is a bloody long time.'

'What went wrong?' I could sense from her tone that she didn't mind talking about it. Perhaps every retelling dispersed a little more of the unhappiness.

'He had an affair with this woman he worked with. The fact that it's such a cliché doesn't actually make it any less miserable when it's happening to you. In fact I think it makes it worse, because you feel ridiculous as well as heartbroken.'

'Poor you,' I said, with rising inadequacy. 'How did you find out?'

'I think I always suspected. I don't believe people who say they have no idea. I think you always know.'

'Really? Do you think it's impossible for a man to deceive his wife for long?' This conversation was beginning to make me feel uncomfortable.

'Yes, I do. I knew for a long time before I actually caught John out. We were in the car one day and he pointed out one of those coffee house chains and said, "*That's* the shop I was talking about the other day." Only he hadn't been. Not to me. He got a bit flustered and tried to pretend I had forgotten the conversation, but I *never* forget conversations. Even after that I was frightened to confront him, because I didn't want to precipitate a huge crisis. I kept thinking, if only I do such and such, he'll realise what he'd be losing, but you just end up running round in circles trying to be the perfect wife, and getting more and more demoralised.'

'I'm so sorry,' I said. Penny offered me the coffee jug, but I shook my head. My heart was hammering enough already. The fact that Wart, who had pursued her so hard and lured her away from Christian when she was at her most vulnerable, had gone on to discard her seemed to me an outrage.

'I thought, perhaps if I showed more interest in all the things he's into, like Formula One, and modern jazz. He always used to accuse me of being an intellectual snob and looking down on his interests. But it didn't work. I used to go round to my sister's all the time and say, "What can I do? How can I make him love me? Just tell me what to do and I'll do it." And eventually she had to sit me down and say, "Look, mate. He doesn't love you any more, so nothing you do is going to work. And if he leaves you it's not going to be for a saxophone-playing racing driver, because love isn't logical like that.'"

'Well, that's true,' I said. My face was burning. Partly with embarrassment at listening to Penny abase herself so frankly, and partly at the hypocrisy of my own expressions of sympathy. I had always been able to appease my bad conscience over Geoff's wife with the thought that our situation was utterly unique, and beyond the scope of conventional ethics. We were no common adulterers: I was no scheming home-breaker. The impregnability of his marriage was a given for both of us, and I had never wanted it otherwise. I didn't feel jealous or resentful of his wife; indeed, I felt a sort of sisterly warmth towards her, and something like regret that we could never meet. I imagined myself, in short, to be the sort of nice, untroublesome mistress that any woman might be pleased for her husband to have. I had been deluding myself, clearly.

'So that night I waited till Cassie was asleep,' Penny was saying, 'and John was slumped in front of the telly – it was *Farewell, My Lovely*, funnily enough – and I switched it off and said, "Do you want to leave me?" And he sat looking at the dead TV for about ten seconds and then said, "Yes please."'

'Just like that?'

'Just like that. It was unbelievably civilised.' She gave a little snort of self-mockery. 'So I said, "In that case you'd better go while Cassie's asleep." So he packed a bag and was gone within ten minutes. And then I lay down on the floor and howled like a beast.'

'Oh no!'

Penny laughed at my tragic expression. 'It's okay. That was more than two years ago. I'm fine now. Good riddance. I'm just a bit overweight from all that comfort eating.' She patted her hips. 'And I'll tell you something. That first year of being alone was a lot better than the last year of our marriage.'

'What's the moral of this story?' I asked, sensing that further demonstrations of pity were superfluous.

Penny drew her features into a mask of deep consideration. 'I'm buggered if I know,' she said.

I WONDERED IF SHE WOULD EVER GET AROUND TO ASKING about Christian, or whether I would have to bring his name up myself, but eventually, after enquiring about Mum and Dad, and hearing their stories, she said, 'Now tell me about your brother.' She had gathered, from that feature about me in the *Guardian* that we lived together in eccentric seclusion, shored up by a rigid structure of routines and rituals, and I was able to confirm that this had, until lately, been the case. I didn't, couldn't explain about Geoff, but I did tell her about the new and unwelcome influence of Elaine.

'So having given him the best years of your life, as it were, you are now facing imminent eviction, physical and emotional,' was Penny's blunt diagnosis of my predicament. 'No wonder you're pissed off.' Put that way it made me sound rather selfish.

'I'm not pissed off with Christian,' I said, trying to frame a defence. 'I'm delighted that he's happy. I just can't seem to hit it off with Elaine. And that's going to be a barrier between us.'

'Poor old Elaine,' Penny tittered.

'Why poor old Elaine?' I said. 'Poor old me.'

'I'd hate to have you as an adversary. You'd be worse than ten mothers-in-law.'

'What do you mean?'

'Well, you've got that same unbreakable bond with Christian, but you're also young and smart and pretty and sarcastic and opinionated. Oh no, my sympathies are all with her.'

'You don't paint a very flattering portrait of my character,' I said. And you don't even know the half of it! I thought, beating back a tide of self-disgust.

'I've always been your biggest fan,' she replied, glancing at her watch, and then jumped to her feet. 'God, is that the time? I've got to pick up Cass. You'll stay till we get back, won't you? She's dying to meet you properly. Make yourself at home. Oh, and can you keep an eye on my tree-man? If he comes down see if he wants a cup of tea.' And she snatched up her keys and bolted out of the door. It only occurred to me once she'd gone that there was no good reason why I shouldn't have accompanied her, and I felt an inexplicable twinge of resentment at having been abandoned.

There is something slightly menacing about the silence of an unfamiliar house. I paced from room to room, in search of an innocent diversion. It was almost impossible not to pry. My wanderings took me back to the kitchen, where I read all the correspondence tacked to the memo board – mostly spelling lists for Cassie, school newsletters, reminders about piano exams and dental appointments, party invitations and lists of emergency phone numbers. So much administrative support for one small girl!

I noticed on the window ledge the agate egg displayed on a pewter napkin ring, and wondered whether Penny had produced it especially for the occasion: it looked somewhat less dusty than the surrounding ornaments.

To make myself useful I did the washing up from lunch, managing in the process to splash my suede skirt with droplets of eggy water from the omelette pan. In the course of putting the crockery away I located the dishwasher, hidden in one of the units. As I filled the kettle, another express train roared through the cutting, slaughtering the peace of the afternoon. High up in the poplar the tree-man swayed dangerously, balanced, legs apart, between two of the slenderest vertical branches that could possibly support a man's weight. He was working with his back to me, and a combination of woolly hat, earphones and the buzz saw made him deaf to my shouts from the patio, but I could see he'd nearly finished, so I carried his cup of tea down the garden, my high heels collecting a ruff of mud and grass with each step.

A cold, low sun was shining in my eyes as I approached the piles of fallen branches. I could see the decapitated trees silhouetted against the platinum blond of the sky. Far above me the man reeled in his chainsaw and in a sweeping stroke sliced through the one remaining bough. Too late I realised it wasn't roped; too late the man turned and saw me; too late I struggled to free the heels of my boots from the sticky clay into which they'd sunk.

'Look out!' he shouted, futilely, as the branch came down like a javelin, catching me on the shoulder and knocking me to the ground. Trees, sky, man: all disintegrated in a blizzard of pain. My hand raged as if on fire; I could feel the wetness of blood pooled in my palm, and then, worse than all, I tried to move my legs but nothing happened. I started to scream and scream.

A voice said, 'Are you all right?' then '*Esther!*' and the coloured fragments slowly reassembled themselves before my eyes to form a face I recognised.

'Hello, Donovan,' I said to the tree-man, who had now entered my dream in this strangely transfigured state. 'I think you've killed me.'

40

MY CLAIM TO BE MORTALLY INJURED TURNED OUT TO BE AN overstatement, but my identification of the culprit was spot on, and so there came about an additional reunion that day which, though unexpected on both sides, nevertheless could not properly be called a coincidence.

It was Donovan who reassured me, once he'd lifted the amputated branch from my legs, that my inability to move them was due not to paralysis, but to the spiked heels of my boots, which had bent back to snapping point as I fell, pegging me to the ground. The absurdity of this image was something I could only appreciate later: pain tends to override subtler sensations.

It was Donovan who helped me to hobble up the garden, and made me run my hand under the cold tap until it ached. The burning and wetness I had experienced turned out to be attributable to nothing more gory than spilt tea.

'I didn't realise it was you up there,' I said, flexing my

fingers. Every time I tried to withdraw my hand from the stream of tap water, Donovan took my wrist and firmly put it back again. 'Penny never said.'

'Well, it's nice to see you again, Esther,' he replied. 'Though perhaps not in these circumstances.' As soon as the shock of emergency was past, his apologies began to contain an element of reproach. 'You know it is actually considered quite dangerous to stand under a tree while it's being cut down.'

I gave him a baleful look, but he just smiled. Now that the fog of pain had dispersed I could see clearly how little he'd altered. Unlike Penny, he was just as I remembered him, his skin maybe slightly weathered from a life spent out of doors. In fact, when I tried to picture his eighteen-year-old self, I found I couldn't visualise anything but the face before me. Strange the way memories age to keep pace with the march of time. Voices, of course, never change, and although there was nothing particularly distinctive about Donovan's – classless, regionless – I would have recognised it anywhere.

'Do you do this sort of thing for a living?' I said. 'Or is it a one-off?'

'Both. I do gardening for a job, but this is just a favour for Penny. I didn't know you were going to be here. I didn't even know you were still in touch.'

'We weren't – until this afternoon.'

'Ah. That explains why Penny was so adamant that the trees had to be done today,' Donovan said, as much to himself as to me. Having decided that my hand was sufficiently chilled, he set about making us a cup of tea, assembling the necessary ingredients in a manner that showed complete familiarity with the contents of the cupboards. He even knew where the paracetamol lived. It occurred to me, with a spontaneous surge of dismay, that perhaps he and Penny were a couple.

'You seem very at home here,' I said, watching him dump the mashed teabags in the bin. 'You must know Penny quite well.'

'I do. We'd exchanged addresses that time she ran my car off the road – for the insurance claim. And then about a year later she got back in contact. I went to their wedding. We've been good friends ever since. In fact, I'm Cassie's godfather.' He said this with a hint of pride that I found completely disarming.

'I didn't know you even believed in God,' I said, accepting two paracetamol and sending them on their way with a gulp of hot tea, which made tears spring to my eyes.

'Ah, well, there's a lot you don't know about me,' he replied. My hand, which was palm up on the table, had started to hurt again now that it was dry. As I looked at the red scald mark my fingers gave an involuntary twitch.

'Is that still hurting?' Donovan asked.

'It's okay. I don't think I'll be able to work for a day or two though.'

'Oh God, of course, you're a painter aren't you?' he said, looking stricken with guilt. 'That's going to be a bit of a problem isn't it?'

'I wasn't thinking about that,' I said, pinching an imaginary paintbrush, and making a few experimental strokes. 'It's the waitressing I'm worried about.'

'You do waitressing? Really?' He seemed surprised by this, although to my mind it was no more menial than gardening. I started to tell him about Rowena's, and that led on to an account of my life with Christian, to which he listened with an almost unnerving attentiveness.

'You must be some kind of saint,' he said. 'Don't you ever feel bitter about all the opportunities you've missed because of living with Christian?'

'No, no, it's not a sacrifice. We're like best mates.'

'But do you have to do everything for him? Even personal stuff?'

'No, he's not helpless. He can do most things himself. And he's got a carer. He can get around in his wheelchair fine, he can do housework, cooking. He could go out more: he's got a specially modified car, but he doesn't like going anywhere too far on his own because there's always a chance he'll get stuck, and he'd rather die than ask a stranger for help.'

'I should have come to see him,' said Donovan. 'I must have been down at the caravan when it happened, and then I went off to the Pyrenees with some friends and lived there for a while, so I didn't even know until ages after the event.'

'What were you doing there?'

'Fruit-picking, cleaning cars, odd jobs, begging. There were four of us living in a VW van. It wasn't very civilised.'

This was how Penny found us when she returned with Cassie – sitting at the kitchen table, talking away like the best of friends.

'Jesus, what happened to you?' she demanded. 'Did Donovan push you into a ditch?'

'Practically,' I replied, ignoring his indignant expression. I suppose my appearance had deteriorated in her absence: I had discarded my crippled boots and snagged tights, and there were grass stains and welts of mud on my white shirt and suede skirt. I began to think living above a dry-cleaner's might not be such a bad idea after all.

'You didn't mention you were expecting company, Penny,' Donovan said drily. 'I expect you forgot.'

'Oh no,' she replied sweetly. 'I thought it would be a nice surprise. I didn't think you were going to beat her up. That wasn't in the plán.'

'Hello, I'm Cassie,' said Cassie, who had stood by unac-knowledged for what was, to an eight-year-old, an uncon-scionable length of time. 'You came to my school.'

'Hello, I remember you,' I said. 'You asked some very intelligent questions.'

Satisfied, she turned to Donovan. 'You said next time you came you'd put up my mirror.'

'Done it.'

She beamed. 'Are you sleeping over?'

'No, I am not "sleeping over", madam,' Donovan replied. 'Haven't you got any homework to do?'

'Only piano practice. You can come and listen if you want.'

'Excuse me,' he said to us, removing his boots and follow-ing her down the carpeted hallway in his socks.

'They get on brilliantly,' said Penny, as the plink-plonk of an elementary two-handed exercise issued from the sitting room. 'He's great with kids. He and his wife couldn't have any of their own,' she added in a whisper. 'Did he tell you that?'

I shook my head. I was thinking how defenceless men look without shoes. 'We didn't get on to him,' I said. 'I was too busy talking about me.'

'They did all these tests,' she went on, 'and they couldn't find anything wrong with either of them individually. But they seemed to have this one in a million incompatibility, like their genes were allergic to each other.'

'How awful. Can't they adopt?'

'Unfortunately it didn't come to that. I think the marriage

was under too much strain. When John left me Donovan was spending a lot of time round here propping me up, which didn't exactly help, and then his wife had an affair with a guy she met at the gym, and she got pregnant, like straight away. So that was that.'

'Eek.' What a bunch of amateurs we had turned out to be in the art of relationships. Two wrecked divorcees and someone's bit on the side.

'Anyway, we sort of helped to scrape each other off the floor,' said Penny, flexing her long, ringless fingers.

Oh really? I thought.

THE CONDITION OF MY HAND AND SHOULDER MEANT driving was out of the question, so various possibilities were put forward, which would result in both me and my car getting home.

Finally Penny, the great organiser, decided that Donovan should drive me in the truck, while she and Cassie followed behind in my car. Donovan would then bring them both back to Weybridge. Beyond that, she didn't elaborate: perhaps he was, after all, 'sleeping over'.

I had rung Rowena to warn her I wouldn't be coming in to work and she had accepted my excuses with a very ill grace. 'Friday night,' she wailed. 'Where am I going to get someone at this short notice?' And then, 'What's wrong with your other hand?'

In what was left of the daylight, Donovan sawed the lengths of poplar trunk into logs, and dragged the thinner branches up the garden to the front of the house. Penny helped him feed them into the shredder, which chewed them to a coarse sawdust and sprayed them into the bed of the truck. I was excused on account of my injuries, so

I played Yahtzee with Cassie instead, and then acted incredulous while she ran through her repertoire of card tricks.

'Shall I tell you how I did it?' she'd say, when I'd overdone the bafflement.

'No – magicians never tell,' I said. 'It's a rule.'

'Oh.' She looked disappointed: she'd been desperate to give up her secrets. 'I've already told Lauren,' she added, in a worried tone.

'Who's Lauren?'

'My best friend. I hate her,' she replied, managing to distil the curious and complex flavour of childhood attachments in six short words. I could feel the idea of a book struggling to be born. The cover illustration was clearly before me: one of my scratchy pen and ink drawings of a girl with a blue-black nimbus of rage throbbing about her head. It wouldn't be a pretty-princess sort of book, but it would be true.

'Do you think you can love and hate someone at the same time?' I asked her.

She had begun building the bottom layer of a house of cards, making rows of trestles, supported at the sides and bridged, one to another. I held my breath. It was such a flimsy structure. 'Yes,' she said, without needing any time to think. 'Daddy.'

'Oh. Right.' I didn't know whether it was wise to reopen this particular wound, but she pressed on. 'When he left I hated him for upsetting Mummy. But when he came to take me out he was just the same as he always was. Actually he was nicer; he didn't ever tell me off or smack me.'

'I used to know your daddy,' I said. 'A long time ago.'

'I know. Mummy told me. Did you know Donovan, too?'

'Yes. I've known Donovan since I was, well, younger than you.'

'I wish Donovan would marry Mummy,' she sighed, beginning on the second storey. 'Then he could stay here all the time.'

Again that stab of dismay. 'Do you think he will?'

'No,' Cassie shook her head with a look of resignation that seemed to convey all the wisdom of antiquity. 'Nothing I want to happen ever háppens.' Her hand trembled, and the card she was holding snicked the corner of the structure so that the whole thing caved in, flopping gracefully onto the carpet.

'I HOPE HER DRIVING'S IMPROVED,' I SAID, GLANCING FEARFULLY in Donovan's wing-mirror as Penny got behind the wheel of my car and pulled out into the road behind us. 'I've only got third party insurance.'

Donovan laughed. 'Could be an expensive day out for you. First I ruin your clothes, then Penny writes off your car. You may end up wishing you'd stayed in bed.'

'Oh, I wouldn't go that far. It's been a very interesting day. Cassie even gave me an idea for a book.'

'She's great, isn't she?'

'Yes, she comes out with these little gems in such a solemn voice. And what's weird is, she looks more like Penny than Penny does. If you see what I mean.'

Donovan smiled at this observation. 'Better she takes after Penny than Wart.'

'You don't like him?'

'Not much.'

'Penny told me all about their break-up. It seems like he treated her pretty badly.'

'And what she doesn't know is that it wasn't the first time. Or the second.'

'How do you know that?'

'He used to tell me. We'd play squash and go for a pint every so often, and I'd hear all about the latest woman he was screwing. It put me in a really difficult position.'

'I can imagine.' We were having to talk in awkwardly raised voices because of the noise of the engine. The interior of the cab smelled of petrol and rust; and there was a snaking crack across my side of the windscreen, giving it a curious, bifocal effect. A gust of cold air blew through a gap at the top of his window where the rubber had perished. Between us the gear stick juddered madly. Donovan had to catch it and calm it down before he could change gear.

'Then it got so that he would have a quick game of squash and then rush off to meet whoever-she-was-at-the-time,' he went on. 'I said no way was I going to be his alibi, and things were a bit cool between us after that. Penny was always more my friend than him.'

'Do you still see him?'

'No. I reckon in the last two years I've lost at least fifty per cent of my friends to divorce – theirs or mine. It's like the Black Death.'

I couldn't help laughing.

'It's true. Sharing out the Wedgwood and the fish knives is a breeze. It's carving up your mates that's the real killer.'

'Penny did mention that you'd been married,' I said, instinctively turning round to check that they were still following. Cassie returned my wave.

'I suppose she gave you all the sordid details,' Donovan said, frowning.

'Oh, well, more or less,' I admitted, since indiscretions were already flowing freely.

'It was all that infertility treatment that caused the problem. Endless, endless tests, and the monthly dashing of hopes. We were perfectly happy before that. But it seemed to poison every part of our lives.'

'I'm sorry to hear that. You'd make a good father, I'm sure.'

'Well, Dad provided me with an excellent model of what not to do.'

'Anyway, it's not too late. It's never too late for a man.'

Donovan gave me a sideways glance. 'Have you never felt the call of motherhood? Or is it another sacrifice you've made for Christian?'

We were on to the M25 now, and the need to project our voices and occasionally repeat ourselves wasn't ideally conducive to exchanging these confidences. 'Sometimes I think it would be nice,' I replied. 'Like seeing Cassie today. Anyway, my circumstances are a bit complicated. My boyfriend is already married to someone else.' I shouldn't have brought Geoff into the conversation. I should have known that after what we'd been discussing it wasn't a revelation that was likely to impress. But Donovan had spoken frankly and I felt obliged to reciprocate. Besides, I wanted to correct any impression I might have given of being immemorially unloved.

'Oh?' Donovan sounded quite taken aback. 'Does his wife know?'

'God, no. Of course not.'

'Have they got children?'

'Yes – a boy and a girl. Teenagers. I don't know them: we've never met.'

'How long has it been going on?'

'Four years.'

'Four years! Does he keep promising he'll leave her, and then not doing it?'

'No, no, nothing like that. I don't want him to leave her. I don't want her to be hurt.'

Donovan shook his head over this, flummoxed. 'I can see what's in it for him. But what's in it for you?'

'Well. It's a relationship. Friendship. Sex. Conversation. Admiration. You know.' Ahead of us I could see ranks of brake lights flashing. Gradually the traffic slowed to a crawl and then stopped altogether.

'Where did you meet him?'

'He was my GP. He's not any more,' I added hastily. 'He made me switch surgeries immediately, for ethical reasons.'

'So he takes his professional oath seriously, but not his marriage vows. Interesting.' I could sense disapproval coming off him like static. It was the second time today I'd been made to feel like a social pariah, a peddler of misery in the same camp as the despicable Wart, and I didn't like it one bit.

'You sound shocked,' I said.

'You weren't expecting a round of applause, were you? I've been on the receiving end of adultery and it sucks, believe me.' He wasn't ranting in any way, but the friendly atmosphere had definitely chilled.

'You can't compare individual cases...'

'Plus, I saw what it did to Mum. So did you. It destroyed years of her life.'

In a minute I was going to be blamed for Donovan's rotten childhood. 'That's why I'm very anxious that Geoff's wife never knows. I'm not a threat to their marriage. I'm really not.'

'How do you know she doesn't already suspect? Aren't women supposed to be gifted with all this intuition?'

'You said yourself that Penny didn't know about all Wart's other women,' I reminded him.

'Okay,' he conceded. 'But she found out enough to wreck the marriage in the end.'

'Anyway, strictly speaking, I'm not the one committing adultery. I've not broken any vows.' A more feeble piece of self-justification it would be hard to imagine. Donovan raised his eyebrows and gave me a cynical, side-long look.

'What do your parents think?'

I was forced to concede that I hadn't actually told them.

'Ah, so you obviously do have a troubled conscience.'

'Of course I do,' I said impatiently. 'But if I did tell them I know what they'd say. What Jesus said: "Let he who is free from sin cast the first stone," and all that.' I thought this was an inspired riposte, which would silence him on the subject for ever.

Donovan nodded. 'Yeah, but he also said, "Go and sin no more…"'

'Look, I didn't intend to get into a discussion about my morals,' I snapped. 'I wish I'd never mentioned it now.' I slumped back in my seat and stared out at the columns of traffic trundling forwards, inch by inch, as though shackled together. Just my luck to be stuck in the front of a truck in the rush hour with a religious zealot.

'Sorry,' said Donovan. 'It was an interesting subject. I got carried away.' Silence settled over us. I continued to gaze out of the window at the necklace of red and white lights threading away into the dusk – an infinity of little tin boxes on wheels – and I thought what I always think when driving on a motorway: so many people whose lives will never intersect with mine.

At last we reached the Caterham turn-off and Donovan spoke. 'Will Christian be in when we get there? It'd be great to see him.'

'Until very recently I'd have said: "It's Friday, so yes, he certainly will." But he's in the grip of New Love right now so his behaviour's no longer predictable. All his routines are up the spout.'

'Lucky him,' said Donovan.

'He used to be a complete hermit. And wild horses wouldn't have got him inside a theatre. Now he's off to the Barbican every five minutes. He can't get enough of old Shakespeare. And someone in the house is reading W.B. Yeats, and it's not me.'

'God,' said Donovan. 'It sounds terminal.'

'I think it may be. He's been going out with Dad for a curry and some man-talk every Thursday for at least a decade, and last week he forgot. Just completely forgot to turn up!'

'How is your dad, by the way? He was always so good. A saint, really.'

'He's fine. Retired, pottering about.' I explained about his breakdown and recovery, and his and Mum's unorthodox living arrangements. 'Since Mum's gone he's rediscovered fun. He actually spends money on himself. Little treats like dates and Belgian chocolates and parmesan.' I described the incident with the designer trunks.

'Good for him,' said Donovan. 'I love spending money.'

I glanced at the decaying interior of the truck and thought that could hardly be the case. As usual the lay-by on the dual carriageway was strewn with trash, and not just windblown litter either. Old tyres, prams, plastic sheeting, pipes, planks, a mattress – at least a skip's worth of refuse had been dumped up against the hedges. For some reason I felt obliged to apologise for its presence.

'How's your mum, anyway?' I asked. We were nearly home now and I would soon have to start giving directions.

'Living quietly in sheltered accommodation in Bournemouth. Secretary of the bowls club. Pillar of the church choir—'

'Are you serious?'

'No, of course not. I had you going for a minute, though. No, she actually lives in Totnes with a potter called Peter. She's involved in a long-running feud with her neighbour, which seems to take up most of her time.'

'That sounds more like Aunty Barbara. What's it about?'

'It was a boundary dispute over a tree, originally. Unfortunately it's escalated in Mum's capable hands. She fires off about six letters a day to her MP and the local paper. Between that and flying back and forth to the States visiting her old lags on death row, she's kept pretty busy.'

'She's still doing that, then?'

'Very much so. She must have been to more executions than Madame Defarge.'

'Did she actually marry that bloke – Kapper? I noticed she'd taken his name.'

'Oh yes, she married him all right. I think it was political rather than romantic. She did it to get publicity for the cause.'

'Did it work?' I asked, directing Donovan to turn left at the lights.

'Yes. Too late for him though. But her name is in the cuttings file now, and every time there's a death row story in the news someone from the *Daily Mail* rings her up for a quote.'

'And she's happy with this potter? Or is that political too?'

'No, no. Romantic, as far as I know. He's ten years younger than her.' This made him about the same age as Geoff. 'And he's very good to her,' Donovan went on. 'He does all the practical things Mum can't cope with, and when she's in one of her rampaging moods he shuts himself in his studio and works on his pots until it's safe to come out. He won't give her the satisfaction of a blazing row. I like him.'

I was still considering the unsettling fact that Aunty Barbara and I were attached to men the same age, and wondering if this could be right and proper, when we reached our turning and I had to jump out and open the gate.

There were lights left on all over the house, but no sign of Christian.

'I don't know where he's gone, or how long he'll be,' I said, as Penny drew up in my car. 'He might be back in half an hour, if you can be bothered to wait.'

Donovan looked to Penny for a ruling. It was eight o'clock; they had at least another hour's journey back to Weybridge before Cassie could go to bed. It occurred to me that no one had eaten since lunchtime. 'Stay for supper,' I said, praying that there would be something in the fridge. Tomorrow was shopping day, so it was by no means guaranteed.

'Just a quick bite then,' said Penny, which pleased Cassie, who could see her bedtime receding still further.

'Warm in here,' said Donovan, following me into the kitchen, shedding garments. Newcomers to the house are always overpowered by our underfloor heating, which is on full all year round. Growing up in the glacial surroundings of the Old Schoolhouse has left Christian and me with a morbid fear of the cold. Besides, he prefers not to be burdened with too many layers, and especially dislikes wearing shoes and socks.

'Everything's so modern and clean,' Penny said, looking around in admiration. Perhaps she still expected to find us living in cobwebbed squalor. 'There's something Swiss about it.'

'Christian designed it,' I said. 'He wanted it to be as plain and uncluttered as possible, with white walls and polished floors and everything accessible at his level. Have a look around.'

While they went on a tour I hunted for food. Luckily there was the remains of one of Elaine's asparagus quiches in the fridge, and a lettuce that was quite acceptable once I'd snapped off the frozen outer leaves. No one wanted alcohol so we had bottled water and ruby grapefruit juice (Elaine's again – I would have to apologise and restock tomorrow).

Once the food was eaten and Christian still hadn't put in an appearance, Penny said, 'We really should be going,' and within seconds, as if in one movement, everyone was on the doorstep saying goodbyes and thank yous, the door was shut and I was alone again. From the hallway I watched Donovan walk down the drive to the truck; there was something heartless, it seemed to me, in that brisk, confident stride. He had asked to be remembered to Christian, nothing more. Penny had promised to call, without taking my number. Only Cassie turned and waved at the blank face of the house before getting into the truck beside her mother.

I sank down on the couch, suddenly overtaken by exhaustion with the unaccustomed effort of socialising. So much talking! Such a torrent of words! The paracetamol had worn off: my hand and shoulder ached, and somewhere inside was a rawness that wouldn't be named or soothed.

After half an hour of stewing, I dragged myself into the kitchen to clear away the supper things and found that Donovan had left his jumper on the back of the chair. It was a black, zip-neck thing, which had obviously seen active service: it was ripped up one side, bristled with embedded sawdust and smelled strongly of creosote. Aha, I thought, a hostage. And felt instantly better.

Then I knew what was bothering me. It was the aftertaste of that conversation we'd had about Geoff. I'd made such a poor job of explaining or defending myself, and Donovan was out there somewhere disapproving of me, despising me, and there wasn't a thing I could do about it. I thought of Penny, lying on the floor and howling like a beast, and felt another pang. Suppose even now they were discussing me: perhaps Donovan had already told Penny I was the sort of woman who had wrecked her marriage and his mother's marriage and lured his father away from their happy home, and who was somehow to blame for the ocean of tears wept by deceived wives and deserted children everywhere.

These melancholy thoughts were interrupted by the arrival of Christian and Elaine, home from their latest spree. They had been shopping and to the cinema, and appeared to be on a high from overspending. Happiness streamed out of them, and it was impossible not to envy the cocoon of mutual adoration they'd spun themselves. Elaine waved aside my apologies about the absence of quiche, and went to run a bath, her musky perfume haunting the room after she'd left it.

Christian fixed himself a bowl of Frosties – his regular after-supper snack – and only then stopped to consider the implications of my being there. 'Why aren't you at work?' he said, mid-mouthful. 'What's happened to your clothes?'

'You'll never guess who I met today,' I said, ignoring his question. 'You'll never, never guess.'

'Correct,' said Christian. 'So tell me.'

I took a deep breath. I wanted to see his immediate, authentic reaction. 'Penny. And Donovan.'

His eyebrows went up, betraying surprise and moderate, rather than ravenous, interest. 'Really? How come?'

I explained the encounter with Cassie that had led me to Penny, and Donovan's role in my dishevelled appearance.

'Well well. How is old Donovan? What's he up to?'

'Gardening mostly. He's divorced, no kids.'

'Gardening? We should get him round to sort us out some decking.'

'Penny's divorced too. From Wart.'

'Wart.' Christian coaxed out another avalanche of Frosties. 'She married him then? God. Wart. I bet he's as bald as a badger now. He was losing it back then.' He shook his head over this memory. 'Funny how things turn out.'

'They both sent their regards. They were hoping you'd be in when they brought me home. They hung around a bit, but . . .'

'Oh well. Looks like I had a lucky escape. You know I think I'd rather just hear what people are up to, second hand, rather than have to make conversation myself.'

His lack of curiosity was truly humbling. He hadn't asked a thing about Penny. It dawned on me that he had

something else on his mind. Elaine appeared in the doorway bringing a gust of tropical air from the bathroom. She
was barely decent, in a flesh-coloured, short, satin robe and
matching slippers. 'It's ready,' she said.

The self-conscious way she was standing, with her left
hand on her hip, fingers splayed, drew my attention to a
lozenge-sized ruby on her third finger. The direction of my
gaze must have been unmistakable, as Elaine said, 'Oh,' and
blushed as red as the ruby.

I DIDN'T GET TO SLEEP UNTIL GONE THREE. THE CELEBRATORY
champagne I'd drunk to toast Christian and Elaine's engagement was still racing round my bloodstream trying to trick
me into feeling happy. As I sat in bed, staring through the
unread pages of my book, replaying the events of the day, I
wondered how I could possibly have thought I knew what
was best for Christian, when I didn't even know what was
good for me. My stupid, ill-considered attempt to revisit the
past hadn't deflected him in the slightest from his chosen
path, but it had left me thoroughly destabilised. It struck
me that I had about as much insight into the complexities
of adult relationships as Cassie – less in fact, since she was
already a pessimist, whereas I had fondly imagined that the
world would kindly arrange itself according to my wishful
thinking.

41

'I THINK WE SHOULD STOP SEEING EACH OTHER.'

'I see. Can I ask why?'

'Because you're married, and it's wrong.'

'It's taken you four years to work that out?'

'No. But I let myself believe my circumstances made it excusable. I thought that because I would never leave Christian and wouldn't be a threat to your marriage, it made us a special case. I was wrong. We're not special: we're just ordinary, selfish and bad.'

We were sitting in Geoff's car in a passing place on the Woldingham road, overlooking the golf course. I had taken the highly unusual step of waylaying him after Saturday morning surgery so that we could talk: this couldn't wait another week and a half until our next assignation at the George and Dragon.

I had spent a wretched night, pacing my studio, agonising about what to do, trying to plan some course of action that wouldn't cause anyone unnecessary suffering. To carry on as we were would be wrong, but to end the relationship would be difficult and painful, and wouldn't undo the wrong, which was indelibly there, for all time. I asked myself whether the example of Penny's misery alone would have been enough to prompt this crisis, and had to admit, to my further discredit, that it might not. It was Donovan's disapproval that was driving me to take action, and Donovan's good opinion that I was trying to secure, and I knew, without needing to analyse my feelings further, that it wasn't just because he was right.

To strengthen my resolve I forced myself to do something I had always held to be utterly prohibited. For the first time ever, I drove to Warlingham and staked out Geoff's house. It was one of the big, detached houses on the green. There was a silver Ford Focus parked outside, and window boxes planted with bright pink winter cyclamens, and interesting-shaped clumps of box and ornamental cabbage. The woodwork had been recently painted: it had that glossy, sharp-edged look that doesn't last.

After twenty minutes or so the front door opened and she emerged: the woman whose trusting nature had made our treachery so effortless. Mary. Between her teeth were some envelopes, which she transferred to the pocket of her coat once the door was locked. She had short, whitish-blonde hair, flicked up at the sides, and was wearing a Burberry trenchcoat and navy court shoes. In one hand she held a navy purse, and in the other was a retractable dog lead like a giant yo-yo, on the end of which was a cocker spaniel puppy, turning frantic circles and springing from side to side with unspent energy.

I watched their faltering progress down the street. Every few yards the dog would tear forwards and then come flying back as if on elastic, and the lead would end up in an ankle-binding snarl from which Mary would patiently extricate herself. She was so real, with her belted mac and her letters for the post, and her funny, lawless dog! What a shadow I was compared to her. I got out of the car and started to follow her. She had stopped to talk to an old man who had bent down to make a fuss of the dog. It took her some time to disentangle him, and they parted, laughing. I smiled acknowledgement as he went by, but he walked straight past me without a glance, as if I was indeed invisible.

'NONE OF THIS OCCURRED TO YOU AT THE START?' GEOFF asked. A light drizzle had started to fall. A few fanatics were still out on the golf course, wheeling their trolleys, heads down.

'No, not properly. I was depressed at the time I met you. You came to my rescue: naturally I was going to fall for you and call it love.'

'You're saying I took advantage of you when you were ill?' said Geoff, staring straight ahead. The windscreen grew mottled with drops, obliterating the view, closing us in.

'No, not at all. I take full responsibility for my actions. I'm not blaming you.'

'As soon as you told me about Christian I knew everything would fall apart. I said so last week.'

'This is nothing to do with Christian,' I protested.

'It is. I said you'd realise this wasn't enough for you. You'd start wanting more.'

'I don't want more: I want less! I want nothing, in fact.'

'Look,' said Geoff, seizing my hand and crushing it in his. 'I can't give you up. You're the only reason I get out of bed in the morning. I know I don't make enough time for you and you've never complained. But I can do something about that. I'll make time.'

'It's not a proper relationship. Talk and sex. Sex and talk. I've never so much as cooked you a meal.'

'So cook me a meal! Next week. I'll arrange it somehow. I'll eat two dinners if I have to.'

'No, no, you don't understand. I don't *want* to – I'm just pointing out how insubstantial it all is. It's not real: we'll never get to know each other any better than we do now.'

Geoff hit a switch and the wipers carved out two semi-circles of deserted fairway. He turned to me: his face was grey and drawn and there were bruise-coloured hollows under his eyes. 'Listen. Darling Esther. Tell me truthfully: do you want a baby?'

'*What?*'

'Is this what it's about?'

'*No!*'

'If you want a baby then I can give you a baby.'

'Geoff, I don't want a baby. And you're not free to give me one.'

'You've just had enough of me, full stop.'

'No. I don't want to split up because I want to. I just think we should. We must. That's all.'

Geoff glanced at his watch. The interview was over. Like all our meetings it was ruled by that stern time-keeper, duty. With smooth, symmetrical movements we plugged in our seatbelts and the drive home passed in what I took to be the silence of resignation and acceptance.

42

ON SUNDAY I STAYED IN BED ALL MORNING FEELING SORRY FOR myself. Even when I did get up a pall of lethargy seemed to have settled over me and it took all my strength to haul my carcass to the bathroom. Once in there I noticed some little touches of Elaine around the place: a new, brilliant-white bath mat, a row of chubby gold candles on the window ledge, a light-pull in the shape of a sea-horse. More and more of these badges of occupation were appearing every day. In my bedroom I stood in front of the open wardrobe gazing at my selection of clothes in a state of mystification. There was Donovan's unclaimed sweater. I put in on, with a pair of jeans. It felt amazingly warm and comforting, in the way that vastly oversized garments do, and still gave off a blokeish smell of wood and creosote and work.

I went into the studio and pulled the blinds to let in the milky afternoon light. It was a beautiful room, with windows on two sides, and a long bench with wide wooden drawers where I stored all my paper and completed work. There was a draughtsman's adjustable drawing-board, which I used instead of an easel, and a chest with lift-out sections where I kept my pencils, paints, Rotring pens, brushes and inks, all in meticulous order, so I could put my hand on anything I needed without any scrabbling around. On the wall was a pinboard covered in source material for the book in progress: photos, magazine cuttings, sketches, postcards, samples of other illustrators' work that I only needed to glance at to feel inspired. Mervyn Peake, Kit Williams, Helen Oxenbury, Janet Ahlberg. Soon I would have to start packing up and moving out.

Perversely, thoughts of my imminent eviction fired me up to get to work on a fresh painting. I only had three left to do to complete my current job, *Jack's Journey*, a treasure-hunt book about a lost glove. I had already planned what needed to go in each picture: it was just a question of committing myself to its execution. Starting is always the hardest bit. Sometimes I could sit poised over a piece of virgin cartridge paper for a whole day and never make a mark, but today I could feel that rare and exciting urgency to begin.

I'd just assembled my materials, and located my original sketches and the section of text I was supposed to be illustrating, when the doorbell rang. I left it for Christian, frowning with the effort of maintaining concentration. It rang again, and I remembered that Christian and Elaine had gone to the garden centre to help Dad choose a tree to replace the sumac that had come down in the most recent hurricane. I slammed down my pencil. If it was someone flogging replacement windows or trying to get me to change my energy-supplier they were going to get a gobful. I snatched the door open, primed for a row.

It was Donovan. He was holding a bunch of tulips in one hand and a rope-handled carrier bag in the other.

'Hello,' he said. 'Am I disturbing you?' He looked faintly amused, and I realised to my horror that I was wearing his jumper, and that I had less than half a second to decide between providing some sort of plausible explanation, and carrying on blithely as if nothing was amiss. As there was no explanation that didn't make me sound demented, I opted for the latter.

'No, I was just working,' I said, standing back. 'Come in.'

He stepped into the hallway and looked self-consciously at his boots, which were caked with cement dust. He bent down to unlace them.

'Don't take them off,' I said hastily. For some reason I couldn't bear to see him in his socks. 'There's no carpet.'

He straightened up and handed me the carrier bag, which bore the name of a boutique in South Molton Street that I would never have presumed to enter. Inside was a brown suede skirt and white shirt, approximating to the ones that had been ruined, but five times the price. 'I had to get some advice from Penny on sizes,' he said, while I gaped in surprise and gratitude. 'But I've left the receipt in there so you can take them back.'

'This is very kind,' I said. 'I thought we'd established it was all my fault.'

He shook his head. 'And these are to say sorry for my outrageous comments on the way home,' he added, passing me the tulips. They were dark aubergine in colour: black in a certain light.

'What comments?' I asked. I knew very well, but I thought I might eke out the apology a little. It was such a pleasant sensation.

He looked uncomfortable. 'The stuff I said about your
...private life. What an arsehole. I don't know what I was
thinking. You should have told me to sod off and mind my
own business.'

'Didn't I say something like that?'

'No, you were far too polite. Anyway, I've been cringing
about it ever since. I told Penny about the conversation on
the way home and she was horrified. She said I was
completely out of order and I'd better come round and
grovel.'

'Do you do everything Penny tells you?' I asked with a
smile.

He considered this for a moment. 'Only in matters of
female psychology where I'm out of my depth.'

'The funny thing is,' I said, 'the moment you'd left, I
thought of all the things I could have said.'

'Such as?'

'Well, for instance, there was a time when you didn't
think a married woman was out of bounds yourself.'

Donovan looked suitably embarrassed. 'Like I said: what
an arsehole.'

'But you were completely right, of course. It's no way to
carry on. And in fact I'm not.'

'Not what?'

'Carrying on. I ended the relationship yesterday.'

'You didn't!'

'I did.'

Donovan was appalled. 'Jesus!' he said. 'Not on the
strength of my interference, I hope.'

'Not entirely. It would have ended anyway. It was talking to Penny and you that woke me up though. I must have
been sleepwalking before.'

'God, I feel even worse now,' said Donovan. I could see he was rattled.

'Are you coming in?' I asked. We hadn't advanced further than the hallway.

'I can't stop. I've been laying a base for a shed.' He held up his cement-grey hands for my inspection. 'And I've got to get the mixer back to the hire shop by five. I just thought I'd better drop the clothes off, in case you had nothing to wear.' He looked pointedly at my top half. 'But I see you managed to find something.'

'Oh, ha ha,' I mumbled. 'I'm sorry about that. It just came to hand.' I couldn't even whip it off, as I wasn't wearing anything underneath, a fact I was glad to have remembered in time.

'Keep it,' he said expansively. 'It looks better on you.' As he turned to go I felt the same twist of disappointment as before. It seemed imperative that he shouldn't just vanish.

'I'm afraid you've missed Christian again,' I said, for something to say.

'Ah well,' he replied. 'It was you I came to see.'

'He'll be sorry not to have been here,' I said, taking desperate liberties with the truth. 'If you're ever passing this way again, perhaps you'll drop in?'

'As a matter of fact, I've got to go and price a job in Godstone next Saturday. I could call in when I'm done, if you like.'

'Good. Do that. I'll try to make sure he's around,' I said, and I was able to wave him off with a sense of relief that I had managed to spare myself the frustration of an indefinite farewell. As soon as he'd gone I put the tulips in a vase on the window sill. Black: strange colour for a peace-offering. Then I tried on the blouse and skirt: they fitted

rather better than the ones I'd bought myself. That's money
for you. When I looked in the mirror I noticed my face was
strangely flushed.

The glowing ember of creativity that had been interrupted by the doorbell was now a roaring fire, so I went
back to my drawing board and worked with feverish concentration for what must have been hours. When the sound of
the key in the lock brought me round I realised dusk had
fallen and I was sitting in darkness, the only source of light
that old wax lantern, the moon, and the reflected white-
ness of my paper.

43

THE FOLLOWING MORNING, MONDAY, I WOKE UP FEELING
terrific – full of energy and optimism, and brimming with
goodwill for the world. Even the prospect of going to investigate the flat above the dry cleaner's couldn't depress my
spirits.

'Hiya,' I called to Elaine, who was out front, planting the
acer that she and Christian had picked up at the garden
centre the day before. 'It's a beautiful morning.'

She looked at me warily. 'You're very cheerful,' she said,
teasing out the potbound rootball. 'Where are you off to?'

'I'm going to check out a flat on the hill. Or rather a
room,' I said, bracing myself to withstand a storm of advice.

Elaine dropped the tree into the hole she'd dug and shov-
elled the displaced earth back in with her strong, smooth
hands. On her third finger the ruby glowed as if lit from
within. She sat back on her heels and squinted up at me,
sweeping her long, woolly mane off her face, leaving crumbs

of compost clinging to the hairs. 'There's no rush for you
to move out,' she said.

'No, I know,' I replied. 'But I may as well start looking.
See what's out there.'

'If you don't find anything suitable, there's always my
house in Oxted. It's a three-bedroom semi. You could live
there. It's not too far from here, and it's never going to be
any use to us because of the stairs.'

'But you could sell it. It must be worth a fair bit.'

'I don't want to sell it. I'd rather keep it as an invest-
ment.'

'Then you could rent it out for way more money than I
could afford.'

She considered this. 'You could give us whatever you'd
be paying for a single room somewhere, but have the whole
house.'

'That's very generous of you, Elaine,' I said, taken aback
by the spontaneity of the offer. 'What's in it for you?'

'I'd be getting a reliable tenant. Anyway, there doesn't
need to be anything *in it* for me. We're going to be family,
after all.'

'It seems a bit of a weird arrangement.'

'The arrangement it's replacing's not exactly what you'd
call normal,' she replied with a smile.

'I suppose not.' Something held me back from committing myself. Perhaps it was the life-swap element that
disturbed me. Or perhaps I simply distrusted any solution
that seemed too neat.

'Well – go and look at your flat on the hill,' she said.
'But the offer's there to fall back on.'

'Was it Christian's idea?' I asked, suddenly wondering if
he'd put her up to it.

'No, Esther,' she said, patting me on the arm. 'I managed to think of it all by myself.'

AS I'D FEARED, THE FLAT WAS GRIM. I WAS EXPECTING IT TO be cold – once you've become acclimatised to the fug generated by our hypocaust, most places are – but this place was cheerless in the extreme. The available room was approximately eleven feet square, unfurnished, and without a single attractive feature. An oblong picture window, aluminium-framed and dressed in nets of such forbidding opacity that they could have served in the blackouts, gave directly onto the street. Over all four walls Artex had been whipped to soft peaks, and on the floor there was a bran-coloured carpet, once fitted, but now stretched into ridges and furrows by repeated cleaning. There was a faint smell of bleach. I couldn't see how I would ever fit the contents of my bedroom and studio in the available space or, once there, that I would ever feel inspired to work. The state of the shared bathroom and kitchen – soulless, functional and not entirely clean – did nothing to convert me, and I could hardly concentrate on the landlady's spiel about the individual electric meters in the hall cupboard, and not drying clothes on the convector heater, so eager was I to escape.

'It's very nice,' I said when she was done. 'But I've got a few other places to see.'

'Well, I've got a few other people coming in to look,' she retorted, and we smiled at one another across this impasse.

When I got home there was a message on the answerphone from Rowena, asking if I had any intention of dragging my arse back to work in the foreseeable future. I thought that was a bit much, given that I'm hardly ever ill and have never taken my full holiday allocation in all the time I've worked there. I was inclined to let her stew, but instead I rang back and left a message saying I would be off for another week. I wasn't sure why I was so recklessly courting unemployment. It must have been the fever of change coming over me. I'd lost my lover, and was about to lose my home: why stop there?

THE GIVING OF PRESENTS MUST BE ONE OF LIFE'S FINEST pleasures. The bestower feels purified; the recipient feels cherished. Both sides are enriched. It was with these elevated thoughts in my head that I went shopping the next day to find something that would repay Donovan's generosity – or rather symbolise repayment, since I couldn't hope to match him pound for pound.

While I was browsing in House of Fraser, flitting promiscuously from Homewear to Small Electrical, to Cosmetics, I came across a cast-iron skillet for making crepes and some highball glasses for Christian, and a long, fringed velvet scarf in peacock blue for Elaine. I also bought a Diana Krall CD for Penny, and a sequinned snake-belt for Cassie.

In the Menswear department I noticed the identical twin of Donovan's zip-neck sweater, which I had now appropriated as a painting overall. As a reciprocal gesture it could hardly be bettered, so I paid for it and started to make my way out of the shop.

It was only as I was passing through Sportswear and my eye fell on a pair of Nike swimming trunks similar to Dad's that I remembered with a sickening jolt that it was Tuesday, and I was supposed to be at the Holiday Inn pool. In fact – I looked at my watch – it was now past lunchtime and the Evergreen session would be long over. I ran all the way back to the car, the cast-iron skillet clubbing the side of my leg reproachfully, and drove with furious disregard for public safety to the Old Schoolhouse (now *Beltrees*). Dad opened the door, his hair still damp and vertical from his lonely swim.

'Oh, there you are,' he said with relief. 'I thought something had happened. I've left a few messages on your phone.'

'Sorry!' I bleated. 'I completely forgot. I just lost track of the days.'

Dad looked at me narrowly. 'Never mind. As long as you're all right.'

'I went shopping,' I went on in the same apologetic tone, and then with a flash of inspiration: 'I bought you a present.' I handed over the Diana Krall CD. Penny would have to go without.

He looked surprised and touched. 'How kind,' he said, turning it over and studying the cover notes. 'I keep telling myself I must go out and buy one of those CD players...' I struck my forehead with the heel of my hand, but he carried on. 'You're just in time for lunch. I was going to have a boiled egg, but since you're here we might as well have something nice.'

While he prepared us a plate of prosciutto, and opened jars of pickled artichokes and mushrooms and sun-dried tomatoes, I gave him a detailed account of my reunion with Penny and Donovan, bringing him up to date with Aunty Barbara's undimmed eccentricity.

'Well, well, well,' was his judicious reaction to the news. 'That's all very interesting. Very interesting indeed. And it just goes to show that happiness can turn up in the most unexpected quarters.'

'He didn't actually say she was *happy*,' I admitted, but Dad just smiled at me. 'How did you get on with your future daughter-in-law?' I asked, chasing a glossy mushroom around the plate. After Sunday's excursion to the garden centre the three of them had come back to the Old Schoolhouse for tea so that Elaine could meet Dad properly, and visit the scene of Christian's childhood. I'd had a version of it from Elaine, but wanted to hear Dad's side. She had claimed they got along famously, and pronounced him 'a treasure. An absolute sweetie.' I didn't pass this on.

'Oh, yes, very nice girl. Woman, I should say,' said Dad, with his usual tact. 'I'm sure she'll be very good for Christian.'

'Did she offer you any wise words of advice?' I asked innocently.

Dad made throat-clearing noises to indicate demurral. 'She does have a certain zeal for organisation,' he conceded, 'but that's no bad thing.'

'I'm coming round to her,' I said. 'She's actually pretty kind.' I told him about her offer of accommodation, and he sat up.

'Really?' he said, pulling meditatively at a sprig of eyebrow. 'We were discussing your...er...circumstances over tea. I'm rather concerned that you're getting a raw deal.'

'Oh? How?'

'Well, you're thirty-two—'

'Thirty-four,' I corrected him.

'Yes, and you've no house, no savings, no pension, no career, not much in the way of income, and no one to support you.' I opened my mouth to protest but he raised his hand to hush me. 'I'm not in any way belittling your achievements as an illustrator. You know I'm extremely proud of you. But these are the facts. And the point I put to Christian is that you have contributed to that house over the years in much the same way as a wife.'

'That's ridiculous,' I replied. 'He paid for it with his

windfall and I've lived there rent-free. He doesn't owe me a bean. Quite the contrary.'

'You've arranged your working life to accommodate Christian, and you've cared for him and put him first, and done his laundry and cleaned and shopped, and redecorated the rooms and bought things for the house when you could have been setting up a place of your own and advancing your own career. And in all that time the value of the property has more than doubled, and you've missed your chance to buy. I just think that needs acknowledging.'

I sagged under the weight of all this praise.

'So if Christian and Elaine do make you any such offers in the near future, I recommend you accept,' he said, with a final tug of the eyebrow.

We shared a farewell hug on the doorstep. 'I'll be there next week,' I promised. 'Bang on time.'

'Don't worry,' Dad replied cheerfully. 'I mean, if something more exciting turns up . . .' Sometimes I honestly don't know what he's on about.

ON THE DRIVE HOME I WAS SO PREOCCUPIED WITH WHAT DAD had said about my dizzying lack of financial security that I failed to notice the dark green saloon parked outside. As I let myself in Christian emerged from the sitting room, making urgent signals with his eyes, but saying in a voice suitable to be overheard, 'You've got a visitor, Esther.'

For a second my heart sprang to attention. A tall male figure stood up when I entered: with his back to the light he seemed to loom over me. It was Geoff. This was unprecedented. There was a discreet click as Christian shut the door on us.

'I've left Mary,' he said.

44

I GAVE A GASP AND STARED AT HIM, OPEN-MOUTHED IN SHOCK and disbelief.

'You haven't.'

'I have.'

'Why?' Blood roared in my ears and I thought I was going to faint. I sank down on the couch and put my head in my hands.

'Because I can't bear to lose you, and if it's the only way we can be together—'

'How could you?' I wailed. 'After I'd told you it was over.' It wasn't Geoff I was thinking of, but Mary, lying on the floor in her Burberry raincoat, howling like a beast. Now my name would be poison on her lips for ever. If I'd had the strength I would have run out of the house and kept right on running, but I was too breathless to move.

'I know I've put you in an impossible situation for years, and I'm sorry. I totally understand you've reached the end

of your tether, and you're such a lovely person you don't
want anyone to get hurt. But someone's bound to get hurt.
Someone always does. The important thing is that we love
each other, and we can try to salvage something from all
this awfulness.' Geoff was ashen-faced and sweating from
the effort of delivering this speech. He looked like he might
have a heart attack at any moment. The room swayed
around me as if I was drunk. The worst had happened. My
belated attempt to do the right thing had backfired in the
most hideous fashion.

'What about the children?' I shrilled. 'It'll ruin their lives.
They'll despise you for ever.' *I have become Mary*, I thought.

'They're sixteen and seventeen. They're practically
adults.'

'Oh my God, this is a nightmare,' I moaned. 'I never
wanted this.' How could Geoff have mistaken the finality of my intentions so disastrously? 'When I said I wanted
to end the relationship,' I said, my voice quavering treach-
erously, 'I meant exactly that. It wasn't a ploy or an ulti-
matum: me or her. I couldn't have made it plainer.' Panic
and indignation made me hard. 'I don't want you, Geoff.
Married or divorced or any other way.' And then I started
to cry, great cowardly sobs with my head on my knees.
Any minute now, I thought, I'm going to feel his arm
round my shoulder, comforting me, and I'll have to shrug
him off, because he'll interpret anything less than cruelty
as a lack of resolve. I couldn't sit up: my face was welter-
ing in snot and tears and I didn't have a tissue, but I had
to eventually, and when I did he had gone, and Christian
was tapping at the door, saying, 'Esther, are you all right?
Can I come in?'

* * *

CHRISTIAN HELD MY DAMP HANDS AND LISTENED TO THE whole miserable story.

'Shit,' was his verdict.

'Exactly,' I agreed. 'It couldn't be worse. Poor Mary.'

Christian squeezed my hand a little tighter. 'Your empathy for Mary is all very worthy,' he said gently. 'But it's about four years overdue, and it's no use to anyone now. I mean, you've been risking an outcome like this every time you and Geoff met.'

'What can I do to fix it?'

'Nothing now. What you certainly mustn't do is go back to him out of a feeling of guilt.'

'You don't like him, do you?' I said – something that had never occurred to me before.

'I don't dislike him. He's a good GP. But you could do so much better.'

'One of the things that attracted me to him was that he wouldn't ever try to take me away from you.'

Christian looked horrified. 'That should never have been a consideration. All that skulking about. Keeping him a secret from Mum and Dad. You've sacrificed too much for me, Esther.'

'Why didn't you ever say anything before?'

'No point. No one ever listens to advice in matters of the heart.'

'That's true.'

'Wait here,' he said, 'I've got something for you.' He left me sitting there, puzzled, while he went into the study. Presently he returned holding a folded piece of paper, which he handed over with an air almost of apology. It was a cheque for £50,000 and it was made out to me.

'What the hell's this?' I demanded.

'It's for you. To help with moving out.'

'You don't owe me any money, Christian. It's your house. I'm just a squatter here.'

'No. You've contributed plenty over the years. I don't mean financially. If we were married, for instance, I'd have to buy you out,' he said.

'This is Dad's bright idea, isn't it?'

'We did talk about it, but I'd already decided.'

'So this is my divorce settlement?' I said, looking at the row of noughts on the cheque in wonderment.

Christian laughed. 'If you like.'

'I don't want it, Christian.'

'You may not want it, but you certainly need it. And you're entitled to it – and more probably.'

'How can you possibly afford to give away this sort of money?'

'I've been earning all this time without any mortgage to pay. I've been saving and investing since I got my first wage slip. Plus, Elaine's got a house and savings of her own. Don't worry about us.'

I put my arms round his neck and he patted my back. 'If only all divorces could be like this,' I said.

HANDWRITTEN ENVELOPES ARE THE ONLY KIND WORTH opening, Dad always said. This one must have landed on the mat after dark as it was there first thing next morning, before the regular post arrived, and I'd been awake since dawn and heard nothing.

Dear Esther
Please try not to be angry when you read this: I couldn't think of another way. Maybe you won't be angry: maybe

you'll just be relieved. I don't know.

What I told you this morning was a lie: I haven't left Mary, or told her anything about us. I'm sorry for the distress it caused you. I only said it because I honestly hadn't a clue from our conversation in the car what it was you really wanted. I thought if I told you there were no obstacles to our being together, I would know from your reaction whether it was our situation you'd had enough of or just me. Now I know. Thank you.

In case you're wondering whether I would have gone ahead and left Mary if your response had been different, the answer is yes. But that's irrelevant now. I hope you will spare me a kind thought now and then. I don't regret the time we spent together, and I don't feel any anger or bitterness towards you, Esther, only tremendous love and tremendous sadness.

Geoff

45

THE TEMPERATURE DROPPED AND THE WEATHER FORECAST promised 'serious snow' for the end of the week, which caused Elaine some anxiety on behalf of her acer, and sent Christian into a mood of despondency. A heavy fall would represent too great a challenge for the wheelchair and leave him imprisoned indoors until there was a thaw. As one not personally inconvenienced by it, I couldn't help harbouring a disloyal excitement about the prospect of snow, tempered on this occasion by concern that bad driving conditions might deter Donovan from calling in. But by Saturday morning, in spite of icy air and a mushroom-coloured sky, not a flake had fallen.

When I warned Christian about the intended visit he was infuriatingly non-committal. 'It's you he's coming to see. Will you be in?' I asked him, while he whipped up some pancake batter to christen the skillet.

'I don't know. We're supposed to be going out looking

at wedding venues sometime,' he said, vaguely. 'Depends how long it takes Elaine to get ready.' Her protracted preparations and resistance to chivvying were already the subject of much affectionate teasing by Christian.

'Can't you wait till after lunch?' I asked. 'It'll look funny if you're not here.'

'Why didn't you agree a time?' Christian wanted to know. 'I don't want to hang around all day.'

'It was just a casual arrangement,' I tried to explain.

'So he may not turn up at all?'

'Possibly.'

He rolled his eyes.

In the event, Donovan arrived mid-morning while Elaine was at Waitrose and I was taking an overseas call from Mum. She had heard about Christian's engagement from Dad and wanted the full story. 'What's she like? Is she reliable? Does she know what she's taking on?' she said, firing off questions in threes to save money. There was a disconcerting delay on the line, so each exchange sounded hesitant and unspontaneous, as though something was being held back. In addition, Mum's hearing had deteriorated in the last few years, and I was reticent about bellowing my opinions, however anodyne, within earshot of Christian. 'Why don't you ask him about it?' I suggested.

Silence. 'I will in a minute. I want to talk to you. Have you decided where you'll live?'

'No.'

Silence. 'You could come out here. They always need volunteers, even unskilled ones.'

'Thanks.' The irony got lost somewhere between Caterham and Nepal.

Silence. 'Don't thank me. It's no picnic, I can tell you.'

She talked some more about life at Dhankuta. She was getting over a bout of bronchitis and only just starting to feel well again. Her knee was misbehaving. She promised to come home for the wedding, whenever it happened to be. 'Put Christian on if he's there,' she said at last. 'Let's hear the good news from him.'

When I went into the study to give him the phone I found Donovan was already there, being given a demonstration of the latest PC game Christian was developing. They must have rattled through the polite ice-breaking protocol in double-quick time, if they'd bothered with it at all, as they were now deep in one of those technical discussions about computers that Christian enjoys so much.

'It's got to be as compulsive as *Tomb Raider*, but less arbitrary,' he was explaining. 'The problem-solving needs to be more logic-based.'

'Like *Myst?*' Donovan suggested, browsing the shelves on which Christian's encyclopaedic range of games was displayed.

'Yeah, but with three hundred and sixty-degree view and completely free walk-through. Plus film-quality graphics, and a really strong narrative. So it's a bit like being inside a classic thriller.'

'But with infinite possible outcomes?'

'Yeah, exactly. Not much to ask is it?' They turned to me expectantly.

'Mum,' I said, passing Christian the handset. Donovan and I politely withdrew to the hallway.

'Hello,' he said.

'Hello,' I replied, and with that two-word exchange I suddenly knew with absolute certainty that it was me he had come to see, and that it wouldn't have mattered to him, or me, whether Christian had been there or not.

'Are you fully recovered from your ordeal?' he asked. I looked at him blankly. I felt as though I'd been through so many in the last week I wasn't sure which one he meant. 'Your hand?' he suggested. 'Your shoulder?'

'Oh, yes. Fine.' I wriggled them to prove it. On the settle next to me lay the replacement jumper, still in its bag. I passed it across. 'I put that top of yours through the wash,' I said, absolutely deadpan. 'It's come up quite well.'

Donovan looked at it and then me, and laughed. 'I can't decide what you and Christian remind me of,' he said thoughtfully. 'Hansel and Gretel perhaps.'

'What do you mean?'

'I'm not sure. You're like something from a fairytale. Brother and sister living together happily ever after in your little gingerbread house.'

'There's nothing mystical about it,' I said. 'I'm just the lodger.'

'I can't put my finger on it,' he went on. 'It's as if you've made your childhood go on and on. You both even look young for your age.'

'I suppose we are a bit juvenile at times,' I admitted, self-conscious all of a sudden. I was remembering the way Geoff had laughed at me once at the Coliseum when I'd folded up my coat and sat on it, like a child, to get a better view of the stage – even though I'm five foot six.

'No need to be apologetic. It's quite appealing.'

I considered the dampening effect of the word 'quite'.

'Are you busy today?' Donovan was saying.

'Busy? Well, there's the gingerbread house to clean, and then I have to make dinner for the elves...'

'Okay, okay,' said Donovan. 'I've got another garden to look at, down in Sussex. Do you want to come for the ride? We could get some lunch on the way.'

'Do you always work on Saturdays?'

'I work all the time if there's work to do. You lose so many days to bad weather in winter, plus the dark evenings, that you have to.'

'All right then.'

Christian came out of the study, shaking his head. 'Mum is so cheerful,' he said, with heavy sarcasm.

'Go on. What did she say about you getting married?'

'She said, "Congratulations! Have you made a will?"'

'SHALL WE TAKE MY CAR?' I OFFERED, AS I PUT MY COAT AND scarf on. I was remembering the Spartan comforts of the truck.

Donovan shrugged. 'If you prefer.'

But when we got outside I saw, parked behind my elderly Ford Fiesta, a new-looking Audi TT, shining like a polished stone. Even Christian came out to have a gawp. 'You always did have bigger, better toys,' I grumbled.

'When I found out my wife and I couldn't have children my immediate reaction was to go out and get a sports car.'

'Logical,' said Christian.

'Unfortunately hers was to go out and get a new husband.'

'Logical again.'

I walked round it admiringly. 'Gardening must pay better than waitressing,' I observed.

'Well, when I said "gardening"...' Donovan replied. 'I mean, there's more to it than raking up leaves.'

Christian waved us off from the driveway, one eye out for Elaine's return: they were going off themselves later, scouring the county for a wedding venue.

'It's a designing and landscaping business, really,' he explained, once we were on our way. 'My sister Pippa – Dad and Suzie's daughter, I don't know if you ever met her – she does the designing, and the planting plan, and I do all the actual work.'

'A slightly Hansel-and-Gretelish arrangement, if you don't mind my saying.'

'You see – we've got more in common than you think.'

WE STOPPED FOR LUNCH AT THE BELL IN OUTWOOD. THE SKY had a sickly yellowish tinge, and as we crossed the car park a flurry of dusty snow blew up from nowhere. Donovan insisted on paying for lunch, and dismissed all my counter-insistence. Short of having a stand-up row at the bar, there was nothing I could do. Another debt to be settled later, I thought. As I watched him laying into his gammon and chips I had an involuntary flashback to those all-day break-fasts he'd bought with Aunty Barbara's money, at the pavement café near St Paul's. But reminiscing is a risky indulgence, and I wasn't going to be the one to unleash its mischief.

'I'm such a coward,' Donovan suddenly announced.

'Why do you say that?'

'When Christian opened the door, I just said, "Hi, good to see you." And he said, "Great to see you. Come in." And it was so obvious that the last time I saw him he was walk-ing and now he's not, and I never even mentioned it. I feel terrible.'

'Don't worry about that,' I said. 'I'm sure Christian was much happier talking about computer games. Which is something he certainly can't do with me.'

'Are you sure?'

'Absolutely. In fact I think the reason he doesn't like meeting people is because he doesn't want to go through the whole "how I cope" rigmarole every time.'

'Would you say he's reconciled to his ... condition?'

'Not completely. He still reads up all the latest research on the internet, and he still hopes they'll find a cure. But he's not as consumed by it as he used to be.' Especially not now, I thought, with a surge of affection for Elaine. I couldn't help thinking how different it felt, sitting here openly with Donovan, instead of skulking in the corner of the George and Dragon with Geoff. But this again was something I couldn't share.

'Where are we actually going?' I ventured to ask as we emerged from the smoky warmth of the pub to the raw air outside. Fine wet snow was falling vertically now, melting as it landed, refusing to settle. It was a relief to get back in the car.

'Ardingly.'

'I've heard of that. Why have I heard of it?'

'There's quite a famous public school there.'

'That's right. Didn't Wart go there?'

'Possibly.'

'And you're going to look at a garden.'

'Correct. You can give me your advice.'

'What do you want my advice for? I haven't got a clue about gardening. I can hardly tell a daffodil from a dandelion.'

'You're an artist. You must have a good aesthetic sense. I know you have – I've got one of your books.'

'Have you? What on earth would you be buying children's books for?' I asked, realising too late that this wasn't a terribly tactful remark. Donovan was oblivious.

'Because it had your name on the front.'

I laughed at the unexpected compliment, and couldn't for a moment think of any suitable reply. 'I'm surprised you remembered it,' I said at last.

Donovan gave me a pitying look: he wasn't even going to dignify such a craven piece of fishing with a reply.

'I used to work there,' he said, a little later, as we passed a sign for Wakehurst Place. 'Nice job. Terrible pay.' We were deep in the Sussex countryside by now and appeared to have left the snow behind.

'You always said you wouldn't ever work in an office.'

'And I never have. I'm a man of my word, you see.'

On the outskirts of Ardingly we turned right down a stony track past the church. It reminded me of the approach to the Old Schoolhouse, before it was done over and turned into luxury flats. The vicar was just coming through the gate with a fat Labrador on a lead. He gave the car a cheery wave, which Donovan returned.

'Friendly place,' I said. We bumped down the track as far as it would take us and stopped just beyond the last of a row of terraced cottages. Donovan's truck was already parked outside. I must be very trusting or very dim, because I didn't even put two and two together when someone emerged from one of the neighbouring cottages to put a milkbottle on the doorstep and called out, 'Hello'. It was only when Donovan produced a set of keys and let himself into the house rather than ringing the doorbell that it dawned on me he owned the place.

'You live here!' I accused him.

'I never said I didn't,' he replied. 'Are you coming in?'

I stepped into a large, open-plan living room, extending the length and breadth of the ground floor. At the far end was a kitchen area with a door into the garden, and against the party wall was an open-tread wooden staircase. There were polished oak boards on the floor and the walls were bare brickwork and white plaster, hung with a variety of prints and engravings. Two old red brocade sofas sat opposite each other across a stout coffee table. In the large stone fireplace an arrangement of logs and paper spills had been laid in the grate but not lit. The floor, the window ledges, the lintels, the rafters, everything was pleasantly wonky. It smelled of fresh paint and brickdust.

'Goodness, this is grown-up,' I said.

'Well, I'm thirty-seven. What were you expecting? *Thunderbirds* wallpaper?' He put a match to the firelighter in the grate and waited until the nest of newspaper sticks had caught.

'It's very tidy,' I said. 'You don't seem to have thirty-seven years' worth of clobber.'

'That's divorce for you. My ex-wife got custody of the clobber. I kept the car. Anyway, I've only just bought this place, so I haven't had time to trash it yet. I've been doing up the inside in every spare moment for the last three months. I haven't even started on the garden yet. Come and have a look.'

He opened the back door and we stepped out into a wilderness of knee-high grass and thistles. Its position on the end of the terrace meant that the cottage benefited from a disproportionately large garden, extending around three sides of the house. In the middle of the lawn was an ancient pear tree, not yet in bloom, and in the corner, sagging against the boundary fence, was a dilapidated lean-to with a moss-spattered roof. Far below in a shallow valley I could see a cloud of cold, brittle trees, and the metallic glint of the reservoir. 'What a lovely view,' I exclaimed. 'And it's such a big garden for the size of the house.'

'I know. That's what attracted me.'

'It needs a bit of work though. It's not a great advertisement for your gardening skills in its present state.'

'No,' he laughed. 'But it's a blank canvas. That's more fun than having to work round some existing feature that can't be touched.'

'What are you going to do?'

'Knock down that shed and replace it with somewhere waterproof to keep all my tools and stuff. After that I don't know. What do you reckon?'

'The first thing you need is a rope swing with an old tyre on the end,' I said. 'And then maybe a nettle patch.'

'I knew you'd be full of good ideas,' Donovan replied, giving me a sideways grin.

'Do you still go for your moonlight rambles?' I asked, forgetting my own veto about reminiscing. 'You used to be practically nocturnal.'

'Yes, I do as a matter of fact, though not as much as I used to. I get these bouts of insomnia now and then, and one thing I can't stand is lying in bed awake. I have to get up. So I go off and plod round the reservoir. I haven't been here long enough to get bored with the route.'

It was too cold to linger outdoors: a few downy snowflakes were falling and my face was starting to ache, so we retreated to the kitchen. As Donovan was closing the door, a fat tabby cat extruded itself through the gap, and made for the hearth, where it stood, pawing the rug as though flattening long grass.

'Is he yours?' I asked. 'Or is he just a local?'

'He's mine – don't go near him. He's vicious. Aren't you,

Weazlewort? Ever since I took him to the vet in a chilly box because I didn't have a proper cage.' He looked at my expression. 'There wasn't an ice pack in it at the time,' he said.

'Weazlewort,' I said, cogs grinding. 'Where have I heard that name before?'

'I don't know where you heard it,' said Donovan. 'I know where I heard it. It's the name of my dad's solicitor. I always thought it was wasted on a human.'

The cogs connected; the machinery began to turn. Yes, I thought, smiling to myself at the strangeness of it all: that's where I heard it too. I was remembering something Alan once said to Mum: *If there's ever anything I can do for you.* And he knew my parents well enough to realise that an anonymous gift was the only sort they wouldn't be able to return. I wanted to say something, but I knew I couldn't. Hadn't I always been the guardian of the Fry family's secrets?

Donovan made coffee in a percolator on the hob. When he opened the fridge to get the milk I could see it was well stocked with proper food – another intimation of maturity that brought before me the practical, self-sufficient teenager he'd once been. From a tin on the slate countertop he produced a date and walnut cake, and cut off two fat slices.

'Lovely,' I said. 'Just like a bought one.'

We sat on opposite couches by the fire, which was still giving rather more colour than heat, and drank our coffee. It was so strong I could soon feel my heart galloping in my ribs. I told Donovan about Christian's forthcoming marriage, assuming correctly that this wouldn't have come up during their earlier conversation.

'So things have moved on pretty quickly in the last week,' he said.

'Not half,' I replied. 'What a week.' I found myself telling him about Geoff's unexpected reappearance and fake claim to have left Mary, my unsuccessful attempt at flat-hunting, and Christian's generous handout. 'Anyway,' I said, conscious that I had talked of nothing but myself, in greater detail than might have been interesting, 'what have you been doing with yourself?'

'I've been thinking about you most of the time,' he said evenly.

I looked up from my coffee dregs to find Donovan studying me with those green granite eyes. Currents flowed between us as I held his gaze in the silence that followed. Before I could frame the perfect reply, the doorbell rang and we both started.

Donovan stood up first, catching his knee on the table and making the plates rattle. He strode over to the window to get a glimpse of the caller, and I saw his expression collapse, from one of annoyance to one of utter defeat. 'Oh, Jesus, no,' he said, putting his hands to his head and seizing fistfuls of hair as though scalping himself might afford some relief. He opened the front door to admit a whirl of dry snowflakes and a figure swaddled in a moulting, floor-length coat, and a leather aviator's cap with earflaps. Aunty Barbara.

'Hello, Donovan,' she said, patting his chest. 'The roads are absolutely appalling, and your map was hopeless. I'm shattered. Get my bags in, will you?' She handed him the keys and began to shed outer layers.

'Mum, it was next weekend you were supposed to be coming,' said Donovan, with more than a hint of impatience. 'You've got the date wrong.'

'Have I? No, we agreed the fourteenth.'

'That *is* next weekend.'

'Is it really? Oh, *bugger*. Then I'm going to miss the Proberts' ruby wedding. Oh, well, it can't be helped.' She noticed me for the first time. 'Hello, dear,' she said, abstractedly, and then took a second look. 'Esther!' she pealed. I stood up and she bore down on me, and pressed her icy cheek to mine. Her hair, now that I could see it, was an attractive, variegated grey-white, though seriously mauled by the aviator's cap. Under the shaggy coat she was dressed in black trousers, a long, embroidered shirt and a waistcoat that must have been made on a hand-loom. Her fingernails, and their immediate hinterland, were painted purple. I could feel them digging into my wrist. 'Did you come especially to see me?' she asked.

'I didn't actually know you were going to be here,' I admitted.

'Neither of us did,' Donovan reminded her.

'Oh, no, of course not. Never mind.' She sat down on the couch and pulled me down next to her with surprising strength. 'While Donovan's getting my stuff you can sit here and tell me how your poor brother is getting on.' Donovan, thus dismissed, made throat-slitting gestures before disappearing out to the car.

I provided Aunty Barbara with the briefest possible résumé of Christian's physical and mental condition, ending with an account of his recent engagement.

'It's surprising how often you hear about men marrying the woman who nursed them,' she mused. 'But you don't hear of women marrying their doctors so much. I wonder why.'

'In my experience the doctor is usually already married to someone else,' I replied tartly.

'How old did you say Christian is now?'

'Thirty-nine.'

'Thirty-nine! There you are, Donovan, it's not too late,' she called in the direction of the open door. The phone rang. I took the liberty of picking it up, in case an answer-phone cut in. It was Penny. 'Oh, hi Esther,' she said without a trace of surprise, before I'd identified myself.

'I've just come to look at Donovan's garden,' I said, feeling that my presence required some explanation. 'Aunty Barbara's here, too,' I added, for good measure. 'Do you want to speak to Donovan?'

'No, you can give him a message. He was going to come over tomorrow and dig up a tree root for me with his special chomper, but there's no point now because there's about four inches of snow outside. Have you got much down there?'

I looked out of the window at the white lacework appearing on the roofs of the cars. 'Not yet. It's only just starting to settle.'

'Well, don't get stranded,' she warned me. 'Unless you want to, of course.'

'I—'

'Just tell him to call me some time. Byeee.' And she hung up, leaving me frowning at the receiver.

Donovan came in from reparking Aunty Barbara's car, which had been blocking the neighbour's gate, and kicked the door shut behind him. He was carrying a Gladstone bag and a trolley suitcase, which he took straight up to the bedroom, his footsteps echoing on the wooden stairs. Aunty Barbara was poking around, opening cupboards. 'So this is the new house,' she said to no one in particular. 'Very nice, but a bit blokey. Needs a woman's touch.' I remembered

Aunty Barbara's 'touch': brimming ashtrays, pilfered cosmetics, and miniature vodka bottles under the bed.

'Penny rang,' I said, when Donovan rejoined us.

'Oh?' he said warily. 'What did she want?'

'She said not to bother about the tree stump tomorrow
– they've got deep snow.'

Donovan looked guilty. 'That's lucky. I'd completely
forgotten.' This admission cheered me greatly. You don't
love her, then, I thought.

Aunty Barbara wanted a tour of the first floor, so while
the kettle was boiling for tea we all trooped upstairs. It
didn't take long: a small, white bathroom, two double
bedrooms with identical iron bedsteads, made up with blue
and white checked covers – one neat, the other left as
vacated. I averted my gaze: there's something too intimate
about an unmade bed. Both rooms had wooden wardrobes
built into the eaves, and the larger of the two contained a
desk, computer and filing cabinet, all covered with paper.
The windows were so low off the floor that you would have
to bend double to see what kind of day it was.

Aunty Barbara sat down on the neat bed, beside which
her cases stood, bouncing up and down to test the mattress,
then she went next door and did the same. 'Do you mind
if we swap?' she called. 'This one's harder. Better for my
back.'

'Whatever makes you happy,' Donovan replied amiably,
at the same time shooting me a matricidal glance.

Over tea, Aunty Barbara – who had supplied her own
teabag, which smelled of compost – cross-examined me
about Mum and Dad, and I was forced to provide abridged
biographies, all the while conscious that, having met
Donovan only eight days ago, I was already repeating myself.

At last, when I had brought her up to date, and couldn't bear the sound of my own voice any more, I said, 'I'm a bit worried about this weather. Penny said the snow was quite deep where she is. I don't want to get stuck.'

Donovan seized on this with elation. 'You're right,' he said, standing up. 'I'd better take you home. I would have said come for the ride, Mum, but it's only a two-seater...'

'No thanks,' said Aunty Barbara. 'I've been on the road all day. I'll stay here and have a lovely bath.'

'Good idea,' Donovan replied, heading out into the back garden, returning a moment later with snowflakes in his hair, carrying a shovel. From one of the kitchen drawers he produced a torch. He slung both in the boot of the Audi and then patted it. 'You beautiful car,' he said meaningfully.

IT WAS ONLY AS WE APPROACHED THE M25 THAT IT DAWNED on us we were in trouble. The snow down in Sussex had been nothing like as bad as it was here. It must have been falling steadily ever since we'd left in the morning, because even the main roads were treacherous, with deep ruts and ridges, and minor roads were completely impassable to vehicles. We sat in a traffic jam at the Caterham junction for an hour and a half, as more and more cars tried to join the motorway and fewer and fewer dared to turn off onto its snowbound tributaries. Dusk fell, and we'd advanced only a few yards. 'We should have set off earlier,' Donovan said, drumming the steering wheel. 'I'm really sorry.'

'It's not your fault,' I replied. 'I'm just worried about your mum. Will she feel abandoned?'

'No, she'll be quite happy, snooping through my things.' He gave her a ring on his mobile all the same, to explain the delay. I could hear her twittering away in the background. 'I don't possess any bubble bath. Try washing-up liquid,' was his closing remark.

'I should have brought emergency rations,' Donovan grumbled, foraging in the map pocket and the glove compartment, turning up nothing but a lone tic-tac in a box. At the sight of it a memory of Grandpa Percy rose up before me, and I could hear again the distinctive rattle that always marked his progress.

'Donovan,' I said impulsively, before I could change my mind. 'I owe you an apology.'

'Oh? What for?' He looked puzzled.

'I once accused you of stealing some money. But it wasn't you.'

'I know it wasn't me. Who was it?'

'Grandpa. We found it hidden in his room when he died.'

Donovan raised his eyebrows in surprise. 'What made you so sure it was me?'

'I saw you on a stool, with your hand in the jar.'

'Oh. Well, I suppose that might have looked pretty incriminating. I was probably just putting back the deposit for that garden strimmer. Or taking it out, or something.'

'I worked that out. I think I saw you putting it back. Grandpa must have seen you taking it out, and thought you were trying to nick it. So he went back a day or so later and moved it to a safer place.'

'I'm surprised he didn't break his neck.'

'He could be pretty strong when he got fixated on some task.'

'Why didn't you tell me you'd seen me at the time?'

'I don't know. Stupid teenage games. Anyway, it's been on my conscience.'

'I'm glad it's cleared up at last. Though I must admit I haven't spent every waking moment fighting to clear my name.'

'No. Such a trivial thing, really.' But it wasn't at the time, I thought. Back then everything was livid with significance.

At last we gained the turn-off: ominously no other cars followed suit. The Audi crawled up the hill, slewing from side to side. I'd never seen the bypass so deserted. Abandoned cars lay at the roadside. The central reservation had become a fat, white bolster. The higher we went the harder it was. Twice Donovan stopped and dug a channel in front of each tyre to give us some grip, but the third time the wheels just churned hopelessly, and he switched off the engine.

'Come on, we're walking,' he said.

'Will the car be all right, just left here?' I asked.

'I don't think anyone's going to be able to steal it,' he pointed out, as he went to fetch the torch. Reassured, I opened the door and stepped out into the blue-white dusk.

Snow is a kind of miracle, capable of transforming even our pebbledash subtopia into a scene of beauty and wonder. The dual carriageway had become a sweeping glacier; even the piles of discarded trash in the layby were smothered in lush drifts. Below us in the dip, and away up the hill, lights twinkled in the houses, all the hard edges softened and blurred. There was a holiness about the silence: traffic, car radios, voices, all the raucous sounds of human interference had been muffled by the mysterious power of snow.

'It's beautiful isn't it?' I whispered. 'It makes you feel a bit...unhinged.'

'You've been having that effect on me all day,' Donovan replied. 'Come on.' He took one of my hands and we

half-ran, half-stumbled along the road, leaving deep,
powdery furrows behind us. I was laughing like a drunk.

A dark shape shot out of the trees at the roadside, straight
across our path, and stopped. A fox: its eyes flaming in the
darkness. It seemed to hold our gaze for ever, and then it
turned and loped along, just ahead of us, as if leading the
way.

'Someone left a mangled fox on the bonnet of Dad's car
the night you ran away,' I said, as the memory surfaced. 'I'm
not suggesting it was you,' I added. Donovan looked at me
as though this was fresh evidence of my insanity. 'What are
you on about, you crazy woman?' he said, without breaking
his stride.

'Nothing,' I muttered. 'Forget it.' I really know how to
slaughter an atmosphere.

There was just the thinnest paring of moon visible in
the sky, but the snow emitted a ghostly light of its own,
and the torch sat unused in Donovan's pocket. 'You won't
be able to get back tonight, you know,' I said, it having
only that moment occurred to me.

'Well noticed,' said Donovan.

'You'll have to "sleep over",' I said, smiling at my own
private joke.

Donovan looked at me through narrowed eyes, then took
hold of the two ends of my scarf and pulled me towards
him, and kissed me at last, and I was fifteen again, barefoot
and clueless in the hot garden. We stayed there kissing for
a long time, and I thought, I'll always remember that it
started here, standing in the fast lane of a dual carriageway.
But it hadn't of course, it had started years ago, before we
even knew that there were such feelings. At last we drew
apart.

'You're gorgeous,' he said. 'I've been dreaming about you all week.' We carried on walking, hand in hand, towards the roundabout, or at least the undulating snowfield that had taken its place. Pavement and road were indistinguishable: several times I missed the kerb and sank in up to my knee. Neither of us was particularly well-shod for this hike. My socks were soaked through and my toes felt scalded. I thought how miserable I would be if I'd had to make this journey alone, what a joyless ordeal it would have seemed, and yet with Donovan it had become an adventure – the fulfilment of a childhood dream.

CHRISTIAN AND ELAINE HAD ALREADY GONE TO BED WHEN we reached home. Enjoying the comforts I can't provide, as Dad might have put it. I indicated their closed door and put my finger to my lips as we peeled off our wet coats and scarves. I led him down the passage to my room, our snow-crusted jeans leaving pools on the warm wooden floor.

'A single bed,' said Donovan, when the modest dimensions of my room were revealed. 'I might have guessed.' He sat down on it and looked up at me expectantly.

'There'll be plenty of room as long as we lie very still,' I said, trying not to smile.

'I wouldn't count on that if I were you,' Donovan said, pulling me onto his knee.

I WAS WOKEN SOME TIME BEFORE DAWN BY THE SCREAM OF A fox. When I came to, Donovan already had his eyes open. 'Oh good,' he said. 'I've been awake for hours. Now you can entertain me again.'

'I thought you said you couldn't lie in bed wide awake. I thought you always had to go for a walk.'

'I find I can put up with it much better when I've got a beautiful naked woman lying on top of me. I don't know why.'

'Enough compliments already,' I said, trying to sound cross. 'I'll be thinking I'm something special.'

'You are special to me,' he replied, and I couldn't help smiling, because he'd used, quite unconsciously, exactly the same words he'd written and then retracted half a lifetime ago.

'You know what you were saying earlier about moving out and flat-hunting?' he said, when we'd shifted into a more comfortable position for conversation. He was propped on one elbow, stroking me with his free hand. 'You could move in with me if you like. I've got space.'

'That would be a bit sudden, wouldn't it?' I said. 'We've only spent one night together. Half a night.'

'You're not going to say we hardly know each other?'

'No, but ... move in. As what? Your lodger?'

'As whatever you like.'

'I don't know, Donovan,' I said, soberly now. 'People are offering to put me up, right, left and centre, but I feel I ought to make the effort to find a place of my own. I've got to start being more self-reliant.'

'Okay. It was just an idea. I was lying here thinking how nice it would be to see you every day. That's all.'

'Anyway, I'd drive you mad. I've got so many annoying habits.'

'Such as?'

'Well. I still have to sleep with a light on.' We looked at the closed door. Not a glimmer was visible from the hallway. For the first time ever I'd forgotten.

'You see, I've cured you,' Donovan said. 'See what a good influence I am.'

* * *

AT LAST WE WENT OFF TO SLEEP AGAIN, A NECESSARY TANGLE of limbs, and it was broad daylight when I awoke to the metallic sound of shovel on concrete. Donovan was sitting up, tweaking at the blinds.

'What's going on out there?' he asked.

'It looks like Dad's clearing snow off the driveway,' I said, peering over his shoulder. 'I wonder how he got here.'

Donovan was appalled. 'Why is your seventy-year-old father clearing your driveway?' he demanded.

'He's probably worried that one of us might slip, and he knows Christian can't do it, so—'

'But *you* could do it,' he said, tipping me out of bed as he clambered past. 'Or did I just dream that conversation about self-reliance?' He began pulling on his clothes, so carelessly discarded the night before.

'If you think Dad will give up that spade without a struggle . . .' I called after him from the floor.

A moment later I heard movement from the direction of Christian's room and flew into the bathroom before Elaine could commandeer it for her hour-long ablutions. I turned the shower on full and let the water beat down on my back like buckshot, revelling in the pain. Perhaps it was the distorting effect of Donovan's compliments or the clouds of steam fogging the mirror, but my thirty-four-year-old body looked fine this morning – really quite symmetrical and pleasant. I thought how my circum-stances had changed in just a couple of weeks. Nothing was predictable any more. Everything was shifting. Ever since Christian's injury my attitude to life had been essen-tially wary and fatalistic: happiness was at best precari-ous, and disaster lurked in the shadows like a mugger. Any change to my routine was a threat to be fought off. Now

I could see that life could throw up some happy accidents too. I started to sing: tuneless optimism came bouncing back at me off the walls.

THE DRIVEWAY WAS CLEARED AND DAD AND DONOVAN WERE in the kitchen eating breakfast by the time I was dressed. The milk had frozen on the doorstep and came out as a plug of cream followed by a slurry of ice crystals over my cereal. Christian came in as far as the doorway. He was holding a piece of paper in his hand and was white with shock.

'Are you all right?' I said. 'You don't look very well.'

'Have any of you spoken to Elaine?' he asked. He unclenched his grip and I could see that the scrap of paper was crumpled around the ruby ring.

'No. Why?'

'She's done a runner.'

'What do you mean? Have you had a row?'

'No. Nothing at all. She got up to make some scrambled eggs and then a few minutes later I heard her car start up. When I came out I found this by the telephone.' He held up the ring and the note, which bore one word: *Sorry*.

'I don't understand it,' he said. 'In bed this morning she was talking about booking the honeymoon.'

'You didn't criticise her, or disagree with her or anything?'

'No.' He sagged in his wheelchair, utterly bewildered.

'Did you say she went in her car?' said Dad. 'Because she won't get far. The roads are terrible. I had to walk from the roundabout. The gritting lorry's done the main road, but—'

'Do you want me to go after her, Christian?' I interrupted. 'And find out what's going on?'

'Would you? I'd go myself if I could. Just ask her to come
back and talk to me. Whatever she's done I forgive her.'
He sounded so desolate I felt like crying myself.

'Don't worry, I'm sure it's nothing. Just pre-wedding jitters.'
I was already squeezing past him to get to the door, grabbing
my coat, pulling it on as I ran up the newly swept path. I
could see from the zig-zag tracks which way she'd gone:
madness to attempt to drive. The surface of yesterday's snow
had hardened to ice. I kept to the edge of the path where it
was deep and softer; it creaked and crunched beneath my
boots as I ran towards the security gate, which had been left
wide open. Our road gave onto a hill, about halfway up.
Whichever way Elaine turned she'd have been in trouble.
Please, God, don't let her have gone skidding down onto the
main road and under a truck, I prayed. But as I gained the
corner, I saw her red Volkswagen about fifty yards away, pointing back up the hill towards me. The tyre marks in the snow
described its hectic progress from side to side before it had
spun through 180 degrees and ground its rear end into an
ornamental lamp post, which was now at a slight list.

She looked up as I approached, and wound down the
window, dislodging a wedge of snow which fell inside the
car onto her lap. 'Oh fucking hell,' she said, despairingly.
'What have I done?'

'Elaine. Please come back,' I said. 'Christian's distraught.'

'I knew this day would come,' she said. 'And I just can't
face it.' Her brimming eyes overflowed.

'What are you talking about?'

'I've been carrying this burden around with me for so
long. You've no idea.'

'What burden? Are you saying you don't want to marry
Christian?'

'No. Of course I want to. But he won't want to marry me.'

'Why not?' A wild thought flew into my head. 'You're not a man, are you?' I'd said the words before I could stop myself. Elaine looked at me as though I had finally lost my wits, and then started to laugh through her tears.

'Now I know what you think of me,' she said, wiping her eyes and nose on a rag of tissue.

'No, I don't,' I spluttered. 'I just couldn't think of anything else that would change Christian's mind. He adores you. You've turned his whole life around. He's crazy about you. He wants you on any terms. Please come back and talk to him.'

Less than a month ago I'd been hatching a plot to remove her, and here I was, grovelling and pleading for her return. And meaning it.

'Do you think he'd forgive me if he knew it was my fault he's in a wheelchair?' Elaine asked, looking up at me with troubled eyes.

Before I could begin to work out what she could possibly mean by this ridiculous claim, I heard running feet approaching.

'Ah. Here he comes,' Elaine said quietly, and for a mad moment I thought it must be Christian, brought to his feet by this crisis, but it was Donovan who slithered to a halt beside me.

'Is everything all right?' he asked, then looked at the figure in the car and gave a jolt of recognition. 'E-laine!' he said, amazement and awkwardness making him stumble over the name.

'Donovan. Hello again,' she replied, and, dull witness to these mysteries, I felt the ground tilt under my feet, as past and present rose up to meet each other.

46

CAN A MAN DIE OF GUILT? DOES THE TRUTH ALWAYS SET US free?

AS ELAINE UNBURDENED HERSELF IN THE CRIPPLED CAR THAT bright cold morning, it struck me that ignorance is a gift whose blessings can never be counted. I sat beside her, the woman for whom Donovan had once jumped from a train and hiked across rain-lashed fields, whose nakedness he'd kept, preserved between the pages of a novel, and I felt I was seeing her properly for the first time.

'I just can't get over it,' Donovan was saying. 'You, here, engaged to Christian. I mean, what are the odds of that?'

'It's no coincidence,' Elaine assured him. 'I was sent.'

'How? Who by?' I remembered Penny's words: nothing that happens here is a coincidence.

'My ex-husband, Stuart. I told you we were separated in my twenties, didn't I? Well, Donovan was the reason. We'd been miserable for ages before that – Stuart was a bit of a depressive – and we'd probably have split up anyway, but me having an affair with a sixth-former certainly hurried things along. It cost me my job, too,' she added as an after-thought. 'But that's beside the point.'

'I didn't know that,' said Donovan. 'Sorry.'

'Not your fault,' Elaine said, shaking her head. She was no longer crying, but she seemed to have developed an allergy to her own tears: her cheeks were raked with red tracks. 'We separated around the time you called it off,' she said to him. 'I didn't have much contact after that, but I used to send his mum a Christmas card: we'd always got on pretty well. Then a couple of years ago she wrote and said he was ill. She didn't say how ill, but I got the message, so I went to see him, just to be friendly, you know. We'd never got round to divorcing, and neither of us had a partner, so there was no one else's feelings to consider.' She paused as a couple of kids passed the car, dragging a plastic sledge. They peered at us – we must have looked pretty peculiar, parked there, slantwise against the bent lamp-post – but Elaine faced them down with a blank stare before contin-uing. 'He had cancer of the stomach: he knew it was curtains. There was a reconciliation of sorts; I gave up my job and looked after him right up to his death. Quite near the end he said he'd had something on his conscience for years. He thought he might have killed a man.'

My heart lurched. I knew what was coming. Behind me I could sense Donovan holding his breath. I couldn't look at him.

'It was the weekend you came to see me to say it was all finished. Stuart was supposed to be away on a cricket tour, but he came back early and staked out the house in case you turned up. When he saw you leaving he decided to follow you. He ended up driving all the way to Kent, to the Fairchilds' house, but it was such a long journey, his anger had worn off by the time you stopped, so he just turned round and came back.

'Jesus,' said Donovan.

It was getting colder in the car; we couldn't have the engine on because of the crumpled exhaust. Elaine's teeth chattered as she spoke and the words emerged in frozen clouds. 'But a few nights later we had a huge row – about nothing, but underneath about you, obviously – a major, plate-throwing row, and he stormed out and I didn't see him again until his illness. He told me he'd driven all the way back to Kent and parked near the house, sort of churning with rage. It wasn't premeditated. He only had a cricket bat in the car because he hadn't got around to clearing his bag out from the weekend. He wasn't going to do anything, but suddenly there you were, coming towards him. Even in the darkness he recognised you by your hat. Anyway,' she blew out a long breath, 'you know what happened. He swore he'd never have used the bat. He just wanted to scare you. When he saw he'd got the wrong person, and that he was badly injured, he panicked and ran for it. He did call an ambulance, which was something, I suppose. But after that he never mentioned it to anyone. He was terrified he'd be done for manslaughter, or attempted murder or something. But he said he'd never stopped feeling sick to the stomach about it. Those were his actual words: "sick to the stomach". It makes you think, doesn't it?'

'Oh no,' said Donovan in a wretched voice. 'This is terrible, Elaine.'

'I know,' she replied.

'Christian took my punishment.'

'I'm sorry to have to tell you. But I've been living with it for months.'

I tried to picture it: Donovan in a wheelchair; Christian walking, jumping, taking life at a raking stride, but somehow I couldn't reel in the last nineteen years and replay them any other way.

'We always assumed it was a reprisal for that Janine Fellowes business. Nothing like this ever entered our heads.' It occurred to me as I said this that there was one beneficiary of this grim story: Dad. Absolved of his guilt at last.

'Why would it?' said Elaine, plaiting and replaiting the fringed ends of her scarf. 'Anyway, Stuart asked me if I could try to find out what had happened to the boy who fell out of the tree, and see if there was anything I could do for him, or the family, if he hadn't survived. He left everything to me, you see: he didn't have anyone else.'

'So you deliberately tracked Christian down?' I said.

She nodded. 'It wasn't hard. I went to the library and checked local newspapers for August 1983, and there it all was. Once I had a name it was easy. Falling in love with him wasn't in the plan at all. I just wanted to find out what his life was like, and how he could be helped.'

'Well, you have helped him, Elaine,' I said. 'And you can't just vanish now.' I looked at the blotchy face of the woman who had once been the object of Donovan's fantasies, and the real shock – that their affair should have had such monstrous consequences – was momentarily buried under a wave of jealousy.

'I know, I know,' Elaine was saying. 'When he told me he was in love with me I was so happy, but I knew I'd have to tell him everything, and I just couldn't bring myself to do it. And the longer I left it the worse it got. Our relationship was so new, and so fragile, and had so little encouragement from any other quarters.'

I flinched at this barb, but I couldn't deny the justice of it. 'I'm sorry I wasn't more welcoming,' I said. 'I should have been nicer. It was just possessiveness, I suppose.'

'And then, this morning I looked out of the window and there was Donovan, come back to haunt me. I just freaked. I thought: I can't do this. I want to run away.'

'But you won't, will you?'

'Would it bother you that much?' Elaine asked me, with her frank, questioning stare. 'You could go back to the way you were: just the two of you in your cosy little world.'

I thought about it for a second or two: that was all I needed. 'No, I couldn't. Everything's changed.' I glanced at Donovan, immemorial source of all upheaval, and for a moment I saw in his devastated expression the child Donovan, watching his own mother jump from a high window. He reached for my hand and crushed it in his – a gesture that might have been love or anguish or apology or all three. 'Christian loves you more than he loves me, Elaine.' The truth of this struck me forcefully, as did another insight, long overdue. Christian had never quite reciprocated my love in full measure. Even when he was at his lowest and most needy, I had always needed him more. I would do this last thing for him – I would bring him Elaine. 'But I know him better. And I know he won't blame you for what happened to him. He might blame your husband, but how much can you really hate a dead man?'

Elaine let out a gusty sigh. 'Right. I'd better go and do this, then.' Her hand rested on the door catch. 'Will you come with me?'

I nodded. 'Are you coming, Donovan?'

He looked at me absently, lost in thought. 'What? Oh, no. If you don't mind. I think I'll just stay here, see if I can do something with this car. It's a bit dangerous sticking out like this.'

Snow was falling around us, impossibly, from a clear blue sky, as Elaine and I walked up the hill together. Not falling then, just blowing from roofs and treetops. At the corner I turned and saw Donovan, squatting to examine the stoved-in rear of the Volkswagen: a practical man, glad to have something he could fix.

47

IN AUGUST 2002, IN WHAT I CAME TO THINK OF AS A PERFECT act of reconciliation, Christian James Fairchild (bachelor of this parish) and Elaine Sarah Harding (widow, St Andrew's, Oxted) were married by the Reverend Gordon Fairchild in the church of the Holy Trinity, at Knot, where nineteen years earlier, Stuart Sidney Harding (deceased) had avenged himself on the wrong man.

'This is a special day,' Dad said, in his opening address to the congregation. 'There are not many men who can say they have married their only son.'

Mum came home from Nepal for the wedding, but couldn't be persuaded to buy herself a new outfit for the occasion. 'No one's going to be looking at me!' she protested. Which might have been the case, if only she hadn't decided to disguise one of her old dresses with a hideous hairy poncho, which looked as if it had come straight off a yak. She was planning to go back for another four-month stint in Dhankuta, but it would be her last, she said, to Dad's great joy. She was starting to feel her age, and they needed younger, fitter workers.

Donovan sat beside me in the front pew, gorgeous and unfamiliar in a suit and tie. I couldn't help thinking, as I'd watched him dress that morning, that there was something heartbreaking about a man putting on cufflinks. The last time I'd seen him in a suit he was eighteen, setting off for work in the Cannon Street bunker. During Widor's 'Toccata' he passed me a minute scrap of paper, torn from the Order of Service booklet, on which he had written one word: *Always*. I smiled, and kept it rolled up, warm in the palm of my hand.

'Did you love her very much?' I asked, as we stood in the churchyard afterwards, waiting for the photographer to set up a shot without the wheelchair: Christian and Elaine sitting on a bench in front of the West Door.

He shook his head. 'I can't remember. Probably not. Does anyone know anything at seventeen?'

'Tactful reply,' I said, but I'm not sure I believe in the myth of youthful ignorance, or that we acquire wisdom incrementally, year by year.

The reception was held in the back room of the Fox and Pheasant. When Elaine realised how few people they wanted to invite she had scaled down her search for a venue. The men, following Christian's lead, whipped off their jackets and ties as soon as they were in the pub, and we sat down to a beer and a ploughman's and it was all so relaxed and informal and unlike a wedding, that I caught myself thinking: that's just how I'd do it, hypothetically speaking, in the unlikely event . . .

There was no best man and no father-of-the-bride, so

the only after-dinner speaker was Christian. 'I won't stand up, if you don't mind,' he began, and then he made this extraordinary speech abut the significance of the number three – the Trinity, the three states of matter, and the stability of tripods, for example – until I started to wonder if he hadn't had too much Guinness. But he ended by saying, 'I'm very fortunate indeed to have the love and support of, not one, but three exceptional women: firstly, someone who has never put herself first: my mother, secondly, my sister, Esther, who has been the best friend and companion I could ask for, and finally my wife' – he paused to acknowledge the collective murmur of approval, and to subdue the lump in his throat – 'who has brought me the sort of happiness I often dreamed of, but never expected to find . . .' Here he lost it completely and had to wag his hand to let us know he was done. The assembled company responded with noisy applause and much thumping on tables, and then the music came back on and Christian withdrew gratefully from the limelight.

When it was time for the newlyweds to leave Elaine made a point of throwing me her bouquet, then, two minutes later, wound down the car window and said that on second thoughts could she have it back as she wanted to press the flowers.

I moved out of the Caterham house three months ago, and I'm renting a tiny cottage in Ardingly at present, about two hundred yards from Donovan. I've quit the job at Rowena's to give some proper attention to my illustrating work. After mature reflection, I've decided it was only my indiscipline and lack of application that made it unviable as a career before. The quality of my stuff was never a problem, just the quantity, but Donovan's work ethic has inspired me to greater industry, and I've finished *Jack's Journey* and fired off a dozen letters to different publishers offering my services as a jacket artist, while I try to get a commission for an illustrated book of my own, without Lucinda Todd and her forty per cent. Christian's money won't last for ever, so I'm giving myself two years, and if I'm not making a living by then it's Teacher Training College for me. Now *there*'s an incentive.

I still see Christian quite frequently, or we talk on the phone, but not by arrangement: only when the mood takes us. We've agreed not to fall into a fresh set of routines. The main casualty of my new situation is the weekly swim with Dad. It's just too far to be viable on a regular basis. He's been fine about it: apparently, my lack of technique in the pool was holding him back, and now he can clock up his thirty lengths in half the time.

One person I don't see as much as I'd like to is Penny. She's not exactly on the doorstep, and her weekends are taken up with Cassie, I suppose. Maybe she sensed that a resumption of a close friendship would have made Christian uncomfortable, or maybe she never intended any such thing once her task, as she saw it, was done.

Donovan has repeated his offer to accommodate me under his roof at least once a week. It's crazy, he says, paying for two places. We're in and out of each other's houses and beds all the time. He's offered to build me a studio at the bottom of the garden, overlooking the reservoir, so I can have some space and peace to work. His onslaughts of charm are hard to resist, so maybe one day. But for the moment I'm quite enjoying the novelty of having a place of my own. It makes me feel that at last I've left home and joined the ranks of grown-up people who know how to turn the water off at the mains, or bleed their own radiators. We have an arrangement where we switch on the light above the front door to let each other know if we're in and want to be disturbed. It's supposed to safeguard our privacy and our rights as individuals not to be drawn in by the mere force of passion to a relationship that might become all-consuming.

I leave mine on, mostly.